PATHWAY

PATHWAY

Peter Bunnett

Book Guild Publishing
Sussex, England

First published in Great Britain in 2012 by
The Book Guild Ltd
19 New Road
Brighton, BN1 1UF

Typeset in Baskerville by Ellipsis Digital Limited, Glasgow

Printed in Great Britain by
CPI Group (UK) Ltd, Croydon, CR0 4YY

A catalogue record for this book is available from The British Library.

ISBN 978 1 84624 654 8

Prologue

It was early morning in the year 2000 when I walked across the beach towards the mainland, my feet sinking in the wet sand as I left the island. I had been through a considerable amount in the last couple of months, a life-changing experience.

I had travelled back to the seventeenth century and watched as the poor, unfortunate inhabitants of the island made a meagre living. I had seen the notorious Captain Vicary treat his crew with contempt, having taken more than his share from their smuggling exploits. Travelling back to war-torn Britain, hoping to use this period in time to obtain a fortune for myself in fine art, I had watched with understanding and pride as the people dealt with the rationing and shortages, learning to cope with all difficulties facing them. Moving forward to the 1980s I had assisted in plans to saves the lives of two people, with careful planning and strategy.

There were people waiting on the mainland. Was I the object of their patience? At this point I had no idea; soon I would find out. My biggest concern was to do with what I had seen: who would believe anything of what I was about to tell them? I hoped there was one particular person there who would have the courage to confirm what I was about to inflict on the world. Whether I was part of some vast event that had changed history forever, I was about to find out, for good or bad. My step quickened in anticipation of what was to come.

1

It was late March when I moved into my bungalow on the South Devon coast, situated in Ruby Bay. A dream had been fulfilled, later rather than sooner. As a boy I had visited this area with my parents, and it was my favourite seaside location. Throughout my working life I had always vowed to retire to Ruby Bay, and this dream had come to fruition. My move might have been earlier, but the Lottery can be a cruel mistress.

Although there was unpacking to be done I decided to take in the delights of my new home. I sat on the veranda and looked towards the small island about 400 metres from the mainland. To get to the island one had to walk across the sandy beach, except when the tide was in, when the journey was completed on a large sea tractor, an awesome piece of equipment.

On the island there were only three prominent buildings, the inn, the hotel, and a dilapidated building on the top of the island. All were to be significant in the story that follows. Looking at the inn, little did I know how infamous the place was. I was soon to find out at first hand. I had visited the hut at the top of the island during my childhood; the long climb up was never worth the effort. It was suggested it had been a lookout station during the Second World War, but to me it was just a broken-down building that smelt of urine.

Stationed at the slipway onto the island was the sea tractor. It had large wheels and a passenger deck, which was about 12 feet above ground level. I watched as the driver started the engine; a puff of smoke signified the engine had activated and it roared into life. It was obviously just a maintenance check, the tide was out so the island was reachable on foot across the sand, but the monster was going to be required that evening. I had always suspected that driving the tractor was a desirable job, working for only a few hours a day. It was thought that the job was passed down from father to son, very much a closed shop. The present incumbent was a relatively young man, so a vacancy was unlikely to occur for a long time.

It was quiet as I sat on my veranda, the summer season had not yet begun. Soon the beach would be full of tourists, enjoying the ice cream, taking in the beauty that this bay offered.

I was suddenly aware of a man in my garden; it was my neighbour.

'Hello, I'm John Campbell. I'm sorry for any interruption,' he said.

'There is no need to apologize, I'm glad to make your acquaintance,' I said.

We shook hands following the introduction. He had the appearance of a military man, his demeanour bore this out, he confirmed this when he told me of his Army background, spending most of his adult life serving the Crown, finally retiring as a high-ranking officer. We chatted for a few minutes.

'I have just completed my time as a police officer, I'm now happily retired. I visited Ruby Bay during my childhood, it was a place I always enjoyed visiting, ideal for a small boy equipped with a bucket and spade; the large beach was paradise for a boy with imagination. My father was expert at building cars with the sand, he patted the sides with his surf board to make the car square and compact. During my adult life these fond memories kept coming back,' I said.

John seemed at ease with my previous career; not everyone was friendly towards policemen.

'This place is indeed an ideal place to retire, but not the

place to find work, not that is until the summer months,' he said.

We had both had visions of retiring here; it was a dream come true for me. For John it became more of a necessity, but that is another story.

Having only spoken to John for a few minutes I decided I liked him, and hoped we were to become firm friends. John eventually left, making it known he was willing to tell me of the history of the area, he gave the impression he was something of an expert. His expertise did not in fact come from what he had read and what the local inhabitants had told him, but from a different source which, as I was to find out, was more sinister than I could ever have imagined.

Although John Campbell was unaware of this fact, I had some knowledge of the local area; although not an extensive knowledge it is true. Most of what I had read related to the small inn on the island, the Smugglers' Inn, a very apt title if what I had read was true from the stories that had been handed down from generation to generation. The location of the inn was fortuitous, situated on an island that was regularly cut off from the mainland due to the tidal activity of the sea. It allowed the islanders to commit many nefarious acts during the hours of darkness, which they were happy to carry out. Nowadays, the sea tractor transported people to the island when the tide was in, but in those far-off days the island was only reached by boat. This was not a recommended method of transport, particularly as the islanders were very wary of strangers. The seafaring islanders of the past were men of courage and guile – with the emphasis on the guile – lawless and caring little for people not on the island.

Very few people lived on the island now, just the landlord of the inn and his family, the residents and some of the staff of the hotel, but there was only a skeleton staff at the hotel at this time of year. The summer season had not yet begun; when it did the hotel was usually packed, which also provided excellent trade for the inn. Both were open all year, but trade in the winter was sparse.

The Smugglers' Inn was a popular haunt with locals, an ancient house with original oak beams, no doubt visited by ghosts of a bygone time, ghosts with salt in their blood. The hotel was a modern edifice in comparison, no more than 70 or 80 years old, built I believe in the 1930s, a relative youngster on this island. Many famous stars of stage and screen stayed at the hotel, which satisfied their craving for seclusion and tranquillity. The hotel's expensive tariff explained its rich, eccentric clientele.

The area of Ruby Bay was well known to me, not only because part of my childhood had been spent on the vast sandy beach, but it was also a place I was always glad to visit even in adulthood; when visiting Devon, a trip to Ruby Bay was always crammed into the schedule. Now I was here permanently, a dream fulfilled. Retirement had brought me back to my spiritual home.

My new bungalow was perched on the top of the cliff, overlooking the island and the beach. I heard the sound of the waves lapping against the rocks below, increasing in noise as the tide came in; it was a wonderful sound. My first day was almost over. I had not ventured from the bungalow, and had all my unpacking yet to do, so I decided to venture out and rediscover Ruby Bay tomorrow. I was not expecting any shocks; the place looked the same as I remembered it, beautiful and unspoilt. The holiday season would certainly change that, and the crowds were expected at any time.

The decisions I had made during my working life had reaped their rewards investing in the right companies, occasionally taking chances which fortunately worked out, saving when possible. My bungalow had been bought outright, with the joy of no mortgage to pay, allowing me the luxury of taking early retirement with an ample pension. Life at this point of time was good.

Today had been a strange day, moving into this wonderful bungalow, but appreciating that my retirement plan had succeeded as I had hoped, I had a warm feeling of satisfaction inside me.

Add to this the acquaintance I had made with John, someone I warmed to immediately. I had no idea at this stage what lay ahead for me; I had not anticipated what was soon to become a reality.

My second day dawned, the sun shone in a cloudless sky, a reminder that summer was on its way. But my adventures were about to begin, as the postman dropped a letter through the letterbox, the first to my new address. It was from Colin Wickham, the solicitor who had done the conveyancing work on the bungalow. He wished to meet me that morning, and stated that he was to call on me at my new home. I was certain I had paid everything that was due, but my initial thought was this visit still had something to do with an unpaid bill. Perhaps this letter showed the personal touch, something that is possible when the solicitor does not have many clients. I got my cheque book ready for the visit.

Dismissing the correspondence from my mind, I went about my business, preparing breakfast to be consumed outside on the veranda, which I did with great pleasure, looking over the calm sea, watching the seagulls swooping beneath the rocks. I looked towards the beach, where a solitary dog and owner were enjoying the morning sun; the inevitable stick was propelled through the air, and quickly and efficiently the dog retrieved it.

'Morning, Pat, how are you this morning?' came a voice from the garden.

I looked up and saw John standing there.

'Not bad to be honest.' I said.

'What are your plans for today?' said John.

'I don't have any pressing plans,' I replied.

John appeared very cheerful, more so than the previous day

'Why are you so cheerful today?' I asked.

'There is no particular reason, I try to be cheerful every day. It is difficult not to be cheerful living where we do, I think it is fair to say we have chosen an ideal retirement place,' he said.

'I agree, this is an ideal location, we needn't have a care in the world, life here is idyllic. I think, John, we have both earned this, we have served our time in the service of this country, in different ways perhaps. The peace and tranquillity of Ruby Bay is our reward. You are right, if it's not possible to be cheerful in a place like Ruby Bay, what hope is there for anyone?' I said.

'I was thinking of taking a wander around the village. I don't expect it to be any different from my last visit, although as I said it was many years ago. But I now have to change my plan as I'm expecting a visitor. It is the solicitor chap, Colin Wickham, I had a letter from him this morning and he wants to see me. Maybe there's a discrepancy with the bill. You know what these solicitors are like when they are owed money, very quick off the mark,' I said.

'I must say that doesn't surprise me, but I think you will find it has nothing to do with the bill. I can't tell you how I know, but I think there is another reason for the visit. Colin has to discuss this matter with you, nobody else but Colin,' he said. 'I am more than happy to offer you the Grand Tour once your business with Colin is concluded. I will introduce you around the village; they are quite a friendly bunch of people and I'm sure they will make you welcome, they did me. Maybe after that we can go to the inn for a drink, then I will tell you what I know of the history of the place. But that will all have to wait until after your meeting with Colin, he has something important to tell you, it is something only he can tell you,' said John.

On that note John left. He clearly did not feel comfortable talking about whatever Colin wanted to discuss, in fact he did not seem to want to talk about Colin at all. I sensed there was some history between the two of them, as John was quick to go when he knew Colin was turning up. The whole situation had an air of mystery.

I looked towards the island, where the sea tractor driver was again at his post, yet another maintenance check. The tide was out and the vastness of the beach was apparent, stretching along the island coastline

I walked towards the door on hearing the doorbell, I had a

good idea who my visitor would be, although I had never met Colin Wickham. I opened the door to find a well-dressed man in his early fifties, looking every bit the solicitor. We shook hands and made our introductions.

'Please call me Colin, that is if you don't mind? This is a close-knit community and everyone uses first names,' he said.

'Of course I don't mind, my name is Pat,' I replied.

'Do you know the reason for my visit?' he asked.

'I have no idea. I thought it was a bit sudden, as you know I only moved in yesterday.'

'I must apologize. I thought maybe John had said something to you. I take it you have met your neighbour John?' he enquired.

'I have indeed met John, he introduced himself soon after my arrival. But I still wonder why this visit is necessary so soon after my arrival,' I said.

'John knows the reason for this visit, and although I didn't expect him to tell you he may have let it slip.'

'Actually, John was reluctant to talk about the subject of this meeting. He was adamant that it was some sort of legal point that only you could deal with,' I said.

Colin nodded his approval. 'The matter is not very serious, in fact I would call it trivial, but it is something in the deeds which I am obliged to discuss with you.'

'I suspect the fact that you have called on me so soon after my arrival means this matter is not so trivial, but I will wait until you tell me before I decide just how trivial it is,' I said.

Colin opened his briefcase and started to shuffle with the papers inside, pulling out several sheets and then returning them to his case. I sat patiently watching. Finally he smiled, it looked like he had found what he was looking for – success at last. I smiled back to allay his embarrassment. He placed a piece of paper on the table and said nothing, indicating with his eyes that he wanted me to read the text. I picked it up and started to read the transcript in my hand, but having read it I was no wiser. It was written in old English, so I had no idea what it was or what it was saying.

'I appreciate you letting me look at this piece of writing. I have tried to make some sense of it without success. I have no idea what language it is written in, let alone what it is supposed to say. Maybe you could tell me in plain English what it is all about?' I asked.

'What this page from an ancient deed is saying, is that you have inherited something because you purchased this bungalow.'

This was news to me, I had never been informed of such a windfall, if in fact it was a windfall. I was immediately suspicious of my new-found inheritance. I was someone who did not like surprises; this was one of them, and I felt this was going to be a bad inheritance.

'You're saying I inherited something when I bought this property, something I've never been told about until now? I find that a little strange, surely this is not the way to do business, is that just me or do you agree?' I said.

'I agree it is not the usual way to carry out business, but in this case the circumstances are far from normal. The deed attached to the bungalow does not allow the purchaser to know of the inheritance until the sale is completed, then the details can be passed on, which is the reason for this visit. I am informing you at the earliest opportunity. I apologise for this, but unfortunately the deed does not allow me to tell you beforehand. I have no choice in the matter, I have to abide by what the deed stipulates. I'll tell you all I know of the whole situation, then of course you'll be at liberty to ask me whatever questions you want, and I will do my utmost to answer them.

'The bungalow you have bought belonged to the Vicary family, descendants of the famous Captain James Vicary, a name familiar to anyone who has spent time in Ruby Bay. He was the leader of a notorious pirate gang that ruled on the island in the seventeenth century; his family lived on in the area. This particular inheritance relates to a small piece of land on the island, believed to have been owned by Captain Vicary himself. This piece of land was passed to his descendants, although the history books know very little of these people. It was assumed Vicary had no relatives, but the will proves otherwise. Who these relatives were is unknown to this day. They must have been very distant and he never divulged their identity. In respect of this legacy bestowed on you, there are a few provisos attached. This piece of land cannot be built on, nor can it be excavated, nor can it be sold separately from the property, in other words your bungalow. Another stipulation, which you are now aware of, is that the details of this piece of land cannot be mentioned until the property is sold. The deed has been checked by experts, it is quite legal. Do you have any questions for me?' he enquired.

I made my position clear. 'I am far from happy, it feels like I have been duped in some way. I expect honesty from others, I always treat people with honesty. It feels like I have been deceived. I can see no good reason why the inheritance cannot be declared at the point of selling the property, unless, as I suspect, there is something to hide, something which I assume is of an unpleasant nature.'

'Your inheritance consists of a piece of land on the island. It is very small and serves no useful purpose. The latter-day Vicarys just wanted to get rid of it, so they attached it to the deeds of this bungalow,' said Colin.

'Why are the provisos attached in respect of not building on it? Why make any such stipulations? It all sounds very strange.'

'I am happy to show you the plot of land, then your best bet is to forget about it,' he said.

I had no idea why he thought that a solution; if it was put in the will then surely it had some importance, or at least Captain Vicary had thought so. My curiosity was aroused.

'I was going to go for a walk with John around the village, maybe it's best I cancel that, then we can go and see my inheritance.'

'I'm sure John will show it to you, he knows where it is.'

'So John knows about the piece of land? That was probably the reason he didn't want to stay,' I mused.

'John visited the plot with Alan Donald, the previous owner of this bungalow. When he inherited it just before you, he felt exactly as you do, confused yet a little curious, but having seen it he realized it was useless, as you will,' he said.

'What's your opinion on inheriting a piece of land on which nothing can be done?' I asked Colin.

'I find it strange, I have never come across a deed with anything similar,' he said.

'Why it could not just be ignored is beyond my comprehension, particularly as it cannot be touched in any way,' I said.

'Maybe in the fullness of time you may find a use for it,' he said.

My immediate thought was, did he know more than he was saying? But I was too angry about John's betrayal to ask any further questions.

Colin then handed me a large metal key, in a leather pouch. 'This is the key to the lock on the wooden door, the door that covers the plot of land. It is thought it may have been the door to Captain Vicary's cellar. But before you get too excited, previous owners would testify there is no treasure inside, it is just an empty hole,' he said.

'All right, I will go and see the hole on the island, and, as you say, no doubt John will come with me. I apologize for my attitude towards this inheritance, I appreciate you are only doing your job. I know you have no control over what the deed stipulates, but I'm someone who doesn't like surprises,' I said.

We shook hands and Colin left. He left a copy of the deed, advising me to keep it safe, which I agreed to do. I still felt that Colin knew more than he was saying. I was keen to join John on our walk, to a destination he knew more about than I did. As Colin reached his car, John appeared at the front door.

'Why didn't you tell me what the meeting was about? Colin told me you knew what was going to be discussed, you could have warned me,' I said.

'I did know, but it was not my job to tell you, that was Colin's job. He held the deed so he was the only one who could pass on that information. Colin has no doubt told you it's a lot of fuss about nothing. I'm happy to show you the plot of land but there is a condition: after seeing it we go to the inn for that drink,' said John.

'That sounds a great idea. Colin said the plot was of no use,' I said.

John nodded his agreement. He asked if I had the key, and I showed him the large rusty object, the key to the door covering the plot. If it had a door and a key it was obviously not too large a piece of land, at least that part of the story appeared to be true. John confirmed the key was necessary for the door.

'I am confused that someone thinks it necessary to lock a door on something everybody thinks is useless. There must be something to hide. The more I think about it, the more puzzling it seems.'

'Alan opened the door and found nothing inside, I expect you to have the same result,' said John.

'If I'm honest, it's the result I expect. It has been left abandoned on the island, locked up. Surely if anyone was interested in the contents it wouldn't be difficult to force the lock. But, as you say, there is nothing inside to tempt anyone to break into it,' I said.

There was more to this plot of land than anyone was telling me. Useless and insignificant? If that was the case, why continue with the charade for each new owner of 2 Ruby Bay? Perhaps the past might be the answer to the present. I decided to enquire into John's expertise of the area; if he was such an expert, surely this plot of land was significant in the history of the island.

'Colin is the best man to ask, his knowledge is greater than mine. He could offer you more detail on your so-called inheritance, that's if you still want to know any more?' said John.

But Colin had left very hurriedly and did not allow me the chance to ask. I felt Colin was somewhat embarrassed about what he had told me, similar to giving a death message; say it and get out as quickly as possible, I hoped the similarity ended there. He was also very keen that John should show me the plot. There was definitely something strange about his whole approach to the matter.

'Is there something you're not telling me, John? Do you know more about this inheritance than you are sharing with me?' I questioned.

'I can only tell you what I've been told; most of that gossip comes from the inn. The story I heard was that Captain Vicary – he was, as you know, a notorious smuggler and pirate – was the owner of the plot of land. This was about the time the inn was built, which was the central point of all the island's affairs. It was obviously the meeting place for the crew, who gathered there every night, drinking their ill-gotten booty from their smuggling trips. It was also the place where the missions were discussed: each mission had only one goal and that was to get cheap alcohol from the French traders in the Channel. On each occasion the next meeting to exchange goods was arranged.

'Vicary was the main man in everything; being the captain meant that his word was law. He apparently held court at the inn each night. He was a vain man who liked to be worshipped by his crew. Vicary wanted his crew to be there, and they never went against his wishes. Whether he did not trust his crew is unclear, although it is unlikely he trusted them; he wanted to know where each man was and what he was up to. Vicary was very insecure about his position, and kept his eye on the crew to stop them plotting against him. Either way, the whole crew congregated at the inn every night, even the married men.

'Vicary's inheritance is not known for certain; it was believed to be in the cellar of his hut. Vicary might have provided himself with part of the smuggling booty for his own personal use, hiding it in the cellar; details are very sketchy as to why Vicary needed a cellar. We know he had the largest hut, which of course befitted his position. He bequeathed the plot of land to his relatives with certain provisos, which I believe Colin spelt out to you; not ideal terms, so maybe he hated his family. It appears Vicary wanted the plot to stay in the family, but nobody seems to know what family he had, and he did not appear to be married. Research has shown there was nobody related to him on the island, so these relatives must have lived somewhere on the mainland. His personal life is very sketchy, either unknown or made up; stories that have been passed down are not always the truth. So this useless piece of land was passed to his mysterious family, with the provisos we know about stubbornly attached,' he said.

'There must have been something to hide, why else did the deeds stipulate the plot was not allowed to be built on or excavated? There was definitely something of importance there at the time of Vicary's death, although whatever it was is likely to be long gone by now – he's been dead hundreds of years. Perhaps there was something beneath the cellar, that's why the conditions were imposed about no excavation. Maybe there is treasure deep underground, or maybe that is just my imagination running away with me,' I said.

I then asked John how these provisos were put into place, but was surprised by his answer. Vicary had in fact left a will, not something that was expected during the seventeenth century. The deed was part of Vicary's will, which was why I was unable to understand the content; it was in the language of the time. Surprisingly, Vicary was not illiterate as I would have expected.

'It sounds very fishy to me, why did he want to keep it in the family? Over a short period of time he might want that to happen, making sure his relatives got whatever was in the cellar, but this is three hundred years later. Why are these provisos still in force after all this time? I think there is more to this piece of land. The next puzzler is why the land needed to stay in his family: how long did Vicary expect his family to be around? There is nothing stipulated about the land passing outside the family, maybe at the time he did not consider that. It is also difficult for me to understand that the plot is on the island, but my bungalow, to which the deed is attached, is on the mainland. Can you explain that?'

'It is because Vicary's descendants owned your bungalow when it was first built in the 1930s. They were the ones who attached it to the deeds, possibly it was their way of offloading it, or maybe there was some reason why they had to attach it to the home they owned. Perhaps a close scrutiny of the deeds might throw some light on the problem, although finding someone who is able to read the whole thing could prove the biggest obstacle. Stating that the owner was not told about the plot until after the sale, allowed them to offload it quite legally. Your present bungalow was built in 1995, the old house was demolished, but the deeds still referred to 2 Ruby Bay, which is why the plot is still attached to this newer property. It might seem easy for me to say, but I think it is a case of grin and bear it,' John said.

' I assume that if I decide to sell the bungalow, the same criteria must apply: the new owners will not be told about the plot until everything is signed up,' I said.

'Are you thinking of selling, then?' said John.

'Of course not, I still need to unpack! Although moving again would save the chore of unpacking . . . Don't worry, John, I am not going anywhere for the forseeable future. I am unable to understand why this plot of land needed to be attached to anything, unless it possesses secrets we have yet to discover. Colin said the plot is covered by a wooden door, is that correct?'

'Yes it is. It has a lock which I believe Colin gave you the key for. It is a substantial door, but over time it has started to rot.'

'It is a little difficult to believe it is the original door, the one that Captain Vicary put there; no wooden door was likely to last for three hundred years, I know craftsmen were good but not that good. I can only assume it has been replaced and a new lock and key fitted,' I said.

We decided the lock was merely a safety issue, to stop people falling down a gaping hole. Alan had asked the same question; with no treasure there was no need for security. But the owner was not allowed to fill it in.

We chatted as we walked, a lot of questions needed to be asked.

John knew some of the answers but I felt Colin was the authority and was likely know a great deal more. I intended to get to the bottom of this inheritance; it was bugging me. Why was there so much fuss about something that appeared to be of no use? There was more to this than I was being told; that phrase was to rear its head on many occasions during the forthcoming weeks.

I questioned John about the Vicary who was the last in line to own the bungalow, in the 1930s. He had gone off to war in 1940 and never returned, assumed killed in action in Norway, but he left a will. He left the house to his son, strangely enough, not to his wife. The son had little interest in the place and it was put up for sale, but failed to be sold until 1946, unsurprisingly, as the men were at war and it was not a buoyant market. The son never saw the property, and the local agent sold it on his behalf. A relatively wealthy elderly couple bought the property in 1946. Their daughter inherited it in 1956, but she had no interest in the property, and sold it almost immediately. The new owners did not stay long, a couple of months or so; why they left after such a short period in the idyllic setting begged a further question, but leave they did. Over the next 30 years the bungalow changed hands on a regular basis; nobody seemed to stay more than a couple of years. Eventually it was bought by a builder. He knocked it down and rebuilt it, and the present bungalow was the result of his labour. Alan Donald bought it about a year ago.

'I am a little concerned that nobody has settled here for more than a couple of years, then they suddenly uproot and leave. If as you say the locals are friendly, perhaps there is another reason which I need to consider. Perhaps this bungalow has some sort of stigma attached to it,' I mused.

'I appreciate what you are saying, it is a little confusing. But perhaps the locals are too friendly – they might frighten someone new away,' he said.

I wanted to know more about my predecessor, Alan Donald. John said he didn't mind me asking, he was happy to tell me what he knew of Alan, though he said Colin probably knew more.

Alan had moved in just under a year ago, and John introduced himself, exactly as he had done to me the previous day; he felt it was the neighbourly thing to do. They got on well, socializing together, including visits to the inn, the culmination of their daily walks. Then Colin turned up to see Alan, a private meeting which John was not privy to, and the relationship changed drastically between Alan and John. Shortly after this visit the bungalow was put up for sale. John tried to find out what Alan was doing but he had already left the area. He had only lived there for six months. He asked Colin why Alan had left, and what he was told surprised him.

Alan had received a telegram stating there was a death in the family, requiring his immediate departure to join his family in Manchester. This bereavement was such that Alan had no intention of returning, and Colin was instructed to sell the house on Alan's behalf. All monies were to be paid into Alan's bank account. It sounded plausible, yet a little bizarre. Why didn't Alan tell him himself? Surely that was the polite and respectful thing to do. What was also strange was that Alan disappeared during the night: John was faced with an absent friend the following morning. Something like this was unlikely to bring about an instant decision to leave in the middle of the night and sell up.

He felt let down when Alan left, but he got nothing more from Colin. Perhaps Colin was being honest and telling John everything he knew. People caught up in the grieving process do make strange decisions. The fact that Colin had never mentioned the situation since was a pertinent point: in Colin's eyes the incident was closed.

John was visibly upset. 'I had become good friends with Alan. Over that five-month period we had become inseparable, then we suddenly started to drift apart. Colin started to make long visits to Alan; they talked for hours. I rarely saw Alan in those last few weeks, and when I did see him he said very little to me. To my surprise he said he did not have time to visit the inn any more. It was like talking to a different person. Life for him did not appear to be fun any more, he was more intense, it was as if something serious was bothering him, but he did not confide in me,' he said.

'Why is it you do not appear to get on very well with Colin? Has there been some sort of disagreement between you?' I asked.

It was all connected with Alan: he did not believe the facts about the bereavement, he was sure there was something else going on. 'I was aware of the contents of the deeds, but that information I treated with utmost confidence. It was these chats between Alan and Colin, that I wasn't privy to. I had tried to approach Colin, but he stuck to the bereavement story. I am convinced that was a lie, but I have no idea why the lie was told. There is no way I can discredit the story,' he said.

'I agree the story is a little strange, but surely it is possible for someone to uproot and leave under those circumstances?' I said.

'It is just not like the character that I knew Alan to be. If he did go in the night, he would have made contact with me later, either by telephoning or dropping me a line. But I've heard nothing from him. I have tried in vain to discuss it with Colin; he either changes the subject or reverts back to the original story. He then says he is only doing what Alan instructed him to do. I think he has lied about Alan. I also think he knows where he is, and I don't think that he's in Manchester, but somewhere I am not to know about. I think the Manchester story is some kind of ruse, but I have no idea why,' he said.

I could see he was unhappy and hurt that his friend had uprooted and left so suddenly, and had not contacted him, and I understood his feelings. John treated people with respect, expecting the same in return, and on this occasion he had not received this consideration. I was also concerned about the way Colin and Alan had met without him, it was as if they were plotting something they did not want him to know about. I did not feel it appropriate to broach the subject again, unless John decided to talk about it.

From what I had been told, Colin knew more than he was

saying, although it was not for me to comment on the issue. I was certainly confused, but confident that Colin had a responsibility to explain all, I let the subject go. I had not known Alan Donald, so perhaps there were two sides to this story, and maybe John was holding back on something. Changing the subject seemed appropriate.

'When did you move to Ruby Bay?' I asked.

'I moved here in 1981, following the death of my wife. I did not want to remain in the house I had shared with her; there were too many memories of the good times together. It was a long time ago. Time heals so they say,' he said.

He said it was a long time ago, but I saw in his eyes that the wounds had not healed. This piece of news made me feel even sorrier for him

We walked along the cliff top and joined up with the path leading to the beach. The seagulls gave out their familiar cry, swooping low to find food, the harvest was quite slim at the moment; the tourists made it more bountiful for the birds, as they were always a good source of food. The day was sunny and cloudless, quite still except for a slight breeze from the south west. The beach was being lapped by the surf and I was able to smell the sea air, always a pleasant smell, one I had missed during my time away.

John appeared happier now; he had put what we discussed to the back of his mind, and this was an adventure. On reaching the beach we found it almost deserted, the tide was well out, just a few locals walking our canine friends, quite oblivious to what was happening around them.

Our crossing to the island was straightforward, no sea tractor was required. As we trundled across my feet sank into the wet sand, leaving impressions behind me. John was quiet except for a comment on the weather, a typical British remark I thought. I was starting to look forward to seeing my plot of land, not sure what to expect: just a big hole was my first thought, nobody had been very complimentary of my inheritance. But deep down I felt I was going to be part of a sequence of events, and that my inheritance was likely to play a part in those events. I did not know that these events would have an impact that would change my life forever. Had I known at that point, the initial step was unlikely to have been taken.

The slipway to the island lay ahead. Standing guard was the large sea tractor, still and primed, waiting for the tide to turn. The island was about 400 metres across, rising to a peak some 50 metres above sea level. At the top of the island was the small stone building, without a roof now. This was about 8 metres square, possibly a gun emplacement during the Second World War, a theory that everyone seemed to agree with. This building was reached by a series of paths, each one giving a different route to the top, each one well-trodden by the feet of tourists; the locals rarely ventured past the inn.

To my left as I looked at the island was the hotel, a white building of a considerable size, fenced in to provide privacy for the wealthy guests. A little further around the rocks was a small house, precariously perched on a rocky foundation above the high tide line; a small boat house lay below it. To my right was the Smugglers' Inn, a place where time stood still, except when it came to purchasing alcohol, a groat was unlikely to buy a drink in this place. It was our intention to visit these premises when my inheritance had been located and examined.

I looked towards the dilapidated hut at the top of the island. John saw me looking.

'I think it was an observation point in the last war,' he said.

'I think you're right. That was the general feeling when I came here as a child, not that anybody was certain it was fact, but the story remained. I remember from those days that the hut is of little interest, and I doubt that has changed,' I said.

John indicated the way towards the hotel, which was not where I had expected the captain's hut to be. I had anticipated his abode to have been closer to the inn, if what I knew of the man was true. We walked briskly towards the fence surrounding the hotel,

John striding ahead with purpose. He seemed interested in getting the job done and retiring to the inn, and I was starting to agree with him.

We walked tight against the security fence. It was a narrow path, invisible under the overgrown bracken, but I felt it was there somewhere. The bracken tugged against my clothing, making it a slow ramble for me. John did not appear much deterred as he stormed ahead. He apologized several times for the route.

'There's no need to apologize, it is not your fault unless you constructed it three hundred years ago. I shouldn't think the spot is likely to be visited by many people, only people like us who have an interest. I agree it was unlikely a local rambler would anticipate finding the hole, so maybe the door does serve a purpose,' I said.

I pulled away at the forest of greenery, and at last I saw a wooden door. The door was a metre square, with a lock at one side. I pulled out the key, it fitted the lock perfectly. I started to turn it, expecting not to be that successful, thinking the lock might have been rusted, but surprisingly the key turned easily. I lifted the door to find a hole a metre deep and 2 metres square.

I had brought a torch and was able to inspect the whole area beneath the door. It was empty except for a small wooden box. I pulled the box from the hole and was pleased to see it was a small, ancient chest. I looked at John and smiled. The box was not locked, but to my disappointment it was empty. I did not really expect to find anything inside, and I was aware many would have opened this box before me, but it had to be opened to reach that conclusion, and at least my curiosity was satisfied. I returned the box.

The next suggestion was the best, my lost treasure was to be the main topic over a drink at the inn. The entrance to the Smugglers' Inn had a latched wooden door, split across the middle, allowing each half to be opened separately. By the look of it, it was the original door. It was a wonderful example of basic wood-craft, no frills, built for a specific purpose. Opening this door was an art form: one had to open the top half and then place one's hand inside to release the latch.

The inside of the inn had the smell of stale tobacco and alcohol. On entering the bar area I was impressed by what I saw, it was like going back in time, although the door had definitely been a clue. There were large wooden beams in the walls and ceilings, misshapen and worn by the ravages of time. These beams were probably part of the original inn. The floor was slate, uneven to walk on but no doubt cool on bare feet. A grand fireplace was located by the outside wall, a large log burned, and not all the smoke went up the chimney, but somehow that seemed right, nobody was complaining. All the walls were an off-white colour; the smoke from the fire had no doubt caused the discolouration. The bar was made of a dark wood that had centuries of ale spills embedded into it; it smelt wonderful. This was a part of the history of the place, no doubt Vicary stood exactly where I stood, ordering his grog from the barkeep, preaching to his crew.

John asked my opinion of the place.

'It's everything I could have hoped for. I think everyone who enters must be impressed with the interior. It is everything I wanted to see, but I did not expect to find it so well preserved,' I said.

'I'll see if I can find the landlord. He knows a great deal about the island; I think he will increase your knowledge by leaps and bounds,' he said.

He moved away in an attempt to find the landlord, and I stood there in awe at the condition and authenticity of the place. An array of pewter mugs hung behind the bar, some bent and twisted, others dented although usable; all were discoloured from lack of care. I had my doubts whether these were the ones used by Vicary; it was an unlikely yet romantic thought.

'Pat, this is Tom Maxwell, the landlord of this beautiful inn,' said John.

I shook hands with Tom who said he hoped I was to become a regular in his establishment.

'I feel certain that I will; it is the only pub for miles around and you appear to have cornered the market. I was a regular visitor to Ruby Bay during my childhood, but not to the inn of course,' I said.

'Are you the one who has just bought the Vicary place?' said Tom.

'That's a strange thing to say: Vicary has been dead for several hundred years, his family has not owned the house for over sixty years, and to my knowledge Captain Vicary never even owned my bungalow,' I said.

'I know it seems strange, but he is the area's most famous son and anything to do with the man is important to the inn, as well as the local area of course. As you say, Captain Vicary only ever lived on the island, but the tourists love to hear any story connected with him. Don't worry, I never mention your bungalow in my chats, they only want to hear about his dastardly deeds. In fact he spent most of his time propping up the bar in here; mind you, he had a right to, he supplied all the booze that was drunk, illegally of course,' he said.

'So this was the same James Vicary who bequeathed me a hole in the ground?' I said.

'I'm afraid it is, I can see you now peering into that empty hole, like many people before you. Maybe in the distant past someone was lucky enough to find treasure. It is a mystery why the piece of land is attached to your bungalow,' he said. He showed us to a small table near the log fire, but not so close as to inhale the smoke. He asked if I had an interest in Captain Vicary, apart from my house purchase, as John had told him I wanted to know more.

I said my knowledge of the man was quite sparse, any addition to this was appreciated, particularly as I had now started to feel like a family member.

Tom then started his story. Whether it was the scripted one for tourists, I did not really care.

I was to imagine the island several hundred years ago, in the middle of the seventeenth century: the inn had just been built, the hotel was obviously not there. The island was littered with small wooden huts, the homes of the islanders, haphazardly scattered, many where the hotel now stands. My hole was probably the foundation of Vicary's hut. The huts had slate floors, much like the inn's floor. The walls were packed with peat to protect them during the winter, which was extremely cold on this island. Tom said he knew that from experience: the wind chilled to the bones. Walking around the island, the smell must have been worse than bad; these people did not wash, sanitary conditions were non-existent, and health-wise they were probably in a bad state of being.

Our illustrious captain was in charge of the smuggling operation on the island. How it started nobody knew, but it was the lifeline of the island, and kept the people fed. All the islanders were involved in some way or another, all of the men were members of the crew, except the inn's landlord: he was in charge of selling any surplus goods. There were about 100 people living on the island, including wives and children. They had one ship, anchored in the deep water at the far side of the island, away from the prying eyes of the Revenue men, who were much feared

The strongest possibility was that the crew got to the ship by rowing around in small boats. But it was rumoured that there was a secret passage at the far side of the island, used by the crew to get to the ship. It was suggested that gold and jewels were hidden somewhere in it, and many had tried to find it, but none had ever succeeded. Tom believed the secret passageway was something made up by treasure hunters to add a bit of spice to that period in time.

Smuggling in the time of Vicary was a capital offence: the only punishment if caught was the hangman's noose. In fact, most offenders were punished in that way in those days; they were strung up for any wrongdoing. This form of deterrent kept the islanders very vigilant, never trusting strangers, always believing them to be Revenue men, which they usually were. It was not known if any of the strangers were killed, but it was quite likely that any Revenue man coming onto the island was at risk. Unfortunately the islanders had little choice, it was smuggle or starve. It was a poor choice, but what else was there for them to do?

If only they had stuck to smuggling. It was their tried and tested way of making a living; not a particularly good one, but a living nonetheless. The only person who actually made money from smuggling was Vicary; the islanders certainly did not. The change to this lifestyle was probably brought about by Vicary. He was a greedy man, and intelligent enough to realize that his fortune was unlikely to come from smuggling. Hardly anyone in the crew was capable of reading or writing, none of them had any sort of education, and Vicary's use of long words impressed them. They had no idea what he was talking about but they trusted his judgement in all things.

Vicary told the crew he had an idea to make them a lot of money. Those words alone made them sit up and take notice. Vicary knew that merchant ships passed along the Channel on a daily basis, most headed for the ports of London. Some of these ships were from Spain and France, and some were thought to carry gold. These ships carried more valuable cargo than they did on their smuggling trips. That was Vicary's theory, which he told the crew

I asked, 'So is this when they became pirates, changing their whole lifestyle for instant wealth?'

'It was not quite that simple, taking up piracy was a big step. I will explain the sequence of events,' he said.

Vicary knew he had to persuade the crew to change their way of life. Greed was a prime incentive, which he used to wet their appetite for the venture, but he needed more. Vicary's talk of great wealth was not enough for all of the crew; some of the slightly brighter expected more details, and wanted to know the risks. Both smuggling and piracy carried the death penalty, which was not the issue. But smuggling was done by arrangement with both parties, whereas piracy was not. Some members of the crew suggested that the ship they attacked would certainly resist. The crew were not happy at putting their lives at risk, and they wanted some assurance from their captain. He was unable to give this with any degree of honesty, but honesty played no part in his life.

Vicary had to convince them that there was little risk. Some of the men did not like him, and at that time he was skating on relatively thin ice with certain crew members. Vicary was astute enough to know his crew, and there was one man he needed on his side, the first mate Charles Landon, who had ideas of taking on Vicary's mantle as captain. Landon was the man everyone in the crew feared, even more than they feared Vicary. Vicary knew there was some unrest among the crew; he needed Landon on his side. The crew did not have the courage to question what Landon told them to do; he was perhaps more of a legend than Vicary in his day, but only Vicary is down in the history books. He had a private meeting with Landon, explaining that there was money to be made by becoming pirates. The risks were there but most of the merchant ships carried skeleton crews, because the sailors were required for the Spanish and French navies, both still embroiled in war. Vicary offered Landon a substantial share of whatever was taken, the details of which the crew were oblivious to and Landon quickly agreed to this deal. Landon was also greedy, he looked after his own interests rather than anyone in the crew.

Following this agreement Vicary called the crew together; they of course met at the inn. Vicary needed to convince the men there was no danger; he needed to make the venture sound easy and lucrative. He put the idea to the men, who were in a foul mood. Vicary tricked them into believing he knew what cargo each ship carried, and that the riches would be great. He then played his trump card and got Landon to speak to the men. Landon was forceful, telling them the risks were minimal, and the riches were estimated to be ten times what they got from smuggling. Vicary was now in a position to blame Landon if things went wrong.

Vicary explained to the crew that some of the goods needed to be held onto; the sensible move was to sell when the price was right. It was Vicary's intention to sell the goods at a good profit, but to tell Landon and the crew he had got considerably less; his profit was to increase at the expense of the crew. He was pleased Landon had not thought this out. Vicary had deceived Landon: it was his intention to hide the booty, he was not going to tell Landon where it was. He had many hiding places, known only to his most loyal crew members, and they had no intention of informing on their captain. Under normal circumstances any sensible man might fear the wrath of Landon, but Vicary knew better than that: Landon was not in a position to harm the man who was holding his share of the booty. This was Vicary's insurance policy, he knew Landon was unable to harm him before the share-out took place, a share-out that Vicary never intended to honour.

'Is that when they became pirates, was that the moment?' I said.

'Unfortunately that is as far as I can go at the moment: I have licensing hours to consider. I appreciate this was not a problem in Vicary's time; they never closed the bar. But I will continue when you next visit,' he said.

Tom picked up the glasses and moved to the bar. We said our goodbyes and left, promising to return that evening to hear the rest of the intriguing tale.

I already knew something of Captain James Vicary's history. He was born in 1600 in Dawlish, South Devon. He came from a relatively poor family, and his father worked as a merchant seaman aboard a ship out of Dartmouth. His father made sure James received some sort of education before he went to sea at the age of 15. James worked aboard with his father until his father tragically died at sea. This event changed Vicary's life; he left home intent on making his own way in the world. He ended up on the island at Ruby Bay, not far from his home town. The year was 1640 and James was 40 years of age. He worked on the small ship that the islanders possessed, until he had a dispute with the captain at the time. During the altercation Vicary killed the captain and immediately took on the role of captain, the islanders accepted their new leader without question.

Charles Landon was born in Plymouth in 1615 of a good middle-class family; his father was a captain in the Royal Navy. Charles decided on the same career and was commissioned in 1635. He served with distinction and started to rise through the ranks, and a wonderful career appeared to be his destiny. In 1645 during a spot of shore leave he got into a fight with another officer, resulting in his death. Landon did not wait around for the court marshal, he made his way to Ruby Bay and joined up with Vicary. Landon was a powerfully built man, over 6 foot in height, broad-shouldered and muscular. His time in the Royal Navy had not only made him an excellent sailor, but he was also able to command respect with ease.

John and I spoke as we walked towards the tractor; there were a few questions I wanted to ask him. We both agreed that Tom was an interesting man, but I wondered how much of what he told us was true.

'I suspect there is a lot of folklore attached to these stories, and I expect they change each time Tom tells them. I don't think anyone can say for certain what the truth is. I can understand why the tourists flock to the inn to hear such tales, Tom is a good storyteller,' I said.

I was hoping some light would be thrown on my inheritance, and this alone gave me a good reason to hear more. Vicary had thought the hole in the ground to be of great significance, and somewhere in one of Tom's tales might lie the answer.

I was glad when it was time to visit the inn for the evening storytelling, confident I might learn something to my advantage. We reached the sea tractor on our side of the beach as the tide was starting to come in. We climbed aboard the monster; we were the only outward customers tonight. Within minutes we had reached the island, where the beach was well covered by the murky sea. We thanked the driver and made our way up the slipway, then it was just a short walk to the inn.

The inn was empty when we entered. Tom stood behind the bar, and nodded to us as we sat down.

'What can I get you?' he enquired.

We ordered a couple of pints and he continued the story with enthusiasm. I listened intently, hoping to learn something new.

The next thing was to pick their first target ship, it needed to be a reasonable haul, otherwise the crew were likely to feel cheated, as they remembered the promise of wealth. Vicary knew there was plenty of shipping in the Channel, but what cargo they carried was down to pure luck. Every ship carried something of value, and most carried a certain amount of gold to be used in emergencies, payment for any repairs and the like. An important problem arose: how to stop the other ship. The French and Spanish ships were faster than the ship Vicary had. He needed a foolproof plan, for any sort of failure would make him look bad in front of the crew, and this could not be allowed to happen.

Vicary and Landon met to discuss a course of action, and yet again Vicary used this to his advantage, suggesting that Landon informed the crew of the plan. If the plan worked, Vicary's position was likely to be enhanced; if it failed, Landon would be seen to be the originator and his position was likely to slump. The meeting between the two of them lasted some time, and eventually a plan was hatched. It was decided that a distress signal was to be used by the hoisting of signal flags. No ship refused help to another showing the distress flags. This message was guaranteed to bring at least one of the ships alongside, giving Vicary's men chance to board the other vessel. Going on the premise that these ships had minimum crew numbers, there was a strong possibility that the plan might work. But there was no way of knowing that the ships were undermanned, it was really only a wild guess. The plan was in place.

Landon told the men, emphasizing the skeleton crews on the intended target, and that the islander's ship would outnumber the enemy's paltry force, and the crew assumed that he knew this to be a fact. It was agreed. The last thing to do was to name the day: that was the easy part, as the Channel always had merchant ships passing through.

Everyone met at the inn on the night of the first piracy voyage, waiting for the midnight tide. The trip to the part of the Channel where merchant ships were plentiful was about six hours' sailing, and the mission had to be completed as quickly as possible. All had to be done before the sun came up: daylight would be their enemy, allowing any ship coming to the aid of the merchant to follow Vicary's ship, and it was unlikely they had the speed to outrun these larger ships.

The ship slipped anchor just before midnight, and returned about ten the following morning. The ship that returned was not theirs, it was a Spanish galleon, much larger and without doubt faster. They had changed ships during the mission, probably moving the Spanish crew onto their ship which was then scuttled, killing the Spaniards and leaving no witnesses. A superior vessel was now at their disposal, better equipped and much faster, the targets within their reach had increased, and they also had a few Spanish cannons on board.

All the islanders felt this was a turning point in their lives, the first act of piracy had gone off without any apparent hitches. But when they checked what cargo they had stolen, this first haul was something of a disappointment, consisting mostly of silks and spices. Although these items were sold at a considerable profit, it was not the untold wealth Vicary had promised. The crew received about three times more than they got on their smuggling trips, and this satisfied the majority.

What was never told to the crew was that this galleon also had a strongbox, no doubt containing gold coins. Vicary told Landon he was going to hide the strongbox; its contents were to be shared by them later. Landon did not see the strongbox disappear, he was too busy with the offloading of the cargo, he also misguidedly trusted Vicary, a grave mistake on his part. Landon went along with the idea, believing at that point he could trust him, a big mistake as it was to turn out. From then on Landon stayed close to Vicary, but still the gold was not shared with him. Vicary refused to tell Landon where the gold was hidden, stating it was for security reasons. This is when he started to distrust Vicary, believing he intended to keep the gold for himself.

Keeping close, Landon thought Vicary might lead him to the strongbox, but Vicary was too clever for that. He wanted all the gold, and it was never his intention to share with Landon. He started to get agitated by Landon's constant presence. Landon had to be disposed of. This option was not easy, as Landon was too strong to be met face to face the plan needed to be a more subtle, and had to be thought out carefully. And Landon was too valuable at that time in their activities.

Vicary had a problem: because that first raid had not brought the wealth they had expected, it was necessary to carry out another. This time he knew Landon would be watching very closely, having learnt a valuable lesson. It was decided to carry out a similar raid, using the same plan as before. The crew thought it a great idea the first venture had been easy, and nobody wanted to go back to the smuggling days. It was only Vicary who appreciated that being a pirate in the English Channel was not going to be a long career, for as well as merchant ships, the Royal Navy patrolled these waters.

It was going to be some time before the galleon they had plundered was to be notified as missing, so a few more trips before lying low were a possibility. The authorities might accept that the galleon was lost at sea with all hands, but if they plundered a few more ships in the same way it was unlikely that all these losses would be accepted as unfortunate; piracy was the only likely explanation. Yet the crew believed they would be able to plunder ships indefinitely, not being fully conversant with normal life outside the island.

The problem for Vicary was as before: he had no idea of the cargoes. He knew he had to find a bigger haul, but he had no idea how. Perhaps a French ship had the potential for greater wealth. Losing the loyalty of the crew was unthinkable, and he spoke to them and told them everything was going to plan. Vicary was also aware that Landon was waiting in the wings: any slip-up at all, and a new captain was likely to be presented to the crew.

Vicary announced to the crew that he felt it necessary to carry out two acts of piracy a week. He explained that the first haul was a disappointment, but they had to sell to the first buyer. With two trips a week, some of the haul could be kept in reserve, waiting for the price to rise before selling. The talk of high finance impressed the crew; they had no idea what it meant, but they understood that the whole idea was to make them richer. Even Landon went along with the plan, but his reasons were different from the crew's: the more trips, the more chance of finding the hiding place. Landon had now passed the stage of being bought off, he wanted all the gold for himself.

'Did the piracy continue with a vengeance, plundering more ships?' I asked. Tom continued his story. 'Not quite as many as the crew had hoped. The smuggling did continue, as did the two piracy trips a week, but no great fortune was forthcoming,' he said.

The next trip was similar to the first: plenty of silks and spices with a small amount of gold. The gold was again hidden by Vicary; Landon had taken his eye off what was happening. The gold was hidden by a member of the crew loyal to Vicary, but Landon was watching Vicary. Landon was again told by Vicary that the gold was to be split between them at a later date and Landon had no choice but to accept those terms, as he had no idea where the hiding place was.

On their third excursion into the field of piracy, the cargo changed the life of every islander. Boxes of gold and silver were the haul, along with an assortment of fine jewels. It was what the crew had wanted from the start, their fortune made in one haul. Vicary was eager to take the credit, but events were about to conspire against the crew.

History shows that this particular ship was in the wrong place, it was far off its predicted course when Vicary plundered it. Had the vessel been on the right course, it would have been closer to the French mainland than the English mainland, an important factor. The only ships carrying such wealth were doing so for a very specific reason: this cargo was intended for the British government, a payment from the French. The reasons for it are unclear, possibly an incentive to declare war on Spain. Either way, the cargo was valuable, particularly to the government, and it created serious problems for the islanders, bringing the full force of the Royal Navy into play. Such acts of piracy on government ships were treated seriously, and the Royal Navy had an obligation to search high and low to bring the pirates to justice. Anyone found in possession of such gold was unlikely to receive anything other than a meeting with the hangman.

'Were the crew aware of what they had done? Surely they saw the gold was stamped? I appreciate they were simple folk, but common sense must have played some part?' I said.

'It was unlikely they knew what they had; to them it was just a cargo that had made them rich. But it appears Vicary was aware of the blunder and I have no doubt he shared this knowledge with Landon. I feel sure Landon already appreciated the seriousness of the problem. All the gold and silver was in ingot form, clearly marked with the coat of arms of France. None of their usual fences, if I may use that modern-day description, were in a position to touch the merchandise – they knew the consequences if they were caught with it. The cargo was impossible to dispose of; the Royal Navy were now going to be patrolling the Channel as never before. Going out to plunder another ship was out of the question, and their second option of smuggling was going to be too risky,' he said.

'So what was done with the cargo, what effect did it have on the islanders?' I said.

It appears that the cargo was hidden by Vicary and Landon. Vicary had no problem with Landon knowing this new hiding place, as the cargo was no good to them, not at that stage anyway. Vicary called a meeting at the inn, as the crew needed to know the seriousness of the situation. He explained it in the simplest of terms, making sure even the thickest islander understood. Quite a few of the crew did not accept what he said, they thought they were being double-crossed and demanded their shares. Landon then stepped in and told them what Vicary said was true. Even after Landon had spoken to the crew they still demanded their share, so Vicary gave into pressure, telling the crew that the merchandise was to be checked, and they were entitled to their share which would be available for them in two days, once the loot had been divided accordingly.

This would give him the necessary time to make other arrangements. Both Vicary and Landon knew the loot was not saleable, and they were delaying the crew long enough to make their escape. The life they knew on the island was over. Now it was a matter of facing whatever consequences befell the islanders, and these would be dire indeed.

The crew met at the inn as instructed by their captain. They waited, but neither Landon nor Vicary arrived; they were long gone. Neither man was ever heard of again, it was if they vanished from the face of the earth. It was impossible for them to have taken the last haul with them, there was too much for two men to carry, so it was assumed that the loot never left the island. None of the haul ever turned up on the market, not a single ingot.

Some of the islanders were eventually caught by the Royal Navy, trying to make a living by returning to smuggling. One of the crew admitted that the gold and silver was somewhere on the island, and this condemned many to an untimely death. The island never recovered: those that were able to get away left and the island was deserted for many years. Even the inn closed for a while, as the landlord had no business without his smuggled booze.

'How many of the crew were actually executed?' I asked

'I think most of them: the Navy made a big thing out of executing the men, using it as a deterrent, a warning to future pirates. It seems Vicary and Landon were never heard of again; they disappeared completely, as if they never existed. Historians are convinced they were both murdered by the crew, which seems a strange thing for them to do, as only Vicary and Landon knew where the treasure was hidden, so it is not a view shared by everyone. I think they probably just left the island, as there was nothing left for them. The strange thing was that their names never appeared again in the area. We knew Vicary and Landon were sailors, and that being the case they would have signed aboard ships, but there is nothing; nobody knows where or how they ended their days. Their deeds are recorded in the Museum in Plymouth, but their final location is unknown. Maybe the islanders did kill them, that could be the reason they were never heard of again. That is why people have been searching every nook and cranny on the island, convinced the treasure is still there,' said Tom.

'Where do you think the treasure is, Tom?' I said.

'If it is anywhere – and I am not convinced it exists – the far side of the island is the likeliest place, but many have tried looking there. Some of these people have turned up with sophisticated pieces of machinery, but no one as yet has been successful. It has been suggested there was a secret passage at the far side of the island, many people have tried to find that without success.'

'I wonder when Vicary's will was read? To do that there must have been a reason for knowing or suspecting he was dead. But I appreciate we will never know the answer to that. Do we know for certain that the piracy took place, or maybe that is folklore?' I said.

'It is a matter of record, this record is in the same museum in Plymouth. There is an inventory of what the French ship carried on that voyage, the gold and silver ingots are registered. The descendants of those executed returned to the island, obviously a long time later, but they were familiar with the details of the raid as it was the reason their descendants had left the island. I think it is certain that it happened, but there is no record of the loot ever being found. It is almost certain that something serious happened to the islanders, something that drove them away. Whole groups of people do not just leave their homes for no good reason, they were frightened into doing so. I believe, as many do, that the piracy caused this mass migration.'

My first thought was that disease might have been the reason, as it was not uncommon in those days for typhoid or the like to strike. They were unhealthy people, and disease was a possibility, but if that was the case some record of such a disaster would be available. Although there were no records of any disease on the island, it was a more logical reason why they left the island. The treasure story was certainly more romantic, but was it true? Tom's story was acceptable to the tourists, and he had no intention of frightening them off with tales of disease; his story had a romantic side, and he had decided to stick with it.

2

I awoke the next morning with a hangover, brought about by consuming a lot of alcohol the previous night; this I attributed to Tom's story-telling. I pulled back the curtains carefully, the glaring sunlight was there as expected, and it felt like the back of my eyeballs were burning. Another sunny day in paradise. Breakfast on the veranda was the only option, a gourmet breakfast affectionately known as a fry-up.There was a great deal to think about. Tom's story was fascinating, but how much was true I did not know. A tale passed down through the ages can change considerably, and it probably bore no resemblance to the actual events. If a large amount of gold and silver was taken, common sense said that it must have turned up somewhere. For there to be no trace put the whole tale into disrepute. Only the people who had repopulated to the island said the loot existed, and they were probably nothing to do with the original islanders. Like anyone else I wished that the events had happened, it gave an air of mystery to the island. History states the ship was robbed, it was attributed to Vicary and his crew, but what if some other pirates carried out the robbery, and Vicary was merely the scapegoat?

And the eventual whereabouts of Vicary and Landon remained unknown: they were either killed, or left the island. If they had left the island surely someone had some knowledge of their whereabouts. I believed the crew had murdered them, and thrown them overboard.

My thoughts were broken by the ring of the telephone. The voice on the other end was Colin Wickham; this man was haunting me. He invited me to his house for dinner that very evening.

'That's strange, Colin. What is the reason for this invitation?' I said.

'Everything will be revealed at dinner.'

His reply was a little confusing, 'I had no idea something had to be revealed,' I responded.

'I thought you might be interested in a short history of the island. I appreciate you have spoken to Tom at the inn, but I feel I can give the subject more depth. I think you might learn something to your advantage. And don't worry, it is not another inheritance,' he said.

I accepted his invitation. The time was arranged, and Colin gave me directions to his house a short distance away. A pleasant walk, I was told.

I was still sitting there, mystified by the invitation, when John appeared in the garden. Was he tapping my telephone? I was glad to see him, and felt his advice on my recent telephone conversation might prove invaluable.

I asked how well he knew Colin. I was aware of the differences between the two of them, and I did not want John to go over that ground again, but fortunately he did not and was forthright in his answers.

'What do you know about Colin, John? I know he has a good reputation in the village, no doubt because all the houses in the village have been conveyanced by him. I appreciate it is unlikely to find anything detrimental about the solicitor who does the conveyancing for your property, apart from the fee of course. In such cases people are satisfied if the deal goes through without any hitches,' I said.

'Why are you asking about Colin?' he said.

'He has invited me to dinner tonight, he said he wanted to discuss the history of the place. I don't know why he said that, I have never mentioned to him about such an interest. He also said I might learn something to my advantage, but made it clear I had not inherited anything else. Which is a shame, I wouldn't mind inheriting the inn. What do you think, John?' I said.

'Perhaps you should go and find out; you have nothing to lose,' he said.

'You're right, but can I ask you if you trust Colin?'

He paused at this question, whether that meant he did not trust him I did not know. 'I'm not quite sure what you're saying. I do not think an invitation to dinner should be treated as some sort of deception on Colin's part. It does give you the opportunity to hear Colin's history lesson, see how it compares to Tom's version.'

'Of course you're right, he might have details of what happened to Vicary and Landon. He might have other details of the gold and silver, perhaps he got rich because he found it,' I said.

'I have known Colin since I moved here in 1981, he handled my house purchase, he carried that out in an efficient manner, I have no complaints about that part of our relationship. Even before Alan arrived I have only had a few conversations with Colin. He always seemed too busy to talk, moving from one appointment to another at breakneck speed. I think he deals with the outlying villages as well. He always nodded when he saw me in the village, or if he was showing potential buyers around your bungalow. Then Alan bought your place about a year ago, and the rest of the story you know. I do not think there is a problem in going to his house for dinner.'

'It does not appear that either of us know him very well, perhaps dinner might change that, it'll give me an opportunity to know him better, to find out if he has any skeletons in the closet,' I said.

'I think it will be to your advantage, I think he probably has a proposition for you. I don't think Colin just makes friendly gestures,' he said.

This proved to me that John knew more than he was saying, but he obviously wanted Colin to tell me, as he had with the inheritance.

'Colin's house is huge, which is surprising because there are only two occupants – Colin, of course, and his very attractive wife, Jane. Jane is much younger than Colin and I've only met her twice in all the time I have been here. She works in Colin's office, although she is a qualified accountant. The job market is somewhat limited for her; she is hoping to get into banking, but at the moment she does the paperwork for the office. She is definitely the attractive part of the business.'

John was influenced strongly by Jane's beauty, she was mentioned several times in this short conversation. I asked him how well he knew Jane, he stated not very well, she was rarely seen out and about, Colin kept her under wraps.

I promised to give him a full report of my dinner at Colin's palatial house. He left with a smile on his face, whether that smile was because he was thinking of Jane, or whether there was something else on his mind, I was to find out that night.

It was just after 7.30 when I took the road to Colin's house. I had been fully appraised as to the route, which was supposed to take only a few minutes. Strange that I had never noticed a large house before, but this of course depended on John's definition of large: each person has different ideas on that. I had decided to dress in collar and tie, no dress code had been mentioned so I assumed it was not a formal gathering, but I took the safe option which also showed a certain amount of respect. The private road to his house was clearly marked, but I had failed to notice it before. Ruby Bay house was an impressive building, John had been correct on that score, and it was well off the beaten track.

I rang the doorbell, and Colin opened the door, he was also wearing a collar and tie. I was invited into a large hallway and then through into a larger lounge, beautifully decorated; someone in this household had taste. A tall, slim and very attractive blonde lady stood in the lounge, this was obviously Jane. John was right in his description of her: she was a stunner.

'Pat, may I introduce you to Jane?' said Colin.

We shook hands and exchanged the usual pleasantries. She was about 6 foot tall, well dressed and much more elegant than I had expected. Colin was a little taller than Jane and quite a bit older, exactly as John had said, but they looked good together.

The inside of the house appeared a lot larger than I had expected. I saw six large oil paintings on the walls of the lounge, and I decided not to appear both rude and ignorant by asking if they were originals.

'They are originals, I am assuming that was the thought that crossed your mind? The artists are not significant at the moment, but who knows about the future. They are an investment, hopefully a good one,' she said.

Maybe she was hoping their prestige might rise in the future, or maybe she just liked the subject matter.

'I'm afraid we are not all appreciative of art,' she gestured toward Colin when she said it. 'He has no understanding of culture, he is not keen on these paintings, he is a Philistine when it comes to art. I hope you are not the same?' she said.

'I like some art, but I am in no way an expert,' I responded.

Colin smiled, and did not appear to think of it as criticism.

The room we stood in had wonderful decor, obviously not Colin's choice, decorated to the taste of a woman. Jane offered to show me around the house after dinner, and I gracefully accepted her kind offer.

'This house appears large for only two occupants, I don't wish to be impolite but it is a large house,' I said.

'You are right, but part of the house was originally designated for office space for the overflow from the business. In fact we use that space to store important paperwork. It has five bedrooms, which I suppose it a bit excessive. We have a pool to the rear of the property, a sauna and a snooker room, and a separate games room. It is a bit over the top but it is something we both wanted in the house.'

I thought of Jane playing snooker, which was a pleasant thought, worth paying to see.

'You must have sold a lot of houses to buy this place, I didn't think it was that profitable in a village like Ruby Bay,' I said.

He knew I was probing him for information, and he was happy to flaunt his good fortune, in fact he clearly relished the opportunity, whereas Jane stood by silently.

'This house is not the result of me selling a lot of houses, I think you knew that when you asked the question. Once we've had dinner I will answer all the questions you have, even to the extent of explaining how a poor solicitor can maintain such a house. Be prepared for a feast, Jane really is an excellent cook. But I will let you be the judge, I don't think you will be disappointed.'

We moved into the dining room, yet another impressive room with wonderful decor, and a chandelier as its centrepiece. The dining table was capable of seating 12 people comfortably, yet the room was not dwarfed by the table.

I was seated at the head of the table. Was this a dubious honour, or was it just the polite thing to do? I suspected this was something I was to find that out in the next couple of hours.

Jane left the room to fetch the first of the five courses. She was indeed an excellent cook, Colin had landed on his feet with her. He remained seated throughout dinner, as Jane scuttled backwards and forwards to the kitchen.

Once dinner was over Jane showed me around the house, it was indeed luxurious, and she was proud of her design. We returned to the lounge and Jane left the room; it was obvious that Colin did not feel she needed to be present. I thanked her for the meal before she left, and I received a lingering smile in return.

Colin asked me to take a seat and make myself comfortable, then started to seduce me with his fine Cognac. It was a winning combination. I still had no idea why this meeting was taking place, nothing had been mentioned to give me any sort of clue, and he avoided talking about anything but the meal, then I felt a pang inside me. I was a retired man with a moderate income, perhaps this was some sort of scam he was about to pull off, and he needed my police experience to find out how legal it was, that must be it.

Then Colin said what he was about to tell me was going to need my full attention. This had the makings of a scam, and I prepared myself to reject any offer he made.

'What I am about to tell you will sound fantastic, it may in your mind appear to be the ravings of a lunatic, but I ask only one thing, please hear me out before I answer any of the many questions you will ask. What I am about to tell you is the truth,' he said.

I nodded that I understood what he had said, I was to remain silent until he finished pitching his scheme. He was going to have difficulty persuading me if it was illegal, and I intended to tell him that, if what he was about to say made it necessary.

'What do you know about the history of Ruby Bay and the island?' he asked.

'I had a small amount of knowledge, but this was increased greatly by what Tom had told us at the inn. I am not sure how much truth there is in his story, these tales change over time, to make them more exciting. I understood that Tom was merely relaying what he had been told. I have an open mind on the subject,' I said.

I then narrated in detail what Tom had told us at the inn, endeavouring to leave nothing out.

Colin listened intently to what I was saying, then he smiled when my account was completed in full.

'The names of the characters are correct, but then I expected Tom to get that right – nobody doubts that Vicary existed, the area abounds with stories of him. As far as the events on the island during the time Vicary was around, Tom was more or less correct. The smuggling trips and the acts of piracy, they actually happened, as did that fateful raid on the French ship, with the haul of gold and silver bullion. As you were told, it was impossible to sell the bullion, and, of course, nobody wanted to be involved in the mess the islanders had found themselves in. The poverty that followed for the islanders was horrendous, there was only one option for them, not a viable option, that was to go back to smuggling booze. They knew if they did that the Royal Navy would surely catch them – it was suggested that was how they were eventually caught and executed.

'This may surprise you, but the story is untrue. What Tom did not tell you was that Landon returned to the island after leaving with Vicary, while Vicary never returned. His fate is unknown; even to this day it was assumed he was killed by the crew. Landon told the crew to wait for Vicary to return – he would tell them where the gold and silver was hidden, but this was a lie, because he knew exactly where the gold and silver was. He had no intention of sharing this with the crew, he wanted to move it to a secret place known only to him. He was able to remove enough, during the hours of darkness, to give him wealth for the rest of his life. Once he had enough he told the islanders where the remainder was to be found and they shared it out amongst themselves, but once they tried to use it they were arrested and executed. Landon disappeared, and although he had hidden a stash for himself, it was too much for him to move, so some of his stash remains hidden on the island. Landon was able to smelt what he did get out, hence the reason he never got caught,' he said.

'I enjoyed Tom's account, but your account has so much more detail. How do you know what you have just told me about?' I asked.

Colin had been pacing the room as he told the story. He suddenly stopped and looked out of the window. It was a prolonged silence, and he appeared deep in thought.

'This is the most difficult part of the evening, how to persuade you that what I have said is the truth. There is a good reason why I have so much knowledge of the events I have described, and you will think this is a crazy thing to say. It is best I just come right out with it and tell you why I know. I know what happened in those times because I was there. That is the reason for this dinner tonight, to tell you what I know, and to convince you of my sincerity in this matter, because I need your help to return to the past,' he said.

He was now facing me, waiting for some kind of reaction, but I was numb with anxiety for his sanity. Was this some kind of joke played at my expense?

His face was serious, not even a glimmer of a smile. He actually believed what he had just told me. I had no idea what to say so I said the first thing that came into my confused head.

'I must thank you for the meal, which as you promised was superb, now you can tell me the real reason for this invitation. What you just said can't be the reason. Your story was very good, but I realize it is just a story,' I said.

'I have explained the true reason for the invitation. I know it is difficult to believe,' he said.

'Did you seriously expect me to believe that tale? I had hoped you would credit me with more intelligence than that,' I said.

'I accept what you're saying, I know it sounds unbelievable, but the facts are as I have told you. All I want is a chance to prove it: surely you can allow me that opportunity. Listening to what I have told you must sound outrageous, and if I were in your position I would think the same. I do not expect you to accept this concept without proof, but I can offer that proof if you indulge me,' he said.

'Alright, I am prepared to listen, but I warn you it'll need to be very persuasive, as I'm convinced it is a ridiculous idea,' I said.

'My proof is simple, it requires that you take the trip with me, back in time, to the island inhabited by Vicary and his crew,' he said.

'To be honest I am not convinced this conversation is taking place, it feels like I am dreaming this part of the evening. Do you actually think I am just going to accept this crazy idea? I am starting to feel a little concerned for your sanity. If this trip is possible, why don't you just go? Why have you decided to tell me about the idea? Am I to assume from this conversation that maybe you are three hundred years old? Or is that a silly thing for me to say?' I said.

'I am the age I look. The only way I can travel back is to go with the present owner, that is of course you, Pat. I am a previous owner so I can travel, but the present owner must travel as well. I cannot travel without you, Pat. You do understand why that puts you in a privileged position?' said Colin.

I asked, 'I know you said you travelled back in time, but how are you going to convince me of that?'

'It is possible because the deed mentions the time travel phenomenon. You have not seen the complete document,' he said.

He then produced the missing part of the deed. 'I once owned the bungalow. I took my single trip to Roman times. I was able to locate a few coins which I knew were going to be valuable in our time, this was how I could afford my house. John then bought the bungalow, we then travelled back together, John as the present owner, and me as a previous owner,' said Colin.

'That's a surprise, John has never mentioned that to me,' I said.

'We went together and visited 1941, but we did not complete the mission we wanted to. Whilst there we discovered something quite unexpected – this will provide us both with riches if we take the trip. The trip to 1941 was for a completely different purpose – I wanted to save someone's life, someone very special to me. I will tell you more if you agree to the trip. When Alan bought the bungalow I tried to persuade Alan to go, but he decided to return to the past on his own. John is not aware of that, which is why I had to use the bereavement in Manchester story. The strange thing is, Alan has returned to Vicary's time. He intends to remain in that time because he was frightened by something to do with owing money to people in Manchester. It appears it was a large sum of money they wanted to collect; he mentioned they were not nice people, his life was at serious risk if he did not repay the money. I tried to help but he would not hear of it, stating it was his problem alone. He did not confide any details of the money as he felt the risks were too high, so he was left with little choice but to take the massive step into the past. The Manchester story I told John was untrue. This was at Alan's request, he just wanted to get away and he didn't want to involve John.'

'It really is a good tale, but my instincts tell me time travel is a thing of fiction, it does not happen,' I said.

'I understand how you feel, I thought the same as you, but let me tell you a few more facts, then you can rethink your opinion. A traveller, or hopefully us, is able to travel to one particular time and date in history, that is apart from Vicary's time, which I will explain to you. This single trip is done by using the key I gave you for the plot of land – it acts as a time travel key as well as an ordinary key. Once on the island the key is set by pulling out the sliding piece, the date is then set and the key is activated. The key can only be used on the island, it only allows the owner a single trip, returning them to the island after the trip. Before travelling to a particular time all travellers must visit the island first. It is like a staging point before making the designated trip, but the island is in the time of Captain Vicary, and this was the cause of a problem for John.'

'So John knew about this time travel? He would also know what was to be discussed at the dinner, is that correct?' I asked.

'That is correct. John was once the owner of your bungalow, he had also been invited to dinner as you were, the discussion was the same. John was more amenable to the time travel discussion, not necessarily believing it to be true, but hoping it was for his own reasons, thinking he might return in time and save his wife. I understood why he wanted the whole concept to be true. There was a slight problem in making the trip, as it was only possible to go to one destination after reaching the island; we disagreed on where we wanted to go. I wanted to go to 1941, as I wanted to save my father. I will at some stage explain the reason why, that is provided you agree to the trip. John on the other hand wanted to go back to 1981 which gave him the opportunity to save his wife; that is something else I will tell you at a later date. In order to make more than one trip, something called the Pathway had to be found. I had already made my single trip to Roman times, that was when I was the owner of your bungalow, I then accompanied John as the new owner. 1941 was John's single trip, although he wanted to go to 1981. It was our intention to find the Pathway, which would allow us to make numerous trips, but we were unable to locate it, so we had no choice but to return to the present. As I said, the single trip was possible by using the key. This opened up and a date was selected, including a return date. The button was pressed and that became the destination for the single trip, the portal opened automatically when the return date was reached.'

'I assume this Pathway is in Vicary's time, is that correct?' I said.

'I will explain this later. All I will tell you is that to make the trip back in time, one has to pass through the portal. This opens four times a year, it is the entry point to the past. It will open again in one month. If we do not travel then, we will have to wait another three months, that is the way it is,' said Colin.

I was trying desperately hard to understand what I was being told, it obviously sounded too fantastic to be true. I had no idea why I was still listening, did I think it was just a nice story?

'This really is a bit much to take in. Do you really expect me to accept what you say after this short conversation? If you want to convince me I think you will need some strong evidence,' I said.

'I completely understand your scepticism. Perhaps if you speak to John? He has no reason to lie, and he has made the trip back in time,' he said.

I was shocked. John had said nothing about these events, he never mentioned owning my bungalow, and he lied about Colin, he said he had hardly ever spoken to him.

Colin then went on to explain about the trip with John. They went back to 1941, it was something he needed to do, then they were going to get the Pathway and go back to 1981 to help John's wife. Getting the Pathway was not as easy as they originally thought, and they gave up and returned to this time. John sold the bungalow and moved next door, hoping the property's new owner would be in a position to help us. That was Alan Donald, but he had other ideas.

'So let me get this straight, you want to go back to 1941, a time both you and John have visited, but John had wanted to go to 1981 to save his wife, but because it was a single trip you were unable to travel to both times. If you want to convince me I would need more of an explanation, I am not in a position to decide without all the details,' I said.

Colin nodded to show he understood what I was saying. 'It appears John's wife was killed in a car crash in 1981, and this is something that we have the power to prevent. John moved to Ruby Bay following this incident, it was his way of trying to forget, although he informed me that he could never forget her. No doubt you agree with me that it would be the decent thing to do, to reunite John with his wife, the person who is still the love of his life. As you know I wanted to return to 1941, my reasons were twofold: one of these reasons was going to benefit both of us; the second was of a personal nature, I intended to save my father,' he said.

'Surely we only have the ability to make one trip, if I believe what you are telling me. It is either go to 1941 to complete the tasks you want, or we go to 1981 to save John's wife, is that the crux of the matter?' I said.

He nodded. 'That is the choice. I'll explain what I know. Once we enter the portal to go back in time, we always go back to Vicary's time, from there we move forward to our chosen destination, be it 1941 or 1981. The key is what is used to choose that destination, the shaft slides back and the date is selected. If we want to go to both 1941 and 1981, we need to locate the Pathway. This is a small tubular metal device, believed to be located in Vicary's cellar. Unfortunately it is in Vicary's time. On my last visit with John we believed it was too risky to attempt to find it. Vicary is not a nice man, can you imagine him finding you in the cellar of his hut? Not a pleasant thought,' he said.

'Am I correct in assuming my inheritance is in fact Vicary's cellar?'

'I am pretty certain that is the case, although neither myself nor John has actually tried it in Vicary's time. It is an important part of the plan that the key to the door is transported with us, as this can then be used for the single trip if we are unable to find the Pathway,' he said.

'I am very doubtful that my key is likely to fit Vicary's three-hundred-year-old cellar door, but fortunately the extra function of allowing us the single trip seems to be the reason for it being part of the deed. Before tonight I thought time travel was for the movies; I'm still not convinced it belongs anywhere else,' I said.

'I am fairly certain it is the original door you tried the key on, but obviously I cannot confirm that. We did not try the lock on our last visit to the island, for the reasons I have explained. The page of the deed explained all I have told you, I can only assume the text is correct,' he said.

'What about the small wooden box I found in the hole, do you think it is significant?' I said.

'I believe it probably held the Pathway at some time, but just like you, all those before you have found it empty. I will at a later stage discuss the properties of the Pathway; needless to say many trips can be made if you possess it, but it is better to wait until we have it, then its true worth can be appreciated.'

He went to his bureau and brought out several pages of ancient manuscript, which he handed to me. I was unable to decipher most of the words, although I recognized the word 'Pathway', which showed he was right about one thing, but the rest was not a writing I was familiar with.

'How do you know what is written on the manuscript? I am having difficulty deciphering a single word.'

'A friend of mine deciphered it, he is an expert on Old English.

The text describes the Pathway in good detail and how to use it if we ever find it,' he said.

'Can you explain in layman's terms what the text said?' I asked.

'From what he said Vicary was the instigator of the deed, which relates to the plot of land on the island, which we believe to be the cellar of his hut. It also states it is valid for any property connected to the plot of land. Vicary was aware his family were not on the island, from extensive research we still do not know what family he had or where they lived. It is obvious Vicary did not see the deed falling into the hands of someone outside his family. How many people have read the deed over the years is unknown, as well as how many of those people actually understood it. From the little we know it is unlikely Vicary's descendants either read or understood the deed, or they would not have been silly enough to attach it to the bungalow, thereby allowing more people access to the power of the deed. I appreciate this is difficult for you to take in, but the portal to the past does work. Both John and I have returned to the time of Captain Vicary and Charles Landon, and in fact I have drunk with both men at the bar of the inn. How would you like that experience?' he said.

I was listening, but it was impossible to believe what I was being told. I had a brief vision of propping up the bar next to Captain James Vicary, then my daydream ended.

'I will need to brief you fully if you decide to go. The things that you will find on the island, going back three hundred years are not something you take on board lightly, the people there are simple folk. As we pass through the portal, our clothing takes on the appearance of the fashion of the day; not that appealing but it allows us to blend in. There are also physical changes, again it helps us to fit in; we become someone who is already on the island. We go through the portal together and have no idea of the other person's identity when we reach the other side, although I believe I know what your identity will be. The reason I say that is simple: on my first visit I was the monk, as was John when I accompanied him. I assume Alan was the same, so it is very likely you will be the monk too. On my second visit I became a member of the crew, it is like a pecking order, the monk being the lowest form on the island. I have no idea how many visits are required to become Vicary. The pecking order system can be changed; I will explain that later.

'This situation only arises when you take the original trip from the present to the island. If you leave the island and make your one trip to the past, you have to return to the island before returning home and you remain as the person you were on the island, in your case the monk. It is only in the time of Vicary that your appearance changes, this is simply to fit it to what the islanders know. The monk is the spiritual leader on the island, but he serves no useful purpose, bearing in mind that these people sin daily and are not too religious. You may be required to perform a funeral. These are normally at sea and only a few religious words are required, nothing more than that. The monk has been known to stray as well; it seems all right as long as he doesn't get caught,' he said

'I must admit I do not feel comfortable with the position of a monk, a religious leader to an irreligious community. Not that I believe anything you are telling me. Well maybe just a little. If I am the monk, what is your disguise?' I asked.

'This is where everything gets a bit complicated, but hopefully I can explain,' he said.

On his first visit he was the monk. He believed he was competent in that role, life continued around him, he was watchful of the goings-on but never intrusive. He remembered his history of the place and wanted to wait around until the crew became pirates. He had no idea how long he had to wait until that took place; at that stage they were still smuggling off the coast of France, not very lucrative but at least it was safe. One day he got into an altercation with a member of the crew outside his house. The crewman was drunk and just wanted to fight someone and the poor old monk was the closest to hand – he tried in vain to persuade the man otherwise. The crewman eventually pulled a knife and a struggle ensued. He lunged at Colin but he was unsteady and Colin got the better of him, disarmed him and stabbed him in the chest, with fatal consequences.

This concerned him greatly, he was certainly not a murderer, but justice at the time was swift and usually final. He threw down the knife with the intention of running off into the darkness, there were no witnesses. Suddenly the man he had killed disappeared in front of him, he had become that man, the monk was gone. Before he returned to the present he made a point of checking on the monk – he was safe and well, he had no knowledge of the fight. A lesson had been learned, a very useful one. On each trip you rise up the ranks of the crew, if you kill someone you take on their identity, the person you were returns. If you kill someone you must make sure he is higher up the ranks than the person you leave behind.

He returned with John, who was now the monk; Colin was the crewman he had killed on his previous visit. He kept an eye on John from a distance, but he thought that if I decided to make the trip, it was important I knew his identity, this was likely to make our stay easier for both of us. Colin had instructed Alan when he went on his own that he needed to obtain another disguise other than the monk, as he was likely to be returning with the new owner of the bungalow. That new person was me.

'If you are considering taking the trip, if you believe what I have told you, you must think seriously about what you are letting yourself in for,' he said.

'I do have a concern, about Alan's identity. I hope he took your advice, otherwise the island will have two monks when I turn up. I feel it is a chance we cannot afford to take, two monks would definitely look suspicious,' I said.

'I am confident Alan has changed his identity as I advised him to do; I made him aware of the implications if he remained the monk. If you make the trip, there are several things to bear in mind. Both Alan and I would know your disguise, but you would not of course know ours. I think we need to arrange a meeting place, so that you know who I am, in case you require help. Although I was a particular crewman on my last visit, I might get promoted on this visit. That is why we need to meet on the first day. I have no idea what role Alan has taken. It is possible he has left the island and chosen some destination in the past, although that is unlikely unless he has found the Pathway. The key was needed for the single trip out of Vicary's time, but I have the key as he never took it. It is likely Alan is still on the island and he might in fact help us to find the Pathway, providing we are able to locate him, which is really down to him. The key can be opened when we reach the island of the past and it will signify the month and year of the single trip. It will only open on the island, any further trips, as you know, require the Pathway,' he said.

'I really hope Alan makes himself known to us, but I am concerned about that. Why would he want to make himself known, and how would he know we were there?' I asked.

'Perhaps the following explanation will clear up a few points. On the two occasions I had been back, time starts at the same point. I listened to conversation I had heard before; I was able to predict what was about to be said. The best way is to say we turn up on Monday, then we leave and return back home on Friday. If we returned with a new buyer it would revert back to Monday. If Alan is on the island he will know a traveller has arrived. The islanders will have no idea time has gone back, it is only travellers that appreciate this phenomenon. The time going back only occurs for new arrivals from the present, it does not happen if you take your single trip and return to the island. That is because you are already a traveller, although in theory we have left the island. Alan might try to locate us to lend assistance and he would know the monk is going to be one of the visitors,' he said.

I asked the question which was bugging me a little, it concerned Colin and Alan's new identities.

'So, to be clear, if you kill someone on the island you then become that person, he disappears and you take on his role?'

'Having experienced it first hand I know it to be true, although I will confirm this with Alan when we meet him. If everything has gone to plan, I have no doubt that at some stage Alan has taken a life. But don't worry it is not really murder, these people get their bodies back when we have finished with them. It is the only way to rise up through the ranks, that is where the so-called pecking order changes. If you started as monk on your first visit, then on your second visit you were the lowest crew member, then on the third visit the senior crew member. But you can by-pass this system. On the first visit you are the monk, you kill the senior crew member, you become him, on your next visit you will be higher than the senior crew member, because each new visit entitles you to promotion,' he said.

'So what you are saying is that these people are having their bodies taken over without their knowledge, something they are still unaware of when their bodies are eventually returned to them?' I questioned.

'Exactly so, but the killings are infrequent. It is only travellers who have this power, the real crew would actually commit murder. If you decide to return with me, I will automatically be promoted from my last position on the crew, so at this moment I have no idea of my new position, but I believe it will be quite senior, simply because of who I was on my last visit,' said Colin.

I had great sympathy for the monk, his body seemed to be in permanent use by someone else. Alan was the only person who was in a position to answer the resurrection question with any certainty, perhaps that might be our first question when we meet him.

'I have not yet made a decision on making the trip. Talking about it does not make it fact, and it really does sound too horrible to contemplate. I have to say it was not in my retirement plan to travel back three hundred years, and live in poverty there. But it might provide me with the opportunity to be part of history, to know these characters from the past first hand. Let us just suppose I decided to go with you, is this the situation? We both return to the island in the time of Vicary and Landon, our clothing will be of that time. We both take on the appearance of someone who was alive at that time, in my case the island monk, while you are to be someone whose identity we do not know. Alan will also be someone we do not know. He will know someone has arrived because time has gone back and will assume you have returned with the new owner of the bungalow. The islanders will know nothing of what is going on, it is only travellers who are aware. We will meet on the first night at a pre-arranged location, hoping at some stage that Alan will make himself known to us. We will then try to locate the Pathway so we can travel to several locations. You want to return to 1941 where you have a plan to make us both rich, a plan you are able to carry out now but were unable to do with John in 1941. Is that just about everything?' I said.

'That's just about it, but I should tell you more, then you will appreciate why John and I could not carry out the plan in 1941. Are you interested in making the journey to the past?' he said.

'It sounds exciting, as well as dangerous,' I said

'There is one more thing I need to tell you, it is an important factor. If you make the trip, no matter how long we stay in the past, the duration of our stay is only one night in our time.'

'What about when we travel from the island on our journey: who do we become?'

'You will look the same as you do now, unfortunately we do not get any younger. It is only on the island that we look different.'

'Before we go, if indeed I decide to go, there are many things to discuss, the top priority is probably your sanity, but that's another question. So we enter the island, I assume during the smuggling period, no acts of piracy have yet been committed. We then have the option of remaining there until the big acts of piracy occurred. I am imagining getting gold bullion from the seventeenth century. Bearing in mind this raid caused the death of many of the crew, I feel it prudent to have some idea when it took place. When would the raid occur? Perhaps Alan might be able to help if he has already been through the robbery period?' I said.

'I do not know exactly when we are likely to appear on the island; based on my previous experiences, I know the fateful raid is going to occur, but I have no idea when. Just like you, I think Alan is the most likely person to be able to help,' he said.

'Once we get onto the island we need to remain there for two weeks, that is when the portal opens again on that side. Those two weeks can provide us with valuable time to locate the Pathway, essential to complete more than one trip. I am confident that if we get Alan's help we have every chance of locating the Pathway,' he said.

'I wish I had your confidence, we do not know whether we have his help to count on.'

'I want to change something else from the past, apart from the trips to 1941 and 1981. It is something I will need your help for, but I will discuss that with you at a later date. Is there anything in your past you want to change?' he said.

'I appreciate your offer, I certainly need time to think about that, but there is nothing that springs to mind. There seem to be a lot of discussions to be had sometime in the future, but at the moment I am in the dark on all aspects of each of our so-called missions,' I said.

We agreed there was no point in discussing anything until we had the Pathway; at the moment we were confined to a single mission.

There seemed to be a lot of unanswered questions, too much supposition about what might happen. It appeared this Pathway was the real stumbling block: with that we would be able to help John, without it we just either got rich in 1941 – I had no idea how – or we helped John's wife and forgot about getting rich.

'There is another aspect of this operation. If what you have said is right, John was also in a position to make the trip, being a previous owner, is that not the case?'

'That is correct, but I can assure you John has no intention of returning to the island. His experience of that time was not to his liking. There is no way at all we can persuade him to return.

I want to return, and I beg you to consider the trip. If successful, it is vital to my well-being.'

I said it was something I intended to consider as a serious proposal, but I needed to speak to John first, he appeared more sane than Colin, and if what had been discussed had really happened, John was part of the last trip.

The possibilities if this crazy scenario was true were infinite; it might even be worth taking the chance. I could see a prize-winning book coming from this experience, a work of fiction about the journey back through the portal, as no one was going to believe such a tall story.

My brain was working overtime. What if Colin was telling the truth? Although very unlikely, this was a golden opportunity I did not want to miss. Many eminent scientists have pondered over time travel, several have even written about it, and although nobody seriously believed the theory, the stories were delightful. My mind raced. What if time travel was possible, as described by Colin? I decided to put a proposition to him, and if he agreed with it, I was going to accept his ridiculous plan.

'I think the idea is too ridiculous for words, yet I have nothing to lose. I have no immediate plans for the next few weeks, so let's say I'm interested. I will go along with the plan on one condition: I want John to be part of this expedition. I appreciate he does not want to travel, but I want him to assist. I ask that we do for John what you both failed to do on your last visit, so I will agree if you accept my terms. The Pathway therefore has to be found before we venture into 1941, I will then have the knowledge of knowing we can help John in 1981. If we are unable to locate the Pathway, the single trip will be to 1981 to save John's wife. Do you agree to those terms?'

He had little choice really, without me there was no trip. He knew that, and therefore agreed readily.

'I think this is a good opportunity, if John is part of the team, to explain Alan's disappearance to him, something I have failed to do so far,' he said.

I felt sure that John was going to agree to the plan, it was in his interest, and he was not being asked to go back to the island merely to assist us. I told Colin I felt it better that I speak to John first, the proposition was possibly more acceptable from me, the disagreement between the two of them had not yet been resolved. The way he had treated John was not the way of a caring man. I think he knew that, and hopefully when the three of us got together this would clear the air between them.

'Once John is all right with the plan, we need to discuss all aspects of it at length; there is much to talk through as you will soon find out. I have mentioned a few things briefly; how primitive the place is, with somewhat primitive laws. I am familiar what awaits us, but I need to prepare you. The people of that time are no respecters of human life, it means very little to them. They use force to get what they want, so you have to be made aware of these facts.'

'I think you will fit in quite well there, you have already admitted to murdering someone on the island, in such a way that the body disappeared, to where nobody knows,' I said.

He smiled. I left Colin's place still puzzled by the whole evening, even more confused that I had agreed to this strange and unbelievable plan. It was a story I wanted to believe in; retirement was boring on many levels without a little adventure. But from what he had said this was no little adventure, it appeared monumental in its proportions: a trip back to 1941, a war zone in one of the largest wars mankind had ever witnessed. It was unlikely Ruby Bay was on Hitler's list of bombing targets, crazy though he was he may well have thought it unnecessary to bomb a seaside resort. The idea that a fortune awaited us was a strange concept; during the war people were rationed on everything, there was little of value around, and if there was it was used for the war effort.

I awoke the next morning refreshed, but I approached the day with some trepidation, a reaction no doubt to the previous night's discussion. I was still wondering if it was a practical joke and I was the victim. My discussion with John that day was certainly going to be interesting he had negative feelings for Colin, and he did not appear to have a sense of humour, particularly when it involved Colin.

The doorbell interrupted my thoughts, and I felt it was certain to be John, which it was, grinning in anticipation of learning about my previous night's experience. I had promised to tell everything, although I suspect he already knew some of what I was about to say. I felt slightly embarrassed by the fact I was starting to believe what I had been told. This was strange as I had never before believed in the concept of time travel; a great idea I thought, but not possible.

'You do not seem yourself, was the meal a disaster? If it was I must say I am surprised, Jane is well qualified in the kitchen department. Was the meal really that bad?' John asked.

'It has nothing to do with the meal, it was of course excellent. Your description of Jane was very accurate, she is in any language stunning. I had a discussion with Colin after dinner. Am I right to think you knew what the discussion was about?' I said. At this comment John looked sheepish. 'What concerns me is that you did not prepare me for the shock I was to have. A few words from you might have softened the blow,' I said

'I apologize for that, it was up to Colin to explain things. It was a bad experience for me, no doubt Colin told you that. Did he tell you what happened to Alan?' he said.

'Colin told me that Alan had returned to Vicary's time. He wanted to go alone and Colin was not allowed to accompany him.'

'Why was returning to that godforsaken place the only way out for Alan?' he enquired.

'Colin had said it was for financial reasons. He apparently owed money to some people in Manchester and he had obviously been threatened in some way, enough to make him want to disappear to the island. Although he had no knowledge of the place, except for what Colin had told him, it probably seemed to be the only solution to his problem,' I said.

'I was not aware he had any problems, financial or otherwise. Alan never gave the appearance of somebody with major problems in his life. But some people have the ability to hide personal things from others,' he said.

I told him the crux of the matter, that Colin wanted me to go with him, back to 1941, where there was a fortune waiting. I then relayed to him the full extent of our discussions the previous night. He listened quietly and without comment.

Once I had finished I waited for his reaction, there were no questions, clearly because he knew exactly what had been discussed. I asked him what he thought of my story, but he remained silent. I wondered why he did not say it was pure fiction; this would be the reaction of any normal person on hearing such a tale. But he knew it was not pure fiction.

Then he started to open up. 'If Colin told you all this, then you know what I think. Is it a preposterous story? Of course not, but you already knew I was going to say that didn't you?' he said.

'Colin had said you had once owned the bungalow, giving you the access to the deeds and what they represented. You went to dinner as I did, Colin told you the same story, but you readily accepted the tale, taking the trip back with him. I understand now how you knew so much about Jane's cooking, but I also understand your reasons for not telling me. Just answer me a straightforward question: does the time portal work?'

He looked me straight in the eye.

'It does work, I was sceptical about the trip, but I had a good reason for wanting to make the journey, the best reason of all. I so desperately wanted to get back to the past, I felt that even if it did not work I had lost nothing by trying. Everything that Colin has told you is true, it is possible to travel back in time, I have witnessed it at first hand but it was not a pleasant experience for me. Colin had promised me something from the trip which he did not deliver, and this has been the cause of the animosity between us, for which I am unforgiving,' he said.

'Perhaps both Colin and I can ask a favour of you, that is to assist us on this trip, I know you have no intention of making the trip, but your assistance on this side of the portal could prove invaluable. I hope you will accept this offer in good faith?'

'I assume from what you have just said that the idea does not seem bunkum any more. If you are making these plans you have most definitely decided to make the trip,' he said.

'You're right, although I am not entirely convinced, but I feel it is a wonderful opportunity if it is true, and worth the humiliation if it fails,' I said.

The telephone rang. It was Colin: he was coming over, he was very insistent. I agreed to his visit, and I told John, who was happy to meet him. It only took a few minutes for him to arrive, he entered the house and shook hands with both of us. He smiled at John, but this was not reciprocated. John wanted to hear his excuses before he put the past behind them, I understood that.

I started the conversation by saying John had agreed to help, but his intention not to return to the past remained the same, his help was to be restricted to the present, assisting us in our preparation.

Colin then stepped forward and said he owed John an explanation, which he was happy to give, along with an apology. John sat down ready to listen, I was interested in what he had to say.

'John I have misled you, something I felt was necessary at the time. Alan requested that you were not involved in his problems. This had nothing to do with not liking you, he did not want you involved in something from his past, something he was not proud of, but that nevertheless had happened. He felt that leaving as he did was his only option. I had some knowledge of Alan's past, as much as he told me. He owed a very large sum of money, he never said exactly how much, but the people he owed the money to were not very nice; he said they were the wrong people and they were not very forgiving. That was his reason for the hasty retreat to the past,' said Colin.

'I appreciate you telling me Colin. I had no idea Alan had

money problems. Perhaps you can find out a bit more, if you meet up with him on the island?' he replied.

They smiled at each other and shook hands again.

Colin had his views on what John's part was going to be in our mission. He felt his value by remaining here was an important aspect. On previous visits it appeared the trip lasted only one night, no matter how long one is in the past, so on our return John would be in a position to confirm this. We also needed someone to make excuses for our absence to the locals, not for the night we were away, but for the time we were stuck inside preparing for the journey. Our base was to be my bungalow for the period of time prior to departure. Colin stated there was a great deal of preparation to be made before taking the giant leap into the past, and it was beneficial to remain in one place. Any visitors to the property might wonder where either of us was; John could give them a cover story. John was happy to accept that role. Having been back in time he obviously did not enjoy the experience, he was happy to remain on this side of the portal.

I wondered how Jane might react to Colin being away for that time, but he said she was visiting a friend, fortunately for two weeks. Both John and I had no such problems, we only had ourselves to worry about.

Colin then asked if I had any questions before we prepared for our adventure.

'Why is it that you went back to 1941 but you were unable to complete your mission? You said you were unable to locate the Pathway on your last visit because it was too risky, so why is there no risk on this visit?' I said.

'There are still going to be risks, but we have two weeks to uncover the Pathway, hopefully with the assistance of Alan, and as I have already been on the island I am better prepared on this occasion. I have to admit the trip to 1941 was not wasted, valuable information was obtained which is likely to assist this trip, making the mission that much easier. But I agree the Pathway is our priority if we want to save John's wife as well.'

Colin had already heard my terms for the trip, but for the benefit of John, I explained that although I was interested in the fortune in 1941, I felt John's wife was more important. I was happy to take the trip if one very important criteria was met: if we did not discover the Pathway our one trip had to be to help John's wife. We had to find the Pathway before deciding on our destination.

I then brought up a problem not previously discussed. Initially we thought John was to remain at the house when we left on the trip; when we returned he would let us know if we had been away just the one night. But I pointed out that on this forthcoming trip things were slanted in a different direction. If we completed our plan to save John's wife, our changing of that piece of history was to have a significant effect on our return: John might not be there when we returned, he might be with the wife we had saved.

I watched as the impact of what I had just said registered with the both of them. John smiled in recognition of my statement. Colin agreed, it was a salient point. We decided we hoped John would be somewhere else on our return. I was in full flow and had further questions that needed answering.

'Although I am excited about the fortune waiting in 1941, I wonder how it is going to be transported into the present, as I have little idea how large this fortune is,' I said.

'Actually there is no need to bring it back, it will remain in 1941. It will be hidden away to be retrieved in our time,' he said.

His answer was a surprise, I was even more confused by this fortune. I was informed yet again that everything was to be revealed in due course.

Colin asked if there was anything I wanted to do in the past, with the Pathway we had the ability to travel to any time or date. I still had no idea on that subject; if that changed I intended to let him know.

I was unable to stop myself asking more questions; I had many concerns, and when these concerns arose I had to speak.

'I thought we went through the portal together, but you tell me I have no idea what your identity will be on the island. If we go through together, surely we will reappear together, or am I being slightly naive?' I said.

'We enter the portal together, but we do not come out directly on the other side of the portal. All I know is that we will reappear somewhere on the island, but we are unlikely to be together. Maybe I will appear at the top of the island, and you could reappear outside the inn. There is no way of knowing, but this is quite a minor problem. If we meet on the first night as I suggest we do, then we will both know the other's identity. This is more for your benefit that mine, as I believe you will be reincarnated as the monk. On the path from the inn to the top of the island there is a very large rock, it is easy to find as it is huge in comparison to the other rocks, we will meet behind it at midnight.

'I will try to find out what guise Alan has taken. If I can find him I will bring him along to the meeting, it will give us added strength in numbers – only three of us, I know. I did advise Alan to dispose of one of the crewmen, thereby taking on his role on the island, hopefully he has done that; I think he knew it was important. Alan will be aware that the monk was one of the new arrivals, and with time going back for him he will know we have arrived. He might in fact approach you. I am hoping Alan might have some idea where the Pathway is, as he is aware of its importance. Another important aspect is where the islanders are in the course of history. Maybe Alan has already witnessed the act of piracy, and although time has gone back he will know what lies ahead. It will make Alan an interesting person to talk to. Now we get to the serious part of our venture, the preparation for going back three hundred years. John is aware of what I am about to say, this is for your benefit, Pat,' he said.

The discussion started with the environment to be encountered. It was vital to adhere to certain rules. Basic though these rules appeared they were important for my well-being; I was emphatically told not to stray from the guidelines I was about to be given. The first thing I was likely to encounter was the lack of sanitation, no inside bathrooms in these huts, in fact no outside structures either, a bush or a ditch serves as a toilet. The people were not shy, they did not care who was watching, to them it was a tedious bodily function, carried out at the location they happened to be at the time. Whatever I thought of this I was not to look shocked to see someone crouching in a bush.

The stench on the island was unbearable, hopefully this was something I would acclimatize to as quickly as possible. I was never to complain to anyone about the smell of the place, the islanders are not aware the place stinks, such a comment was likely to arouse suspicion, and such a remark was only uttered by outsiders. Outsiders are treated with utmost contempt, they are usually Revenue men, or people passing information to the Revenue men. I was not to expect even the luxury of a wash; water is a valuable commodity, not to be wasted on washing, something islanders rarely do. Needless to say the people and their clothes did not smell good, I needed to be made aware of this point. This was something else I must not comment on: turning one's nose up at the smell of a person would be very unwise. Unkempt and dirty are the normal state of affairs, this was a state we needed to adopt before we left: smelling bad was a good thing on the island, it showed you belonged there.

That was why we needed to stay in one place, away from decent members of the public. Colin suggested we stop washing for at least three days before we leave, nobody on the island was to encounter the slightest whiff of deodorant, being dirty might just save our lives. On his last visit he had decided to throw himself into a murky pool on the island, just to smell more disgusting.

It was also important not to shave before we went, the only unshaven people on the island were women; that did not necessarily include all of them, but he felt that was something I might discover for myself.

I understood we had to be in sympathy with our environment,

we needed to cover all possibilities. I was subtly informed that although I was unlikely to be in the company of prostitutes under normal circumstances, these were not normal circumstances. Although I had the appearance of a monk, nobody on the island for one second believed him to have the convictions of his office. If I was offered the services of one of these ladies, it was unlikely that these ladies expected to be paid.

It was perhaps even classed as impolite to refuse this service, but he stated he was going to leave that to my conscience. The locals did not expect to see me in the company of a prostitute, this was unlikely to please them, I therefore needed to use discretion if I wished to indulge. Perhaps I could tell the islanders I was trying to save the lady. He left it for me to sort out this kind of dilemma, which was not exactly what I wanted to hear.

Food was another important aspect of life on the island, although this did not unduly affect me as my position allowed me several privileges, and my food was provided at the inn free of charge, it was some sort of penance from the landlord. Unfortunately the food was far from good, but Colin warned me about being tempted to find my own food. 'Accept the penance and look as though you are enjoying it' he said, which he felt was very unlikely. There was livestock on the island, wandering free, but I was not to be tempted by the possibility of a chicken supper, the livestock were not mine. Stealing a bird was treated swiftly and painfully by the inadequate judicial system on the island, my calling would not save me from the wrath of the islanders. His advice was not to touch any livestock. One very important point was that both livestock and dogs are very likely to be disease ridden, I was to avoid touching them; the dogs probably had rabies. Begging for food was normally an accepted practice for a monk, but in this situation not so, as the landlord fed him. It was suggested I avoid begging.

Colin's advice was to stay out of everyone's way, not to speak unless someone spoke to me, and most importantly not to offer an opinion on anything, because someone would surely disagree.

The consequences of this sort of disagreement could be serious, as these people make their own laws, usually as they go along, I was not to get caught up in any dispute. He then asked if I had any questions.

'There is nothing that I feel is urgent, it sounds like a place I am really going to enjoy: no talking and making no comment on anything! You say our stay will be for a few days, maybe even weeks, so where do I sleep? A pew in a church or a tent in a field maybe?' I said.

'I'm afraid your sleeping arrangements are unknown to me. Both John and I spent only a short time as the monk; we were never on the island during the hours of darkness. There must be a monk's hut somewhere, but at this stage I have no idea where it is located. It is one of those situations where we need to wait until we arrive on the island, then hopefully I will obtain some information about your abode. In respect of the working life of the islanders, that is easy to explain, everyone is involved in the smuggling expeditions, that unfortunately includes you. On board the ship you will be giving spiritual guidance to the crew. You must prepare yourself for some rough seas, the ships of the time lacked any sort of stability in the water. They were small and in the case of this particular ship, very small,' he said.

'I am concerned about my duties on board ship, I find it difficult to visualize the monk climbing a rope or splicing anything,' I said.

'The short answer to your question is simple: you are unlikely to do anything at all. The captain only wants the monk on board in case there is a God, he wants to cover all possibilities, these people are far from God-fearing folk. As I already mentioned you might be expected to perform a funeral at sea; you must be prepared, a few religious words are all that is needed, these people have little idea about whether such a service was right or not. You must realize these people are very unhealthy, their staple diet consists of rum and more rum, and they are likely to keel over at any moment,' he said.

The account of life that he gave was honest, although not pleasant, but it was better to be prepared. Finding out these things when I was there was not the way to do it, and would be an enormous shock. I thought maybe if I made myself familiar with the funeral service it must prove beneficial.

Colin confirmed the islanders had very little in the way of personal possessions, they had their huts and the clothes they stood up in; in most cases only one set of clothes, that was apparent from their smell. Their swords and pistols were their priced items, more valuable than any member of their family. Any confrontation was likely to necessitate the use of one of these items, that was why he kept warning me about confrontation.

Colin described how the business of the island was carried out at the inn, which was permanently open, as there were no licensing hours. The inn was crowded every night, crooked deals being carried out in the corners and recesses, each crewman trying to make a living as best he could, not concerned how he did it.

'Vicary has pride of place at the bar. He doesn't make deals with anyone, he is the law on the island, anything he wants he takes. Landon is at his side, watching over him, ready to pounce on any member of the crew who disagrees with their leader, although this is very unlikely. Landon is superior in both physical strength and swordsmanship to any member of the crew; they are not going to challenge his authority. Landon is better equipped for the captain's job than Vicary, yet it suits him to be second in command, but will that situation last? I feel Landon is in a good position to take over the helm any time he wishes, but he chooses not to. Being second in command allows Landon not to take responsibility for anything, especially if it went wrong. Landon is clever and educated, rare qualities indeed on the island.

'The only real problem for the islanders are the Revenue men, who do occasionally visit the island. Their arrival is well advertised, allowing time to hide any contraband. There are never any serious searches carried out. The Revenue men usually leave with a gift from Vicary; in those days bribery was carried out by everyone. The visits are infrequent, this allows the islanders to go about their business without too many interruptions. The only money on the island comes from the smuggling, most of this is in Vicary's and Landon's pockets, but the crew have enough for their few needs. Nobody dares to complain about the shares they receive. Landon has his own way of settling disputes, and the results are inevitable. Both Vicary and Landon get a share of the profits from the inn, where the crew spend their money. Pat, do you have any questions about what I have said?' he said.

'I think you have explained it very well. It appears the order of the day is to live like a tramp, smell like a dog, therefore emitting the same odour as the rest of the islanders, and most importantly not to utter a word to anyone. I only have one question: when do we depart on this adventure? I am excited beyond belief,' I said.

'In eight days' time, that is when the portal will open. If we fail to meet that date, we will have to wait another three months.'

'I really don't want to wait another three months, I want to get the experience of the island out of the way. Hopefully we can find the Pathway and then come and go as we please. We won't need to stay on the island very long, just passing through on our way to our next destination, or on our way home,' I said.

'What is my part in this plan, bearing in mind that if you save my wife I am unlikely to move to Ruby Bay?' John said.

'You're right, John. If we save your wife you are unlikely to be here on our return, and you are also unlikely to know who we are, if things go according to plan, which we hope they do. So I will give you a letter before we venture on the journey, asking you to be present in Ruby Bay on the morning of our return. I hope the letter would persuade you to be here, if merely out of curiosity,' said Colin.

'I will be pleased to take the letter, and promise I will be here on your return. My presence is inevitable, as I have a curious side to my nature,' he said.

Colin and I decided we had earned a holiday, somewhere out

of contact: Florida was the agreed destination. John hoped we enjoyed our fictitious holiday in Florida, but I was starting to think I would prefer that to what we were about to experience. Colin then asked if John was happy to make the visits to the village for food, as we should not be seen if we were enjoying the sun in Florida. John agreed to this. We intended to live at the back of the bungalow by the veranda, using only one room during our preparatory period. John was to cook all the meals. Colin and I agreed to stop shaving and washing. I was going to miss my daily showers, but the venture was more important than my personal feelings, I wondered if eight days' accumulation of dirt was enough. Colin proposed a toast to the adventure that lay ahead and the riches that hopefully awaited us, which we agreed to share with John.

I decided to go to the village with John, possibly the last occasion I expected to do this for some time. He said he was going to introduce me to some of the locals, and I thought this a good opportunity before I was locked away at the back of my bungalow. Colin waited for us in the living room. Perhaps this was also the chance to mention I was off to Florida for a holiday, just in case the locals were interested.

The first place we went was the general store, a shop which sold everything, I tried in vain to think of something not sold there. The owner was called Otto, he was Austrian from Vienna, he had settled in Ruby Bay after the war. He was a pleasant man who welcomed me to the area in the most boisterous of terms, his voice was several octaves above the majority of men I had met. Our next port of call was the Post Office and bakery, two for the price of one here. This was owned by Vera, this was not her real name, which was unpronounceable. She was from Czechoslovakia, and she also had arrived here after the war. She showed pleasure at meeting me, hoping I was to have a long and happy retirement.

We loaded ourselves down with supplies, struggling back to the bungalow and a well-earned rest. Colin was still in the lounge, and we sat down to continue the discussion.

'What about the riches that are there for the taking, what do they consist of? Where are these riches to be found, and most importantly, why are we the only ones able to obtain them?' I said.

'I think it best that John tell the story, I need to go to my house to get something,' he said.

I sat down, and John told me that he knew very little. He and Colin had gone back to 1941, where Colin wanted to save his father from making a grave mistake. He said little more on the subject, and at the time John did not know what the grave mistake was. Colin went to the mainland on his own he said. He was going to be gone only a few hours, then they were to meet up in the bar and he promised to tell him everything. John stayed in the bar of the island hotel. After an hour John heard a large explosion on the mainland, like all the guests he peered out of the window.

A house on the mainland was ablaze, and it was assumed a stray bomb had caused the explosion and subsequent fire. He later found out that the destroyed property was 1 Ruby Bay, the house next to mine. People assumed it was a stray bomb, but because of Colin's departure to the mainland he felt he might be responsible for the explosion. It seemed a logical conclusion as he was adamant about going to the mainland alone. The unlikely conclusion in John's mind was that Colin was a demolition expert of some sort, blowing up houses on mainland Britain. Colin returned to the bar an hour later and asked John if he had seen the explosion; bearing in mind it shook the foundations of the hotel the question hardly needed answering. He said he was near the house when it was struck by a bomb from a German aircraft returning home, not thought to be intentionally targeting Ruby Bay: the aircraft had returned from a raid on Plymouth, the bomb was left over from the raid. Asked if he had sorted out the problem with his father, Colin said he had seen him but had not sorted out the problem, that was something for another day.

I got the feeling that this trip was that other day. I now knew the reason for our return was in some way to help his father, but I still had no idea where the alleged fortune was coming from, only Colin had those details. John had no idea about any fortune in 1941, this was not information he had been privy to. I agreed that with eight days to kill, there was plenty of time for Colin to divulge all. I was going to nag him until he told the whole story. We sat on the veranda drinking coffee, and Colin appeared in the garden. He walked into the house and poured himself a coffee, the aroma wafting from the lounge.

'John has given his side of the story, but he knew nothing about the wealth you talk of. Maybe it's time you told us both, Colin?' I said.

'Of course, you're right. I will tell you the full and true story. The fortune was not available on the last visit mainly because I had no idea it was there. It was after the bomb dropped that the realization came, then it was too late,' he said.

His father worked for the War Office in Plymouth, but was not around in Colin's childhood. His mother had said he was killed just after the war. Colin's later research revealed that was true, his father was executed in 1949, the year of Colin's birth, as a spy. He dealt with sensitive information in Plymouth, he was trusted and well respected in his position. Somehow he was compromised, the offer of some sort of wealth from the Germans, and information he passed to the Germans may have assisted them in some way. The office in Plymouth became suspicious of him, but it was what happened in 1941 that was to bring his eventual downfall. Although it took many years to put the information together, the records stated that something found in 1941 sent him to the gallows.

Colin went back to try and persuade his father that he was close to being found out, he knew he had bought 1 Ruby Bay, his late mother told him that was where the evidence was eventually found that convicted him. 1 Ruby Bay was bombed on the night in question, and never rebuilt. When Colin and John went back, they arrived months before the bombing, which was fortuitous, as John's house was up for sale – which was something he intended to explain later.

The night he left John at the hotel he went over to check out his father's house. He waited on the hill overlooking the house, until his father appeared and went into the house. He was about to go and confront his father, when the strangest thing happened. His father came from the house carrying a large envelope, walked into the cellar, came out without the envelope, took off the padlock and left it on the ground. He then walked away from the house, Colin was mystified by what he had seen. He stayed where he was, trying to fathom out what was going on.

Then a figure appeared on the side of the cliff. He walked slowly towards his father's house, looking around in all directions as he did so. He reached the house and immediately went into the cellar, he came out with the envelope, which he put in his jacket pocket, then he shone his torch in the direction of the cliff. Three or four men appeared from the cliff carrying bulky items. They went to the cellar and left the items there. All the men left, and the one with the envelope snapped the padlock to secure the door.

Colin watched them as they reached the cliff edge. He was then aware of a silhouette out at sea, it was a submarine. He kept watching, to check where these men went. After a few minutes he was able to see a rowing boat heading towards the submarine, this was obviously our visitors. The only possible reason for this clandestine operation was that the envelope contained information for the Germans, and the goods transported were the reward. He realized that his father was without doubt a spy.

He waited for his father to return, to see what he had to say about the evidence in his cellar. He waited a good half an hour, but he did not return. Then it happened: he watched as the bomb hit his father's house and exploded. Whatever deal he had made, the goods he had received were lost forever, but the information had been passed.

I wondered what it was the Germans had left for this information.

Colin knew exactly what it was: they had left paintings, but not just any pieces of artwork. The works they left were by artists with great reputations, Franz Marc, Emil Nolde and Max Beckham, but in Hitler's Germany these artists were denounced. Hitler called them 'degenerate artists', and their works were removed from galleries throughout Germany. It was therefore easy for the Germans to give his father these pieces of artwork, as they were not wanted in Germany. These are now all well-respected artists, their work in today's market is almost priceless and fetches astronomical sums at auction, because a lot of it was destroyed by Hitler. Colin knew about the artwork because pieces of the canvases were found in the ashes. From those pieces the experts were able to identify the paintings, which were supposed to have been in Germany, languishing in a museum cellar. The main evidence that convicted Colin's father was the German art in his cellar and the fact a German submarine was seen in the waters off Ruby Bay. It all added up to prove his guilt.

Our plan was simple, he had witnessed everything first time around, he knew there was more than an hour from the paintings being locked in the cellar to the bomb dropping, plenty of time to remove the paintings. That is where John's house came into the plan: we would take enough money or its equivalent to buy the house, we then store the paintings in the cellar, to remain there until we picked them up in the future. There was no need to bring the fortune back, it remained there and eventually came to us. It was without doubt a brilliant plan.

But we also we had somehow to prevent the information being passed to the Germans by Colin's father. He was prepared for that, apparently the man who took the envelope did not open it, he just put it in his pocket. Maybe he did not have the clearance to read it. Colin was adamant that the contents of the envelope were not read, he had watched closely and he assured us the envelope was not opened. this was vital to the plan. He was going to take a similar envelope containing a few sheets of blank paper; he intended to swap the envelopes before the Germans arrived.

We all felt it was a good plan that had a strong possibility of success.

I was still not sure what I had let myself in for, but it was a decision I had no intention of going back on; for John's sake more than anything else, he was pinning his hopes on us. Although I had not known him for very long I believed him to be a genuine, caring man. He was somewhat lost without his wife, he had been lost for many years, and I hoped we had the power to bring his nightmare to an end. The previous night's pep talk had not made me feel confident about the trip, Colin had been honest, that it was not going to make it a holiday of a lifetime. In fact it had all the makings of a holiday from Hell. I wondered whether either of us had the mental capacity to survive long enough to reap the rewards. What if someone took an instant dislike to me?

The next morning I decided not to shave but to shower, using an unscented soap. The heat of the shower relaxed me, but this luxury was to become a thing of the past. The idea of using only one room of the bungalow was a good one, there was no point in the rest of the place smelling. At least the windows to the veranda were opened, that allowed us to help to improve the quality of the air. Colin and I decided not to wash at all for about two days before we left.

John arrived and said he was going to prepare a hearty breakfast, another pleasure that was soon to be a fond memory. We tucked into the fry-up on the veranda, it was a sunny morning with a slight breeze. The food was excellent and I savoured every mouthful.

'The meals that you will have on the island will all be the same, it is a stew of unknown origin. It is difficult for me to describe, needless to say it ranks as a minus Michelin Star,' he said.

'Your beard is starting to look good, Pat,' said John.

'Thank you, but this stubble is starting to itch. I know I will need to put up with it, for the sake of the trip,' I said.

There were only a few days left, I had my doubts about taking the trip, but felt it a golden opportunity, to see something from the history books. I was about to meet these characters from 300 years ago, although I did not intend to have a conversation with anyone. This would be very ill-advised in the cases of Vicary and Landon; merely to be in their presence was enough.

I was both nervous and excited, and wary of what was about to change my life. John appreciated my apprehension, his one visit was enough for him not to repeat the experience, he made that perfectly clear and I respected him for his honesty.

'Common sense tells me I am living in the present, there is no other time period out there, the past has gone forever, there is nothing we can do about that. I have no idea why scientists believe there are other dimensions, thinking we can travel to the future, a time that has not yet happened, and these are supposed to be educated men. If as you both say time travel is possible, maybe the Pathway can move us forward in time, making pick up the winning Lottery numbers, or even the Grand National winner in the future. But I appreciate all this is supposition, we need to find the Pathway first,' I said.

Colin sat quietly thinking, he was someone who looked for opportunities to make money; had I given him an idea he had not thought of?

We again went over the plan; our meeting at midnight on the first night was agreed, at the large rock in the south of the island, it made me feel better. Colin felt it prudent to make contact early and I agreed; he had been there before so his knowledge was invaluable to me.

I pointed out the rock formation to John.

'Why don't you look up there at midnight on the first day, John, you may be able to see Colin and me, what do you think?' I said.

John smiled, realizing the stupidity of the comment.

'Colin, if we are able to locate Alan, surely that may be to our advantage, as he might know the location of the Pathway. To be honest I would feel better if there were two of you watching over me, that would stop me making silly mistakes,' I said.

'I agree, but unfortunately I have no idea who Alan is. I'm hoping he will make himself known to us, but bearing in mind the reason for his leaving our time, he may not want to be found,' said Colin.

'I very much hope that is not the case,' I said.

'If I can locate Alan, I will persuade him to come to our meeting,' he said.

'Thank you, that does give me some comfort,' I said.

The closer the day of departure, the more I worried. This was a terrible place I was about to visit, with people unlike any I had encountered in my life. Colin was adamant that what we knew about travelling back in time remained between the three of us, not that anyone was likely to believe the story. He was of course correct that we must keep our travelling to ourselves; just imagine what might happen if this was made public. Yes, it might be beneficial to me, I would be able to sell my bungalow for millions. But if the story got out and people started moving between time zones, changing events as they went, the world had every chance of becoming different to what we know it to be. Yet surely we were about to change history in 1941? Not a vast amount, though, we were simply retrieving something that was already there, stopping it being destroyed.

Colin again stated that history must not under any circumstances be changed, I was expected to go with the flow of what happened on the island, any change can have dire effect on the future, like a ripple in the water it gets larger as it moves outward. I understood what he was saying, I had no problem with that, I had no intention of making even the smallest ripple, I feared too much for my life to do that. It was my intention to watch and learn, I was not going to speak to a living soul, but I still felt that by retrieving the paintings we were changing history.

Colin and I stayed at the bungalow and John called around each morning. He only visited us on the veranda, but he willingly provided our meals each day. As each day passed I became more uncomfortable. I had stopped washing and my hygiene was an itchy problem, but as the day of reckoning was getting closer, it worried me that Colin's plan was going to become a reality.

My beard had improved beyond the scruffy stage, Colin's was at the magnificent stage. I decided to remain in the same clothes for the days leading up to our departure, as did Colin; all the clothes were to be burned along with the sleeping bags. John had volunteered to be the arsonist. He was playing an important role in this operation, he also agreed to remove all odours we had left when we departed. His minor role in this enterprise was growing by the day; his support was vital. I think he knew that, but he was glad not to face the dangers beyond the portal. John kept his distance but took on every task we asked of him, both Colin and I agreed this venture was impossible without him, we told him so, he accepted the praise with his usual shyness.

The days turned to hours, everything had been discussed in the minutest detail, and it was departure day. All three of us met for our final breakfast on the veranda, cooked by our resident chef. I had not seen my kitchen in four days; he assured me it was spotlessly clean.

I was still half convinced I was taking part in some sort of fantasy, but if that was the case, why was I so nervous? Colin also showed signs of worry about the trip; this was not what I needed. John continued to support us through the last few hours, giving us confidence about our ultimate goal.

It was time, the sun had started to drop in the sky. Hopefully the beach was deserted, we did not require onlookers. It was now time to meet my destiny.

Colin said we had better start preparing, he knew it was only a short walk, but felt it was better to be there too early; missing the portal would mean our preparation was in vain. He handed me a leather pouch containing a few Roman coins, and told me to put the key into the pouch. He had a similar pouch around his neck, he explained only items carried in the pouches could be transported through the portal, these pouches formed part of the will, Colin had some coins and papers which he felt we needed in 1941. He said he was going to tell me about them at the appropriate time. The weather outside was lousy, pouring rain and howling wind. Colin said the weather always became stormy, it was a sign the portal was about to open, and it kept people off the beach, except those who had a reason for being there.

I was ready to take on this adventure. The three of us left the bungalow, striding out towards the beach, the storm was raging, a perfect cover for the events that were about to unfold. We walked towards the island, nobody said a word, everything had been said, we then reached what was to become the portal. Colin turned and spoke to John.

'John, do not read this letter until this time tomorrow. I have written the time and date on the back. I cannot explain the reason, but all will become clear. Thanks for what you've done, we both appreciate it.'

We both shook hands with John. Colin asked me if I was ready to be part of history, I thought I was so I nodded. He asked if I had the key to my inheritance, which I had around my neck in the pouch with the Roman coins.

I wondered if the first part of the journey was going to be successful, travelling back to the time of Vicary, exactly as predicted by both my colleagues, now I was going to take those steps. Although not fully believing it was going to happen, here I was waiting to make this historical journey. Soon if all went well I was going to another period in history, to a period I knew a little about. I had only a vague idea what awaited me in Vicary's time, and I was hoping the stay was going to be a short one.

The Roman coins Colin had given me were part of our finances in 1941. Numerous television documentaries told us of the horror of this period in our history, the devastation to the lives of those involved. Both civilian and military personnel suffered; my feelings were that the civilian population were worst hit. I was about to take a giant step into that time too, with little knowledge of what awaited.

Colin had two goals to achieve in this time, only one of which was to involve me. I was only along because he had no choice. I had the feeling John was fine with the 1941 period of history, but he did not want to endure the island again, that was understandable, having spent a short and unhappy time there. My trip to 1941 was going to be a journey of discovery, seeing first-hand what affect the war had on a small community like Ruby Bay. They may not have suffered as others did from bombings raids, but rationing and the like affected everyone.

It was late evening, the storm was now in full swing, I had never witnessed such a storm, heralding what was about to unfold into an adventure beyond my wildest dreams, or nightmares. I wondered what I had let myself in for, I knew I was going to find out very soon.

We looked at each other, the area of the portal clouded over in a dense mist, we shook hands with each other, we both walked into the mist, forward into the past. I was in limbo between two dimensions.

3

The clouds around me started to clear, slowly at first, then speeding up to give me a clear picture. It was not what I expected. I was standing on the island, near the top on a footpath. Colin was nowhere to be seen, but then we had expected to be parted at this point. Most of the landscape around me I did not recognize, although I knew where I was; the inn was prominent in the distance, but the hotel was gone. Stone and wooden huts covered the island, many where the hotel was situated in my world. We had actually succeeded in our venture, we had actually gone back. I was mad with myself for doubting the two of them.

The island looked like a very desolate place, which I had expected. I looked towards the mainland; there were no houses at all, just huts as on the island, although the buildings on the mainland looked more substantial, possibly brick construction rather than wood. The buildings on the island were single-storey, built from either wood or slate, covered with a haphazard kind of thatched roof. They were arranged in no particular order. They looked very random, a case of finding a spot and putting up a hut. There were about 30 of these buildings covering the island, in different states of repair; some looked like they were about to collapse and I hoped my abode was not one of them, that was something I needed to find.

I looked towards the inn, there was a great deal of noise from within, and this was obviously where the crew was congregating.

Colin had said the inn was the hub of the island's activities, and it sounded busy tonight.

I had been told I would take on the guise of the monk, and for the first time I looked at my attire. Colin was correct, I was indeed a monk. I had a long brown flowing habit, very dirty from my first analysis, tied around the waist with a rope, which I believed might once have been white. The previous owner of this ensemble was not a clean man, the cloth needed a wash as a matter of urgency and I had a pair of unkempt sandals on my feet. These sandals had either belonged to a man who had walked thousands of miles, or he had owned them for over 20 years, but I have to say they were comfortable if not a little chilly.

At that moment I became aware of my own body odour, but this paled into insignificance as I appreciated the smells around me, all extremely pungent. The island had a smell that was almost indescribable; the closest comparison is an open sewer, but I do not think that was a strong enough description. Perhaps there were a few rotting bodies around that I had not seen.

The livestock Colin had referred to, were very scrawny, none of them looked like they were able to provide a good meal, not that I was tempted in the slightest. Knowing these creatures belonged to someone, I had no intention of making enemies on my first day.

I moved towards the inn. Now was as good a time as any to meet my flock. I reached the door of the inn, I was amazed to see the same door that John and I had encountered in our time. I opened the latch, and not knowing what lay ahead of me inside, I moved forward with trepidation. This was a defining moment.

I entered the drinking house, it was noisy and crowded, everyone dressed as I expected for that period, just like a picture of a pirates' den. Everyone had donned either a hat or a bandana, and knee-length boots. Shirts were a mixture of colours, although from the dirt it was difficult to ascertain the original colour. I was glad to see beards were the order of the day. Considering we change into some other person, it was not necessary to grow a beard.

I noticed that the smell of the island was replicated inside the inn, but it was not as powerful because of the tobacco smell. The crew were in a poor state of cleanliness and no doubt health. Dentistry had not come to the island, and those who had teeth had their mouths filled with black and grey tombstones, but most of the crew had no teeth at all. The crew were winners in the ugly stakes, as well as stinking in unison. Imagine the stale smell of sweat, but times ten worse. Sitting there I wondered about my decision to visit these tortured souls. How long would I be able to stand the living conditions these people took as normal?

All but two present had a bandana type of headgear, the other two had large triangular type hats; I assumed Vicary was one of these, the other was almost certainly Landon. Both these men were tall and powerfully built; no wonder the crew never argued over their decisions. The remainder of the crew were tiny in comparison, but I think both Vicary and Landon were freaks of their time: men over 6 foot must have been unusual, and they had obviously used this to their advantage. A quick glance at these two men allowed me to decide which was which, as my history lessons had told me Landon was considerably younger than Vicary. Vicary was a little shorter, he had long black hair tied into a ponytail under his gold-rimmed hat.

I walked to an empty table near the door, as my instincts told me it was safer to have a quick route out if things got serious. I looked towards the bar and the landlord nodded. I nodded back as it seemed the right thing to do. Almost immediately a plate of some sort of stew appeared in front of me, with a glass of what I assumed to be rum. The landlord nodded again and left the table, and I thanked him for the repast. I looked at the meal before me, there were definitely creatures swimming around. I was grateful we had eaten before we left but I knew I had to consume this gruel; failure to do so was certain to cause offence to the landlord. The meal was consumed with gritted teeth. God knows what my digestive tract was about to encounter. The liquid was indeed rum, the strongest I had ever tasted. I might bring some back I thought, a sort of duty-free entitlement.

I was sitting in complete disbelief. Just a few yards in front of me was Captain James Vicary, a man whose name appeared in the local history books. This historical figure was within touching distance.

I looked up from my drink to see the person I assumed was Landon coming towards me. I did not look him the eye. What had I done? I thought. Surely I had not been here long enough to upset anyone, it sent a shudder down my spine.

'Where you bin, Pilgrim? Was wondering 'bout you. Let me buy you a grog. Barkeep, rum for our friend,' he said.

I thanked him and he smiled. The landlord called him Mr Landon. So I had just met the man himself, and I had survived the encounter. Nobody in Ruby Bay was likely to believe this, not that I was going to tell them. Landon was a brute of a man, no wonder nobody ever crossed him. He had steely blue eyes, his face was covered in scars, adding to his menace. No doubt these were wounds of previous conflicts, all of which he had obviously won.

Since I had arrived at the inn Vicary had not looked at me once, even when Landon approached me. I suppose in Vicary's eyes I was not important in the scheme of things, I was simply to be tolerated.

I had been at the inn for some time, the timepiece over the bar said 8 p.m., I had to wait another four hours before I met Colin. I was looking forward to seeing someone I was able to have a conversation with. He was probably standing somewhere in the bar, but with no idea of his disguise I decided not to look for him as making eye contact with these men was not advisable. I wondered if he had any information on the length of our stay; the shorter the better was my thought at this juncture.

The landlord of the inn was completely different from anyone else in the place, a portly gentleman, about 5 foot 6 in height, with a round face that was also bearded. He wore an apron which was well stained, but no doubt that was also white in a previous life. He shared in the jokes of all he served, laughing raucously at the smallest comment. This gentleman was keeping very busy, serving drinks from a large cask at the end of the bar, this I assumed was rum, sailors drank rum and this was the tipple I had received.

Of the remaining crew, one man stood out above the others in stature. He was powerfully built but not to the degree of Landon. He was friendly with both Vicary and Landon, and from my knowledge of these seafaring times I assumed this man to be the second mate, Jefferson. These three did not mix with the crew, not unless it was strictly necessary. It appeared that the senior members of the crew gained their positions because they were taller and stronger; the rule of the jungle was alive and well on the island.

To add to the splendour of this place there were several ladies present. I use the term loosely. I had not noticed them initially, but when I saw one of them drape herself around Landon, I came to that conclusion. Landon paid little attention to her efforts, and he carried on drinking and chatting. She moved away when she realized her intentions were not reciprocated, and I do not think Landon was aware of her presence. This particular blonde lady moved amongst the crew, and she was quite willing to expose her ample breasts when requested by the men. Two other ladies confined their efforts to the crew, and both were amply endowed for what I believed was obviously their profession. The crew did not seem keen to spend their hard-earned cash, so the ladies moved into a corner and started an impromptu sing-song. If they hoped their singing might arouse the men they were to be sorely disappointed, as Vicary and his men did not join in. All three ladies I supposed to be in their thirties, and had a dirty appearance, I thought that surely a prostitute was going to be thinking of business opportunities, they would be enhanced if they considered having a wash.

Perhaps I was the agent they required . . . then I remembered how valuable water was on the island.

Although I had been wary of going to the inn, the time passed quickly as I watched the people inside this overcrowded building. Although these people had problems beyond my imagination, this simple way of life gave them contentment.

There was to be a smuggling trip that night, and from what I had heard at the inn my presence was expected on board, a terrifying thought. The crew required a religious figure for the trip, I was the only one on offer. The voyage did not commence until after midnight, very much dependent on the tides. This gave me time to meet Colin before we sailed, and I was hoping he was going to instil confidence in me about the voyage.

I remained at the inn until just before midnight, listening and laughing when appropriate, not that anyone noticed I was there, but this made my departure easy. I walked quickly to our prearranged rendezvous point, it took only a few minutes to reach. It was near to the inn but far enough away to prevent being overheard, an ideal spot for our meeting.

I crouched behind the large rock as I did not want to be seen by anyone, and I waited for my unknown collaborator. I had no idea which form Colin had taken. I heard a voice call me from behind the rock and I knew it must be Colin. The voice was a little different from his actual voice, but this was to be expected as he had taken over someone else's identity.

'How are things going for you?'

'I'm fine, well as fine as possible. I could tell you the meal at the inn was delicious, but that would be untrue; to be honest it was disgusting, but it was free as you suggested, and for that small mercy I was grateful. Landon also bought me a rum, which surprised and frightened me. Is this going to be a nightly ritual?' I said.

'I think it was a one-off gesture. Landon is not about to become your friend, but he occasionally buys the monk a drink, his own salvation. Just like Vicary, it is done just in case religion is a good thing,' he said.

'One of the crewmen said something about seeing me on the ship. From that I assume my services are required for the voyage, is that right?' I said.

'That's correct. I musn't hang around too long, the crew are about to leave, they will be making their way from the inn to the top of the island. Follow them up the hill, prepare yourself for an unpleasant voyage,' he said.

'I am seasick on calm waters. I get the feeling this is going to be an unpleasant experience. I can only hope for calm seas but I will prepare for the worst. Have you located the Pathway yet? I appreciate we have only been here a short time,' I said.

'I have no information about it, but I still feel Vicary's cellar is the most likely spot. Only time will tell if I am right, and just like you I hope our time here is short,' he said.

He asked if the key was still around my neck, and a quick check caused me to panic. I checked inside my cassock, maybe it had lodged somewhere, but unfortunately not. It had disappeared. I told him I must have dropped it somewhere.

'Don't worry, you haven't dropped it, there is a simple explanation, the key is around Vicary's neck. The key will reappear around your neck when Vicary is asleep, it is his key remember,' he said.

'I appreciate the Pathway is our top priority, without that we are restricted to the one trip, that is once I get the key back when Vicary is asleep.' I said.

'We've got two weeks before the portal opens again, hopefully we will have the Pathway and so won't be concerned as to when the portal opens. If we fail to leave in the next two weeks we have a three month wait. I remember that from my last visit here, the island opening of the portal is different from the mainland, although the portal opens four times a year, exactly as it does in our time,' he said.

'The thought of a three-month wait does not fill me with happiness, I think two weeks is long enough. We have time to turn the island upside down to locate the Pathway, especially with two of us on the case, and if Alan is found and persuaded to join the search, our chances of success would be increased,' I said.

Colin agreed that locating Alan could only help our cause. 'From what I remember of my last visit, I believe the piracy is several months away. There is of course no certainty for this supposition, but when it is about to take place, I feel there will be some sort of warning. I think even Vicary and Landon will discuss these matters with the crew. Just for your information the smuggling trips take place twice a week, and tonight is the first for this week,' he said.

'So I have to endure four trips before our departure,' I said.

'If all goes well then yes, but I must stress, you are not in any way to change the status quo of the island,' he said.

'I understand what you're saying, but I have no intention of doing or saying anything that will change the status quo; if it changes it will certainly not be my fault,' I said.

'Just to make you feel a little better, I have found out where your hut is, it is near the top of the island. I will point it out to you when we go to the ship, but don't acknowledge me in any way. By the way, I have been promoted as expected, and I think you might be pleased with the result,' he said.

I understood his reluctance to be acquainted with the lowly monk, but I was starting to feel unwanted by even my closest friends.

'I also have an idea as to Alan's identity, but I am not completely certain and this needs further investigation. I hope it is who I think it is, we could do with his help,' he said.

He left the meeting place, asking me to wait a few minutes before emerging from behind the rock. I waited then walked out onto the path. The crew had started to leave the inn, they were heading to the top of the island. I followed behind some of the crew, as befitted my position. As I walked up the hill I tried to make conversation with some of the crew. Most of them just ignored me, not wanting to talk to such a low-life, a few were talkative but limited their conversation.

It was obvious that the voyage ahead concerned some of the crew. Although they had made this voyage many times before they were still wary, there was always the possibility of being stopped by the Revenue men, the consequences of which they did not want to contemplate. The voyage would take all night, as it required meeting our suppliers just off the French coast.

As we reached the top of the island I was surprised to see the crew filing into a small hut, which was in the same position as the modern-day dilapidated building. This was larger, with a straw roof. At that moment Jefferson turned to me and nodded towards a hut. Now I knew Colin's disguise, and it pleased me that he had a position of authority and was also close to Vicary and Landon. My hut looked small and badly constructed, but at least it provided a roof over my head.

As I reached the hut at the top of the island, it suddenly dawned on me what the purpose was: it covered the entrance to a narrow passageway downwards, obviously to the ship. I wondered what remained of this passage in modern times. I entered the hut and saw a trap door with a wooden ladder going down, each crewman eased himself through a small hole. I heard boots below on what I assumed was stone steps. I entered the darkness of the hole. No sooner had I stepped into the abyss than I was aware of a ray of light shining skyward from below, it was coming from an oil lamp, just enough to show the way, obviously not wanting to advertise the voyage to the Revenue men. This passage was an amazing piece of engineering, the secret passage that nobody had ever found. I kept walking downwards, in awe of this construction, it continued down about 50 feet to the sea, where a wooden gangway led from a rock ledge to the ship. I wondered how both Vicary and Landon had made the descent; both were very large men and the hole was relatively small for their frames.

The ship itself was smaller than I had imagined it to be, there hardly seemed enough room for the crew. Even at anchor the ship was rolling from side to side, there was no anti-roll device on this vessel. My initial thought was this was not going to be a good experience, particularly if the sea got any rougher. I thought this was classed as a calm sea, and my stomach started to turn at the prospect Little did I know that my stomach was to do somersaults many times before this night was over.

I made it on board without too much trouble, feeling very queasy as I stood on the deck. Landon started shouting orders, and the crew hurried around the deck. Suddenly the sails billowed with air. The wooden gangway was pulled aboard and we turned about and headed out. I made myself as comfortable as possible on the forward deck, trying to keep out of the way. I appreciated that my help was of little use to these old salts, the crew was managing perfectly well without my assistance.

I looked at the top deck where Vicary, Landon and Jefferson were standing, with a commanding view over the ship. Vicary looked at me and beckoned me towards him, and I wondered if I had done anything wrong. I moved towards the top deck, my passage made more difficult by the continual rolling of the ship. Both Vicary and Landon found my plight amusing. I eventually clambered onto the top deck, and Vicary indicated that I should stand next to him.

'Now you're up here, Father, give us a prayer to wish us luck,' roared Vicary.

I slowly made my way towards Vicary, not too close, as that privilege belonged to Landon. To say I was nervous was an understatement, I was in the presence of a man who I had read about in local history books. Why did he want me by his side? Surely he was not going to sacrifice me to the sea.

'Perhaps a few words of blessing might provide help from above, Captain?' I said.

I was really getting into the role.

'If you want. It can't do much harm,' said the good captain.

I mumbled a few words, they sounded religious, the crew stood silently during this address, all of them removed their respective headgear. They waited for me to finish and together said 'Amen', probably the only religious word most of them knew.

'Heave to,' shouted Vicary.

At least that is what I think he said. The crew jumped into action without questioning the order.

The crew were now working quicker and more efficiently; I thought the prayer might have had something to do with that. I had survived my first sermon, I was something of a revelation to myself.

I was suddenly aware that our speed had increased, as did the roll of the ship. The swells were getting larger, and we were now some distance from the cliff face. We cut through the water with ease, the sails were fully inflated. I knew there was no way I was going to enjoy the experience, I was terrified by the whole situation.

We had travelled for only a short while when I realized all was not good, my constitution was not up to the trip and my stomach was swelling as much as the sea. I excused myself from Vicary's presence. Vicary was not aware that I had left the deck, I do not think he cared one way or the other.

I moved to the side of the ship briskly, just in time to feel my stomach explode over the side. The crew had stopped work to watch me, and I tried to recover my composure despite the derision of the onlookers. Both Vicary and Landon were amused by my misfortune, and the crew joined in the laughter. I accepted this indignity without comment. During the course of that night many trips were made to the side of the ship, much to the amusement of the crew.

After many hours of sailing the French coast came into view, and the order was given for the ship to slow, the crew were looking towards the coast for some sort of signal, it came in the form of a lighted lantern. The ship came to a complete stop, and the anchor was dropped with a thunderous clanging noise. I looked towards the coast and saw several longboats heading towards us, they were low in the water, indicating that they were heavily laden. These were obviously the Frenchmen bringing the contraband. The crew greeted the Frenchmen as long-lost friends, waving and shouting in French, the greeting was returned from the longboats in broken English, and everyone appeared happy to see their counterparts.

The first longboat drew alongside and was tied securely to the ship. The unloading of the barrels started at once and everyone in the crew assisted in this task, the barrels were heavy and needed several men to lift them. It was back-breaking work for the crew, and it took several hours to unload the three boats. Vicary and Landon watched closely from the top deck, and Landon counted the barrels as they came aboard. During the operation the Frenchmen remained in their boats, hoisting the barrels up to their English cousins, a very smooth operation, something both crews had perfected over time.

When the barrels were stowed Landon left the bridge. He walked to the longboats and spoke in French, he laughed as the men appeared to be sharing a joke, his French was very good. Landon then brought a velvet pouch from his inside pocket, obviously the payment, which he threw to what appeared to be the senior Frenchman. They said their goodbyes and the longboats turned for home. Landon returned to the bridge, shouted further orders and we turned for home.

I was relieved we were going home. The return journey was similar in many ways to the outward journey: a great deal of my time was spent over the side. The crew were now bored of my sea sickness. I craved dry land; even the disgusting place we were heading to was better than this sea journey. To maintain my cover I had to endure these trips, and I thought it unlikely that this was ever going to be a good experience. The homeward journey was quicker, the wind was behind us. The cliffs of the island were in sight. I knew the same trip had to be endured in a few days, but my heart leapt at the thought of this journey ending.

Once we had tied up at the cliff face the unloading began, and this was again an arduous task for the crew. The gangway to the ledge was put in place, then the barrels had to be taken up the stairway to the top of the island. A pulley system was operated but it was still difficult. There was no other way, it was impossible to float the barrels to the mainland side of the island as too many eyes were watching, the far side of the island was the safest. The Revenue men were likely to watch the island from the mainland, and the sight of barrels floating by was going to be of interest to them.

The unloading took over four hours, so these men obviously earned their wages, even though their share was small in comparison to Vicary and Landon's. It was dawn before the task of unloading was complete, and now the barrels had to be taken to the inn. Vicary and Landon took no part in the physical side of the unloading, they merely counted them into the inn. I later found out that the majority of the barrels left the island, sold to local hostelries. That was where the money came from, negotiated by the landlord of the inn.

Like the rest of the crew I went to the inn following the offloading, as I needed to keep up appearances. I was not sure if it was expected of me, but I was not prepared to chance not going. It was a strange time of day to drink rum, but these men deserved their libation. I sat in my usual place and was provided with breakfast by the landlord, it consisted of the same stew I had consumed the previous night, except it was a day older, and it did not taste any better.

I left the inn and went to the hut indicated by Colin. It was dark as I entered, the sun had only just come up and I expected it to be light inside, then I realized the shutters on the windows had been closed, by the real monk. It took only a few moments to realize that the hut looked better with the shutters closed, a wise decision by my predecessor. My main objective was to sleep, the night had been long and tiring, not because of any physical work but due to the evacuation of my stomach at regular intervals.

I was able to see inside my new home, it was deserted except for a bed and a table, this was probably the maximum amount of furniture it was possible to hold, even though this made the hut look crowded. A jug was on the table, it was filled with a watery substance, green in colour. Also on the table was a bible. Having seen what was in the jug I decided to forgo any sort of wash, as I was unable to decide what the liquid was or why it was there. The decision not to wash was a wise one, anyway: what might my crewmates think?

The bed was wooden-framed, draped in what I assume was at one time a blanket, which had a dusky smell and appeared to be alive. Sleeping was going to be more of a problem than I had thought, I had never shared a bed with so many creatures. This was all part of the rich tapestry of life on the island, a life I did not care for very much. I overcame the sleeping problem very well, I slept well without sustaining a single bite. It became a regular routine to check for bites but I never experienced a single one.

That evening I went to the inn, this was of course expected by my fellow smugglers, not that there was a lot else to do in the evening. I was treated to my customary free meal, which had not improved since breakfast. The rum ration also duly arrived, courtesy of our jovial landlord. The crew were reliving the previous nights' exploits and most of their fun was angled at me. Some were graphically describing my misfortune, not what you want to hear with a delicious meal in front of you.

I left before midnight and walked to the designated meeting place. Colin had not been at the inn, and I hoped he was all right. It concerned me as he had not mentioned he had anything else to do tonight. Vicary and Landon were sure to have missed him. I hoped he possessed some information, having spent many hours with those two. I looked forward to meeting with Colin, it gave me the chance of a normal conversation, much better than the grunting of the crew; I was sure many of them were unable to speak. I sat down, hoping he was soon to turn up. Then I heard a rustling behind the rock.

'Colin? I hope that is you,' I said.

'It is me. Have you got over the voyage? Like everyone on board, I could see you were suffering,' he said.

'I'm fine now I am on dry land. I was concerned you did not turn up at the inn. How did you get away with that?' I asked.

'I spoke to Vicary and told him my wife was ill, but he did not understand why that should keep me from the inn, Vicary has little time for wives and children, he doesn't understand the concept of family. He believes men are put on this earth to drink and steal, that is the philosophy of the great man,' he said.

'How is your new-found wife? Hopefully she is a pleasant surprise for you. You do know you are committing adultery and possibly bigamy? Or does it count if it is three hundred years in the past? I said.

'I do not see the humour in that remark. I was actually using it as an excuse to look around near where the ship is anchored, hoping to find one of the many secret passages and hiding places it is thought Vicary had there. It would be nice to know where the pirate gold was going to be hidden, but I couldn't find any hiding places,' he said.

'I am a little concerned that you wanted to find these places, hopefully our stay isn't going to last that long? I hoped we might be gone before any of the gold appeared on the island. Or are you now staying for the piracy phase?' I said.

'Of course not, it is for the future. Nobody in our time has located any of the gold, and this would mean we had the advantage if we knew where the hiding places were. It is a back-up plan,' he said.

It appeared that the wealth we anticipated from the paintings was not enough for him, just in case the paintings only made us mildly rich, in his eyes that was not rich enough.

'Why don't you tell me about your newly acquired wife, a luxury that a monk does not understand,' I said.

He was reluctant at first, whether he was embarrassed or not, only he knew the answer to that. 'Let's just say I do not recommend inheriting a wife, or maybe it is just this particular wife, who I would describe as far from a ravishing beauty. In her favour she is an excellent cook, she does not impinge on my social life, which of course is spent at the inn, she is far more accommodating that the women we find in our time,' he said.

He did not delve further into how accommodating she was.

Although there appeared to be disadvantages with having a wife, he had mentioned a huge plus, she was a good cook, and I craved to eat a decent meal. I suggested he invite me for a meal. Only one meal, and it might neutralize what I ate at the inn.

He instantly rejected this idea, and was quick to state that as second mate, an important position, it was impossible for him to be seen inviting the lowest life on the island to his hut. He had a position to uphold.

'I think you are starting to enjoy your role on the island, that is how it comes across to me. I actually think you're a snob, if such a thing exists here. You are rejecting the only friend you have on the island. No, I understand exactly what you are saying, I just wanted to make you feel bad,' I said.

We discussed Vicary's possible secret hiding places. Colin played a trump card by saying this might accelerate our departure, a cruel trick to play on someone as vulnerable as I was at that moment, but it worked: we decided that one of these secret place must hold the Pathway. I requested that we both made a concerted effort to locate the Pathway; our departure was likely to be brought forward drastically if we possessed it. We knew the gold was something in the future, as those adventures had not started, but if Vicary felt the Pathway was of value he was likely to hide it somewhere other than in his cellar. All along we had assumed the item was in the cellar, mainly because the box that held it was there, but that did not necessarily mean the Pathway was in the box: Vicary had probably removed it and hidden it somewhere else. This idea was a reasonable one. I agreed that to carry out a search, it was easier for me to leave the inn, as nobody cared or batted an eyelid if I walked out. Colin was a man in a position on the island, his absence was not feasible. Although I felt his motives were eventually to locate the gold, it was a task I was happy to carry out. And it meant

I was relieved of the tedium that was the inn, not exactly my scene.

He believed the passages were located on the cliff face, he had checked in the immediate vicinity of the ship, so I needed to check higher up. My mission was to scour the cliff face in an attempt to locate the Pathway.

We walked up to the stone building and climbed down the ladder towards the ship. Colin showed me where he had searched, and I said I was going to give it my best effort to search the rest.

It was strange that this passageway down to the ship had never been discovered in our time. Many people had searched the cliff face; admittedly they were looking for the gold, but it seems inconceivable that no one had found any trace of this passage, I intended to examine the area closely on my return to the present. Maybe the hut that now covered the entrance helped disguise it, and this was something to look into seriously.

We left the hut and returned to our respective abodes: Colin to his wife, me to my six-legged friends. I was not sure who was best off.

The morning broke, bright and sunny. I decided to have a walk around the island, a snooping day; there was no voyage tonight so I felt more relaxed.

I blessed my congregation as I went, some were happy with my benedictions, other completely ignored me, a few were abusive. One young lady misinterpreted my blessing, offering me her wares as some sort of recompense. It looked too big a job for me and I declined her kind offer. I still gave her a blessing, then I moved on quickly. I thought I recognized her as one of the ladies in the inn, but I felt it unlikely as she offered her services for free.

It became obvious that the monk rarely met his flock outside the inn, as the islanders looked at me with some suspicion My position was not respected, given the language used by some of the female parishioners. The women and children were generally unfriendly, they were tending their livestock and wanted no interruptions. The menfolk were still sleeping off the night before, leaving the women to do the daily chores. It was a hard life for these women, and no doubt that accounted for their aggressive attitude towards me. I was able to cover the island in less than an hour, and unable to find other likely hiding places for Vicary to use.

One particular lady near her hut looked at me and smiled, this in itself surprised me, maybe some sort of conversation with possible with her. Her conversation was limited, suggesting the hut I wanted was next door. This was strange, how was she to know I was snooping for secret passages? I walked to the hut and knocked on the door. I had no idea what I was going to say, but the lady seemed sure I required this particular hut.

'Good morning, Father, I didn't think you were going to make it,' I was greeted by a tall attractive blonde lady.

Had I made some kind of arrangement with her that I had forgotten? This seemed very unlikely; the island had done many things to me but forgetting an appointment I think not.

'Please come in for some refreshment,' she said.

As I entered it became blatantly obvious this lady's idea of refreshment did not run parallel to my own. Even a lowly monk was able to appreciate that.

She was not to be deterred by my edging towards the door, and she played her trump card: she started to disrobe. Under the oversized dress was a body of incredible beauty, perfectly proportioned, which may have accounted for me standing open-mouthed. My next thought was whether the monk had his own account with her. How was I going to pay the bill if I took advantage of the situation?

'I think we may be at cross-purposes. I have to say this isn't what I expected,' I said.

But she did not understand my response to the situation. What I saw before me did look like a pleasant way to spend an hour or so, I wondered how I was I going to refuse after she had gone to so much trouble.

'I like your idea of refreshments. Not exactly my idea,' I said.

'Is it not a form of refreshment?' she said.

I was unable to find an argument with that, not that I was trying very hard. The next thing she said took me by complete surprise.

'This has been paid for by Mister Landon, he said I was to take care of you, allowing you to have whatever you want. I hope you will have satisfaction,' she said.

This was very confusing, I had thought I was a complete low-life in Landon's eyes. But whatever the reason, I accepted his hospitality with much pleasure I felt it impolite to refuse the great man's offer. My opinion had changed about the island. I left the hut some time later, happy and refreshed by my encounter. I felt it was disrespectful to go against Landon's wishes, that was my excuse.

The lady next door was still in her garden, she had seen me enter the hut some considerable time ago, and she gave me a knowing look.

I returned it with my 'I know you know but I don't care' look and she turned away.

No doubt my exploits were to get around the island very quickly, but what choice did I have when faced with such a situation? The crux of this matter that I was only acting as a monk, and my real life as a man took over occasionally.

I continued my journey, greeting people as I went. Some were a little cordial, but I was still being ignored by many. This was certainly a thankless job; there was only one lady who appreciated my work.

I located Vicary's hut with relative ease. It was bigger than the others, and also closest to the inn, which did not surprise me. I checked around my neck and found the key had reappeared; this told me Vicary was asleep. I needed to wait until he went to the inn before forcing entry, although I had the tools to pick his lock.

I returned to my hut while Vicary slept. Not an ideal retreat, but it was quiet and out of the way. Most of my good intentions that day had fallen on stony ground. It still confused me why

Landon had wanted me looked after. I was not complaining of course, it was an admirable thought, and I was looked after well by the lady in question. Perhaps he felt sorry for my state on the voyage. I decided to mention it to Colin; his close proximity to Landon might throw some light on the subject.

My decision to clean up the hut was a good one, but limited. It was impossible to wash the blankets, they had to remain dirty. Cleaning the windows was an admirable thought, and this action provided a little more light. The trouble was this extra light showed how bad the hut was on the inside. What a terrible place to reside.

The noise outside told me the inn was open for business, and my view from my newly cleaned window confirmed this. All of the male population were making their way to the inn, and as a member of the crew I felt obliged to join them. As expected the bar was packed. Vicary and Landon were together, Jefferson was in close proximity, and he nodded to me as I entered. I took my place in my normal seat, the barman nodded, the nod was returned, and the ritual stew and rum arrived shortly after.

A quick look around confirmed that my lady friend was present, she smiled and winked in my direction and I smiled back, knowing what was under the dirty clothes. A wink seemed inappropriate. She was plying her trade amongst the crew, and knowing what I knew I was surprised nobody was taking up her offer, it was my best experience so far on the island. But these were ignorant men. It still puzzled me why Landon wanted me taken care of. Perhaps he had found God, maybe I had misjudged this man.

Having checked that Vicary was well into his drinking, I left the inn. I walked towards Vicary's hut, checking about me to see there were no members of the crew lurking. I was, preparing to commit my first burglary, but I believed I had just cause. I took a collection of items I had put together, hoping to be able to fashion some sort of skeleton key. My previous occupation had not been wasted, I had learnt certain tricks from a perpetual burglar I had known.

Listening intently at the door, I realized I had no idea whether

Vicary was married or not, it was generally accepted he was not. But it was quiet, so I assumed the hut was vacant. Entry was gained by using the implements I had brought with me. The light from outside the inn was enough for me to see inside, giving me a good overall view of the hut. It was dirty and sparsely furnished, following the trend of my hut, but it was much larger. There was a large bed in the corner. The only other pieces of furniture that interested me were the two large wooden chests placed together under the window. Both chests were locked, the lock mechanism was not sophisticated, entry was effortlessly gained. Was I about to locate the Pathway?

On opening the first chest I was met with a mountain of paperwork, which related to the ship and the crew. Vicary seemed to know everything about each crewman, even to the point of how many children they had. Why he wanted such information was a mystery, perhaps for some sort of bribery, knowing his reputation. The chest also contained diaries and ledgers, detailing the smuggling operations in fine detail. Why he needed to keep records was also confusing; if the Revenue men got hold of them it would be good evidence against Vicary. The ledgers were well written; Vicary was obviously more educated than I had assumed. I quickly sifted through the diaries, but there was nothing there worthy of further investigation. There was a list of the hostelries which had received goods from the smuggling trips, all on the mainland. It was more damning evidence against him. I locked the first chest securely, leaving it as though it had not been tampered with.

Moving onto the second chest, again entry was easily gained. Inside was a single parchment, Vicary's will. I recognized it from what Colin had shown me, and I was sure that Colin had in fact shown me the genuine article. The parchment was only partially completed, and I still had no idea of its content. My inheritance was a hole, believed to be under Vicary's hut, so the trap door must be in the room I was in, but where was it?

Then I noticed an old piece of carpet under the bed. This must be the cellar. I pulled the bed out to give me access, and folding back the carpet I saw the trap door. It was not the same as the one in my time but to my surprise the door did possess a lock. The key was not needed as it was unlocked. The door had obviously rotted over the years, but the original lock was fashioned into each new door. But that was another problem. I pulled back the door, and it creaked like something out of a horror film. I was able to see inside.

To my surprise the hole was about 2 feet deep. This was my inheritance. There were six small barrels in one corner of the hole, no doubt Vicary's bonus to himself. In the other corner was a piece of canvas covering something which I was unable to see. I was able to pull away this cloth, which revealed something I did not expect to see. There were six rolls of silk. They were not supposed to be there, this was the booty from the first piracy trip, which had not happened yet. I left the cellar as I had found it, closing and locking the door and replacing the carpet, and pulling the bed back into its correct position. I left the hut and locked the door.

Quickly I returned to the inn. Maybe I had been missed. Unlikely though it was, I did not want to compromise the find. There was much to discuss with Colin tonight. I was extremely confused. I had no idea why the silk was there. Why was someone like Vicary storing silk? Maybe Colin had an explanation for this strange phenomenon, because I was stumped for an answer.

Time passed very slowly that evening. I was excited about my find, believing it was in some way significant; how or why was another question. Everyone inside the inn was in their usual place, Vicary and Landon together like Siamese twins, Jefferson on the fringe, all unaware of the crime I had committed. My lady friend was still smiling at me; perhaps she had received a religious experience in more ways than one.

Just before midnight I left the inn, hurrying to our meeting place, hoping to get answers from Colin. He arrived a few minutes after me and immediately asked me if I had anything to report, as if he knew I had something to say. His manner was a little curious.

'There is much to report. I visited Vicary's hut, where I found a couple of wooden chests, of the same style as the small one in my inheritance. The first chest contained ledgers and diaries, recording details of the smuggling trips. The second chest contained Vicary's will: it proves his will was genuine,' I said.

'What is in the ledgers?' he asked.

'They have details of everyone involved in the smuggling: names and dates of local people receiving the booze, names of the crew involved, and how much each was paid. The ledgers would be a godsend for the authorities, it would mean the death sentence for most of the crew. What surprises me is how neat and meticulous they are, not what I expected from Vicary,' I said.

'There is a good reason for the neatness, because they are not kept by Vicary. Landon keeps the records, he is the neat one, Vicary tells him what to write,' he said.

Landon's name brought another subject to my mind. 'There is something else I need to ask you. Why did Landon provide me with a lady, I think you know what sort of lady I'm talking about. Was it to cheer me up after the voyage, or some other reason I don't know about?' I said.

'That was not actually the reason, it was a genuine offer by Landon. I know why he did it but I am not at liberty to say yet. Don't expect it on a daily basis,' he said.

'When you next speak to Landon, can you thank him for me? If it was out of pity, he can feel sorry for me any time he wants,' I said.

He grimaced at this remark, but he had not seen the lady naked as I had.

'Is there anything else you have to tell me?' he asked.

'Yes I do, even more surprising than the prostitute. I got into Vicary's cellar, and strangely it has the same lock on it as in our time. What I found I feel will be of great interest to you, although it is not the Pathway. The small box, which we assume holds the Pathway, isn't there, but there are several small barrels of booze and six rolls of silk.'

His mouth fell wide open, not a pretty sight. We both knew the silk was a result of the piracy, but that had not happened yet, that event was months away.

'You must have imagined it, or saw something you thought was silk,' he said.

'I touched it and I know what silk feels like,' I said.

We both felt it was absurd, the ships carrying such items had not yet been looted. There must be a reasonable explanation, but the trouble was that we had no idea what it was.

He was troubled by my revelation, he tried in vain to find a reason. I suggested we were not the only travellers; perhaps someone had arrived from the future.

'The large chests were in the style of the small chest I found in my inheritance, surely that means the Pathway is from this time, or at least the box is, they must have been a set. I am confused as to why the Pathway does not appear to be where we thought it would be. I understand that the Pathway was removed from the box long before I bought the bungalow, but I thought it would be around in Vicary's time. Finding the Pathway was going to be the solution to our immediate problems. I hope you have a few ideas on how to find it?' I said.

'I think I know who Alan is, and that must be our best option for finding the Pathway,' he said.

We drew the meeting to a close, both still confused. Vicary had silk in his cellar which had no reason for being there. The Pathway was not in his cellar, but it must be in one of Vicary's hiding places, even though it was unlikely he knew what it really was.

'I will try to get some information on the next voyage. I am close to Vicary so maybe I can find out something. It is going to be a difficult task, I will not be able to mention the silk. I need to be subtle. I need to speak to Vicary when Landon is absent, I have no intention of saying something in front of Landon,' he said.

By mentioning this plan, he reminded me that another sea

voyage was imminent. He left and went off to his wife, the one who was a good cook, I went to the hovel I called home, and started to conclude he was much better off than I was.

I spent the next day walking the island; not that exciting but it was exercise. The weather was what some call bracing; it was what I called windy. I hoped the wind was going to drop before we sailed, the ship was unstable enough without any wind. I thought it prudent to keep an eye on Vicary's place, it might possibly give me an insight as to the whereabouts of the Pathway. Watching his comings and goings was easy as he had no visitors. There was a strong temptation to visit my lady friend, but Landon's kindness was probably just for the one visit, and I had no money for a repeat performance.

Many of the other females were becoming friendlier towards me, happy to pass the time of day with me. Perhaps they had heard about my exploits, maybe they wanted some of the action. All this adoration in my own mind was making me something of a sensation, and I wallowed in this for a short time. I started to chat with the female population, and it was surprising what they told me, mostly about the menfolk; some details were very intimate. Many wanted my opinion on the sexual practices of their husbands. I remembered the code I had to live by, not the religious one, but the one that said I was not to give an opinion. It was difficult not to do so, bearing in mind that I was starting to be accepted by the ladies. I merely told them to speak to their husbands on the matter, which did not help their plight. If they thought I was going to do that for them, they were sadly mistaken. I tried to help where possible, without giving an opinion or any advice, although there were many things I was inclined to say. I started to appreciate the predicament some of these ladies were in, their marriages were not enjoyable matches, and from what I heard their sex lives were even less enjoyable. The menfolk were definitely in charge, the women catered for the needs of their husbands. Some of the husbands were unaware of how many children they had, they saw so little of them.

My walk to the inn was a little later than usual. I was mentally preparing myself for the inevitable sea trip, recalling the last voyage and keen to become more of a sailor on this trip. I walked into the bar and sat at my usual table. The food arrived immediately, along with the rum. I looked at my meal, confident that it was certain to reappear later that night.

The crew were excited unlike the last voyage, they seemed particularly upbeat about this trip. Perhaps they were looking forward to my encore performance. My intention not to repeat it was mentioned to a few of the crew, possibly not the best thing to say. When the time came to go I rose slowly from my seat, with little enthusiasm in my manner, but I knew I had no choice. Before leaving I was approached by my lady friend, much to the amusement of the other ladies in the bar. She offered me a reduced rate on my return. Was I to read something into this offer?

As we reached the ship I noticed that the wind had dropped and the sea looked calm, this had the makings of a pleasant voyage. Who was I trying to kid? I had realized the stupidity of my assessment of the situation: the ship was at anchor in a bay, surrounded on three sides by cliffs; the true force of the weather was only likely to hit us when we left the bay.

We eventually left the protection of the cove, and the wind built up instantly. I knew I was in for another tough test, and the crew watched me with anticipation, waiting for the explosion within. It did not take long before I was hanging over the side of the ship, soon to be seeing that meal again. Initially the crew were amused, then they returned to their duties. I was amazed at how the crew endured these voyages, although I appreciated it was only a two nights a week. But they had no other option, their livelihood depended on these trips. I was not invited to the bridge by Vicary on this trip. Perhaps he thought one blessing a week was enough.

I watched Colin with great interest. How was he going to make the approach to Vicary? What was he going to say when he did speak to him? Any backlash from this conversation was likely to have a disastrous effect on his health. Vicary and Landon were side by side, the pair only split up for a few seconds when Landon checked the rigging. Colin was going to find it difficult to get Vicary alone; the only possible chance was when Landon was paying the Frenchmen, when he left the bridge then and spoke to his allies. That only lasted a few minutes, but those few minutes were probably enough.

Then as I watched, Landon left Vicary's side. He walked onto the lower deck, bellowing orders to the crew as he went. Maybe this was the time. Landon looked even fiercer when he shouted, and the crew responded instantly.

Colin started to move closer to Vicary, was this the moment? Vicary looked at him; he was clearly agitated by Landon not being at his side, his body language showed he was worried by the situation, strange for a captain. Colin started to speak to Vicary, but it did not look like it was going well, he was listening and shaking his head, and he did not nod at anything that Colin said. He then turned to face Colin, and started shouting, which caused him to step back. The conversation had not gone as planned, Vicary looked angry. Colin retreated, this appeared to be a wise decision.

Landon returned to his place beside Vicary, and a short conversation took place. Both men looked towards Colin, and Landon did not look pleased with what he had heard. Landon took several glances at him, those steely blue eyes penetrating into his soul. Whatever was said the conversation had been relayed to Landon, I feared Colin's safety was at risk.

The voyage continued with no more incident, the incident had certainly not been forgotten, it was simply a fact of doing the job first. I felt Colin's retribution was close at hand. He kept clear of both men, avoiding eye contact whenever possible, no doubt hoping to diffuse the situation. I feared that was very unlikely in the circumstances.

Suddenly we were at our rendezvous point just off the French coast, this trip had seemed quicker than the last one. The longboats were waiting, the lantern signalled and they came towards the ship. The same format as before was adopted, each longboat in turn was tied up to the ship, and the cargo was unloaded barrel by barrel. Watching this back-breaking work I wanted to suggest a pulley system to the captain, but I decided not to change history, something that I knew was taboo.

This was the part of the voyage I enjoyed: we were at anchor and the sails were down, there was still a little rocking, but that I was able to cope with. On the top deck stood Vicary and Landon, masters of all they surveyed, Landon again counting the barrels aboard, sometimes shouting orders to hurry up the process. Vicary stood silent throughout the unloading, he trusted his second in command to see the process through.

The last barrel was eventually aboard, and Landon moved from his post next to Vicary, moving onto the lower deck Landon moved to the side of the deck, talking in French to the longboat occupants. Several of the crew stood alongside him. This was different from last time. Landon said something to the crew, and they drew their pistols. The noise that followed was deafening, a barrage of shot was aimed at the occupants of the three longboats, it was continual fire until all the Frenchmen were dead.

I was stunned by what I had just seen. Vicary also looked surprised, I do not think he had known what was going happen. Colin was open-mouthed.

None of the Frenchmen were able to return fire, it was slaughter. All three longboats were close when the onslaught took place, it was impossible for the crew to miss their targets. Most of the Frenchmen fell into the sea mortally wounded, their chests bleeding from the shot. None of them survived. It was over in seconds, and their bodies were strewn across the surface of the sea, floating face down. I had just seen a mass execution on a terrifying scale, that memory was to stay with me.

Vicary told several of the crew to sink the longboats. Landon then gave the order, they hoisted the sails and we turned about. Landon returned to his position next to Vicary. They were deep in conversation, Landon no doubt explaining his reasons for the mass murder as Vicary listened intently and occasionally nodded. Whatever the reason, it looked like Landon had persuaded Vicary of its merit.

The crew on the return trip were silent. Not all were involved in the incident, only those loyal to Landon took part, and the rest had looked on in horror. I still did not know why it had happened, but what was certain was that the smuggling days were over. The history books did not record this event, which made the crew look like butchers. I hoped Colin had an inkling about what had just happened, but he looked very shocked by it.

Although grateful this was the last smuggling trip, I mourned those poor Frenchmen. They had no chance to defend themselves, brutally murdered on the high seas. I felt sure the piracy trips were not due to start yet; or had I got my history wrong? I did not understand why Landon had decided on this course of action, he was far from being an idiot, he was aware the islanders needed the smuggling trips, their livelihood depended on this. He had obviously thought it all out, Landon no doubt had a motive.

Sailing into the bay of the island, the crew silently unloaded the barrels. They had no doubt discussed matters on the return trip, and some were bright enough to appreciate the significance of what had happened. Once the unloading was complete the crew went to the inn. I was not convinced all the crew wanted to, but they went anyway. I did not feel in a celebratory mood either, and I returned to my hut.

I was looking forward to meeting Colin at midnight, perhaps he had some answers. But he was as shocked as I was. He had been knocked sideways. History had certainly been changed. I wondered what would happen in these unusual circumstances?

I awoke just after midday and I decided to make my walk around the island. It was going to be a sombre walk today, the memory of the previous night deeply ingrained in my mind. The whole island was deserted, no doubt many feeling the guilt. I appeared to be alone, and I did not like it much. There was no sign of the womenfolk, who were usually around in their gardens. All was quiet, it was like a ghost island. As I walked past Vicary's hut I heard some movement inside. Suddenly the door swung open, and before me stood the powerful figure of Landon. He looked straight at me but said nothing. I decided to open the conversation.

'Morning, Mr Landon. How are you today?' I said.

'Fine, Father. How did you enjoy last night's trip?' he said.

'It wasn't quite what I expected. No doubt you had your reasons,' I replied.

'Because it was destined to happen, Father. You're a pilgrim, I thought you might understand.'

He smiled. I had never seen Landon smile before. It was a strange thing to say, and Landon now explained himself.

'Pilgrim is a term used by men of the church, is it not? But I feel, Father, that you have not been as celibate as you should be. I think you know what I mean,' he said.

He laughed out loud and returned to Vicary's hut, slamming the door behind him. I thought he was quite jovial, saying it was destined to happen. What did that mean? The Landon temper was not there, he spoke softly and precisely.

He was in Vicary's hut, but I did not see Vicary. It was possible that Landon had killed Vicary, and he was happy because he was now the captain. I was now concerned about Colin, maybe Landon had disposed of him as well. My mind was working overtime with numerous possibilities. For me to manage here without Colin was a horrible prospect, he was a much needed ally and confidant.

At this moment I perceived Landon to be a cold-blooded killer, him and certain members of the crew. A ruthless man, how were the crew going to react if he was the new captain? I wondered what the atmosphere at the inn was likely to be that evening, one of harsh reality or just calm.

The day passed quickly and then it was time to get my evening meal. I entered the inn at an important time. Vicary was there, alive and well, talking to the crew. They were silent as he spoke.

Quietly I made my way to my table. He was explaining the reasons behind what had happened the previous night, although I was certain he was not the instigator. That was no doubt the reason for Landon's visit to his hut, probably advising him what to say.

Vicary emphasized the fact that their smuggling days were over, just in case some of the crew had not realized it. The crew in the most part understood that things had changed, whether they had been part of what happened or not.

Colin was at the inn too, and he smiled at me to show all was well. From the information I had on the island's history, this was not the story I had been led to believe. The piracy was supposed to happen later, and not because of the reasons of the previous night. Vicary put forward his plan to start the acts of piracy, and the crew looked confused for the most part, but they accepted what their captain was telling them. They had no choice in the matter. He told the crew that he would inform them of the first piracy venture once he had worked out a strategy.

Vicary was a good speaker, and the talk of great wealth impressed these simple men. But both Vicary and Landon knew that the crew would only make a bit more than on their smuggling trips; the two of them were to reap the greatest rewards. Vicary made it sound as if the slaughter the previous night was his idea, but I was certain that was not the case. This had been planned and carried out by Landon, Vicary was as shocked as I was.

My food and drink arrived on cue, some things never change. Looking around, I noticed that Colin had left the inn, perhaps his wife was ill again. I hoped he would make the midnight meeting, there was much to discuss, we still had not located the Pathway, and we were both hoping to be off the island before the piracy started.

Suddenly the inn fell silent. I looked up, and saw that Landon was the reason. He stood on a chair to address the crew, agreeing with what the captain had said, stating that the days of smuggling booze were over. I think most of the crew already knew that. Nobody spoke, and it was an attentive audience.

'What happened last night was inevitable, it was bound to happen, the Frenchmen have been cheating us for a long time, although none of you were aware of this. Our customers have been complaining about the barrels not being full, they threatened to take their business elsewhere. We have been deceived by the Frenchmen, so we paid them back in full last night. Because our customers had threatened to boycott our operation, we were left no choice. By our actions last night the haul was free, it made up for what the Frenchmen had cheated us out of. I spoke to the Frenchmen, and they were not prepared to negotiate; at this point we realized we could not trust them again.

'These events give us a wonderful opportunity. The idea is now to attack the ships of either France or Spain, they travel near the French coast taking their wares to London, some carry vast amounts of gold and jewels, and the profits will make you all rich men. There is one minor problem: the ships carry armed men, not many, very few in fact, and they will not expect to be attacked, surprise is on our side. They carry the barest crews, and we will easily outnumber them. It is not a very dangerous mission and the rewards are far greater, it is up to you to decide what you want to do,' said Landon.

Landon knew exactly how the crew would vote on his idea, although he spoke as if it was the captain's idea, which he happened to agree with. I knew differently, and possibly some of the crew did as well, but vote they did in favour. The place erupted with a positive yes, they were prepared to take the chance. Landon was indeed someone who had the ability to rouse the crew, they accepted his offer without question. Most of the crew assumed Landon never lied to them; Vicary they were not too sure about. Landon had used his powers of persuasion, with a lot of fear thrown in.

Landon further drove home the point by suggesting that for anyone who did not want to sail, there was work on the mainland. This was a great insult to these men, he knew that and used the point to his advantage. The crew cheered, they were sailors, nobody wanted a job on land, they were fully behind their leaders.

Landon continued by stating that their first task was to capture the ship they were plundering, it was essential to replace their small and slower ship, this allowed them to reach the Channel quicker, and made them a stronger force. The crew liked the idea. They celebrated their new occupation, having no idea of the possible dangers ahead. They did not care, they only thought of the riches they had been promised.

Colin was not at the meeting place, although I had expected him to be there before me. I hoped he was in a position to make our meeting; the events unfolding before me needed serious consideration, least of all Landon messing with history, for we were not supposed to be at the piracy stage.

I heard a noise coming from the rock behind me, I moved around to see who it was. Then I heard a man's voice, but it was not Colin.

'Colin is unable to make the meeting tonight, he sends his regrets, I have come in his place,' he said.

It was a voice I vaguely recognized, I had definitely heard it before somewhere on the island. Only someone who knew our situation was going to call him Colin. I came from my position into the open, I needed to see my visitor. It was Landon.

My jaw dropped, what was he doing here? I was unable to comprehend what I was seeing, this was indeed an unforeseen state of affairs. My first thought was that he had killed Colin, somehow he had found out our situation and decided to tackle me head on. I was not sure if Landon was one of us, I did not intend to reveal my real identity.

'Why don't you ask me why I am here? In fact I insist you ask me anything you want. Colin has told me everything about your visit. I am acquainted with Colin but not on this island. I have tried to drop you hints, but to your credit you never let the façade drop,' he said.

It was then I realized he was Alan Donald.

'Colin was unable to come because he had to visit the doctor on the mainland with his wife. She has been taken ill again, thought to be a minor complaint, but in this time of course nothing is minor. He asked me to come to the meeting place, he knew you would be waiting. I saw the relief on your face when you realized I was Alan Donald and not Landon. That is why I said Colin had sent me. I knew you would be surprised; hopefully you approve of my identity,' he said.

'It is indeed a pleasant surprise, in fact it's better than that, you are someone who has the captain's attention, it is the best disguise ever. But to get that disguise, didn't you have to kill Landon?' I said.

'That's true, but I was not as brave as you think. Landon was asleep at the time, I was incapable of doing it face to face,' he said.

'Even though I know you are not Landon, just looking at you unnerves me a little. Can I ask you at what point in time we have reached, surely we have not reached the piracy stage yet? From your speech at the inn I assume we are about to start on that course?' I said.

'Your assessment is correct. I was the person behind last night's events. I am aware of the history of the island and I know I should not change anything, but my position is unique, I have lived through it all before, I know exactly what the future holds, as no doubt do you. I decided that seeing I was staying in this time, I did not want to know what the future holds for me. If I changed things, that would possibly change the future. If only the crew were aware of what awaited them in the future, I am sure they would thank me for my intervention. I know the history books tell of the crew's demise, most of them were hung following a few acts of piracy. If I can make plans to avoid attacking the ship carrying the Crown's gold, I might just save some of the crew,' he said.

'I understand what you are saying, you are the one remaining on the island, and for that reason you deserve some latitude, but the acts of piracy are still going to take place, just a little earlier than expected,' I said.

'I am aware of that, but it adds something to my life here. I have no idea what cargo the ships will carry, but I know which ship to avoid, which is something in the crew's favour, and at least I can change my own destiny,' he said.

'What about changing history?' I said.

'I feel my actions are too minor to have an impact on the future, it only affects the small community on the island.'

'I disagree with you, but you are the only one who has the right to decide your future. Colin and I are only passing through, perhaps if I was staying I would think the same as you do. Fortunately I am not in that position,' I said.

'When will you be leaving the island?' he said.

'There is a problem if we want to leave before the portal opens; perhaps Colin has told you? We intend to help John, he was your next-door neighbour; that requires going to 1981, but we also want to go to 1941. As you know, to make both trips we need the Pathway. I have searched Vicary's cellar, and it is not there; we have no idea where it is hidden. Do you have any ideas about the Pathway's hiding place?' I said.

'I do know where it is, it's in my cellar. You have been looking in the wrong place,' he said.

'What is it doing in your cellar? I expected it to be in Vicary's,' I said.

'Vicary gave it to me to sell, he has no idea what it is,' he said

'The box for the Pathway was under Vicary's floor, at least that is what I am led to believe. Are you sure you didn't steal it?' I said.

He then explained what history told us of what had happened on the island. Following the act of piracy resulting in the large haul of the King's gold, Vicary left the island with Landon. They took some gold with them, hoping to sell it in the future. They both hoped that when the furore had died down, and the hunt for the gold was given up by the King, they would then get someone to melt it down, then sell whatever was possible to sell without getting caught. Vicary wanted to get all the gold from the island, no doubt intending to double-cross Landon in the process.

Landon decided to return to the island and take up the position of captain, telling the crew that Vicary had abandoned them. He moved into Vicary's larger hut, but then the unexpected happened, Vicary returned to the island. This brought uproar from the crew. Landon had no choice but to give up the captain's position, moving into Landon's hut as first mate. This position was not to last long, as Vicary again left the island and was never seen again. During that short spell of his return he had completed his will and placed the Pathway in the cellar of Landon's hut.

'The Pathway is at your disposal, I appreciate you need it for the two trips. I will assist you in your quest, it is the least I can do. I will be here to assist you on your return as well. For my part I still intend to remain on the island. I will be captain eventually; my position is going to change and I think it is a lifestyle I will enjoy, although first mate is not all bad. Because you have returned to the island, time has gone back, I know what is ahead for me and I am in a position to change what I want, and gain a position of power over the crew. The fateful piracy act is not going to happen, I will make sure of that. I intend to design my own future, a different outcome from the history books,' he said.

'I really want to help John, he is the priority, but Colin wants to revisit 1941, with the Pathway we can make both trips,' I said. 'I have no idea how the Pathway works.'

'Don't worry, I have worked out the rudiments and I believe Colin also knows how it works. The Pathway is a metal tube that opens up, and is then set to the date before pressing the button. It is quite simple to use. If we use the Pathway and you both make the trip to 1941, the Pathway will be available when you return. It will remain in my possession, you can use it when required. Under no circumstances must the Pathway leave the island; if it leaves the island it can never be used again. Once the Pathway has been set it must be returned to me to activate it, as you and Colin walk through the mist. You said you wanted to make two trips? I think you'll find Colin has other ideas, I believe he has planned another trip. No doubt he'll tell you at some point,' he said.

Was this something Colin had told him? Maybe he will get around to telling me I thought. At his convenience, of course, as with all his revelations.

'I take it the acts of piracy are due to start soon? Hopefully you'll avoid the King's treasure,' I said.

'It has to be soon, bearing in mind we have burnt our bridges in the smuggling trade. I know when the King's treasure passes through the Channel, and we will avoid going to sea on that day.'

'As you are the expert on this place, can I ask you if time goes back when we return from 1941? I feel that I need to clarify that, being the monk is not something I want to linger with.'

'Although you travel away from the island, in theory you are still on the island for the purposes you describe. Time only goes back for new travellers, once you go to 1941 you are not a new traveller when you return to the island. Time on the island will move forward when you are in 1941, and it is possible there will have been a lot of changes when you return. No doubt some acts of piracy would have taken place, but the time you spend away does not necessarily equate to the same amount of time on the island,' he said.

'Do you know when Colin is returning to the island? Now we have the Pathway I am anxious to leave, getting out of the monk's habit will be a delight,' I said.

'He will be at the meeting place tomorrow evening. I will be here to assist you on your travels. Don't worry, you will soon be in war-torn Britain in 1941.'

'Strange though it might seem, I expect to enjoy that much more,' I said.

On that note we said goodnight, and agreed to meet again the following night. Hopefully this was going to be one of my last nights on the island.

The dawn brought a bright new day, shining down on the place I despised. I looked towards the mainland; my bungalow was not there. Drawing no strength from my island home, I went to the inn in the hope of getting a free breakfast. I had an idea what was on the menu, but I suppose it did keep me alive. There were plenty of the crew about, this was unusual so early in the day. the fact there was no sailing the previous night helped, but they rarely got up before midday. Landon was nowhere to be seen; my new friend was probably asleep. Vicary was also absent.

I entered the inn and was warmly greeted by several members of the crew. This included Jefferson, who was Colin. Breakfast arrived without my asking, the same delightful dish I had been served on all other occasions. I thanked the landlord, trying not to snarl, which was difficult. I consumed the meal and left, concerned that I was starting to enjoy the food.

I spent the day talking to the crew and their families, everyone had suddenly become friendlier. I felt the announcement the previous night was the catalyst, these people saw the prospect of instant wealth. I had hoped that the islanders had begun to trust me, but deep down I knew that had nothing to do with their euphoria. Most of the talk revolved around the rich pickings that awaited them, some even asked my advice. I remembered what my brief was, no opinion was forthcoming. Not one of the crew were inclined to mention the dangers of their new venture, perhaps they did not appreciate that aspect, maybe they blocked it from their minds. Greed had overridden the brains department. I felt a little sorry for them, lambs to the slaughter.

Hopefully I was not joining their flock. I was hoping to be away from the island before these new adventures began, not only because of the intolerable voyage, but also because I had a good idea that there were many dangers ahead. I had no intention of putting my life in danger, 300 years ago. I tried to pass on my apprehension to the crew but they did not listen, their minds on the financial gain.

I drifted around the island all day, tempted at one point by a lady who was looking in my direction as I passed her hut. She waved and invited me in, but I decided against another liaison.

When it was time to go to the inn for the evening meal I approached with caution. As I entered I saw Jefferson near the bar, but he did not acknowledge my arrival. I was worried that this was the real Jefferson, and Colin had for some reason left the island. I drank my free rum, followed by numerous other rums bought by the crew I had encountered that day. It was the most I had drunk since my arrival, and I had consumed much more than I intended. My lady friend smiled in my direction, but I had no intention of letting her take advantage of me in this drunken state. I was going to approach Jefferson to check his credentials, but unfortunately my legs did not respond as I had hoped.

It was several hours before the midnight meeting, I did not think I was going to be much help at this meeting if I continued to consume any more rum, so I decided to leave the inn, maybe a bit of fresh air was required. I staggered out of the inn, how I managed the door was a miracle, I sat on the stone step outside, and watched Vicary and Landon approach.

'Have you drunk too much?' said Landon,

'I think that is possible,' I responded.

Vicary said nothing, he looked at Landon, wondering why he had spoken to me. Landon then whispered in my ear, making sure Vicary was unable to hear.

'See you at midnight, Colin is back from the mainland,' he said.

Vicary and Landon went inside the inn, and I heard a cheer as they entered. I was pleased Colin was back. Now, leaving this island and pursuing our other tasks was possible. I felt better for that news, but no more sober.

I was suddenly aware of my lady friend standing in front of me, smiling.

'I have something in my hut that might sober you up, if you would like to try my remedy?' she said.

'I think maybe I would,' I said.

This she accepted without further comment. I had a good idea what the remedy was.

I was then helped to my feet, with the assistance of this beautiful lady I was taken to her hut, it was a hut I recognized with fond memories, she kept her clothes on this time. She prepared a liquid concoction. It tasted like cabbage, but I suddenly felt less drunk, this recipe was worth a fortune.

'How do you feel?' She lifted me to my feet; she was surprisingly strong. 'Is there anything else I can do for you to make you feel better?' she said.

'I don't think so, it is kind of you, but I remember quite vividly the last time, it was very exhausting,' I said.

'I thought I would make you the offer, in case you don't pass this way again,' she said.

It sounded like a comment from someone who knew what was going on. Maybe this lady was a female traveller who had decided to stay; but why take on this role? I supposed it was either that or the wife of a crewman; this was certainly the better choice, at least she was able to choose her bedfellows. I made the decision to leave, before temptation got the better of me.

It was getting near to midnight, and I was sober enough for the meeting. I made my way to my rocky meeting place. I heard a noise from behind the rock and both Alan and Colin, appeared in their disguises of Landon and Jefferson respectively. I was glad to see them both.

I was informed that Vicary had consumed a lot of ale; Alan had ensured his sleep was going to be sound. When he was asleep, the key would appear around my neck. It was decided to leave once the key appeared, it was sensible to use for our journey home, in case the Pathway was not available. There was a button on the key which had to be pressed to return to the island, this was done instead of waiting for the portal to open, although pressing it when the portal was open did ensure a return to the appropriate period, it acted as a safeguard to return to the correct era in time. It worked in the opposite direction when returning from the island to the year 2000, after this it was useless unless a new buyers for the bungalow was found. A series of buttons were used to set the date of the period one wished to visit, Colin had set his to Roman times, John had set his to 1941, without the Pathway those were their single trips.

'I am happy to leave but I made a promise to John. We cannot travel to 1941 unless we have the Pathway available on our return,' I said.

'I have it here, but as you know it must not leave the island, I will hang onto it until you return, then all being well you will be able to leave immediately for 1981,' said Alan.

The Pathway was about 4 inches long, tubular in appearance, it looked like brass, with buttons at either end. Alan pressed one of the buttons which opened the tube, it looked like a calculator when open, I saw it was possible to fix a date on the panel. It was similar to the key but appeared more sophisticated.

I was happy with the plan, confident now I knew the Pathway was there to be used. I knew we had use of the key if necessary, but I wanted to keep that as a safeguard in case we lost the Pathway, bearing in mind that Alan was about to embark on a treacherous period for the islanders. I sincerely hoped the key never had to be used.

The obvious question had to be asked, I was the one who asked it.

'How can both the key and the Pathway appear in the will of somebody from the seventeenth century? They are both sophisticated pieces of machinery,' I said.

I looked at both Colin and Alan for an answer, it was obviously not forthcoming. Both of them shook their heads, they had no idea and neither did I, was it just something we had to accept Perhaps it was one of those situations where one does not ask questions, simply accepting what one sees.

I asked Colin if he was ready to make the trip. The key had not reappeared around my neck, but we felt that was not important at this stage as we had the Pathway to use for this trip. We all agreed there was little point in waiting for Vicary to drop off to sleep.

Colin checked I had the coins he had given me, these were my insurance, to be taken to the bank at the earliest opportunity. It was envisaged they were to provide me with a large amount of cash; he said it likely they were valuable even in 1941. Colin had already deposited money in the 1941 bank on his last visit with John, that was foresight on his part, but he also had some coins. We needed to raise enough cash to buy John's house, this was vital to the plan.

Alan was opening the Pathway, fiddling with the buttons. He asked what arrival date was to be set on the Pathway.

Colin said that the bomb dropped on 21st March 1941, but we needed to be there before that in order to purchase John's house. We decided six weeks before was going to give us ample time, so that was to be 13th February. Alan confirmed the Pathway was set to the date required, and we walked towards the portal in excited expectation. The three of us moved towards the entrance to the island, checking nobody was around to see us together. The journey only took a couple of minutes.

I wondered what my tailoring was going to be like in the 1940s. It was certainly going to better than this habit I was wearing. Alan had prepared a food parcel of bread and cheese for each of us, but Colin explained only the small pouches could be carried through the portal. I was looking forward to this trip, leaving the squalor of the island pleased me. I did appreciate there was rationing in war-torn Britain, but even in those terms the food had to be better. I was also looking forward to being allowed to speak, not living in fear of being decapitated for saying the wrong thing. I was trusting in two people who until a few weeks ago had been complete strangers, one of whom had lied to me.

We approached the portal, as Alan continued to make his

calculations. He pointed the Pathway towards the mainland, he pressed one of the buttons. The Pathway started to make noises, a gurgling sound.

'Good luck,' he said as he slowly moved away.

What awaited me in 1941? It was fortunate that Colin had already travelled there. I was returning to a time I did not know about except for the war, eight years before I was born. My father and mother had both spoken about the war years, not in any great detail, both had suffered: my father was abroad for most of the war, my mother was living in Plymouth. I always felt it was worst for those left behind, and my mother often talked about the horror of the bombing. Plymouth did get a pounding from the Luftwaffe, mainly because of the dockyard and the port. My father always felt he was better off fighting than being in Plymouth. I was about to find out what the Home Front was like. Although Ruby Bay was some distance from Plymouth, the rationing restrictions were no doubt still in place. I took a deep breath, I was about to witness an important period in British history.

Colin and I stood still, waiting for the inevitable storm to come. The portal lit up in bright lights and the rain started to fall. The centre turned into a mist, just as it had done in our time. I hoped the calculations were correct, if not we were likely to end up anywhere.

I remembered that I had wanted to ask Alan how the silk ended up in the cellar, before the actual piracy was committed. That was going to have to wait for our return, there were more important issues to deal with first.

'The same principle as when we came here, I think. We will not end up in the same place. If we don't come across each other, I'll meet you in the hotel bar at eight p.m. tonight,' said Colin.

I nodded to Colin, then we walked into the mist and – hopefully – into 1941.

4

It was dark, which was to be expected, it was just gone midnight. It was also very cold; after all, it was the middle of February. I could not make out my surroundings. There were no lights, but no doubt the blackout was in force.

I was unable to do much until it was daylight, then I planned to check if the buildings I expected to be there were in fact there. I made myself comfortable among the jagged rocks on which I had landed, assuming I was on the mainland. I decided to try to get some sleep, although not easy I did sleep quite well. From what Colin had said there were going to be financial benefits in this time, but was that the whole truth? The one advantage of being in Ruby Bay during the war was obvious, this area was not going to be a priority for Hitler.

As dawn broke I heard the familiar sound of seagulls, looking for their breakfast on the beach and rocks. Looking towards the island I was ecstatic to see the hotel, looking whiter than I had remembered it. I also saw the bungalow, not the one I knew, this was the original building which had been built in 1935.This indicated that we were after that time, so it was very likely that this was 1941, and the Pathway had done its job laudably. Next to the bungalow was the house I recognized as John's.

Moving from my rocky bed on the mainland I started to walk, heading towards the village centre. Looking about me I was unable to see anyone else. I hoped I would see Colin. I was pleased to see I was wearing a duffel coat, fashionable in the 1940s as well as the present day.

I thought of food as I walked to the village. I stopped outside the local newsagents, where the daily papers were piled up. I checked the date; it was 13th February, exactly as planned.

On checking the newspaper headlines, I was shocked by what I was reading. 'BRITAIN BROKE – ROOSEVELT LENDS BRITAIN MILITARY EQUIPMENT'. This was to become known as lend lease. America was not due to enter the war until later in the year, it was assisting Britain without officially being a combatant. Other stories contained details of victories abroad, although I fear at that stage there were not too many of those. The newspaper also carried items on what was being done on the Home Front, it was strange to read this when I knew the final outcome.

My thoughts turned to my father; he was in this time 28 years old, fighting for his country somewhere overseas, my mother was living in Plymouth, about to give birth to my older brother. It was a strange twist of fate that I stood here in a situation where I was older than my own father I was glad no meeting with him was likely to take place on this visit.

I checked the six coins I had were safe from the journey, they were and I felt them jangle in the pouch, their true value had yet to be ascertained. Colin had said they were probably worth several thousand pounds each to a collector. He had been known to exaggerate on many occasions, I was hoping this was not one of those occasions. Added to this was the fact there may not be collectors in abundance in Ruby Bay. Little did I know how wrong that statement was to prove; I was in for a surprise.

It was 8.30 a.m. when I arrived outside the bank. It did not open until 9.30 a.m. Several local people passed by and went into the newsagents, most wished me a good morning, some looked at me with suspicion. It was easy to understand why an outsider was going to be looked upon in such a way, rumours of

German spies abounded, even in Ruby Bay. These spies were supposed to be infiltrating all levels of society.

I knew it was to be a long wait for the bank to open; even then I was not sure of receiving funds immediately, the coins I had needed to be valued first. It was imperative I find Colin at the earliest stage, he had the funds to tide me over, and finding accommodation was a top priority.

I walked away from the village, not wanting to arouse too much suspicion by waiting for the bank to open, and hoping to find Colin in the meantime. Ruby Bay itself was not a large area to cover, but there was no sign of him. I decided not to ask anyone if they had seen him, this would show me to be an outsider.

The bank opened on time and I was the first customer. I requested an interview with the manager and was shown into his office almost immediately, no need for an appointment in those days. On meeting the manager I informed him that I was thinking of moving to the area and needed to open an account, telling him I had no money but I had several coins which I believed to be of value.

He examined them closely; he said he was not familiar with their value, but he knew someone who was certain to know, an elderly gentleman who lived locally was a collector. I was surprised to learn there was a coin collector in Ruby Bay. I was asked to wait in the foyer while the gentleman in question was telephoned. The whole meeting was carried out in a cordial manner, customer service of the highest standard.

A few minutes later an elderly gentleman arrived, and he was ushered into the manager's office. I was then invited back in, and introduced to a Mr White, who I assumed was the expert.

'Mr White asked where you acquired the coins,' said the manager.

'They were my father's, they were left to me in his will. My father was an avid collector and although he never told me if they were valuable coins, I always assumed they were. They were not something I intended to sell, but I have had a few financial difficulties that need to be sorted out,' I said.

Whether or not this was the correct approach I did not know at this stage, an unscrupulous dealer was likely to see that as an opportunity to get the coins cheap. Mr White did not appear to be that type, and I did not have to accept his offer, I was quite at liberty to refuse.

'Do you know what these coins are?' asked Mr White.

Fortunately I had been thoroughly briefed on that point.

'I believe they are Roman from the reign of Brutus,' I said.

'I am impressed. You are no doubt aware they are valuable. I am prepared to offer you £4,000 for one of the coins,' said Mr White.

His offer was readily accepted. He made out a cheque immediately in my real name: this was an account I intended to remain open for the foreseeable future.

'I know people who may be interested in the other four coins, if that is agreeable to you?' said Mr White.

'It is indeed, I intend to buy property in the area so I need to sell the coins,' I said.

Mr White said he would check out his contacts, then we shook hands and he left.

The bank manager asked me if I wanted an advance, he suggested £100 which I agreed to. I took the money after opening the account.

My next priority was to find somewhere to live; the manager told me there was a guest house at the top of the hill. I walked up past the three houses, one of which was to become my bungalow, one was to be bombed, and the third was to become John's. In no time at all I was in sight of the guest house.

As I arrived the door was opened by the landlady. She called me by my name which did come as something of a surprise until she explained that the bank manager had telephoned her to expect me. It was a close-knit community.

She showed me to a room overlooking the bay; it was perfectly clean and cosy. She told me that the rent was £4 per week which included breakfast, this sounded a good deal, so I asked her if I might pay for five weeks in advance. Her eyes lit up as I handed over £20. The guest house had only two other guests, so being off season this was a real bonus for her.

I thought it suited my present position, but was it too close to the house that I knew was going to be bombed? I needed to check this out with Colin, I did not want to be blown up eight years before I was born. But he was nowhere to be seen. I confirmed he was not at the guest house; perhaps he had gone to the next village: I intended to check this out as soon as possible.

My settling-in period was quick as there were no clothes to unpack, all I had was what I stood up in. This confused the landlady. My explanation that I had lost all my clothes when my house was bombed was readily accepted, particularly when I said I came from Plymouth. Her sympathy was apparent. Many people had been through that, and my story was both believable and impossible to confirm. I said I intended purchasing some clothes at the earliest opportunity, and she was impressed that I had the means to purchase new clothes; she expected them to be black market purchases.

My landlady confirmed that there were two pubs in the next village; they were the only places that took in lodgers, there were no other lodging houses in Ruby Bay. I needed to change some of the notes I had into change, I was carrying a huge amount of money in this time of scarcity, much more that I appreciated. The whole day was ahead of me as I ventured to the next village by bus, full of hope and anticipation, feeling sure that Colin's plan was going to work, if everything happened as he said.

The passengers travelling with me were going about their daily business, very aware that the country was at war. No doubt some had sons overseas, fighting for their freedom. The majority of the passengers were very chatty, they enquired as to my business, and said they had not seen me around. I was tempted to say I had arrived from the seventeenth century, but wasn't sure they were ready for that. I told them I worked for the War Office, we were concerned at the possible infiltration of German submarines in the area. I showed them the fake identity card Colin had produced for the trip, it said War Office on it. Colin had given it to me before we left the island, stating clearly it had to be carried in the pouch around my neck. They accepted I was not a spy and was here on important government business; no doubt the story was going to do the rounds in Ruby Bay by teatime. Having disclosed this information I thought it was sure to stop people looking at Colin and I suspiciously. I was aware Colin had other documents with him, I had not been made privy to his hoard.

The bus trip was an adventure. Comfort was not a priority on this mode of transport. The trip was marred by the condition of the road and the narrowness of the lanes, and there did not appear to be any suspension on the bus. The regulars accepted it with a cheery disposition; it was incredible how the adversity of war brought the community together.

On reaching the next village I said goodbye to the passengers, lying to the driver as I thanked him for a pleasant trip.

I headed for the Ship Inn, an apt name in this part of the world. The landlord was friendly and the beer was cheap, but it was restricted to half a pint; the pint glasses were only for regulars, he was at pains to tell me. This I accepted without comment. I made enquiries about Colin, he had not visited this pub, although he remembered someone similar a few weeks ago, he was with an older gentleman. That must have been his last visit with John, the time scale was of course irrelevant.

I tried to obtain another half pint; the landlord agreed, but was at great pains to tell me there was a war on.

I replied that this I knew without him telling me. Did he think I had just arrived from another century?

There was nobody staying at the Ship but the Pilchard Inn just down the road took in lodgers, maybe that was where Colin had registered. I thanked the landlord for his service and the history lesson, and leaving the inn I heading down the hill.

The Pilchard Inn was a little larger, the beer was just as cheap, the landlord was again selling me a half pint, and he also informed me of the war situation. From my description he confirmed that Colin had visited that very morning, making enquiries about the local estate agents which was across the road. I left the pub and walked across the road to Merrydown Estate Agents, which had very little property to sell.

Walking in I was greeted by a very attractive lady, slimly built, and I guessed in her mid-forties. She approached me and asked if she was able to assist me in any way.

I explained it was possible Colin had called that morning, showing an interest in property in the area. I mentioned his real name, as we had never discussed changing names.

'I have not registered anyone by that name, that does not mean he hasn't called in. Normal practice is only to register those who are serious about buying a property,' she said.

I was surprised that he did not fit into that category. I described Colin's appearance, although I was unsure what he was wearing. It struck me that the purchasing of a house in these times only fell to the rich, most people were barely surviving.

'I do remember him now. He wasn't in uniform, was he? He asked about a property in Ruby Bay, but I was unsure whether it was for sale or not. I told him I would check and he said he would return to see me. I'm sorry I can't help you, I have no idea where he is staying as he left no details,' she said.

' Could you tell me which property he made enquiries about? Was it 3 Ruby Bay?' I asked.

She looked surprised.

'Yes it was, but how did you know that.'

'He is a friend of mine, who was supposed to meet me in Ruby Bay, but he forgot to tell me where he was staying, that's why I checked with you,' I said.

From that she perked up a little.

'Do you think your friend is still interested in the house?' she said

'It's a certainty he is still interested, provided I can locate him. Do you know whether or not the house is for sale?'

'It is for sale. Are you certain your friend is still going to be interested in purchasing it?'

'I think you can safely say he will buy the property, provided the price is right of course.'

'That is good news, business has been sparse as you can imagine.'

'Expect us tomorrow, that is if I can find him before that.'

I left the shop and decided to spend some of my new-found wealth, buying clothes was a priority. In such times that was not as easy as expected, but I managed to pay over the odds for some items; even in Ruby Bay the black market operated. Having spent the grand sum of £20 I was able to replenish my wardrobe and buy a suitcase; the white fiver in the shop brought strange looks from customers and staff.

Colin had printed up a couple of ration books, but the trouble was, he had them on him. With no chance of finding him I decided to return to Ruby Bay, as we had agreed to a meeting at the hotel that night.

In my new clothes, I was ready to face the hotel bar. I walked across the soggy beach that evening with a spring in my step. I remembered the last time I had made this trip; tonight's outcome I expected to be more pleasing. It pleased me that I was back in a civilized time, except for the horrors inflicted by Hitler. It started to drizzle and I quickened my step, not wanting to ruin my new clothes. I reached the slipway to the island and walked up to the hotel. With a sigh of relief I entered the grounds of the hotel, making my way to the small entrance door. Two men staggered past me and went into the hotel, no doubt clientele from the inn.

On entering the hotel I was found myself in an exquisite foyer; the floor was marble, shiny and clean in the evening light, and the curtains were heavy and expensive. I went to the reception in order to locate the bar, and was directed by a beautiful receptionist. On entering the bar I saw that all the tables were wooden, as were the chairs, each table had a small lamp on it; the heavy curtains were drawn to comply with the blackout.

Colin was sitting near the window. He jumped up when he saw me, offering his hand like a long lost friend, a nice gesture. He waved to the waiter and ordered drinks for both of us.

'Where have you been? I've been hunting high and low for you,' I said.

'I've been staying at this hotel, I am surprised you didn't book in, particularly as we agreed to meet in this bar, I thought you would realize that. When I arrived from the island I came directly here and was immediately shown to a room,' he said.

'I booked into the guest house on the mainland, thinking it was the only place to stay. I did not consider the hotel on the island. Foolishly I have been trying to keep warm waiting for the bank to open, it appears you were the smartest of the two of us. It was just that I considered the hotel a little extravagant, surely we have to consider our finances? We are going to be in this time for a couple of weeks, we need to be prudent,' I said.

'That is quite amusing. Have you sold any of the coins yet?' he enquired.

'I've sold one for £4,000 to a collector,' I said.

'Do you appreciate what £4,000 pounds is worth in 1941? It's a fortune. It is equivalent to eight years' wages to most people. You still have four more to sell. You have the finances to live in luxury at this hotel,' he said.

'You are right, I am wealthier than I thought. I'm going to move into the hotel, a little luxury won't hurt. I must admit I think I deserve it, the horror of the island is still with me. I will move into the hotel in the morning. Now what about this German bomb that is going to destroy your father's house? I am concerned about the people staying in the guest house. I do not want any of them injured, not when we are in a position to do something about it,' I said.

'Don't worry, there were no casualties, and even if there were, we are not in a position to do anything about it. As I've said before, we must not change time. The bomb fell just after midnight, there was nobody around except my father, but he had gone before the bomb dropped. I know he was all right because I saw him the next day,' he said.

'The fake identities work. I used them on the bus to the next village, the locals were very impressed. I told the passengers I had been sent by the War Office, as they suspected German submarines might be in the area,' I said.

'Those identity cards have an important part to play in my plan. I visited the next village as well, I took a taxi. What you told them was the truth in a roundabout way, we are looking for a German submarine. It is good that the locals do not suspect us, we can move about freely, particularly when we go to John's house,' he said.

'I visited the estate agents you went to, the house is for sale.'

'We'll go back there tomorrow. With any luck the deal can be done in less than six weeks, which will give us time to carry out some alterations on the house,' he said.

'What sort of alterations? You're not thinking of putting in a swimming pool are you?'

'Of course not, we need somewhere to hide the paintings. It will be many years before we pick them up. I think we should dig in the cellar, large enough to build a hiding place under the floor. We need to see what the cellar is made of; perhaps we could arrange a viewing?' he said.

'I picked up a card at the estate agents, I am surprised you didn't. It says she is called Julie Merrydown, I assume she owns the place.'

I handed it to Colin, he read it and smiled.

'It does not say Miss or Mrs, I think we should confirm her marital status.'

He smiled a knowing smile, thinking there was an interest in this lady on my part; he was not too far away from the truth, she was easy to take an instant liking to.

'Let's telephone her in the morning, there is a phone number here. We can then arrange for a viewing. Once we have talked to her, maybe we could invite her to dinner at the hotel, and we might persuade her to push through the deal quickly. What do you think?' he said.

'I think it is a great idea. And as she is very attractive, it gives me something other than you to look at!'

I remained in the bar with Colin, who was being well looked after by one of the waitresses. Each time she served the drinks she smiled longingly at him, and he returned her gaze with a lingering, wanton look. This young lady seemed to take an unusual interest in his welfare. Colin explained he had passed the word around that there was a film director staying at the hotel, possibly looking for a location in which to film. It was a government-sponsored film; this brought Colin's identity card into play. He emphasized he did not say he was a film director, he merely let it be known he was working for the government. People could draw their own conclusions, particularly the young ladies working at the hotel. Although his identity card stated War Office, this did not stop some of the ladies believing he was a film director, and he did nothing to stop them thinking that way. I was surprised that some of the staff had been taken in by this, but the reasons were going to become apparent.

'Why aren't you telling these young ladies you are not a film director, when we are supposed to be from the War Office looking for submarines?'

'They are young and impressionable, I have told them I do work for the War Office, but they believe I could be the film director who is staying here,' he said.

'And they swallowed that did they?'

'As I said, they are young, the words "film director" impress them, they are making assumptions which I have no control over.'

'As you started this rumour, perhaps you are looking for budding young actresses for the film,' I said.

'I'm surprised you should think that, but yes it is my intention to take advantage of the situation. I do not think it is in any way underhand, I am not promising these ladies a chance to appear in a film. If they offer me incentives in the belief I can help in some way, I have no choice but to take advantage of the situation. My stay here is short, I intend to enjoy it to the full. To be honest there is little chance of meeting any of these ladies again, not once we have left. If I did meet any of them again they would be in their eighties and unlikely to remember me. This is a chance of a lifetime for a red-blooded male and I intend to enjoy it,' he said.

'You mentioned "ladies", so how many are there?'

'Four at the moment, I expect that to rise in the fullness of time. Once the word has got around, I think my casting couch is going to take a lot of action,' he said.

The search for submarines was something he had forgotten about, so did the ladies in question.

I left the hotel in plenty of time to avoid the incoming tide, walking swiftly back to the guest house. I had booked myself into the hotel for the following day. I also was going enjoy my stay, but my intentions related to the luxurious surroundings, unlike Colin who had other ideas.

The following morning I informed the landlady I intended to move to the hotel, she appeared sad at this news, but when I asked her to keep the rent I had paid her for the next month, she suddenly brightened.

With only one suitcase to carry, my departure was quick and convivial. Making my way across the beach on foot, my luggage was light. The room was ready when I booked in, the porter took my case and took me to the second floor. He was rewarded with a pound note for his trouble and he was overjoyed with his tip. This extravagance was bound to get around the hotel in double quick time, which was my intention.

The view from my room was spectacular, looking towards Ruby Bay. There was a small veranda with a table, but it was still chilly outside, and I doubted if the veranda was going to see much of me.

Turning up for breakfast I was able to join Colin in the dining room. He was getting plenty of attention from the female staff. I was able to work out who three of his ladies were, but there was no indication of who was the fourth victim.

'I have figured out three of the ladies. Who is the fourth?' I asked.

'You won't see her up here, she works in the laundry room and she has another friend there who has shown an interest. It seems the total is rising. If any of these ladies are of interest to you, let me know, I am prepared to share my good fortune,' he said.

'I appreciate your offer, it is very magnanimous of you, but no thank you, I still have some pride. It appears the tip I gave to the porter is showing results, I don't think we'll have a problem with the service,' I said.

'It was a smart move, you are to be congratulated.'

'I will telephone Julie after breakfast, on your behalf. We could walk across the beach and meet her at the house,' I said.

'We are on first-name terms are we? Are you going to be chatting up Julie?' he asked.

'I have no intention of answering that question, I know very little about her or her domestic situation. She might be married with children for all we know.'

The conversation ended there as I went off to telephone Julie, arranging to meet her in an hour, along with Colin as the intended purchaser.

We walked across the beach to the mainland. It was a good idea to check the property out first, and we discussed this on our way to the appointment. We needed to store the artwork somewhere that nobody was likely to look; it was to remain there for many years. We agreed the cellar was the best option, but without seeing it we were not in a position to decide.

Julie arrived early, dressed in a tight-fitting business suit. She looked more like a high flyer from the city than an estate agent; appearances can be deceptive. We both shook hands with her and entered John's house. There was no furniture inside. We politely moved around the house, our main objective was to see the cellar, but it was impossible to show that was a priority, we waited until it was shown to us. The cellar floor was tiled; Colin banged his heel on it. He asked Julie if it had a concrete floor. Julie checked her paperwork, which stated that it was a tiled floor over a wooden base. We knew the wooden floorboards were a plus for our purpose.

Colin said he liked the house, but wanted to know how long the sale was going to take to be completed. Julie was confident it was only going to take three to four weeks; this was ideal from our point of view. Now a price had to be agreed. They both walked away from the cellar, discussing the price as they went.

I checked the floor: it was a little bouncy, indicating that there was no concrete down there, this was good. I followed them upstairs; they were still discussing the price. Then I remembered a piece of the history, which related to my bungalow next door.

I asked Julie if the bungalow next door was for sale, and she said it was. She thought it strange that I asked, as it was only put on the market a few days previously. We did not explain how we had that inside information. It was certain the price was likely to be a lot lower than what I eventually paid, not that such a thing was a consideration; but it made sense to buy it now.

Colin looked at me; he now remembered. The property was passed down to a Vicary who died in the war, then it was passed to his son. The son lived in London and wanted nothing to do with the property.

Colin wanted to confirm this piece of history; he asked why the bungalow was up for sale. Julie responded by saying it belonged to a soldier who had died in action in Norway, he had left it to his son who wanted to sell it. He was actually at the bungalow now if we wanted to have a look around.

This surprised both of us, the story was that the son never saw the place. Why has that changed, I thought? Yet another piece of history had possibly been changed. We agreed to have a look at the place, both aware that the young man was not supposed to be at the bungalow. We walked around to the bungalow, which was to be demolished in the future, and mine was then built in its place.

My thought was that if either Colin or I bought this place and hung onto it, my luxurious bungalow was not going to be built as I knew it. Colin knew the history, so he certainly realized it too.

Julie knocked at the door of number 2, there was silence amongst us. I heard movement from inside, then the door opened, stood before us was a young man of about 16 years of age, the new owner.

Julie asked him if he was James Vicary – not the name I had expected – and he confirmed his identity. She introduced herself, and said she had spoken to him when he telephoned about the property. He explained it had been left to him by his father, and that he and his mother were thinking of putting it up for sale, not intending to spend much time there. He said his mother was out at the moment.

We were invited inside to look around; he stated the place had not been properly cleaned up to accept visitors, we said we understood, more than he was likely to know. We had a good look around, including the cellar, which was certainly a concrete base. We thanked our host and left.

Colin said we would discuss the options before making a decision, and we invited Julie to dinner at the hotel that night. Confident that a decision was about to be made over dinner, she accepted the invitation, unaware that a decision had already been made. We said our farewells to her, looking forward to seeing her again that evening.

Colin and I walked across the beach, discussing what we had seen. He was aware that the purchase of number 2 was out of the question, not only because of the concrete cellar floor; he realized as I did that my bungalow was never going to be built if we purchased it now.

We were confused by the fact the young James Vicary was in

the bungalow, Colin had a theory, it was all to do with changing history, the thing we were forbidden to do. Alan Donald had changed the past, he had started the piracy before time, and that event had a knock-on effect on the future. It was a strange effect though: why did Alan's action result in young Vicary visiting his inheritance? Colin and I discussed it but were unable to see why this was the bizarre outcome of an action 300 years ago.

Together we sat and talked in the hotel bar, thinking about what a momentous time in history we were now living through: 1941, what a time to be alive in. I hoped we were going to live through this war; I felt nobody was safe anywhere.

Colin and I started discussing the fact that both houses were up for sale. If John's house was purchased there was no problem, it was our intention to save John's wife, therefore he was never going to buy the property; we assumed he was going to remained with his wife. Buying my bungalow was a different matter, it was unwise to buy it for obvious reasons. We agreed that it was John's house that was to be purchased, we knew that remained in the same condition in our time. I asked Colin about the selling price: I believed it was an excellent time to negotiate a price. He said he had enough money in his account to cover the purchase price which he had agreed with Julie. It was going to be a cash sale, which always helped with negotiating a selling price, and Colin was confident of completing the sale.

The matter of pushing through the sale as quickly as possible was vital to the operation, we needed time to dig up the floor, prepare it to accept the paintings safely and securely, then replace the floor in the same condition. We decided we needed at least two weeks. We must ensure there was no way the paintings were found, that required virtually rebuilding the cellar floor, not an easy task, but we both felt it was a necessary undertaking. It was a lot easier because of the wooden floor, although we had no idea what lay beneath that.

'I am concerned about someone getting into the cellar and finding the paintings: a burglar or a squatter,' he said.

'I think that's unlikely, I have never in the whole of my police career come across a squatter or burglar who has broken into a property and been found digging up the cellar,' I said.

Colin and I left to change for dinner; our guest was due to arrive soon. He would use his silver tongue to persuade Julie to push through the deal, I was confident this was in his character.

We returned to the bar an hour later, both smartly dressed, me in my off-the-peg suit, Colin in his made-to-measure suit which he had purchased on his previous visit. Julie arrived in the bar dressed in a very fetching black dress, a 'little black number' as we call it today. She was slim and beautiful, looking as elegant as I remembered her. We went to the entrance to greet her, then Colin called the waiter over and ordered drinks.

We sat by the window looking towards the mainland, it really was a spectacular view. She said she had never dined here before; hopefully this was one of many such visits.

She came right to the point and asked Colin if he had made a decision about the house, she was happy for him to think it over for longer if he so wished.

He told her he had decided on the house rather than the bungalow, young James Vicary needed to wait for his windfall.

Then the vital question of price came into the conversation, and although Colin had already decided to take it, a few pounds off here and there was not to be brushed aside; he was persuasive when it came to monetary matters. She quoted a price which appeared very low, but it was the going rate in this time. He nodded as if considering the price, but I knew he really did not care what the price was: he had the money to cover it. He said he was happy to pay the price quoted, but asked that the property be ready to move into within a month, if that were the case it was a cash transaction. He asked her if she was able to make the necessary arrangements for this to happen.

Julie was ecstatic at having agreed the sale, mentioning that Colin appeared in a rush to move in. He then explained that the two of us were possibly going abroad, so he wanted everything sorted before he left. She did not question this: in the time we were living, people were travelling abroad to fight the war all the time. This was a good tactic by Colin; he implied that we were in some way involved in war work. This detail was said in the hope it reached the ears of the locals, he felt it was good for our public image. Some of the locals had already seen my War Office identity, this was going to simply confirm our position.

She said she understood and did not think this sale was likely to be a problem, she intended to do all in her power to push it through within the required period. She promised to telephone him at the hotel the following day, when hopefully she would be in a position to give an answer. The war work ploy had worked a treat: nobody wanted to upset someone going abroad to fight, and I felt sure the deal would go through as we had planned.

We went into dinner and talked about Julie's life. Her father had fought in World War I, he was in his thirties when he went to war, she was born in 1905, making her 36 years old. These details were volunteered; we were not so impolite as to ask her for her date of birth. Her father started the business in 1920, believing that future generations wanted to buy property; he was very astute in this particular fact, but unfortunately he was 40 years ahead of his time. She said the business did not do well, so her father turned it into a hardware store to make a living. He died only a few years before, leaving the business to her. She returned it to an estate agency; her father would have appreciated that gesture.

I was upset that I had thought Julie to be in her forties, no doubt the ravages of this war had taken its toll on her life, and she had also had to contend with the death of her father, someone she obviously cared for very much.

On several occasions she tried to find out what we were doing in Ruby Bay, we showed her our identity cards, showing we were both commanders in the Royal Navy, and she was impressed by our rank. The story of the German submarines reared its head. I told her there was nothing to worry about, we were here as a precautionary measure. I added that in our business it sometimes required us to work late at night, in case we were seen during the night of the paintings arriving. Colin nodded his pleasure at my foresight. Although we did not think Julie to be a gossiper, her knowledge of what we told her was helpful in getting the locals to accept us, it was yet another precautionary measure.

Once dinner was over we returned to the bar. Even with rationing it was possible to produce good-quality food, although paying a high price for it was one of the drawbacks, but Colin signed the bill in his flamboyant style; this was for the benefit of the waitress serving at our table.

Julie reiterated the point that our stay was only for a few more weeks; I did not think she was prying into our business, merely making polite conversation, but Colin felt it was time to say something.

'I think you know better than to ask such questions. Walls have ears, you know,' said Colin.

'You're right, I apologize for asking, but it was because I shall miss you, even though we have only known each other a short time,' she said.

We were both touched by this sentiment, but then we were probably the only men near to her age group in the area. All the men of her age were fighting somewhere in the world. I think our false identities made us look like men of action; Colin was, but his actions were not what she was thinking.

'Instead of phoning you, why not come to dinner again? We enjoy your company, and it is a more sociable way to sort out a deal,' he said.

She readily agreed, possibly because she liked our company, or maybe the quality of the food assisted her decision. I was prepared to accept either reason.

'How do you intend to get to the mainland? The tide is in, you know,' I said.

'The hotel has kindly provided a boat to take people across. I wish there was an easier way to cross.'

'Perhaps they will invent a giant tractor, that would do the job,' I said.

This brought a grimace from Julie as if she did not like the idea. She followed the grimace with a smile, as if thinking it over in her head. Perhaps she was the inventor, and I had just given her the idea.

We said our goodbyes, making sure she got on the boat safely, then returned to the bar. Colin was amused at the giant tractor remark.

His waitress friend arrived with more drinks and he whispered something in her ear, no doubt arrangements were in hand for later that evening. I stayed for one more drink and then went to bed; Colin remained to organize his love life.

I arrived at breakfast early, Colin was already there: he looked terrible, the night had obviously been a tortuous one.

'How are you this morning? Did you have any visitors last night?' I asked.

'Yes I did, I think my energy has been sapped. This particularly lady had an aversion to sleeping. She had more energy than I thought possible,' he said.

'There is something important you did not consider when embarking on this venture. There is an age difference, all these ladies are a lot younger than you.'

'I think I might return to my room for a lie down, hopefully it will prepare me for this evening,' he said.

I planned to visit Plymouth; the main reason was to buy more new clothes, having recently appreciated that I was wealthy, a new wardrobe sounded an excellent idea. Colin also wished to visit Plymouth, but his reasons were a million miles away from mine: he wanted to check his father's present address, as we needed to know that before the bombing incident. Although we knew he sometimes lived in Ruby Bay, if we were to stop him spying, we needed to know his permanent address.

'What are your plans?' I said.

'I intend to visit my father, showing the false identity, in order to persuade him about his future course of action, by that I mean the spying. I will tell him we know what he has been doing, then threaten him in some way to stop it. This prevents him getting caught at a later date, the result of which I am very aware. Although I have not put the finer points on this plan, I feel something along those lines is worth trying. We came back to take the paintings, this was always my intention, but this will rob the authority of their evidence against my father. If we do not visit him and advise him against it, he might continue. By continuing we could not say what information he might pass to our enemies, so we have to stop him once and for all,' he said.

'I agree with you, we need to know exactly where he lives. I think we could devise a plan a bit nearer the date; we have weeks. I understand that you did not have a father when you grew up, hopefully we might be in a position to change that. I know your father was charged with spying and ultimately hanged, but there is a chance we can stop that from happening. We also have the opportunity to stop him spying and making him a good citizen, and then only we would know what his past was. We have to work out a scheme to put to your father, something he has no choice but to accept,' I said.

Colin appreciated my help, I could see it in his eyes. 'Thank you for what you have said. My father was probably not a bad man, he was probably pushed into a corner by his German family ties,' he said.

The following morning after breakfast we took a bus into Plymouth. It was a long journey, and the roads in some places were in need of repair; not a priority, I understood that.

Colin said he was born in an area called Mutley Plain, in 1949, which coincidentally was the same year as my birth. We hoped his parents had lived there eight years previously. We went to the area, which I also knew slightly from my childhood. The first obstacle to overcome was to locate the address, particularly as the name Wickham was not the family name at that time, but was taken on by his mother following his father's execution. His father's surname was Heinrich, but it was unlikely he was using that name in this time, he was using an assumed name. This he did to obtain an English sounding name, knowing that the Nazi Party was gaining favour in his native Germany. He knew if he was to have any sort of career in this country he had to have an English-sounding name. The trouble was, Colin had no idea what it was.

'If we call at the address, it is quite likely my mother will answer the door, a younger version than I remember, but I am certain I will recognize her. We will use the excuse of checking the home addresses of Ministry of Defence personnel, to ensure their accommodation is suitable. If my father answers the door I will know what he looks like, I saw him on my last visit with John.'

'I can instantly see problems with just knocking on the door, the reason for the visit might scare him off. He will go into work the following day and realize he is the only one who has been checked out. This is going to make him suspicious that the authorities are aware of his spying misdemeanours; it is too risky,' I said.

'You're right: we don't want to scare him off until after the paintings are delivered. We need another plan,' he said.

'Why don't we go to the MOD in Plymouth? We have our fake identities, we just need to tell them it is a routine check. If we can check the files on all those who are security checked, this will hopefully include your father. From there we will have his home address. By checking all the files, no suspicion will fall on an individual. What do you think?' I asked.

'I think it is an excellent idea.'

He had made a perfect job of the false identity cards and we expected them to be accepted. They showed we were security cleared. I felt going to the MOD and trying to convince them was a difficult proposition, mainly because we were unaware as to what security was in place. They must have had ways to check our identities, maybe just by telephoning London, but that was unlikely as details like that were never discussed over the telephone. I decided we ought to run with the idea. We must show an air of superiority; Colin had a knack of being able to do that. The assumption we were high-ranking officials would assist our cause. We had a plan, now we had to see it through.

The Ministry of Defence building was near the dockyard, passes had to be shown at the gate, and this was our initial test. The official on the gate checked our passes thoroughly, looking at the photographs before checking our faces. He asked how he might help us. The fake identities appeared to have worked.

We asked to speak to the head of the Ministry of Defence, and he said we needed to wait whilst he contacted him. Our rank as commanders in the Royal Navy, not exactly a lowly rank, was another good move by Colin. The official telephoned and we heard him say he had two Royal Navy commanders waiting, who needed to be escorted.

We were told someone from the Ministry was coming to meet us immediately. In less than 30 seconds a Royal Navy officer arrived. He checked our identity cards and saluted us both.

'How might I help you, gentlemen?' he asked.

'It is routine, we need to check the security of all personnel working in the department, it is a matter of urgency. There have been rumblings in Whitehall, security appears to have been breached. We know the name of the person in question, we just need to check that person is not employed here under a false name. We feel certain he is not here, but we still need to verify that. We appreciate your help in this matter. The request has come from the highest level, the Prime Minister himself,' Colin said.

This made him take a step back. If you had to bluff, it was best to do it in style. 'Gentlemen, would you follow me please,' said the officer. He seemed nervous about our authority.

Colin was wise to say what he had: it was unlikely anybody would have the nerve to check if the Prime Minister had sent us. Even if they did, nobody was likely to confirm or deny it. Colin did surprise me at times, and his train of thought was quick and foolproof. I was confident it was not going to trip us up.

We were taken into the main Ministry of Defence building, where a rear admiral was there to meet us. We told him exactly the same story, saying we needed to see the records of only those with the top security rating.

He asked to see our identity cards before he allowed us to do so. Somehow Colin had found out what the top-ranking security card issued by the War Office looked like, and this is what we had. The rear admiral showed us to a room, stating the files we wanted were on their way up. He was anxious to find out if his department had a leak, and we said we intended reporting to him before we left.

The files were duly brought to the room; there were less than 20. Colin looked through them, it was of little use to let me see the photographs as I did not know what his father looked like. Suddenly he stopped at one file; looking at me he indicated the photograph. He had found his father, who was calling himself Colin Brown. He pointed to the section bearing his father's home address, it was not where we had been expecting: he lived in a completely different area of Plymouth. We now had both the name his father was going under, and his address. Colin noted the new address and put the piece of paper in his pocket.

We went to the rear admiral's office with the files, he looked up as we entered.

'There is nothing to worry about, sir. May I ask you keep this visit to yourself, this was the Prime Minister's request,' said Colin.

'I understand, and I am glad I do not have a spy in this department,' he said.

I was tempted to tell him the truth, but we did not know that for certain, not at this point in time. We left the complex feeling very relieved. Colin had taken us to a place I had no intention of revisiting: if our identity cards had been seen to be false, our arrest as spies was certain to have been disastrous.

I asked him about what he knew of his father's demise. He

only knew what he had read about the incident, something he had checked out years later, going to the archives of the paper. He told me he had read the following account, which sent shivers down his spine.

The owner of Number 1 Ruby Bay was arrested for spying, as a result of forensic checks on the pieces of debris that we knew were the paintings. He was arrested and confessed all; he was eventually executed for his crimes. Colin said the paper did not name him as Brown, simply his German name Eric Heinrich, which they obviously got from him when they interviewed him about the matter, that was when the name Heinrich came to light. Maybe he wanted to make money, but in his eyes he was helping his home country, although he was living in his adopted country.

I was surprised that such a forensic check on the rubble was possible in this time, but there were many things of that time that were never divulged. He was working for a government department in Plymouth, and his job brought him in contact with classified information. He was a trusted employee, although some sort of security check must have been carried out, this check cannot have shown he was associated with Germany. How you can complete a proper security check on someone called Smith or Brown is beyond me, perhaps that is why he chose the name.

He bought the property in Ruby Bay in 1940, to be used a weekends. He must have been earning good money to buy a second home, that was the initial idea. He was contacted by someone who knew his real name, forcing him to spy for Germany; it was a real threat. Brown's blackmailer realized Ruby Bay was the perfect spot to liaise with German submarines, so started the trail of deceit and spying. The house in Ruby Bay was ideal for this purpose, radio communications were easily set up, and nobody was any the wiser, as he was such an infrequent visitor. It all seemed so simple for him to do, he obviously had German contacts in this country, he had access to secret information. Once Colin's father realized he was being sought following what was found at his burnt-out property in Ruby Bay, he went on the run, and was not caught until years later.

Colin was only a few months old when his father was eventually caught, so he never knew him. He had no idea whether or not his father knew what was found at the Ruby Bay address, just that it definitely incriminated him in some way. He may well have thought the envelope he had left for the Germans had been found; either way, he was aware he must leave the area quickly.

I wondered whether he continued with the name Brown, which appeared to be a sensible move; although it was the name he used at the Ministry, there were a lot of Browns in the country. Maybe that was the reason it took so long to find him. Although it took eight years to track him down, his downfall was that he had not changed much; they had the photograph from the Ministry. The government was unlikely to have left any stone unturned to locate a spy, possibly a very significant spy. He was living in Buckinghamshire at the time.

When he was interviewed he told the authorities nothing, he was questioned about who his contact was but he did not divulge that information. The details of the trial were in the national newspapers, so his mother had little choice but to change her name. She chose the name Wickham, then returned to Devon with a very young Colin. He explained that the name Wickham was something his mother thought up; when they lived in Buckinghamshire the nearest town was called High Wycombe, so she used that as their surname, just spelling it differently.

Heinrich was interviewed and admitted the offence; at this point he learned that the remains of the paintings had given him away. He was executed by firing squad, only a short while after the trial. Justice was swift in those days, there was no other punishment for spying.

I was glad Colin had told me the history behind his father's demise, and I think he felt better having confided in me. He had no reason to feel guilty for what had happened but I think he did. This mission was his way of making amends for his father's crimes. He then said there was something else about the paintings: his father told the trial he was being paid with twelve paintings, but on Colin's last visit the U-boat had brought only six. There was the possibility he had already been paid with six paintings, in which case there were six paintings hidden somewhere, six very valuable paintings. Or maybe the next instalment was six paintings, and there was to be another consignment. So were these the first six paintings or the second six?

I wondered whether the trial had delved into this far enough, but Colin said they did not appreciate the significance until after his execution. It also made a great deal of difference to the investigation: if the assignment of paintings was the second six, it certainly meant the information had been passed. I was surprised some smart lawyer had not picked that up. The envelope he left must have been either the information itself, or a confirmation of information already passed.

The MOD checked what information he had come in contact with and recorded, and they were confident he had not seen anything of national importance. But of course we would expect them to say that. Anyone with any sense is unlikely to record information they were about to pass to their enemies, so really there was no way of knowing what had been passed. And the importance of particular pieces of information was relative: everything that came through that department was important in its own way, and sometimes small pieces added up to the big picture.

From what his mother had told him, Colin's father was an intelligent man. It would be easy for him to put together minor pieces of information in the right order to show something was being planned. Maybe realizing that the British had the Enigma machine. Imagine how important that piece of information was to the Germans? Knowing their codes had been broken, they were then able to send messages with the intention of misleading the British code-breakers, vital information indeed.

Colin believed his father had confessed about the U-boat, as the Royal Navy lay in wait off the coast for several weeks. No

U-boats were ever sighted; the Germans must have known he had been compromised. It was thought there was some sort of transmitter at 1 Ruby Bay, and when he failed to respond to their calls they knew he was gone. He obviously never responded as it had been blown up; ironically, the Germans had blown up their own transmitter.

It was a golden opportunity for Colin and me, we were stealing something that did not exist after 21st March 1941, something unique. The art world was going to be ecstatic at such a find. Although these particular works had ceased to exist before I was born, I was confident the connoisseurs had knowledge of them. I, on the other hand, had no idea who the artists were.

We travelled to Plymouth, to check out the address for Colin's father. We left it until late in the day, when his father was due home from work. We thought of knocking on the door and speaking to his mother, but we had no excuse to do that, and if we mentioned our identities as stipulated on our cards, she was going to tell her husband who was certain to become suspicious. We had already decided this was a bad idea.

It was a matter of walking up and down the street until his father arrived, but this in itself had an air of suspicion so we decided to split up and take turns walking on opposite sides of the road. There was nobody around so we felt relatively safe, and we had our identity cards if challenged. Colin's father arrived in the street just after 6 p.m., and he went to the address we had been given for him. Now we knew his home address. This information was to be used after we had stolen the paintings.

We returned to our luxurious hotel on the island in Ruby Bay. We went to the bar and had our early evening drink, and discussed what had gone on since we had arrived in this time. All in all this had been a good day, and everything was in place to complete two missions: the theft of the paintings and the saving of his father, which also meant we were about to prevent the Germans obtaining the information his father was going to leave for them.

'Can you imagine the Germans' reaction when they open that

envelope and find blank paper? This brings another scenario into play: surely the Germans will want revenge for this deceit, and that task might be passed to an unknown contact. Have you considered that?' I asked.

'I have considered that, possible repercussions for my father. If we save his life he must leave the area immediately, which is similar to the original story. The difference being that he is not going to be hunted down by the authorities, but possibly by someone more ruthless. I intend to persuade my father to change his name by deed poll to Wickham, which would stop the likelihood of any other name being used for me. I have a bank account here in that name, can you imagine how difficult it is going to be in the future if my name changes?' he said.

He appeared to have thought it all out, he was certainly looking after himself, but I expected that of him, and his antics in the hotel proved that.

We left the bar and went to our rooms to dress for dinner; this was a prequel to yet another night of passion for Colin. He said he had an appointment that night, with a waitress I had not yet seen; she was keen on a part in his movie. He showed he had very little respect for himself or the ladies, particularly when it concerned his carnal cravings. The waitress in question worked the day shift, which was why I had not seen her.

Tomorrow we were visiting Julie to check on how the house sale was going, assuming Colin was fit enough. She had left a message with the receptionist, apologizing for having to cancel her dinner date tonight.

That evening Colin enjoyed his meal, but he was drinking more than usual, perhaps it was Dutch courage. The lady in question was a lot younger than him, and looking at him I felt sure she was in better shape. We had a few drinks after dinner, he then excused himself, saying he had pressing business waiting. I knew what that was; I wished him good luck.

I sat quietly, looking out of the window at the lights on the mainland. To my surprise I heard a voice greet me, I looked around to see a face I recognized. I rose to my feet at the wondrous site of Julie, dressed this time in a tight-fitting crimson dress.

'I am surprised to see you. There was a message at reception, it said you had cancelled the dinner date,' I said.

'That's right, I apologize but I felt it was only polite I join you for a drink. Is that all right?'

She was showing her good manners yet again; I expected nothing less of her. The waiter approached the table and we ordered drinks.

'Where is Colin, is he going to join us?'

'Unfortunately he is otherwise engaged.'

She smiled at this comment.

'Which lady is he meeting tonight?'

I was shocked that she was aware of the situation. I pretended I did not know what she was talking about, but she knew differently and went on to explain.

'Don't worry it is all around several of the villages. There is a government official staying at the hotel, he also happens to be a film director. I know most of the guests here, that leaves only you and Colin. I am aware you both have government status, so it had to be one of you. You were sitting here on your own, so that leaves the position open for Colin. If I had to choose, Colin is the most likely candidate,' she said.

'I am amazed how quickly these stories filter out in a close-knit community, where everyone knows everyone else's business. I appreciate a film director staying here is going to cause gossip, but it was a rumour started by Colin. He is adamant that he has not told anyone he is the film director, but then he has not said he isn't. Have any of the girls involved said anything?'

'Not to my knowledge. That was not the reason for my visit.'

She made that point perfectly clear, maybe highlighting she had no intentions of visiting the casting couch in Colin's room.

'I want to speak to Colin about the house. The purchase is going through smoothly and quickly, I appreciate that is what you both want, I know you are needed elsewhere, war work and all that. I have negotiated with the other party, and it can be completed in the first week of March. Do you think that is suitable for him?' she said.

'I think he will agree that the timing is perfect,' I said.

She pulled me up on that, telling me in no uncertain terms that I shouldn't have given that information.

I accepted my telling off with dignity, she was of course right in these times. I then decided to take a chance, asking her if she preferred to go to a pub in her village, as I was starting to tire of the bar at the hotel. She agreed it was a good idea.

We left the hotel and walked across the sand. She took off her shoes in case the sand was wet. The tide had only just turned, and it was going to be hours before the beach was covered. On the mainland we got a taxi to her village, entering the Ship Inn for our first drink.

'You can order what you want, as you are in the company of this lady,' the landlord said.

'Do you know the landlord of the Pilchard? We'll go there next,' I said.

She laughed aloud. 'Yes, I know him.'

I was in the company of the most beautiful lady in the pub. I was sure she knew that, but she never acted big-headed.

'Why don't you tell me about yourself? I don't really know anything about you. What are your hopes for the future?' I said.

'The future seems a long way off, I don't want to go on about the war but it does have a bearing on all our futures. I know I'm not actually doing the fighting, but I am affected as well,' she said.

'The war is not going to last forever, it might seem like that now but it will end. Then perhaps we can all look forward to a better world. Only time will tell.'

'You may be surprised by this, but do you know what my biggest concern is, if we lose this war? I read the papers but they don't tell the full story; we are already in the second year of the war, and it was supposed to be all over by now. Have we under-estimated Hilter? I just wonder how much longer it will go on.'

I thought that the politicians in Whitehall must be having the same thoughts; just like Julie they did not know the answer. I felt like telling her exactly when the war would end, as well as the result, but I knew this sort of comment was not advisable. Nor was it likely to instill confidence if I said the war was going to continue for several more years.

We had several drinks, trying hard to forget the state of the nation, but it was difficult; she had relatives fighting overseas, and was worrying constantly about their welfare. She was no different from the majority in Ruby Bay: virtually everyone had a relative fighting somewhere.

She talked briefly about her father; he had been through the horrors of World War I, and like all heroes he talked very little of his experiences, but she knew in his eyes that he had witnessed terrors in those campaigns. He never shared those thoughts with his family; it was unlikely he wanted them to be put them through what he witnessed.

Soon it was time for Julie and me to move on to the Pilchard. We thanked the landlord for his hospitality and for allowing me more than half a pint. He smiled and wished us goodnight.

The Pilchard was very quiet when we turned up, the landlord greeted Julie by name, commenting that she rarely visited the premises. But I knew for certain I was not in the company of a lush.

We sat in a quiet corner. It was difficult to talk about my personal life, all of which was in the future, so the life I told her about was a complete fabrication; I had no choice in the matter.

We got on very well, and there was a moment where she touched my knee to emphasize a point. I enjoyed that but never let on, hoping she was going to do it again.

It was just coming up to closing time when she said something that shocked me. She suggested that it was unlikely I was going to get a boat to the island so late, so perhaps it was a good idea to stay at her house tonight; it was a small cottage down the road.

Before I was able to agree to this extraordinary proposition, she said it was a two-bedroomed cottage. I think she knew what was on my mind, and it was her intention to scupper any ideas I had in that direction.

We walked arm in arm from the pub to her cottage; it was as she had said just a short distance away. The cottage was a beautiful building with a thatched roof, and the walls did not appear to be straight. Inside the cottage the walls were whitewashed, with no wallpaper. It suited the walls with their exposed oak timbers. There were uneven beams in the ceiling.

I looked around the room, which seemed strange: the furnishings were very basic, there was a large radio, and I was surprised not to see a television in the corner. Then I remembered in which time I was. The house was clean and tidy, the carpet was spotless clean but had seen better days; it was of course a time of austerity.

We sat on the sofa and talked about everything that concerned her, there were indeed many things to talk about on this subject. She was nearly 40 and was concerned about her future. She was working too hard, there were no possible suitors around, all the young men were fighting abroad. I understood the problem she faced, as did many unmarried women in that time. I was sympathetic to her plight, and she appreciated that.

The subject of my marital status came up, I told her I had been married but it did not work out. It was her turn to show sympathy, and this she did with great skill.

I mentioned the fact I had seen a television when I was in America. I explained the concept and she was interested, but she felt it was something that was not going to be a success. I did not argue the point.

It was just after midnight when we decided to turn in for the night, and she graciously showed me to the spare room, which looked comfortable. I thanked her and kissed her on the cheek as she left.

What happened next was strange and yet wonderful. I was lying in bed about 20 minutes after Julie had left. There was a knock on my door. She came into the room wearing something long and very see-through, it was a wonderful sight. She asked if it was acceptable for her to have a cuddle, either inside or outside the bed. I pulled back the bedclothes without saying a word, she got in and lay down beside me and got very close. I did not expect my wish to be granted that quickly, it was to be a night to remember.

I awoke to find Julie asleep next to me. She had a smile on her face. My smile was a lot larger. Colin would have been very jealous, although I had no intention of telling him.

I left Julie's house and she promised to be at the hotel that evening for dinner; she was looking forward to having Colin join us. I had decided not to tell him that Julie was aware of his amorous liaisons with the staff; she had the ability to use her charm to dismiss his excuses for not being available to have a drink after dinner. I was going to tell him that she had joined me for a drink; he needed to know that, and he would no doubt want to know what I told her about his absence. I planned to make up some feeble excuse for him, just to watch him fabricate the story. I was looking forward to it.

I was able to make the trip back to the island in quick time, I made my way to my room for a quick wash before breakfast. Colin had not missed me the previous night, embroiled in his amorous engagement. I did not fancy being his neighbour, someone else had that misfortune.

I had just finished washing when there was a knock on my door. I opened it, expecting it to be Colin alerting me to an early breakfast, but I was surprised to see my visitor was a young lady. She asked if I was the film director. She looked ready for action in more ways than one.

I smiled, knowing that Colin was likely to be surprised by her presence, particularly at this time in the morning.

'The room you want is 564, just down the corridor. Just knock and walk in, he is expecting you,' I said.

I watched her wiggle down the corridor. She knocked and

walked into his room, where I assumed he was already entertaining a lady. I closed my door, not wishing to witness an unpleasant incident.

I asked myself whether he had now decided on a day shift to cope with his exploits. I doubted he had been able to get too much sleep, and I felt the young lady I had seen might be too much for him. Or maybe I had underestimated Colin. Either way, he was going to be late for breakfast.

I went down for breakfast, and Colin was not in the dining room. One of his conquests was serving my breakfast and she smiled at me. I guessed she was last night's visitor. Although she was polite and smiled, I got the impression that her encounter with Colin had not been all she had wished for.

He eventually arrived, looking sheepish. He spoke to our waitress who was again polite, and came to the table looking as if he had not slept. He greeted me in the usual manner, then asked if I had sent a young lady to his room this morning.

'She did ask directions to your room, I simply answered her. I assumed you would have wanted me to. Perhaps in the future you can give them the right room number?' I said.

'To be honest it was a bit embarrassing. The lady who called on you had cancelled, she had to work, so I made other arrangements. It appears at the last moment she was not required, so she decided to come after all. I was entertaining someone else when she burst into the room, I had forgotten to lock the door. I got flustered and asked her to come back later, but the lady I was with got offended and left. I thought that was two ladies off the list, but not so. My new visitor was not upset by what she saw, she returned later to complete her mission. Let me tell you she was tireless, she needed a lot of satisfying,' he said.

'I must thank you for leaving me early last night. We had a visitor; Julie stopped by for a drink. I told her you were in Plymouth. She had news about the house; completion is the beginning of March. This gives us three weeks to do the work and prepare for the paintings. I've invited Julie for dinner tonight as I thought you might like to thank her for her efforts. By that I do not mean in your waitress sort of way,' I said.

'I think she is too much of a lady for that sort of treatment, and it is unlikely she would be conned by the film director routine,' he said.

'That just shows how you treat your bedroom guests, certainly not as ladies.'

'They are ladies, they are just more susceptible to my charms. I think you should try your hand with Julie; if you don't, I might. I think it would need more than a little wining and dining to attract her to your room, and to be honest I don't have time for those sort of niceties.'

With what she now knew of him, it was unlikely she was going to entertain his advances. I was hoping I had spoilt any chance he had with her. But maybe it was just a one-night stand and I was not to read too much into it. I believed her to be a refined lady who obviously had good taste, but I kept that to myself. I really did not care what he got up to, I was more concerned with the ladies he was deceiving, but that did not concern him as this morning had verified in abundance.

Colin had no plans for the day, it was intended to be a recovery day from the previous night and this morning's exertions. I intended to visit the bank on the mainland, not only to check my finances, but also to see if my coins had sold, making me even richer in this time. I had also devised something for the future: once I left this time it would be 50 years in the future, so I needed to have something in place to protect my finances. I had devised a letter to serve that purpose. I needed to know that in 50 years' time my money would be accessible to me, and the letter was to be kept on file for that future date. In the future when someone came in to draw from the account, they must quote a codeword which was in the letter. It was going to state that the person may have the same name as me, and it was my intention to teach him to provide a signature like mine. It was unlikely that anyone working there would be still working there in 50 years.

Colin also thought it a good idea. He needed to do something similar for himself, although he was expecting to visit his account before I revisited mine; it was something he planned to explain to me at the appropriate time. Although a little suspicious as to why he would want money from his account earlier, he was talking of another occasion apart from the house purchase, I accepted that he was going to tell me some time. There was obviously another plan hatching in his active mind.

I walked across the beach to Ruby Bay, and my first port of call was the bank. I spoke to the teller, and was taken to the manager's office. He was pleased to see me.

I wasted no time in asking if my coins had been of interest to anyone and was greeted with some good news: the bank had a client who was prepared to offer me £4,000 for each of the five remaining coins. Unfortunately this client was only able to purchase one now, then the remaining four over a period of time. I was asked if I was in a hurry for the money, and whether this arrangement was convenient for me.

I was more than happy, and asked the manager to let his client know the arrangement was acceptable to me. My account, I was pleased to hear, paid an interest rate which was very good for the amount I had in it, and it was likely to increase with the higher balance from the sale of the coins.

I then asked for the letter to be attached the account, only to be opened upon someone asking about the account. The money was to remain there for a few years before anyone asked about it. That was not the truth but how could I say in 50 years' time? I said I intended to leave the money to a relative, and this letter would show if the person was allowed to access it: there was a codeword to verify that person.

The manager said this was acceptable. My business was concluded in a very convivial manner and I left the bank feeling satisfied that I had prepared my account for my future use, soon to contain over £20,000 plus whatever interest accrued in nearly 50 years.

I walked around the village, greeting villagers as I went. It was like being in Vicary's time, except these people did not ignore me. It was a temptation to visit Julie, but I was to see her that evening. It had the makings of an interesting evening, now that she was familiar with Colin's immorality. At Colin's request I took a look at 1 Ruby Bay, the house that was to be bombed, to check if there was a lock on the cellar door, which was situated on the outside of the house. It was probably a place to store coal, the usual fuel in those days. There was a small padlock on the door, nothing that was likely to cause a problem to break into. Colin had said he had a locksmith's kit, and was proficient at picking locks. This lock was not going to cause a problem, provided he was as good as he said he was.

I looked at the predecessor to my bungalow. It had character, and I was starting to regret the fact that it was pulled down. Then I looked at John's house, which was the same of course.

I returned to the hotel, having completed the task I had been assigned, and joined Colin in the bar. We spent the rest of the afternoon in the bar area, as it was too cold to go outside into the lush gardens. We drank copious amounts of coffee and chatted about our venture. Looking around it seemed that Ruby Bay was not affected by the war, yet just 20 miles away in Plymouth the war was very real and very frightening.

Colin the suspected film director was under constant scrutiny from the female members of staff. If he looked around there was a waitress to take his order, smiling as they approached. This man was a local phenomenon. I was not completely sure all these ladies worked at the hotel, the staff was surely not that large. Every time he ordered something he made sure it was debited to his room, and emphasized his room number. I felt sure the whole female population of Ruby Bay would have no difficulty in telling you his room number.

'Do you have enough strength to dig up the cellar? What does your diary have in store for you this evening? Are there any appointments in room 564, or do you have a free evening, bearing in mind we are expecting a dinner guest?' I said.

'I have nothing definite fixed up, I have hopes for the blonde lady at reception. She has shown an interest in me, saying she was interested in some film or other. I have no idea what she's talking about.'

'At this point, Colin, I think I need to inform you of something you may not be aware of – there is no film, maybe you should tell these ladies you started the rumour.'

'As I told you before, I have never said I was a film director, I may have hinted at it, but that was all. We will never pass this way again, I am going to enjoy the company of these ladies, they come to me after all. I appreciate they have this dream which they think I can fulfil, and I feel it is my duty to let them feel good about themselves, let them think they have encountered a movie maker. It's only for a couple of weeks,' he said.

'I hope you can sleep at night. That's a silly comment, you are starting to look like you're getting no sleep. It has to be said, you are dedicated to the task of bedding as many women as possible. You are starting to believe it is your duty not to let these girls down, you have lost all sense of reality,' I said.

We left the bar in plenty of time to prepare for dinner, with the added attraction of Julie as our guest. All the staff smiled at Colin as he passed. He stopped at reception and spoke quietly to the blonde lady; she did not slap his face, so I assumed a time had been fixed. He looked at me and gave a thumbs-up. Yet another victim. I felt sorry for the look she gave him as he left.

I arrived in the bar early, just in case Julie was there already, which she was, sitting by the window. She was wearing yet another figure-hugging dress, this time in pale blue. But she was capable of looking good in overalls.

'I'm sorry I wasn't here to met you,' I said.

'I am very capable of looking after myself.' She kissed me on the cheek, then pushed home her advantage by saying, ' I've even ordered a drink for myself, I think my independence does not make me very feminine.'

'I'm afraid I have to disagree with that,' I said.

'Thank you for your concern, I was not being critical, merely showing my independent streak, which is probably apparent. I take it you never mentioned to Colin what happened between us last night?'

'No, I'm too much of a gentleman for that,' I said. She smiled.

'Why is Colin not with you, is he up to no good?'

'I can reassure you he is on his way, I'm not completely sure what his plans have been for today. I have not mentioned anything to him about the reputation he has in the outlying villages; he is also not aware that you know of this. I told him you had asked about his whereabouts last night, and that I had said he was on a business trip. This obviously gives you the opportunity to have some fun at his expense, if you so wish. I am going to sit back and watch the entertainment unfold. To be honest, there is a strong possibility he has an engagement later with the blonde receptionist,' I said.

She nodded that knowing nod, she was a woman of the world, but deep down I do not think she approved of his nightly adventures. She was from 1941 with the morals, I thought, to match. She then took me by surprise.

'I bought one of your coins from the bank, thank you for allowing me time to purchase the others,' she said.

'Why did you not mention it before, I could have offered you a deal.'

'Was it a Colin sort of deal?'

'I think you know the answer to that: I was going to let you have the coins cheaper.'

'Your original price is cheap, I can sell them for £5,000 each in London. Do you want to change your mind about selling them to me?' she said.

'Of course not, you don't look like a coin collector.'

'What does a coin collector look like?' she said.

'I must admit there is no answer to that.'

'I'm happy to work out a way of paying the money back, it might require you to visit my home,' she said.

'I think you're right; we do need to work out some form of repayment,' I said.

Before we got into the details too much, Colin arrived. He greeted Julie with his normal panache.

'I'm sorry I missed you last night, Julie. It was an urgent business meeting, and it took longer than I thought,' said Colin.

'I'm glad the meeting was successful and no doubt satisfying,' she said.

'I hear the house is progressing well?' he said.

'The house will be completed by the beginning of March; hopefully that satisfies you?'

This was certainly good news, we now had plenty of time to prepare the cellar. We got up and went into the dining room to celebrate this news. Julie had decided to curb her mischievous side, at least for the moment. Colin had no idea she knew of his nocturnal habits; she dealt with the situation with her usual class. Dinner was as usual exquisite: how they produced such food in wartime was amazing. Colin ate heartily, no doubt building up his stamina for the evening session he had waiting. The receptionist did look like a sporting girl, and I felt he was going to have his hands full with this one.

We returned to the bar, where Julie watched Colin closely, waiting for the excuse he was about to use to leave. I had no idea what time he had arranged to meet the receptionist.

'I am enjoying this evening; I hope you do not have any meetings to attend tonight, Colin?'

'I do have a meeting later, but not for a few hours.'

'You seem to have a lot of evening meetings, they must prove very tiring,' she said.

'I prefer the daytime meetings, but most of these people are doing something else during the day.'

'I understand what you're saying, being a receptionist is an important job during the day. May I suggest you do not wear her out too much, she will be needed here tomorrow.'

He looked shocked, then he realized I had told her. He smiled as if to accept the fact everyone knew, then explained he was meeting her at his room in an hour.

He started to give details of his other conquests, and Julie showed a certain amount of disgust at his bragging, but she smiled to hide her embarrassment.

Colin changed the subject.

'Is it possible to get the keys to the property? I am hoping to decorate before I move in,' said Colin.

She agreed to let us have the keys the following day; this would allowed us the chance to check the cellar floor.

I told Colin I would see Julie got off the island safely; he was at liberty to make his appointment without making up any excuse. He said goodnight to us; his lady friend was going to be arriving soon.

I went with Julie to the boat. She asked if I wanted to stay at her cottage that night: we had some negotiations to carry out. She pretended she was talking coins, which I was happy to go along with. It was a silly question, so we both boarded the boat for the mainland, much to the amusement of our captain who had brought her over. He smiled but said nothing. On our arrival on the mainland we caught a taxi to the next village, and decided to stop at the Pilchard for a final drink.

It was then that it happened: Julie uttered those words, 'We need to talk.'

Throughout history, those immortal words put fear into any red-blooded male. They meant some sort of decision was required from the male, not an easy task, we were not good at committing ourselves.

I bought the drinks and joined her at the table. She was in a pensive mood, she smiled but all was not well, that much showed behind the smile.

I sat and waited for her to start the conversation; she was the one who wanted to talk. It was strange, as we had only spent one night together, but these were unusual times for the inhabitants of 1941.

'I know we have only spent one night together, but I feel there might be something between us. You are different from other men I have known, in a good way,' she said.

Little did she know how different.

'I cannot promise anything, what with the present situation, I know you are not asking for any sort of commitment, to be honest I can't give that. Once the war is over I will return to see you, then we'll take it from there,' I said.

I did not want to lie to Julie, but how was I to tell her that the next time I was going to be in Ruby Bay was many years in the future? Of course I had no intention of saying that.

'You will be the first person I look up when I return to Ruby Bay,' I said.

I intended to keep that promise; hopefully she was not going to recognize me, but it was the truth nonetheless.

We went to her cottage and spent the night together. Julie felt I had made some sort of commitment, but I knew it was not the sort she expected. It was all I had to offer unless I decided to stay in this time.

I again left in the early hours. I did not want Colin to know about this relationship, not that he was too bothered, he had enough problems of his own in the female stakes.

I met him at breakfast, and he asked me to pick up the keys to the house from Julie. We were going to meet at the house. He was drained from his night's exertions; he felt it was inappropriate to see Julie in that state. I thought she was likely to laugh at him, and he wanted to keep his macho image intact. But he was right, she did not deserve that.

I met Colin after collecting the keys, and we entered 3 Ruby Bay, John's house in our time. We had torches as our time was to be spent in the dark cellar. The cellar door was under the stairs in the hallway, there was no key to open it. We agreed to remedy that.

We moved slowly down the steep stairway. In the cellar we saw the tiled floor; Colin had brought a few tools with him and he carefully took off some of the tiles, beneath them was a piece of hardboard. Beneath that were the floorboards, the whole floor of tiles now had to be removed. We stacked the tiles up against the wall. Once the artwork was secure, it would be a simple task to replace the tiles, and nobody would be any the wiser.

Once the floorboards were clear of tiles and debris, Colin brought a jemmy into operation. The boards came up easily. Underneath the floor was a space 4 feet deep, ideal for our purpose. We sat on the floor to consider our options. We needed to work out how to hold six such pieces of artwork securely; these pieces needed to be protected for many years. We decided to build a box framework, using good quality wood, on a concrete floor. It was to have a wooden top, then we would concrete over the top. Colin estimated how large the paintings were, based on seeing them carried by the Germans on his last visit. The box was to be a lot bigger than that estimate, to be sure all paintings fitted into it. The wood and concrete was to be purchased from the local store. The wood which was unlikely to arouse too much suspicion, as the locals would be made aware that we were doing up the place, although we needed a story for the concrete. We decided to say the cellar's wooden floor was unsafe; hopefully that would do the trick.

The local store was prepared to deliver the concrete; the wood we carried. We decided not to build the box until after the concrete had arrived, as the delivery man might be suspicious of a large box in the cellar.

While we awaited the delivery, I took the opportunity to look around the house, hoping I might find somewhere else to hide the paintings that was unlikely to necessitate so much work. There was nowhere. The concrete arrived late in the afternoon, and we decided we had enough time to lay a large floor area.

Colin was quite adept at the task, he had obviously laid concrete before, although that was not what he preferred laying. His energy levels had returned.

We arrived back at the hotel in the early evening, tired and dirty. Dinner was of the same expected high standard.

'I have nothing arranged for this evening, hopefully I will get a full night's sleep. I believe it is the height of rudeness to turn anyone away from my door, particularly if they made the effort to knock on it,' he said.

The drinks arrived without delay, the smiles towards him showed his chances of a full night's sleep were diminishing by the second. That knock on his door was something he was going to get, whether he wanted it or not.

'How did it go with the blonde receptionist, was she all you had hoped for?' I asked.

He smiled as he thought of the previous night.

'She was far from a disappointment. Did Julie get off home all right? I don't think she should make that trip alone, perhaps in the future one of us should accompany her. What do you think of that suggestion, Pat?' he said.

A large smile crossed his face. I had forgotten his window overlooked the bay: he had seen me leave with her.

'I am seriously pleased for you. She is someone very special, let her down gently in respect of our leaving,' he said.

'That is what she wanted to discuss last night, where the relationship was going,' I said.

'How did you get out of that one?'

'I'm not sure I did. I told her that although we had only known each other for a short time, I really did like her. I mentioned the war in relation to our forthcoming mission, promising to see her on our return. We both know that's not going to happen, at least not in the foreseeable future.'

'That is the advantage of my system, no commitment necessary. I am unlikely to fall for any of the women I've been seeing. They have given themselves too easily.'

His next suggestion was one I did not expect him to make:

'There is an obvious solution to your problem, you could remain in this time with Julie. Of course that was going to bring other problems, getting a job for one thing. Although we are about to obtain a fortune in artwork, it is not worth anything in this time, the value lies in the future, partly because these paintings are believed to have been destroyed by Hitler. It was going to be decades before they were worth anything, can you wait that long?' he said.

'You're right, the only good thing about staying is Julie. Is that enough? Maybe it is. I would not be in a position to support her in any way, there is also the façade of being an official with the War Office to overcome. I just can't say they don't want me any more. I have no choice really, I must continue with our journey.'

The following morning we returned to the house, the quick-drying cement had set, and we started constructing the wooden box, a long and laborious task.

Once the box was complete we spent the next three days cementing it into place; the cement for the top was not needed until the paintings were inside. The floor tiles were still stacked against the wall, the floorboards were to remain lifted. There was nothing more for us to do, the floorboards and the tiles were to be put back the day after the bombing. All we had left to do was wait to get the keys officially, and then await the Luftwaffe.

We enjoyed the facilities of the hotel; Julie visited the hotel regularly as our dinner guest, and Colin occasionally slipped away for more business meetings, much to the amusement of Julie. I do not think he believed Julie was going to be one of his conquests, after our discussion on the matter. He had thought at one stage that he was going to be in with a chance, like most other males was something purely in the mind, with little chance of coming to fruition.

Our relationship blossomed. She was waiting until after the war, but to me it was not quite that simple, I was unable to tell her the truth of what lay ahead. Julie and I explored the local area, and when the weather was fine we sat in the gardens of local pubs and chatted for hours. We both avoided the subject of the war, it depressed her, so I was reluctant to mention it.

As time passed she did mention my departure, did I have any idea where I was going, how dangerous it was, and most importantly when I was going to return? It filled me with sadness that I was unable to tell her the truth. The chances of us meeting after my departure were very slim, and I just wanted to enjoy what little time we had together. The days at the hotel were pleasant; we used the garden occasionally, when the weather allowed it, but this time of the year provided more cold weather than anything else.

Then the house deal went through, Colin got the keys and we returned to the house. He had no intention of moving from the hotel, telling everyone he needed to decorate first. This story satisfied the local populace.

We had three weeks to wait before the bomb landed on 1 Ruby Bay and we spent time at the house, mainly hoping to see Colin's father, but he never turned up. Colin wanted to go inside his father's house to check if there was some sort of wireless; he must have contact with the Germans somehow, it was only logical. We knew the cellar was not going to contain the equipment, so it must be hidden in the main house. It was also possible that we might find some sort of code book, which would assist the Allies. The problem with that was if we handed it over to the authorities, we would be questioned as to how we got it.

We decided to make it a night mission. Colin had his burglary tools with him, and he was dressed completely in black; he had been watching too many films. But then, he did think he was a film director. We approached the front door, he picked the lock with consummate ease, and we were in the dark hallway. I illuminated one of the two torches we had brought. Our route took us to the rear of the property, checking each room as we went. All the rooms were completely empty, not a stick of furniture to be seen. It was obvious that his father had not bought the property to live in, and we knew his motives were somewhat different to that; but at this point in time we were the only people who knew this for a fact, along with German Intelligence.

A strange thought occurred to me: what if our government knew of his spying, what if the building was being watched?

Neither Colin nor I had foreseen this problem, but it was too late now. Here I was, putting myself in a position of being accused of spying eight years before I was born. How could I give my true date of birth to my captors? I did not want to think of capture, we were merely burglars. None of the light sockets had bulbs in; this was in itself significant and indicated that the house was never occupied.

We found the kitchen, a door from which led to the cellar. Colin unlocked this door, again with ease, and we clambered down the steps. We knew the cellar was also reached by the outside door, but this gave us an opportunity to check it out before the operation. The cellar was empty, although this was the best place to hide a wireless receiver. But with no receiver we had another problem: how was he made aware of any drop-off? A look in the cupboards within the property did not provide any wireless equipment, so how did he contact the submarine?

We left the house none the wiser. Maybe there was a portable receiver? Then I remembered it was 1941: nothing was portable in those days. We returned to the hotel to deliberate on what we had found, or to be more precise what we had not found. It was a little perplexing; Colin's father knew when the consignment was due, but we did not know how he knew. There must be some sort of contact.

We decided not to worry too much about it. Our time in Ruby Bay was getting short, the consignment was due, and it was now a case of waiting for 21st March and the bomb that was inevitably going to fall.

We continued to enjoy our stay. Colin continued his almost nightly manoeuvres, but the film was still no closer to being made; he needed more time to find his leading lady. He continued chatting up the ladies; his entourage was now in double figures, all his ladies were willing partners, but of course he had lied to them to get their approval. The mornings were the worst for Colin, he appeared to age daily.

Julie visited and had dinner with us, and Colin was discreet and left us alone. He had some good points, which many of the ladies of the hotel knew. On all occasions that Julie visited, I escorted her home, always staying the night. It was a magical time for me, and I think her life had brightened a little.

I got to know many people in her village, we had become a couple, although the subject of marriage was never mentioned. I think many thought it an inevitability with Julie and me, but she never broached the subject. Our walks in the local area were always greeted by greetings from passers-by, she knew everyone, she was well respected as a businesswoman, 'making it in a man's world', she called it.

I remember thinking to myself, wherever my travels may take me from this point, these last few weeks are going to be the ones I remember for the rest of my life. I had acquired a princess.

I wondered if there was a way of taking her with us. The only logical way was if she purchased my house, but was that fair to her, asking her to come with me into a future more than 50 years away? I discussed it with Colin; he knew I was smitten with her, but he was able to give an impartial opinion, taking into account all aspects of her life. Before she was able to make a decision, I needed to tell her the implications of her decision, and how likely was she to believe I had come from the future? There was very little hope of that. I was not glad to be leaving Julie. I had weighed up all the options, it was going to be very sad for me, but I realized I had no choice. She belonged in this time, I did not. No matter which way my heart went, we were soon to part company forever.

The day arrived; we prepared ourselves to secure a fortune in paintings. It was at last 21st March1941, the day all the planning was to come to fruition, if what Colin had said was true. I had no reason to believe otherwise.

During our hearty breakfast our plans were laid for that evening. Colin looked even more drained than usual. The submarine was to arrive at about 10 p.m., then the drone of the bombers heading towards Plymouth would be audible. We had to carry out the transfer before the bombers made their return journey; Colin said we had a good hour to carry out our mission. We were to go to the mainland in the early evening, and position ourselves on a grassy area above his father's house, in a position to see everything that was happening. Hopefully the night would be too cold for locals to wander around.

We spent the day going over and over the plan, we had only one shot at this, there were no second chances, and we wanted to be gone by the time the bomb dropped. The day passed slowly; I was a little nervous, Colin was confident everything was going as planned. We cancelled a dinner date with Julie, asking her to visit the following night, she agreed to do so but she seemed put out by this decision.

The time had finally come, we made our way to the mainland. It was dark and cold, and we had both wrapped up well for the expedition as we did not know exactly how long we were going to be sitting on the grass; possibly a long time. I had remembered the torches, Colin had remembered his burglary kit, needed to unlock the door of his father's cellar.

I was concerned that his father might return while we were removing the paintings, but Colin was adamant his father had left the area, having dropped the envelope in his cellar. He now had a similar envelope in his pocket, this one contained blank sheets of paper.

We reached the grassy area overlooking the house, we both had binoculars to check on the incoming submarine. It was incredible that an enemy vessel was going to pass so close to the mainland, but I doubt anyone was looking for a one-submarine invasion force. Colin checked his watch, he knew near enough when this event was to happen, it was just a question of waiting. He knew his father was going to turn up first, and this would give us a clue that things were moving in the right direction.

Suddenly a figure moved across by the house. Colin gave a thumbs-up. I assumed this was his father. The figure unlocked the padlock to the cellar, shone his torch inside, then removed an envelope from his inside pocket. He walked into the cellar and out of our vision. Within seconds he was out again, he closed the door, and placed the padlock on the ground. He then walked into the house, and we saw the torch flickering through the windows, maybe he was contacting the submarine; although we had not found the wireless, that did not mean it was not there. The house was occupied for only a few minutes, he then came out and locked the door, and walked away up the hill towards the village. I watched him until he was out of sight.

Colin indicated the edge of the cliff. This was where the next piece of the puzzle was to slot into place. He then whispered that he was going to change the envelopes; I was to signal with the torch if anyone came over the cliff. He scuttled down the bank and into the cellar, and he took only a few seconds to return with the envelope containing the information. He passed me the envelope and said I was to put it in my inside pocket to keep it safe, which I did. I was confident that we had prevented vital information reaching the Germans.

The wait on the grass continued, my eyes getting accustomed to the darkness. I was ever vigilant for movement on the cliff, occasionally looking out to sea in the hope of seeing the submarine.

Then I saw it; Colin saw it at the same moment. It was an intermittent flicker of light out in the Channel, that must be the submarine. I was unable to make out any sort of shape, it was much too dark for that, but it appeared that the enemy had arrived. Colin whispered that the Germans were preparing to row to the shore. It was going to take a few minutes before they reached the shore, then they had to climb up the rocks to the top of cliff.

One person emerged and went towards the house; he was obviously an officer checking out the area. He had a small torch in his hand, and he was looking around slowly, waiting to move forward when he felt it was safe to do so. He started to move slowly across the grass, looking around him in all directions as he went, moving closer to the house. Colin and I slid lower down in the grass. For him to see us now was something we did not want if we were to secure the paintings.

The man approached the house and the cellar. He looked down at the padlock on the floor, walked into the cellar and emerged immediately. He had the envelope in his hand, and I watched him place it into his inside pocket. He then looked towards the cliff and I saw another figure there. The first man used his torch and flashed the light towards the cliff, two more figures appeared at the cliff, carrying something heavy. All three of these men moved quickly towards the house, and as they got closer I saw they were carrying the paintings, one in each hand. Our fortune was arriving in double quick time. The paintings were put into the cellar, and when the third man emerged the officer padlocked the door. All four men then moved quickly towards the cliff, and within seconds they were gone. The deed was done.

Colin said nothing but rose to his feet, he indicated I had to follow. We reached the cellar door and his burglary kit came out; he unlocked the padlock quickly. We moved into the cellar and switched on a torch, to see the paintings resting against the wall. Colin turned to me and smiled; now we had to get them out.

We decided to make three trips and carry two paintings each, and leave them outside John's house. I picked up two paintings, one in each hand. They were substantial pieces I thought, but fairly easy to transport. As I picked up the last two paintings, Colin locked the padlock.

We returned to his house, or John's house as it was in our time. We moved the paintings one at a time down to the cellar, placing them up against the wall. We were in no rush to do anything with them, we left them for the following day.

I then heard the drone of aircraft overhead.

'Don't worry, they're on the way to Plymouth, the bomb won't be dropped until the return journey, but we should get out of the way and back to the hotel,' he said.

We left the house and made our way to the slipway. A small

boat transported us back to the island. The trip back to the island was quick, and we went straight to the bar. The view out of the window was going to be spectacular; I had never seen a bomb demolish a house before. We sat in our usual place by the window, waiting to hear of the drone of the bombers returning. Some of the staff were nervous, they had heard the bombers going over. I found it strange that they thought Ruby Bay might get attacked by the Germans, as I doubted Hitler was able to see any military significance in that. The droning engines started to come within earshot and the staff joined us at the windows, looking skyward. Colin and I had our eyes fixed on the mainland.

It was an explosion the likes of which I had never heard before. The building shook a little; there were a few muffled screams, then complete silence. Nobody at this stage, apart from Colin and me, were aware that nobody was hurt. The staff at the hotel were shocked by the massive explosion, their first thought was the possibility of casualties, and they feared for the owner and his family. I was still finding it difficult to comprehend that everything Colin had said had actually happened, this was a momentous night in my life.

At that point my thoughts went to the people of Plymouth, no doubt many had lost their lives tonight. It was to be a shocking night for many of those families. I sat at the window and watched 1 Ruby Bay burn, a house that was going to cease to exist after this night. Colin ordered some more drinks, and some of the staff remained at the window watching the flames.

Eventually a fire engine arrived, no doubt from some distance, and the men started to hose down the fire. I knew they were not going to save anything of the house. Had it not been for Colin and me, his father would be on the brink of a death sentence. We had saved his life and the artwork, and the paintings were our spoils of war.

We sat there quietly watching the events unfold on the mainland, we did not know what to say to each other, we had just become very rich men, but it was not something we had an opportunity to share with anyone else. Colin's half-hearted attempts to chat to the female staff members were not reciprocated. He was about to have a quiet night tonight; most of the ladies were concerned with what they had seen on the mainland, unable to believe there was nothing to worry about. We stayed in the bar for the remainder of the evening, and the fire had been extinguished by the time we left. The house was still smoking against the night sky; tomorrow we would visit the site and see for ourselves.

The receptionist smiled at Colin as he passed, perhaps it might not be a quiet restful night after all. He returned her smile, but perhaps she just wanted some kind of reassurance from him. His idea of reassurance was unprintable.

Following breakfast Colin and I made our way to his new house. Today was the day we were going to seal the paintings in the cellar. It was going to be many years before they would see the light of day again, appreciating in value as they lay under the floorboards. We called at the hardware shop first, purchasing the grouting for the floor tiles, a few nails and a hammer to secure the floor, along with a piece of hessian to protect the paintings.

Everyone was talking about the bomb that dropped, grateful that nobody had been killed. Colin said we had been at the hotel when it happened, and it was a terrible shock.

We left and headed towards the house. The cellar was as we had left it, six paintings stood against the wall, this was the first time I had seen them properly. I looked but did not think they were to my taste no matter how much they were worth. We wrapped the paintings, placing them one at a time into the wooden box of the cellar, taking great care not to cause any damage. The box was plenty big enough for all six pieces of work. The wooden lid was secured, nailed down by Colin. Now we mixed the cement to cover the box, and it looked just like concrete floor. Nobody was likely to know what lay below the floor, the deception was complete. We started on the tiled floor, the tile grouting took over an hour, we wanted it to look good. Once the job was complete we both stood back and admired our work, we had made an excellent job of the whole cellar. We changed upstairs in the house, leaving the work clothes in the cellar.

Today we intended to visit Colin's father, to let him know we knew what had occurred the previous night. This was the second part of our mission. Outside, a crowd was looking at the bombed out shell of the house. Police were there to prevent anyone looting the property, not that there was much left.

At that moment I saw Colin's father, he was in conversation with the policeman. This was going to save us a trip to Plymouth, and the meeting could be more private. Colin suggested that I approach him, show him my false identity card, then let him know we knew about his unscrupulous lifestyle. Our approach was to be sympathetic to his plight, an offer of something alternative to arrest. Colin was not going to approach him, and I realized his reasoning: this man was to become his father, so he did not want to be recognized in the future. He pulled his hat down to cover the top part of his face.

I approached the man known as Mr Brown, and showing my identity card I asked to speak to him in private. He was very nervous; I think he suspected we might arrest him.

We moved away from the crowd, Colin standing close by. I spoke in a low voice so that no bystanders heard our conversation. I informed Mr Brown that my colleague and I were from the Intelligence Agency. I was unaware whether or not such an agency existed, but it sounded impressive, and there were so many departments during the war that it was unlikely his father would know either.

'Do you know why I am speaking to you? I do not want to arrest you unless it is really necessary,' I said.

The word 'arrest' stopped him in his tracks.

'Why would you want to arrest me, I've done nothing wrong?' he said. He was trying to bluff.

'A German submarine has been seen off the coast, it has been monitored closely. We watched the sailors row ashore; items were brought to your house, to the cellar of your house to be exact,' I said.

Mr Brown's face visibly drained of colour. He now knew we were on to him, and he waited for me to speak again.

'We have monitored you while you have stayed at Ruby Bay and it is obvious to us that you are passing information to our enemies. Your reward for this is the artwork that was left, brought from the submarine. We have those pieces of artwork, they will be transported to Whitehall for a full assessment,' I said.

I paused to see his reaction; he was visibly shocked that we had so much information on him. He must have assumed his life was at an end, that it was impossible to survive this ordeal.

'I don't know what items you're talking about,' he said.

Maybe he was just good at bluffing.

'I may be able to offer you a way out of this situation, but it is only possible if you do everything I tell you to do. Do you understand I am saving your life?'

He nodded. 'I will do whatever you want, I want to protect my family from this. You may not understand it, but I had reasons for doing what I did.'

'Our department knows everything there is to know about you, we have been watching you for some time. This is where it ends; I am offering you the only way out. You are to continue working for the Ministry of Defence. Nobody there knows of our involvement with you, except a few people whose job it is to watch you, and they will never make themselves known to you. It is possible that at some point in the future we are going to call on your services, to pass certain information to the Germans. In two months' time you will ask for a transfer to another part of the country, with this transfer you will change your name. It is to be Wickham, spelt W-I-C-K-H-A-M. Have you understood everything I have said? Any deviation from what I have told you will result in your arrest and ultimate execution for spying,' I said.

He understood but wondered why he had been let off.

'You are going to be more use to us if you remain active, but only when we decide to use you. You must not do anything without authorization from me, do you understand that?' I said forcefully.

'Thank you for giving me this second chance, I will become a model citizen. I will do whatever you ask of me,' he said.

'You must be patient; you will be informed at the appropriate time. With any luck you may live through this war without any further incidents. Just become the good citizen you have promised to be, but be ready in case you are called upon,' I said.

Colin's father was genuinely grateful that we had given him his life back, he kept thanking us, vowing to help when called upon. The ploy had worked perfectly.

We walked away.

'You were very convincing, he was petrified of the consequences if he strayed again. Your performance was excellent. Thank you for giving me my father back,' he said.

Colin went to the bank, and I stood and watched as the few embers of the burnt-out house died away. We had completed our two missions in this time, and soon we were to return to Vicary's time. I contemplated that possibility with dread, hopefully our stay was to be short as we had another job to do, to go forward to 1981. The loss of his wife had devastated John, and I was now in a position to help him. It was a pleasing thought that I was to see John again, I appreciated he would of course be 20 years younger.

Colin and I met in our usual place, the hotel bar, to decide our strategy. We had to meet up with Alan to use the Pathway, which hopefully would propel us into 1981. Colin had the time and date of the accident: we needed to be in that time several weeks earlier, not only to locate John's house in Plymouth, but also to check on his wife's routine. We decided we needed to leave in two days. Now it was time to say goodbye to Julie. It was at this point I asked what I thought to be a pertinent question, I had no idea what John's wife was called, she was simply referred to as his wife, that appeared a little impersonal. John told me she was called Ann, that satisfied my curiosity.

We invited Julie to dinner the night before our departure. She had been a friend to both of us; more than a friend to me. Our final dinner with her was a sombre affair. I knew I was probably never to see her again, and if I did she would be a very old lady. Colin, on the other hand, had no scruples about not seeing his ladies again, I think he was pleased with that prospect, he had used lies to obtain their favours, not that they were innocents in this respect.

Julie sensed that all was not well, and she realized we were leaving soon, it was our last meal together.

'When are you going? Unless that question breaches the Official Secrets Act,' she said.

'We'll be leaving tomorrow, there is important business to take care of, something that cannot wait; someone's life depends on us being there,' I said.

'It sounds serious. Do you know when you're coming back?' she said.

A difficult question to answer, the truth was that we were, but she was unlikely to be the young and beautiful woman we remembered when we next set foot in Ruby Bay.

'I don't think it will be for some time.' At least that was honest.

'Is "some time" a long time in the future?'

I thought this a strange comment. 'Colin and I want to thank you for all your hard work in securing the house so quickly.'

She looked a bit bemused. Her comment made me think she knew exactly who we were, she had made several comments that made me suspicious. But how was she to know we were travellers? I had almost dismissed the thought when she said something else which surprised me.

'Why have you decorated the property?' she asked. 'It just seems a strange thing to do when neither of you will be living there for sometime. I think there is an underlying factor in this purchase, I thought you both might have trusted me. I don't think you told me the true reason for buying the house, perhaps it is something to do with your job. I can be trusted, and I hope I am not being deceived in some way. I wish you had told me the real reason for buying the property, I might have been able to help. But if you don't tell me anything, how can I help?' she said.

'The property is Colin's and not mine; the chances are he will be away for a long time. I only have the next mission, whereas Colin has more to do,' I said.

I was struggling with what to say, how could I tell her the truth. Colin was now obviously wary of Julie, as she seemed to indicate she knew as much as we did. This was the last chance to discuss it with her, I wondered if perhaps coming right to the point was the best course of action: just ask her outright what she thought our job was. But Colin and I both remained silent on the subject, wishing to avoid a situation which had the possibility of backfiring on us. We sat down to the meal and chatted generally.

My mind was racing with endless possibilities. Was she about to appear as a prostitute in Vicary's time? Was that to mean a discount in my role as the monk?

'It's a shame we can't find work for you, Julie, our department does have a shortage of females. Do you have any skills that might prove useful?' I asked.

'I am good at filing, unless you think I am good at anything else?'

She glared at Colin; she knew what his suggestion was going to be.

'We are not really at liberty to discuss our work, although I am confident you would not say anything, Julie,' he said.

'I have no idea what your work is, apart from Colin's fictitious film director role, but I think that is more pleasure than work, if what I heard was true.'

She had a sharp tongue when necessary and he was slightly embarrassed by this remark. If she knew anything she was being clever, hinting but giving nothing away. Colin had jumped in at the right moment and I decided not to press the subject, we were to be gone tomorrow.

She got up to leave after the meal, and I offered to escort her home. We all felt sorrow at this last goodbye.

'I am sorry you are leaving. Whatever work you are both undertaking I wish you luck, and please take care of yourselves. Look me up when you hopefully return safely.'

Colin was deeply moved. She knew he was something of a rogue, but had genuine affection for him, and he appreciated that. He waved as we left the island.

Julie and I walked slowly as we reached the village, it was as if the slower we walked the slower time was passing. We walked hand in hand to her cottage, neither of us spoke.

We slept together for the last time. I knew that to be the case, she thought that maybe there were to be other times. I did not tell her the truth. Neither of us slept very well, we lay in the bed holding onto each other. Julie hoping I was not going to be killed in the war, whereas I knew I was unlikely to see her again.

When morning broke it was time for me to leave. It was an emotional farewell, I was losing someone I really cared for. She was indeed a true lady. I walked away and decided not to look back.

I returned to the hotel and was in time to join Colin for breakfast, I wanted to discuss Julie. He was happy that she was not a traveller, he was able to explain all her comments.

Next we had to pay the bill and pack our suitcases. We had no chance of passing through the portal with a couple of suitcases, so we decided to leave them at Colin's house, safe there for the next 40 years, knowing only the pouches around our necks passed through the portal. The clothes were likely to be fashionable again by then. The staff at the hotel were sad to see us leave, we promised to return in the future, we did not tell them how far in the future.

We made our way to the mainland. We were to remain in Colin's house until that evening; if we left just before midnight we would only spend a short time on the island. Our rendezvous with Alan was arranged for just after midnight and I hoped he was going to be there, the less time on that island the better. He would have the Pathway, and we were then to leave immediately.

I hoped Alan would be there with the Pathway. It made the trip more difficult, having to count on it being on the island each time we went back. I trusted Alan when he said he was going to be there for us, and I knew the Pathway would lose its power if removed from the island, but there was a temptation to want to know exactly where it was. We were trusting him with our lives; he was going to calculate when the portal was going to be open for our return, he was going to set the Pathway for today's date. Whether we were ready to return or not, we had to return to the island this very evening.

'I hope we can help John out on our next trip, it is going to mean so much to him,' I said.

'I know the time and date of the accident, along with the location. There is no reason to miss it, but just like the paintings we only have one shot at it. The Pathway will be set to return us to the island after the accident, possibly a couple of days afterwards. That way we can check on Ann's welfare, knowing beyond doubt that we have succeeded in our task,' Colin said.

'I gather there is another mission you want to carry out. Perhaps now is a good time to discuss it?' I said.

'I need to make another trip, after the one on which we are about to embark, but I can only do it with your help. If I do not get your help I will not go ahead with it.'

'I am hoping you don't want to go back to the Stone Age and collect rock samples,' I said.

He had motives for all his trips but they were not always the best of motives.

'This trip is very personal to me, something as serious as saving John's wife Ann. I will reveal everything to you in 1981, but the destination for my venture is 1985,' he said.

I really did not mind what the trip entailed, it was in a civilized time, that was an important factor.

We spent the day chatting generally, hoping our arrival was in time to save John's wife, knowing this was going to mean so much to him. It was also going to mean a lot to me, as I had promised John we were going to do our best.

The time for departure dawned, I put on my scruffiest clothes, knowing they were to disappear when I reached the island. They were easy to pick out I had worn them to dig up the cellar. My thoughts turned to the cellar, was there really a fortune there? I only had Colin's word for that, I had no idea who those particular artists were. To be fair he had been correct on everything he had said so far, and his timing over the bombing was spot on.

We walked across the deserted beach, Colin was looking towards the entrance of what was to be the portal, the calculations for opening the portal was in Alan's hands, several centuries in the past. The storm clouds gathered, and the portal took shape ahead of us, Alan had done his job as promised, the time was exactly as Colin had asked for. We shook hands and entered the portal. The island awaited us. Was it going to be a changed island? We expected it to be, as it only returned to the beginning for new arrivals. I wondered whether the islanders had become fully fledged pirates yet. Soon all was to be revealed.

5

I appeared at the top of the island, quite close to my hut, my monk's habit was as expected, still very dirty and smelly. I made my way to the meeting place behind the rock; I did not want to miss Alan, as otherwise our stay was going to be extended, not a prospect that filled me with delight. I wondered what island we had returned to, how far in the future from our last visit. No doubt the acts of piracy had begun. I sat behind the rock, it was cold, my clothing was not warm, although I had thought the dirt on it was going to provide me with warmth.

Then Colin appeared in the form of Jefferson. As I was alone, it was obvious that Alan had not appeared yet. I said I was not sure of the time, perhaps we had arrived early, but it must be around midnight, it was a matter of waiting a little longer. The only way to check the time was to visit the inn, something I did not intend to do. We waited quietly behind the rock, hearing the noise from the inn. No doubt Alan was waiting for an opportune moment to leave, as he did not want to arouse suspicion.

Eventually we heard people leaving the inn, some were making their way home to their delightful wives. Alan was going to arrive soon. Then I heard a noise from behind the rock, and a voice asked if we were there. We assumed it was Alan and responded.

The tall figure that was Landon appeared, and although I knew Alan had taken his form it was still very unnerving. It was something I still had difficulty with, this fearsome figure being Alan.

He asked if we had sorted everything out in 1941; now I was certain it was Alan.

'We have done what we wanted in 1941, we now intend to go to 1981. We'll need the Pathway to do that. Pat has done more in 1941 than he intended; he fell in love with a lady from that time,' Colin said.

Alan looked at me and said nothing, no doubt thinking it was a complicated tale. There was a short silence. I did not feel it was necessary for Colin to relate that part of my life, although he seemed to get some sort of pleasure out of it.

'The Pathway is in my hut; we will go there when the crew have dispersed from the inn. It is obviously not a good idea for me to be seen with you, Pat, I'm sure you appreciate that by now. What date do you need for returning to 1981?' he said.

'The date of the accident is the 11th of March, but we need to be there at least a week before. Things needed to be sorted to make sure the operation is successful,' said Colin.

'Have you told Pat about your 1985 trip, Colin?' said Alan.

'He has promised to reveal all when we get to 1981. Do you know how long we have been gone and what changes have there been on the island?' I said.

It appeared that we had been away for two months, a period which had changed the island dramatically. He told us the story, one that was without doubt going to change history.

'We started raiding ships and to honest it was quite profitable. We stuck to the smaller vessels, except for the first trip, that was a large vessel which we captured for ourselves and it is the larger ship we are now using. Although it is impossible to tell, I tried not to loot ships heading for the Treasury, we know what a bad idea that is. Vicary is still the captain, but in name only,' Alan added with an air of superiority.

'Vicary knows the crew will follow me if push comes to shove, and he does exactly what I tell him. I decide on the ships to plunder, but it always comes across as Vicary's idea. The crew are making a lot more money, and we only go out once a week, we don't want to over-fish. Everything so far is going well,' he said.

'I'm sure you appreciate the situation is not going to last forever, at some stage the authorities will catch up with you,' I said.

'I am very aware of that, and don't intend to continue too long. I know the crew will get caught, it is just a matter of when. I will remain here until you two have done what you need to do, I will wait here until you return to your own time, taking care of the Pathway, then I have my own destiny to consider. I have put enough aside to make me a rich man on the mainland, which is my intention. I will remain in this time as a wealthy man, an aristocrat of the seventeenth century. My stash is hidden on the mainland, I am the only one who knows where it is. Once I have seen you two off, then I will leave and set myself up somewhere on the mainland. I intend to stay in this time, it suits me very well. Most of the people in this time are illiterate, and an educated man, which I think I am, can make a fortune. Think of all the simple discoveries there are to be made, things that in your time you take for granted. I could become a renowned inventor,' he said.

I thought it an interesting career move, from pirate to inventor. The strange thing was that he was right: anyone with an education had the chance to do great things, so perhaps his intention to stay was not such a bad idea.

Once the noise had died down we walked to Landon's hut, he quickly went inside and returned with the Pathway. We then went to the island slipway. Colin and I agreed to meet at his house on our arrival through the portal.

Alan asked us if we were ready for our next journey. I had never been more ready, this flying visit was the ideal situation, the couple of hours' stay on the island was plenty for me. The date was set for 3rd March 1981, our return date was 17th March 1981. We nodded to indicate that we were ready, Alan pressed the appropriate button, and the storm began to build as the usual downpour of rain started. The portal suddenly loomed in front of us, we shook hands with Alan, stating we were going to see him again on our return, and walked into the future.

I arrived on the mainland side of the beach, on the rocks fortunately as the tide was in and the beach itself was underwater. I was glad to land where I did, it was a small mercy. I walked up into the village, I noticed the small stores had different names above their doors. This was strange, as in our present Colin said these places had been owned by the same families since the war. But it was not important, there was more important issues in this time.

I walked to Colin's house, and saw torchlight inside. I hoped it was Colin and not a burglar as I knocked on the door. Fortunately he answered the door, he had laid out two sleeping bags on the floor; he had purchased these in 1941, he was good at thinking ahead. We did not say much, it was just after midnight, and we both settled as best we could to sleep. The sleeping bags were quite warm.

I awoke next morning quite refreshed, I had slept very well. Colin was already up and about, sorting through his suitcase, it had survived time intact. He had checked the floor of the cellar, and it had not been tampered with. The good news was that our fortune under the floor was as we left it.

He suggested we change into something smart to visit the bank. We both hoped our accounts had flourished in the 40 years since we last saw them. Once we had done this we intended to move to the hotel on the island. That was to be our base for this part of our journey. We expected our base to be of the highest quality; it certainly was in 1941.

Colin said he was going to explain the plan over a long lunch at the hotel. That sounded ideal, both the hotel and the lunch. He wanted to talk about selling the paintings, timing was everything in the art world. I was ignorant of such matters, but I was sure he was right. I thought the plan was a good one.

But I told Colin that I hoped nobody recognized him at the hotel. He thought for a moment before answering, but after 40 years he doubted that.

We then walked over to the bank, and I explained to the manager about the account, mentioning the letter that had been left, and giving him the codeword which appeared in the letter. He checked the letter, which I had left only a few days ago, although the envelope had obviously been locked away for 40 years. He checked the information I had given him, and compared my signature with the signature I had left. He was satisfied to allow me access to the account; the relevant cards would be available for me in a few days. Colin went through the same process and was given access to his account.

Both accounts had accumulated a vast amount of interest. Having drawn large amounts of cash from each account we headed towards the hotel, happy that we had money at our disposal, and extremely happy with the interest earned. I requested the letter remained with the account for the foreseeable future, the manager was slightly puzzled but agreed to my request.

Colin was confident he was not going to be remembered at the hotel. The lady on reception was pleased to see us, as the hotel did very little business in March. She looked at Colin closely.

Have you stayed at the hotel before?' she asked.

He looked a little sheepish.

'I stayed here some years ago,' said Colin.

'You do look vaguely familiar,' she said.

'How long have you worked at the hotel?' he asked.

Her reply shocked both of us. 'I started here in 1940 at the age of seventeen, I am due to retire in a few years,' she said.

She pointed to an old photograph on the wall, pointing herself out. It was the receptionist from Colin's past, the young blonde lady he had his final fling with. It had to be said she had a good memory; maybe Colin was particularly memorable to his harem. I saw the resemblance to the lady from 1941, it was indeed one of his conquests. No wonder she thought she knew him, she actually knew him very well.

On seeing the photograph Colin's jaw dropped as he realized

who she was. I was tempted to ask if she had ever been in films, but he was sweating enough.

I asked if anyone else had been working at the hotel as long as she had, and she said the manager had started as a bellboy. It was good this was a male member of staff, not many of the females had got through Colin's net. I thought he was on safe ground with the manager, it was unlikely the bellboy was going to remember him.

We booked in and went to the bar.

'You are aware who that receptionist is?' I said.

'Of course I do, she's worked behind that desk for forty years. I have no intention of rekindling any relationship with her, just in case you decide to ask,' he said.

'You're only saying that because she has aged, not very gallant of you,' I said.

'I have decided to mention that my father stayed here in the 1940s, just in case she twigs what sort of relationship we had. I think she will fall for that, she is unlikely to think I am the one she slept with.'

'I think she is an attractive woman for her age,' I said.

'I do not wish to rekindle any relationship with her, let that be the end of the matter,' he said.

Around the bar area were photographs depicting the hotel in 1941. Several of images were familiar to us; it was only a few days ago when we were in that time. Some of the ladies pictured brought nostalgic memories for Colin.

'How fortunate there are no photographs of the guests at the time,' I said.

'I don't think that's funny, can you imagine if we both appeared together on their wall in 1941?' he said.

He changed the subject, wanting to discuss the plan to save John's wife Ann. At this moment in time it was a week before the accident, and we had all the relevant details to prevent the accident. At least we thought we had, that was why the week's stay before the accident was so important. It gave us the opportunity to check out John's address in Plymouth. We had the details of the car Ann was going to be driving, if we saw it in the driveway of the address which we believed to be John's house, that in itself was a step in the right direction. All these details had to be verified before we helped in the prevention of the accident.

I appreciated that we had changed the past in 1941: we had intercepted the document Colin's father was going to pass to the Germans, therefore changing what had been. Colin asked if I still had the document we had recovered from that time. I said I did, but it was in my other jacket. We were not sure how important that document was, he felt it probably had little importance on the outcome of the war, just a small part in the jigsaw.

To travel to Plymouth, we needed to hire a car. Hiring a car under normal circumstances was considered an easy process, but required a driving licence. I mentioned this small factor to Colin. He had thought through every conceivable problem, and when obtaining our identity cards from his forger friend, he appreciated a driving licence was a possibility and a requirement in this time, these were added to the forged documents he carried in his pouch. I kept underestimating his prowess.

We sat and discussed the plan in detail. We were to wait outside the address and check if Ann left the house on a regular basis. He had told us she did not work, therefore it was logical to expect her at home most days. It was not feasible to knock on the door to check if John lived there, neither of us knew what Ann looked like, we therefore had to wait for him to come home from work. John was not likely to recognize us, as of course in 1981 he had never met us.

We knew the time and date of the accident, John said he had left the house to go shopping, Ann was meeting him for lunch; this meeting of course never took place. The accident itself was about half a mile from the house, she had pulled out of a junction when a speeding car hit her. She stood little chance of surviving the collision. The driver of this car was drunk.

We had somehow to delay her reaching that junction at that time, if she arrived later the drunken driver was going to be well past the scene. The question was how to delay her; even a few minutes was crucial. Colin said were to go to one of these back street car dealers, purchase an old banger, give false details to the dealer, and use this old car as a diversionary tactic. He had meticulously thought through the problem. I was concerned about the old banger: before we used it in the plan, I did not want anyone to see me driving it. He said we had to find an out-of-the-way place near John's address to park up the old banger until we needed it, keeping it out of the way of prying eyes. We needed to purchase something that even the most desperate of thieves were unlikely to steal.

We decided to check out John's house the following day after a hearty breakfast. Colin went to reception to arrange to hire a car, stating quite categorically that was the reason for seeing the receptionist. Why he felt he had to say that I did not know. I watched him approach the desk.

He was speaking to her and she was watching him very closely, her mind was working overtime trying to place this man before her. Even from a distance I saw he was very nervous, no doubt remembering with affection their last encounter. I was hoping we were going to complete our mission and be gone before everything clicked into place for her. He left her still wondering. This was going to be a long week, I felt at some point she was going to remember the face, or possibly some other part of his anatomy.

We had dinner and then sat in the bar, tomorrow had the makings of an interesting day, seeing John 20 years before I had met him; travelling through time brought up strange situations. The evening was quiet by Colin's previous standards, for although there were young ladies working at the hotel, he was reluctant to take on his 1941 role. I think Colin might have taken on that persona had there not been someone still working there from 1941; he felt it prudent not to push his luck.

The car Colin had booked awaited us on the mainland, and

we quickly made our way there after breakfast. It was of little use going directly to the house as John was at work until late afternoon. We decided to run pass the house to check if the car was outside, then the rest of the day was to be spent shopping in Plymouth. We found Eliot Street with relative ease, we also located house number 32, but there was no car in the driveway, although the property did possess a garage. Maybe John had taken the car to work, we decided to return later to see him come home.

We returned to Eliot Street at about 4 p.m., not sure when John finished work. We sat in our hired vehicle, a short distance from the house. It was just after 5 p.m. when someone walked down the road. He was more sprightly than the man I knew as John, and it was soon to become apparent why I thought that: our plan was about to be shattered. He approached the door of number 32, which was opened as he approached. The lady was obviously his wife Ann; they kissed and he went inside. But to our dismay, we saw that this man was not John.

Both Colin and I looked at each other, both realizing at the same moment that we were at the wrong house. This situation concerned us: John could be living anywhere in Plymouth, it was a large city; it was also possible that he had moved out of Plymouth completely.

'If John does not live there any more, surely Ann was not going to be involved in the accident we are trying to prevent?' I said.

'I agree to a certain extent, but to help John we need to be certain that Ann cannot be at the location of the accident, and to do that we must find out where they live. We have the opportunity to solve this. We have to assume the drunk driver is the same person, as well as assuming the location of the accident is the same, and we have to ensure Ann does not meet with the drunk at the location of the accident on the day in question. It is vital we do not leave it to chance, we must know where they live. Let's assume they have moved but still live near their old address. Ann might take the original route to town, which means she is still likely to be involved in the collision. We must know for sure. I think the only way to check is to visit the council offices, check the voters' register,' he said.

He pulled out his War Office identity card from 1941, which was not dated. It was possible to use it in this time, and it had the potential to impress the council officers.

That was the plan, he was to approach the council the next morning, stating it was a case of national security that we trace this man.

The council offices were situated in the town centre. We were dressed in our dark suits which would help to make the appropriate impression. Colin entered first, and showed his identity card to the young lady behind the counter. She was visibly shocked and asked us to wait while she called the manager of the office. We sat down in the foyer of the building, Colin looking around with the air of importance, this was his film director look with the addition of 'look how high-ranking I am'; it was very charismatic, he had perfected this look to a magnificent degree.

The manager arrived quickly; the receptionist had obviously mentioned the words 'War Office' to him, not an everyday occurrence at Plymouth Council Offices. He introduced himself as Nathan King. Colin showed his identity card to him, then looked around to make sure nobody else was listening.

When the manager asked how he was able to help, he lowered his voice, and Colin nodded at him to signify he recognized his discretion in this matter. I was of the belief this manager was an idiot, and Colin used that to his advantage. I looked on and tried hard not to laugh, it was like something from a spy movie, Colin acting as the spy, the manager his secret contact. It was a very bizarre situation.

We told him there was a person who we believed lived in Plymouth that we were trying to contact as a matter of urgency. We were able to do it through official channels but that was likely to cause great embarrassment to both the person in question and the government. We said that Nathan King's assistance in this matter would be noted, and we would pass our praise on to both his superiors and people in the government who were in a position to assist his career prospects. He confirmed he understood what we were saying, which is more than I did.

We walked through to the lift, his office was on the sixth floor of the building. Within ten minutes we had two possible addresses for John, both near to his original address. We shook hands with our host, asking him not to mention to anyone else about this visit. He might receive a letter from Downing Street thanking him for his assistance, but as far as anyone else is concerned we had not been here.

He said he understood, which again confused me. How on earth did he understand? But he was glad to help his country, he was a true patriot.

I wished we might have the opportunity to visit Mr King again, he had entertained me greatly on that visit. I wondered if he would discuss the day with his wife, how he had helped government officials on a matter of national security.

We left quickly on receiving the information. Colin had given a sterling performance, and I was almost convinced he was a spy. The manager had accepted his persona without question, it had made his day. Colin was mildly amused.

Both addresses were near to the Eliot Street address, but the similarity did not stop there: both were on the route Ann was likely to take to pick him up John from work. We needed to locate John's house and prevent Ann making that appointment. Although some things had changed for some unknown reason, we had to assume the accident had not, and we had the power to prevent this disaster happening. I had no idea why John's address had changed from the one he told Colin about, I assumed it had something to do with the changes we made in 1941, although minor it possibly changed the future, in this case John's address.

We went to the first address just before 5 p.m., again there was no car in the driveway but this house also had a garage. We needed to check out the premises again, hoping the car was to appear from the garage. As we looked down the street we saw a man walking towards the house; it was John, no doubt about it. He walked to the front door of the house we were watching. He opened the door with his key and disappeared inside. We had the right house, but had not found the car. We checked the street again to see if the car was parked, we even checked nearby streets.

Time was on our side, there was almost a week before the accident. We scouted the area for a back street car dealer, and to my surprise there were many. We purchased a car with ease and parked it behind some garages on a piece of waste ground. We felt this vehicle was in too bad a state to be stolen.

Our decision to return the following day was a good one. We sat in the hire car just up the road and watched John leave the house, no doubt off to work. He was starting later than we had anticipated, and he did not use the car. Our long wait was rewarded when Ann left the house and went to the garage. When she opened the garage door, there was the car we had hoped was going to be there. The make and registration checked out. This helped us in the plan we had devised. All was due to happen in three days' time.

Ann drove off, and we decided to follow her, just to check on who she visited. She travelled only a few streets away, and she was met at the house she was visiting by another lady. There were several cars in this driveway; it had the look of a coffee morning. We decided not to stop outside, and we returned to the hotel, confident that our planning had been worthwhile.

We celebrated in the hotel bar, knowing the second part of our adventure was about to come to fruition. Our plan was hopefully going to save Ann, but it would also take John out of our lives. I was happy that we were going to help him, although in fact he was never going to know that. That was the beauty of the time travel aspect, nobody had to say thank you for what we did for them, they were oblivious that anything had been done.

But Colin also wanted us to divert to another time, and I took the opportunity to broach the subject of the other trip he wanted to take, the trip he said he needed me for, that was as important as saving Ann. He was happy to tell me now that our other preparations were in hand.

He started saying how important it was to him; it was a part of his life that he had not yet divulged to me, and in fact not many people knew about what happened in 1985, the time that he wanted to revisit: 1985 was particularly sad for him. He was married at the time and living in Plymouth, he had just moved there from a solicitors' firm in London. It was a golden opportunity to run his own business, which was doing well. He lived in a big house with his wife Helen and his daughter, although at the time his daughter was at university, so there were only two of them in the house. That particular point was to become very important in the story.

He had several well-to-do friends, and inviting each other to their houses for dinner parties became the norm, once a week they were either entertaining or being entertained. One night they were due to go to a friend's house, but Helen said she felt unwell, so unwell she did not want to go. She insisted that he went as the person hosting the party was important to his business. Reluctantly he decided to go. He made sure she was tucked up in bed before he left. He telephoned his friend to say his wife was not attending but he would be there on his own. He then said to his host he was just leaving.

When he left the house he realized he needed to purchase some wine to take to the dinner party. He went to the off licence and bought the wine then drove to the party; he did not drink too much as he had to drive home.

He arrived home just before midnight, walked into the house as quietly as possible, not wanting to disturb his wife Helen, he went straight to the bedroom. To his surprise his wife was not in bed, he checked the bathroom but he was unable to find her. He shouted out her name but there was no response, he decided she must have gone downstairs. He was shocked when he went into the study: Helen was lying on the floor in a pool of blood from a head wound. He checked her pulse but it was obvious she was dead. It was the most devastating moment of his life. He called the police, who arrived within minutes with a doctor. He confirmed life was extinct.

There was a small safe in the study, which was open. They had kept some money in the safe and items of his wife's jewellery, the more expensive pieces, but nothing was missing. He had no idea why the safe was open and nothing valuable had been taken, although Helen kept some paperwork in there but he never assumed it was of value to anyone but her. The only thing that was missing was a diary of his mother's, she had given it to Helen for safe-keeping, as his mother did not possess a safe. He had no idea what was in the diary, it was personal to his mother.

The story Colin had told me about his first wife was sad; I had not realized Jane was his second wife.

'May I offer my sympathy, I had no idea what you had been through. From what you say it appears your wife was killed by a burglar, who appeared to have stolen something with no intrinsic value. The only value it had was to the family. You have every reason for wanting to revisit this time, and I am happy to help you in any way I can,' I said.

'Although the time of death couldn't be pinpointed, most such cases are of a domestic nature. I was unable to prove I had bought the bottle of wine. Not that it was likely to prove very much, but I thought it might show I was telling the truth. There was no CCTV inside the premises and I paid in cash, the place was very busy at the time, the clerk was unable to remember me.'

'Were you arrested for the crime?' I said.

He was, being the prime suspect. He was unable to prove conclusively where he was for about 20 minutes after leaving the house, there was no one to back up his claim that he was buying wine. The friends told the police when he arrived at the party, they were being honest about that. Whoever committed the crime was careful not to leave any prints, everything pointed to Colin.

Even though he was completely innocent, the sequence of events conspired against him.

His ordeal with the police was frightening. He was held in custody for several days, they questioned him time and time again, he kept repeating the same story: that was the truth, it was the only story he had. Believing him to be the guilty party, they were keen to get a confession from him, but eventually they had to let him go as there was no real evidence against him. They did not carry out enquiries into anyone else, so the real murderer got away with it.

That was the reason for this next trip, he wanted to find out who murdered his wife, and why they took that diary. He wanted to check the diary, as it was obviously significant in his wife's death.

'Did your daughter believe your story? I only say that because I want to know all the facts, not because I think you did it. I'm confident you are innocent,' I said.

'She believed what I told her, she accepted I would not harm her mother. I was grateful she was not in the house at the time; if she had been perhaps the police would have been dealing with a double murder. I tried to get the police to continue with their enquiries, but they did not want to waste resources when they suspected who the murderer was. All this upset made me decide to move away; the memories of my wife and the fact that nobody believed me,' he said.

'It must have been a terrible ordeal for you, but surely the dinner guests supported you, they were your friends. How did they react?' I said.

'I tried to contact several of them afterwards, none of them wanted to talk to me. The police had put doubt in their minds and they thought I had done it.'

'I understand how important it is for you to clear your name, as well as finding out who killed your wife.'

'There is one more important aspect of this trip. If I save my wife as I hope we will, I will be remaining in that time, I will not be returning with you to the island. I know you look at me in 1941 and think me a philanderer, but when my wife was around I never looked at another woman.'

Strangely enough, I believed him.

'I have discussed the situation with Alan, who will meet you on your return and help you back to your own time. I will be waiting for you on your return to your time, a little older and a little greyer. There is another problem to address if all goes well in 1985: we need to sell the paintings in that time, I would prefer not to wait fifteen years for my share, I hope you understand that?' he said.

'I understand, if you're rich you want to spend it. We can deal with that when we arrive, once we have preserved your marriage,' I said.

'I know someone in the art world, he works at an auction house in London, and would be delighted to get his hands on our pieces of art, for commission of course. The proceeds of the sale would also give you fifteen years of interest at the bank,' he said.

We decided to plan for a longer stay, possibly a month, in 1985. It would take that long to organize an auction for such tremendous pieces of art. Colin was to see to the auction side of the venture.

I was a little concerned about Jane, but if Colin remained in 1985 she was never going to meet him anyway, and with her looks she was never going to be short of suitors. Colin's first wife Helen was obviously the love of his life.

I did not think for one minute that Colin was a murderer, and going to that time was going to prove that point beyond doubt. Once again we had the date and approximate time of the incident, and there was no reason why this incident was not preventable with that information. I felt the police had to be involved, but I needed to persuade him of that fact; this was the difficulty, as after his experience he was unlikely to have confidence in the police. This situation needed meticulous planning, that was a certainty.

The following morning at 8 a.m. we were sitting in our hired car a short distance from John's home address. We decided to watch the routine at the house: when he went to work, whether or not Ann left the house, where she went, whether it was near to the location of the accident. John had told Colin that on the day in question he had been shopping in the town, he had apparently taken the day off to buy his wife a birthday present. I thought that was a nice thing to do, and wondered what he had bought her. Ann was going to meet him for lunch. She did not make the appointment, we now knew the reason.

Our concern was that we did not know if she had come from the house to meet him, or if she had visited a friend first. Colin had not asked him those questions at the time, which under the circumstances was unfortunate. But it was unlikely he knew those details, it was not something he could ask her after the accident. If she left the house tomorrow before the planned time, Colin had another plan up his sleeve, this was to deliberately collide with her car; drastic, but a necessary action.

We decided to stay parked for four hours, a long but we felt necessary time span. Fortunately the heater worked as we sat there, without that heat the vigil may well have been abandoned. We watched John leave the house just after 8.30 a.m., to take the short bus ride to his place of work. Ann saw him off, then returned inside the house.

About 30 minutes later she emerged from the house, went to the garage and reversed the car onto the road. We followed as she drove away, stopping outside a house some three miles away, this was no doubt one of her friends. She was greeted at the door and went inside. We waited patiently outside, at least we had something different to look at now.

About an hour later she returned home and parked the car in the garage. We waited outside until midday, but there was no more movement from the house. We returned to the hotel.

We decided to arrive at the house early the following day. We had to track her movements: no matter what, she was not to be at the junction at the time of the accident, we had to do what was necessary to prevent that happening. If she took the car out we had to be prepared to ram her car at some stage, not forcefully but just a gentle knock that was going to cause her to stop. If she remained at home then the old banger was to come into operation, something I was not looking forward to.

The following morning we had our breakfast early again, leaving the hotel just after 7 a.m. This was the day, the day we were going to prevent the death of another human being. We only had one shot at it.

We arrived at John's house just before 8 a.m., knowing that John was not leaving for work today, and that he did not take the car to go shopping. The old banger we had purchased was only 50 yards away. We had checked it before turning up in the street, the engine started all right; how long it was going to last was another problem. When the time for his wife to depart got closer, I was to pick up the vehicle and park it across her driveway.

John left the house about 10.30 a.m. Not long to wait now, I thought. I hoped our plan was going to work, there were a multitude of reasons why it could fail, but we had done all within our power to bring success. It was now a matter of waiting. We estimated Ann would leave just before midday. The junction was a couple of minutes away and we knew the accident happened at 12.05 p.m., which was what the police report said according to John.

As it approached midday I went to pick up the old banger. I had made sure I left no fingerprints, wearing gloves every time I went near the vehicle. There was no DNA testing at this time to connect me with the vehicle. I parked the car right across the driveway of John's house, making sure there was no room for the car to get out. I removed the keys, locked the driver's door, looked around to ensure there was nobody about, then walked quickly down the road to join Colin, who opened the door for me.

We only waited for about a minute before Ann appeared at the front door. She saw the old banger instantly. Fortunately we were unable to hear what she was saying but the air was no doubt blue. She walked down to the car, to see if she was able to pass it safely. Realizing it was not possible she walked to a neighbour's house. Our delaying tactics were working. A gentleman from next door came out, and tried to open the locked driver's door. He then went to the passenger's door. I had forgotten to lock that door. He climbed inside and released the handbrake and then pushed the vehicle forward; it was a slow process. When eventually the car was clear of the driveway, Ann went to her garage to get her car. It was now 12.10 p.m.; hopefully we had saved her life.

Colin decided to follow the car as it pulled out onto the road, we wanted to be sure the mission had been successful. We followed the car to the junction where the collision took place, she came out of the junction safely and we followed. About 100 yards along the road we saw a car crashed into a tree. The police were handcuffing what I assumed was the driver. Was this the driver who had killed Ann in a different time? We had no way of knowing. It was too much of a coincidence not to be the offending driver. I felt we had successfully completed our mission.

Ann parked her car in a large car park in the city centre, and we parked nearby. John was there to meet her, a meeting we had made possible. I expect she was telling him about the idiot who had parked in front of the driveway. That idiot had in fact saved her life, not that she knew that, or was every likely to know. We were happy with the result of our day's work.

I knew this meant John was not going to be at Ruby Bay on my return, and it was starting to look as if Colin would be absent as well. Who was I going to share my adventures with? He said that he was likely to remember it, because he was a traveller who stopped off, unlike John who had not travelled. But I was returning to my time alone, although Colin had promised to be there on my return.

There were still five days before we returned to the island, this time scale we had no control over. The following day, 12th March,

I decided to take a trip to the nearby village. Colin wanted to relax at the hotel. On arrival in the village I was interested whether it had changed since 1941. There were buildings I still recognized, externally they were the same, but no doubt internally they were very different.

As I made my way along the High Street I was taken by surprise: Merrydown Estate Agents was still there. Was I to see an elderly lady running the place? I was reluctant at first to go in. I looked through the window and saw a young lady at the desk. She was the image of Julie, no doubt a close relative, and she was about 20 years of age. I decided to go into the shop, it was like going back in time.

The young lady approached me as I entered.

'Do you need any help, are you looking for property in the area?' she said.

She had all the mannerisms I associated with Julie. I then started to tell a story, making it up as I went along.

'My father was in the area during the war, he told me he met a Julie Merrydown. Was this lady a relative of yours?' I enquired.

'The Julie Merrydown during the war was my grandmother.'

'You really do look like her,' I said.

'How would you know that?' she replied.

'My father had a photograph of her, he showed me it,' I said.

'My grandmother always said I looked like her in her younger days.'

'Is it possible to meet your grandmother? My father only had good things to say about her,' I said.

'I'm sorry, my grandmother died two years ago, she was seventy-four years old. I still miss her. She used to tell me stories from the war, especially the one when the bomb dropped in Ruby Bay. It was the only one for the whole of the war. She said it was probably a mistake by Hitler. She relived that story many times, but I didn't mind,' she said.

'Did your grandmother ever mention the two men she met at the hotel?'

'She liked telling that story, one of them pretended to be a film director, the other one she liked a lot, they both worked for some department of the government.'

'My father was one of those two men: not the film director. He often talked about your grandmother, I think he had a soft spot for her. He said she dined at the hotel with both of them on many occasions, did she mention that?'

'She did, but I got the impression she did not like the way one of them behaved, it was the one pretending to be a film director, I think he was called Colin. He was trying to impress the ladies of the hotel, by all accounts he was a bit of a scoundrel,' she said.

What a lovely description of him, 'a bit of a scoundrel'!

'I presume your grandmother married? I'm sure my father said she was single when they met.'

'She married an army officer just after the war, she was forty at the time. The war meant that there weren't many eligible bachelors. I think she always hoped your father would return, but he never did. She told me your father was called Pat, is that correct?'

'He was, and he was close friends with Colin, the one your grandmother didn't like,' I said.

She smiled at that comment.

'From what I have learned about 1941 people were supposed to be very reserved, it appears they did not behave like this chap Colin. She said she had a thing for Pat, they seemed to have spent a lot of time together. She said they were both Navy officers, quite high ranking I believe. Your father left after a few weeks, she believed he went abroad to help the war effort. She never heard from him again, she assumed he had been killed. She always thought he was coming back, once the war was over. He promised her he would return, and she believed him. She thought they might marry if he returned, but that is history now. In her mind the reason he did not return was obvious, he had been killed. But I assume your father lived through the war, is that right?'

'Yes he did, like you he told me a similar story.'

'She tried to find out if he had been killed, to no avail. She got a surname from the register at the hotel, at least a surname she thought it might have been, people did not always fill in the register, so the task of checking if he was a casualty was impossible. She told me it broke her heart when he never returned, I think he was the love of her life,' she said.

On hearing the tale I was saddened, but what option did I have? I had to move forward, sad but true.

'Are you the present owner of the business? I thought maybe your mother was. I'm glad to see it bears the Merrydown name, my father would have been pleased about that,' I said.

'What about your father, he is still alive?' she asked.

'Sadly not, he passed away a few years ago, shame they could not have met up again,' I said.

'As far as this business is concerned, my mother is the owner. Although my grandmother married a Browning, she decided to keep the name Merrydown, I think it was because her father had started it, she wanted his name to remain.'

'What about your grandfather, is he still alive?'

'No, he died about ten years ago, killed in a car accident. I never really got on with him very well, he was too military, a retired colonel, and he never stopped ordering us around. He was very strict towards all the family, even though my mother was not his child.'

Suddenly a beacon lit up in my mind. Had I just heard correctly?

'Did you say your grandfather was not your grandfather by blood?' I asked.

'That's right, my mother was born many years before my grandmother married. She would never say who my grandfather actually was, no doubt some wartime romance, and maybe she just wanted to forget the person, we will never know now,' she said.

'What was the year of your mother's birth?'

'I know what you're thinking, maybe it was your father Pat, and if that was the case you are related to our family. But maybe that's why she said nothing, she had a drunken affair with someone she didn't like, possibly this Colin guy. If that was the case she would have wanted to forget it, maybe that's why she didn't tell anyone,' she said.

'I shouldn't think it was him. If she didn't like him surely that would have been that,' I said.

I felt it necessary to protect Colin, who on this occasion was the innocent party, something unlikely for the 1941 Colin.

'I think it was likely to be someone she did not know very well, a sort of one-night stand. My mother was born in December 1941, and I think if it was your father she would have advertised the fact, rather than want to keep it quiet. My grandmother always said he was a gentleman, perhaps he would have been a candidate if he was not such a gentleman.'

She referred to Colin more than this Pat, nobody was sure if she had an affair with either of them. In those days people were usually married before anything like that went on, but her mother was born during the war.

This came as quite a shock. I was sure I knew who the father was. This was possibly my granddaughter. A DNA test could prove it, but did I want to do that, I thought? I understood why she thought Colin might be her grandfather, simply because her grandmother did not want to talk about it did not to me seem a good reason, but it was in her eyes; perhaps Julie had said nothing to throw them off the scent. I would have thought Julie would have advertised the fact her lover was a Royal Navy commander, but obviously there was a reason for her silence, one we will never know. This was indeed a revelation, an incredible shock.

'It has been a great pleasure to meet you, my name is Pat, after my father.'

'My name is Juliette, my mother and grandmother were christened Julie, mine is a variation, it is not supposed to confuse anyone, but it does,' she said.

My mind was racing. It appeared I was related to this beautiful young lady; the question was, what was I going to do about it?

'I'm sorry I cannot meet the man who stole my grandmother's heart,' she said.

She had no idea how close he was.

'Why don't you come back when my mother is here, she will be so pleased to meet you. She knows more about my grandmother's life,' she said.

'Perhaps I will come back, thank you for your time, Juliette,' I said.

But in all honesty I knew I had lots to think about before possibly meeting my daughter. I said my farewells and left the shop, a little disappointed that the Julie I knew was no longer with us. But what if she was still alive? What would her reaction have been if she saw me after 40 years and I had not shown any sign of ageing?

It was probably best that I discussed the whole situation with Colin, he was the most likely to understand, he was the only one who was there in 1941. How was he going to react to this news? I decided to return to the hotel to pass on the story to him, leaving out the bit about Julie thinking little of his escapades. But perhaps that was what he was doing now, casting for yet another film. They always say use methods that are tried and tested, he did very well last time he directed a film.

He was where I expected him to be, sitting in the bar, looking out the window towards the mainland and watching the people on the beach. He greeted me as I entered the bar; he had seen me crossing from the mainland.

I told him I had been to the next village, just to check on the changes in the last 40 years. He knew that was not my motive, but he did not comment.

'I met Julie's granddaughter. The shop is still there, it is the same business bearing the same name, it was a surprise to see it had survived,' I said.

'Was Julie there?' he said.

'No, sadly she died a couple of years ago, she was quite elderly remember. Her granddaughter is the image of her, but Julie's daughter was not there.'

'Did Julie just have the one child?' he said.

'Yes only the one child. I need your advice on something I was told. She married an Army officer, he died ten years ago. They were married in 1947, and at that time Julie had a six-year old daughter, also called Julie.'

I waited patiently for what I had said to register.

'Imagine if she had still been alive, the sight of you would have killed her. Did you think of that when you visited the shop?'

'You're right, I'm glad I didn't have to put her through that. I think she had a good life, she appeared to be well loved by her granddaughter, Juliette. But I think maybe you have missed the point about what I just said.'

Then like a bolt of lightning it struck him. He suddenly appreciated what I had said.

'Are you saying Julie's daughter was born in 1941?'

I nodded, and he looked stunned. He was now looking at the ceiling, I knew he was thinking about his next comment, it did not take long.

'Are we saying you have a daughter in Ruby Bay?' he said.

'Julie's daughter was born in December 1941, it fits into the time we were here, it fits in perfectly to the time I was having a relationship with Julie, so I think she may be my daughter. If that is the case I also have a granddaughter, the girl I met today.'

I thought, knowing him as I did, that he was likely to break into laughter at this point. But he did not, his face was serious, he was starting to see the implications.

'You've done very well, you arrive back in this time and find you have a complete family. Does the daughter know who her father is?'

'From what Juliette said, she had always refused to name him. It was assumed it was someone she met during the war, a wild fling or something. Although Julie mentioned both of us to her daughter, I did not appear in either her daughter or granddaughter's eyes to be a candidate. Juliette mentioned who she thought the most likely candidate was, a one-night stand or something, but we know different from that,' I said.

'It is possible you are not the father, but we both knew Julie, she was unlikely to have a casual affair. Do you think you are the father?' he said.

'I think it is very likely, although I had not known her that long. Perhaps she did have casual affairs, something that she hid from us, although our relationship was far from casual. I still believe I am the parent, and I am not sure how to handle this problem, if in fact I need to handle it. What difference am I likely to make to their lives? They have managed without me for forty years. What do you think I should do?' I said.

'You have not considered the bigger picture. We know we should not change history in any way, yet here we are with two people on this planet, who had not been in the other 1981, this is pretty huge in the sequence of events. In twenty years' time Juliette could have four grown-up children who are married with children; you have caused possibly ten people to be born who had never existed until you appeared in 1941. It is the ripple effect on the water, the ripple gets bigger as it travels outward. We thought if John changed his address then history had been changed, that is insignificant in comparison.'

He was of course right, there were two people in this time that were not supposed to be here, and it was all down to me.

The saving of Colin's father meant he was likely to still be around, the father he never knew, but 40 years older of course. That person was not supposed to be in this time, and that in itself had changed time.

We decided the next few days were to be spent checking out Colin's home address; just as John's address had changed, maybe his had as well. It was his way of taking my mind off a situation I had to deal with at some stage, but we had something else to do first.

These influences on events were all very strange and a bit

spooky. I knew from our experiences over the last few days that Colin's address may have changed, but I really hoped not; I did not fancy visiting the Council Offices again, impressive though Colin was. I assumed the burglar who had killed his wife Helen had chosen his house because it was large, although as nothing much was taken, it was a strange type of burglary.

'I wonder about the burglary at my house. Do you think I may have been the target, and Helen was in the wrong place at the wrong time? Maybe it was me they were after,' he said.

'It is possible, you being a solicitor. Had you ever been involved in any dodgy deals?'

'Not at all, I only dealt with mortgages. I was not a criminal solicitor. There are no skeletons in my cupboard.'

'It seems it was the diary they were after. I think the burglary was going to happen no matter where you lived.'

He was still desperately trying to work out the reason for the burglary, four years before the crime was committed. I was not sure it was a viable proposition, but he was adamant there was nothing in his past that made him a target for a burglar, the diary was the secret to the break-in. Why was the diary was so important, Colin said he did not know.

We had changed history to quite a degree, and perhaps that change had affected his business dealings as well, but at the time of the burglary he was dealing only with conveyancing. We thought it was a good idea to visit his business premises to check his files, just in case he was involved in a different type of business.

He was concerned his secretary was likely to notice a difference in him; merely stating he had had a hard day was not going to account for fifteen years of ageing. He decided to tell her he was wearing makeup for a fancy dress party he was going to that evening.

We decided to sit up outside the building he thought was his house, hoping to see himself come home from work, then we knew the burglary was going to take place at that property. Colin was very nervous at seeing himself, and he informed me that in the laws of time travel the two of them must never meet. I did not ask him how he knew that, I think he saw it in a Science Fiction film, but it did sound logical.

'If you turn up in 1985, what happens to the Colin that was already there? I assume there is only one Colin, although many years older. Is it like the island and the monk who keeps disappearing, only to return when the traveller leaves? Will you become the younger Colin or remain your present age? Why are we waiting for the other Colin to come home, surely you have automatically taken his place by being here? Do you know how this situation works?' I asked.

I was confused about what was happening; I believed there was only one of us in each time scale.

'I think the other Colin will turn up. I will explain that if the other me turns up,' he said.

'If your theory is correct, I also existed somewhere in this time, although in this time I was away from Plymouth, serving in the police,' I said.

A car appeared in the street, Colin's car. We had a clear view of the driveway as he pulled in. The door opened slowly, and sure enough, it was a younger version of himself.

We returned to the hotel to discuss the situation. There had to be a way for Colin to take over the younger one's identity on our next visit in 1985. He said he knew how, once our Colin appeared to someone he knew in that time, the other Colin ceased to exist, our Colin took over until he returned to the island. This problem needed careful thought, we intended to go forward four years and save his wife, and he really had to be there to help, so the timing needed to be correct.

Colin said Alan had told him he was able to take over his former life, an explanation for this was as we had just discussed, but how did Alan know that?

'There is very little else we can do now, the burglary is not for another four years. The most important thing was to locate your house, we have done that. The changing into the other Colin is less convincing, maybe Alan can advise us, although I could see no reason why he would know, he has never left the island,' I said.

'Although Alan has never left the island, he knows the deed inside out, he studied it for several weeks before he came here, so perhaps he found what we need to know,' he said.

He agreed, he thought Alan was able to discuss it more fully, he had checked the deed before leaving on his trip, he knew the deeds better than Colin.

For now, he was intent on enjoying the next couple of days, and he promised to enjoy them without becoming a film director, although he was at pains to point out he never said he was a film director, the ladies made that assumption from the rumour he started. This time I believed him, with good reason: the receptionist would recognize this ploy instantly, the memories of his prowess would come back to her, then his past was in the open for all the guests to see. He had without doubt acted as a blackguard in his previous life.

I suspected he still fancied the receptionist, as he spent a lot of time looking in her direction. I think if the opportunity arose he was almost certain to be tempted. The terms 'scoundrel' and 'lecherous cad' will always in my mind be associated with my travelling companion.

We dined early and sat in the bar discussing what had happened in a short spell of time. Tomorrow we would return to the island of the past, hopefully for only a short spell. The island had bad memories for me: the sea voyages, the terrible conditions those people lived in. But there were good memories too: a young lady of easy virtue was the best aspect of the trip.

I looked towards the reception area, and there was Julie in all her glory. I stood up as she walked towards the table. Colin looked around and his mouth opened. We were both shocked to see her. As she walked towards us, I was speechless.

'Which one of you gentlemen called on my daughter Juliette, enquiring about my mother?' she said.

'That was me. I know who you are,' I said.

We introduced ourselves and asked her to join us, she gracefully accepted.

'It is strange how you both have the same Christian names as your fathers, also the fact you have become friends, just as they were, many years ago of course. Although, saying that, my mother called me Julie, which was her name.'

'You are the image of your mother, I saw the photograph my father had of her,' I said.

'I would be interested to see the photograph at some time, I do not have anything of my mother in her younger days.'

'I'll try to get a copy to you,' I said.

She nodded gracefully to acknowledge my offer

'I apologize for arriving unannounced. Juliette told me who she had met and I wondered if you had any stories of my mother, perhaps your fathers had talked about her? She only mentioned a few things about the war years, and I think Juliette told you everything we know about that time. I hope you might fill in some gaps, if you know anything from your parents. She mentioned your fathers. Anything you can tell me would be appreciated,' she enquired.

We sat and chatted for hours, and she was impressed by my knowledge of the liaison – but then I was speaking from first-hand experience, something she was never going to understand. I felt she was happy to have learnt something of her mother's life, something she had never discussed with her, I think she was pleased to find out the information I imparted. Everything that was said showed her mother in the best possible light, that was our intention.

Colin kept fairly quiet, his character had not received many plaudits from this Julie. Like me he stared at the vision before us, the very image of the person I knew. It was amazing to talk with Julie again, one generation removed, but she had all the good qualities of her mother, the charm and the grace.

I was desperate to ask her about her father, and Colin knew

I was having difficulty mentioning the subject, so he decided it was his chance to rescue me from my plight.

'What do you know about your father? Pat said your mother rarely discussed the subject, is that right?' said Colin.

'I don't mind your asking, the trouble is I have no idea who he was, my mother simply said the man in question had no idea he had a daughter. She was concerned that if he was still alive he probably had a family of his own; she always thought of others before herself. I think she had feelings for my father, she always had a twinkle in her eye when I mentioned him. I had thought that one of your fathers may well have been my father, but mother always dismissed that notion. So to be honest I have no idea who he was. Perhaps just ships that passed in the night; I think that is Juliette's opinion as well,' she said.

It was time for her to leave, we went with her to the ramp to pick up her transport to the mainland, exactly as we had done with her mother, but that was 40 years ago. We informed her that we were leaving the area tomorrow, unsure when we planned to return, I did not feel it appropriate to say the time span was four years.

This lady was going to be in her sixties in my time, she was obviously around when I had bought the bungalow, and her daughter Juliette was going to be in her forties, the same age as the original Julie.

'I wonder if it was possible that you and Juliette could join me for dinner one day in the future? I will be leaving the area soon but I intend to return,' I said.

'That sounds a splendid idea, you know where to find us.'

Once she had left Colin and I talked about how uncanny the resemblance was, as well as the older Julie denying that either of us were the father, was that merely protection, or maybe I was not the father I emphasized.

'Looking at her was like going back forty years, although I was not happy with what her mother thought about me,' he said.

'What did you expect? Your antics in 1941 were the morals

of the 1960s, how did you expect her to understand your actions?' I said.

'Changing the subject slightly, do you have the pouch that the key is in? Alan wants to ensure we take it back to the island with us,' he said.

'The key and the pouch are back at the house, I intended to take it back to the island, knowing it is the only thing that can pass through the portal, but why does Alan want it?' I asked.

'It is not the key he wants, it is the pouch. We will leave the key on the island on our next visit. Alan wants to use the pouch to send something back. He'll explain it to you when we next see him. I don't know what it is, he just asked that we had the pouch with us.'

'Why don't we leave the key at your house? We have the Pathway so the key is no longer required, doesn't that seem the sensible idea?' I said.

'What if something happens to the Pathway, the key must remain within easy reach, as a back up, just in case it is required. If we go to the island we leave it there, when we finally return home it comes with us, remember it belongs with the bungalow deeds, just in case the next owner wants to travel,' he said. I was surprised Alan wanted something bringing back, but perhaps he had changed his mind about staying on the island; perhaps the piracy phase was getting a bit too dangerous and he had decided to return with me to our present. This would make up for not having Colin along.

We decided to check out in the morning and take our clothes to the house on the mainland, staying there until it was time to leave, then wear our oldest clothes yet again to make the trip back to the island. What a treat.

We had breakfast and then paid the bill, thanking the staff for their kindness. Colin left a large gratuity, knowing we were going to be returning in four years' time; he was good at thinking ahead. He said he intended to stay at the hotel for a short time, then hopefully move in with his wife, once that vital information had been obtained from Alan.

I hoped we were successful in saving another life. I felt I was on a life-saving quest, and wondered if there was anyone in my family that needed saving. I thought of no one, and counted that as being very lucky.

We dragged our suitcases to the house that was once John's; he had no use for it now, as his life had changed completely. I hoped his wife survived to my time when we were due to meet again, or in actual fact meet for the very first time – it was confusing. We spent the day at the house. Colin had obtained a small gas heater from the hardware shop, and apart from that there was no heating in the house.

We went to the local cafe for food, where they had no idea who we were. But in 1941 they knew exactly who we were, including our movements around the village and Colin's antics in the hotel.

The time had finally come to leave, it was approaching midnight and a storm was brewing. Colin checked I had the pouch around my neck. We walked across the beach; there was nobody around. As we approached the island we watched the portal take shape as the weather rose in a crescendo, with lashing rain and howling winds. I was soaking wet. Together we walked into the portal, and I shuddered at the prospect of our destination. I hoped it was a short stay.

I had no idea how much time had elapsed since our last visit. What was the situation as far as the islanders were concerned? I was dreading going back and finding the crew had been caught; we knew justice was swift in this time period and I had no illusions that Vicary was not going to protect his crew, quite the opposite in fact, he took care of himself and the crew were merely there to help him get wealthy. Although the crimes they committed were terrible, these poor islanders had no other way of feeding their families. We entered the portal. Destiny awaited, yet again; it was not going to be the last time I thought that.

6

I arrived on the island a little way up from the inn, within easy reach of the rock that was our meeting place. I walked behind the rock, looking across the island in the hope of locating Colin, but nobody was about. I sat down and waited. The inn was full of people, and I did not expect to see Alan until the inn cleared; that was likely to take some time by the sound of the laughter.

There was a rustle behind the rock, then Colin appeared in the form of Jefferson. He looked bedraggled and confused, not his normal appearance. I asked how he was in such a state, wondering where he had ended up. He said he had arrived on the other side of the island, transported to the middle of some gorse bushes, and he had difficulty freeing himself. His appearance showed there had been quite a struggle which he obviously nearly lost. It was usually me who ended up in out-of-the-way places, he always seemed to land at comfortable locations; he was due some of the discomfort I had suffered.

He enquired whether or not Alan had turned up, I told him there was no sign of him, but he appreciated the inn was busy, so it was unlikely he was able to leave until the place emptied. Alan had said he was going to make a point of calling by the meeting place every day after the inn closed, as he had no idea how long we were going to be away; the time lapse was different on the island, not the same as we encountered on the mainland.

We made ourselves as comfortable as possible, it looked like our wait was going to be a long one. Eventually we heard voices outside the inn; some of the crew had decided to make their way home. This was surprising when you considered who they were married to, there were some big women on the island, Colin was in a position to vouch for that. I thought being drunk and incapable was ideal, especially when you had to sleep with one of the monsters that inhabited the island.

The people leaving the inn now became a steady flow, and I felt sure the place was soon going to be empty. As the sound of voices grew less, it was tempting to look over the rock, but common sense decided us against that, having no idea who or what was on the other side. Many of the crew lived near the top of the island and they had to pass our meeting place in order to get home. Most of them were my neighbours; it was comforting in a strange way.

Then a noise from the other side of the rock made my hair stand on end. We remained still and quiet. I heard a voice I recognized, it was Landon's. I hoped this was Alan in his disguise. We responded to the voice, hoping we were right. Then Alan appeared in the form of Landon; it still frightened me to see this monster of a man.

'You have only been gone two days in our time, which unfortunately poses a slight problem. The Pathway can only be activated after seven days from its last activation, so you must wait five days for that. Last time you were gone longer than seven days in island time, but this time it has not worked out in your favour,' he said.

'I am not looking forward to my duty as the monk for five days, particularly living in that terrible hut,' I said.

'To add to the bad news, we will be sailing tomorrow night. This is not a smuggling mission, we have entered the piracy stage, which you realized on your last visit. We have decided on a trip tomorrow, with all the dangers that entails. Fortunately the ship is larger and quicker, we swapped with our victims.'

'I was starting to think this nightmare could not get any worse, then you tell me I am part of a pirate crew,' I said.

'There is the advantage that the ship is larger and more stable.'

'If that was said to make me feel better, it did not,' I said.

'Did you conclude your business in 1981?'

'We did, and Colin has explained the 1985 trip. I am happy to help him,' I said.

'Did you bring the pouch with you?' he asked. I gave it to him.

'Why do you need an empty pouch? I brought the key instead of leaving it on the mainland, just in case we should need it, then I was going to take it with me on my return to my time. It would then be reunited with the deeds, as you are aware this is necessary for the next buyer of 2 Ruby Bay,' I said.

'I will need Colin's pouch as well. As you know I was going to stay in this time. There were good reasons for that decision, reasons I do not want to go into, except you are aware I had some nasty criminals after me. I do not really want to meet with them again, but I now realize I can pay them off and return to normal life. On the island I have a position of authority and respect, something that was lacking in my real life, but that was because I did not have much money, and as you know money talks. I had retired on a modest pension, enough for me to survive, and that was the point, I wanted to do better than just survive. No doubt Colin told you there were people looking for me. I owed them a great deal of money, mostly gambling debts of one kind or another, I learned my lesson too late in that respect. The island life suited me. I didn't need to just survive, I took whatever I wanted, even the women provide their services free. I did not want to be feared, although that came with the position. I have thought about it long and hard. Even though we have carried out only one piracy mission, I have a large amount of uncut diamonds. Vicary and the crew have no idea what they are. In their eyes if it doesn't sparkle it is worthless. What I have already is worth a fortune, and more piracy trips will expand that fortune. I have decided to return with you after the 1985 trip, but could you take the pouches filled with diamonds for me and deposit them in the bank in 1985? When I return with you, I will be rich beyond my dreams. I can pay off my creditors, and live a long and prosperous life.'

The diamonds could only be transported in the pouches, Alan was aware of that. I was glad he had made the decision to return.

'That is an excellent plan, of course we will transport them for you,' I said.

He was unable to transport all the diamonds as the quantity he possessed were more than the size of the pouches, so he was going to transport some more when he returned with me. I was going to bring Colin's pouch with me, Colin did not need the pouch if he remained in 1985. I thought it was a straightforward proposition: the diamonds were to be deposited in the bank in Alan's name, we would return together, he would bring more diamonds with him and become rich.

He then explained his concerns with this plan, namely the different time span on the island; it was vital in this plan. If I returned after the next trip and the island had moved on several months, the piracy was likely to have brought about his capture, closely followed by the inevitable execution. Therefore Alan felt it necessary to make some arrangements for the diamonds and of course the Pathway, which as we knew must not leave the island.

'I have a letter which must accompany the diamonds at the bank. If I do not make it, you and Colin will inherit the diamonds. I'd prefer you both to have them rather than them languishing in a bank vault for eternity,' he said. 'I will show you where the Pathway is. Remember, once it is set it must be placed back in the box after activation; there is enough time to pass through the portal after hiding it. Obviously I hope I will claim my diamonds as we have planned, but it is sensible to prepare for all eventualities. You understand what I am saying?'

'I understand, but like you I hope the second plan does not come into operation. I appreciate none of this will concern Colin if he remains in 1985.'

Alan reminded me to bring the empty pouches on my return,

he was going to have more diamonds to transport, as I would be unable to transport all he had in one trip.

We then made our way to our individual abodes. There would be no meeting the following night as there was a sailing, not a prospect I was looking forward to. Meanwhile we all needed a good night's sleep. The trip would to be more dangerous than any of our previous trips, no doubt the crew was to be heavily armed. A risky business this piracy adventure, and I wished Alan had told us more of what to expect on this voyage. But perhaps if I had asked the question, he may have felt it was better not to know. I was to find out for myself very shortly, anyway.

I reached my hovel within a few minutes, it was a desolate excuse for a home. The smell hit me as I entered; it had not improved since my absence. I tried to sleep, but with little success.

I had hoped to be gone by now, I had been unaware of the seven-day criterion with the Pathway. I think Colin was also shocked by that piece of news, it was apparently in the deed but Colin had paid little attention to that detail. Alan was concerned that if the piracy missions went badly he might not be in a position to make the final trip home. These missions were very dangerous; the government was not going to allow piracy on this scale to go on indefinitely, action would be taken, I had no doubt about that. I hoped this was not the voyage Alan was worried about, the one where everyone was captured. My religious role was unlikely to save me from execution.

Alan had the chance to leave with us, going forward to 1985, yet he chose to remain here and put his life at risk. He had diamonds for me to take back, but he wanted to take back more on my return. Was any sort of wealth was worth that?

The morning dawned, and I walked around the island. I doubted anything had changed since my last visit. I walked near my lady friend's hut, merely to check that she was in good health. She was waiting at the door as I passed, and winked at me as a form of encouragement. I wandered over to her, first checking that nobody saw me.

She invited me in to take refreshment; I knew what that meant in her language. But considering the possibility that tonight's voyage had all the chances of being the last, particularly if we were caught by the Navy ships, I accepted her kind invitation. No payment was mentioned.

An hour later I left the hut, fully refreshed for the day ahead. I saw Jefferson as I closed the gate; he smiled and said nothing. What was there to say? I continued my walk, a little tired from my exertions, and pleased it was only Colin who had seen me. But after all, even a man of the cloth has needs. Colin was probably a little jealous: I knew what awaited him at home.

I passed the time of day with most of the islanders, they seemed a more cheerful bunch since their salaries had increased. I doubted they knew that time was running short, capture was inevitable, followed by the due punishment. I think their lifestyle was such that only today mattered, tomorrow was to be faced when it arrived. In many ways this was a wonderful philosophy, not worrying whether you were in any one's future plans. I was at a loss to see any result of the increase in wages, no new buildings to show wealth, no new clothes for themselves or their children. I wondered how it had affected them.

During the course of the evening at the inn I realized how their fortune was being spent: the measures of rum were usually doubles rather than singles. What a peculiar existence which the womenfolk appeared to put up with; I feared they had little choice. At the inn my food was served, provided as usual by the jovial landlord, smiling and winking. The food was still foul, the rum was a welcome distraction from the food.

All the usual members of the crew were there, Vicary and Landon were in their usual place, Jefferson close to them as was expected, while the crew were trying to find favour with their heroes. I knew the crew would be armed, but with what I did not know. Having witnessed the smuggling I was interested to witness the next phase of the islanders' life, more risky without doubt, but quite interesting, if I survived the ordeal.

The time for departure had arrived, Vicary shouted and everyone finished their drinks. Slowly the crew started to leave, making their way up the hill. They were happy as they strode to the top of the hill, past the place I called home. I followed on the assumption that I was expected to make this treacherous voyage as well. I followed the crew through the passage which led to the ship; it was still a tight fit for me. I reached the ledge by the ship, which was indeed a larger vessel: about three times the size I thought, so maybe the voyage was going to be a pleasant one.

My hopes were dashed as we headed out to sea, this was not a more stable ship, in fact I believe it was worse. My dinner soon made the customary entrance. I watched as the crew went about their business with efficient speed. The sails were billowing and our speed was building up slowly. Even with my small knowledge of sailing ships, I could see that this was obviously a faster vessel than the original.

Once we were on the open sea the crew got their weapons from below deck. Each man appeared on deck with a pistol and a cutlass, and they all seemed competent with these tools of their trade. Vicary and Landon had their weapons brought to them. I had no idea how long we needed to travel to meet our victims, nor did I know what the plan would be when we got there. The activity on deck made me think the moment of truth was getting closer, as some of the crew were sharpening their blades. What sort of fight was imminent? Whatever it was, they were ready to deal with it with ultimate force.

Landon was now scouring the horizon with a telescope, which surprised me as it was pitch black. Then I realized he was looking for lamp lights on the ships. It was obvious that Landon was the main man on this venture. Vicary waited for some sort of signal from Landon, telling him that a ship had been sighted.

At this distance and at night, surely it was impossible to say what sort of ship was in sight, possibly even a Royal Navy vessel. It was only when they were fairly close that a decision could be made to attack or not. This was Vicary's decision.

Suddenly Landon spotted something he liked the look of. He informed Vicary, who shouted the stand-by order to the crew. Without hesitation the pistols were drawn, and the crew crouched on deck, positioned so that they would not be seen by the oncoming vessel. A few drew their cutlasses.

A signal was sent up the mast by way of the flags, I assumed this was to bring the other ship closer. Slowly a ship emerged out of the darkness, moving towards us. The signal had worked. Our prey came ever nearer, the crew remained hidden. One of the crew remained unarmed on the deck, and I soon realized his function: he was ready to tie up the other ship alongside. The crew remained crouching patiently out of sight, looking towards Vicary and Landon, were waiting for their signal to attack. The ship grew ever closer, and eventually it was alongside. A rope was thrown, and it was tied up tightly. I saw only a couple of crew on the other ship, they spoke in what I was sure was Spanish, the lone crewman on deck spoke to them in broken Spanish.

Then the signal from Vicary came. A mass of bodies appeared on the deck of our ship, shouting and screaming, then without warning the shooting began. Two of the Spanish crew fell down with shot wounds. Our crew clambered onto the Spanish ship, firing indiscriminately at the unarmed crew. I counted at least ten Spaniards either dead or seriously injured.

Those who were left held their hands up in surrender; they were herded to the stern of the ship. Then the crew went below deck. I heard several shots, which I assumed were summary executions.

Vicary and Landon did not leave their post, they were waiting until the coast was clear to board the stricken ship. They did not put their lives at risk, not when they had a crew to do that. One of the crew appeared from below deck and shouted to Vicary and Landon that the crew had been subdued.

Now Vicary and Landon would check the prize; nobody in the crew touched anything without the captain's permission. This gave the two of them the opportunity to fill their pockets first, something the crew accepted without criticism. I heard Vicary and Landon shouting orders in the hold, then the booty started to appear on deck, boxes which I assumed held the usual silks and other clothes, a couple of chests this may or may not contain gold. There were many large crates, which were quickly brought aboard our vessel; the offloading took a couple of hours.

I was concerned about the outcome of the Spanish crew; were they to be released to tell their story? I feared for their welfare, and I was soon to find out their fate. Once all the goods were aboard, Landon shouted something to the Spanish crew. They moved to the side of their vessel and they started undoing various ropes, then I saw several longboats being lowered into the sea below. Landon shouted something in Spanish, and the bedraggled crew climbed over the side into the longboats. They did not take the wounded with them.

Two of our crew appeared from below decks on the Spanish ship, and on Landon's signal a fuse was lit. The two men scurried aboard our ship as we made sail, moving swiftly away from the explosion that was about to happen. The two Spanish longboats were also some distance away, no doubt heading for the French coast. I was anxious for the wounded on board the Spanish ship; I was very aware of their cries for help. Vicary and Landon were not sympathetic to their cries, and our ship turned for home.

We were some distance away when I heard the first explosion; the charge had been connected to the stored gunpowder. This was followed by two more loud explosions, and the ship was obliterated before my eyes. All the dead and injured went down with the ship, the sinking was quick and complete, it was unlikely there were survivors. The longboats stopped to watch the destruction. It surprised me that the uninjured crew were allowed to go free, and although glad they had not been brutally murdered, I was not sure why this had occurred. Was Landon responsible for this act of mercy? The problem was that the authorities were now almost certainly going to be alerted to

Vicary's escapades. Surely they had not always allowed the crew to go free? I needed to ask Alan when I next saw him, this question needed answering.

We returned to the island in the early hours of the morning. The task of unloading was long and tedious. I watched this take place, as a monk was not used for manual work. I was very interested in what the cargo was. Apart from a couple of strongboxes, and reams of cloth which I assumed were silk, there were a dozen oblong boxes which bore no markings. I had noticed these boxes had been heavy, causing the crew some discomfort in bringing them up the steps. Their contents appeared to be unknown to everyone. The strongboxes were kept in the care of Vicary and Landon, and the share-out with the crew was to take place that evening. The two men would check their contents in private first, skimming off their enormous share.

When finally the load was on shore, it was piled up in the small hut, and the cloth was taken to the inn for storage. Using his sword Landon forced open one of the oblong boxes. The crew stood and watched, hoping to see gold inside. Landon knew the contents were not gold, that was only in the strongboxes. The box was lined with straw. Landon fumbled inside, then he looked at Vicary, shocked by what he had found.

He had every reason to be concerned, for he pulled out a long musket. All the boxes contained weapons; this was no ordinary consignment, and the vessel had been heading in the direction of London before we stopped it. The situation was as bad as the one we were trying to avoid: in real history the crew had taken gold intended for government officials; these weapons were obviously heading for the same place.

A disastrous piece of piracy was about to bring the government in pursuit of the pirates, the circumstances were different to the original version of history, but the outcome was the same. Landon looked at me. He knew exactly what this meant: the pirates were about to be hunted down by the Royal Navy. He had to think of a plan to avoid a similar fate for the islanders.

Vicary looked surprised by the haul, although I doubted he had any idea of the possible implications.

The crew were excited by their haul; to them these were weapons to be used by them on their piracy voyages, and they had no idea of the implications of what they had done. Why were they to be concerned, when their captain had organized this mission? No member of the crew believed for one moment that their captain would endanger them in any way, he was their leader and they trusted him not to put them at risk. Little did they know.

This evening's talk with Alan had all the indications of being interesting. He was aware how history had dealt with the islanders, was it going to be repeated after this haul? What was his escape plan?

I went to my hut to sleep. Although I did not feel as ill as I had normally been on these trips, I was extremely tired after what I had seen, and worried by the discovery of the cargo. The disgusting hut did not aggravate me as much as I expected it to, as there were too many things on my mind.

Colin and I still had a few days to wait before the portal opened. If the authorities acted quickly, we were likely to get caught up in the consequences. I did not fancy a rope as a necktie. Many things needed to be discussed at our midnight meeting. It now appeared to be the opportune time for Alan to leave with us, taking his diamonds with him. Alan's situation here was in jeopardy, so he had to leave, to avoid arrest.

There was another important point to be discussed. At some time after our jaunt in 1985, I had to return to the island to get back to my present, if all went well this would be without Colin. But what was I returning to, and how long in the island's future was I going to appear? This next return to the island was a worry for me.

I slept well eventually, awaking around midday. I started to feel hungry, so much so that I started to look forward to the stew. I walked down the hill to the watering hole; there was plenty of noise coming from within, the crew were no doubt celebrating what they believed to be good fortune. I was in a position to tell them differently but decided against it.

The meal arrived as soon as I sat down, and the usual nodding ritual took place between me and the landlord. The food actually tasted good. Dare I ask for more or was that too impolite? I consumed the meal with vigour, but I did not ask for seconds. I saw Vicary and Landon at the bar as I drank the impeccable rum. They were deep in discussion, and neither looked happy. They spoke softly so the crew did not hear.

Landon looked towards me and nodded, I returned the nod as someone who knew what their discussion entailed. Jefferson stood nearby, trying unsuccessfully to encroach on the conversation. But he soon appreciated it was better not to disturb these two men. He like myself would find out about this discussion at midnight.

I left the inn to carry out a walk around the island, leaving Vicary and Landon deep in discussion. No doubt Landon was trying to make Vicary see the implications of what had happened, while Vicary saw only profit and not the dire situation the crew had made for themselves.

Most of the islanders I spoke to were ecstatic about the previous night's haul, thinking that most of the weapons could be sold at a huge profit. None of them appeared to understand the mistake that had been made; perhaps their island existence made them oblivious to what went on in the real world. I tried to enjoy the glory with them, but it was difficult, knowing what I knew of the possible consequences. There was no doubt in my mind that neither Vicary nor Landon was likely to tell them the truth; Alan in the form of Landon had plans to leave the island and leave them to it, while Vicary cared only about himself and was surely looking for a way of getting out while it was possible.

I started to feel sorry for these people, soon the Royal Navy were going to come down on them to wreak severe vengeance. Only then were they going to appreciate the error they made, it would be too late when they finally realized it. I was unable to see any way that such weapons were to be sold on the open market; perhaps a few at a time, but that was going to take years. It was also a risk, as one of their many customers might let slip where the weapons came from. I felt the best option was to leave the weapons in storage at the inn. Selling them was an added risk, but these men were profiteers, they wanted these weapons sold. Even if I was given the opportunity to speak to the crew, what impact were my words likely to have?

The islanders on this day were in good heart, no doubt expecting a large gratuity from the two strongboxes that were seized. I did not share their optimism, as I knew that Vicary and Landon ensured they were well compensated first. The loot from the strongboxes was to be divided that evening at the inn, and the islanders were excited by that prospect.

I continued my reconnaissance of my parish. Most of the people were polite, although there was still some animosity towards me; perhaps these people knew of my liaisons with the prostitute.

I decided I was going to try and bring a bit of light into their meagre existence, advertising the fact that I was happy to tell stories from the Bible to the children of the island. The mothers were happy with that, it took the children off their hands for a while. I said the storytelling would be held at the top of the island that very afternoon and all were welcome, including any of the mothers who wanted to be educated.

It somehow made me feel useful. I was not sure what purpose the monk had on the island, as there did not appear to be any religious services held. I had not done so, and nobody complained about that, so I assumed the real monk did not pass the word amongst his parish either. I was looking forward to talking to the children; I had noticed it was rare that anyone spoke to them without either hitting them or scolding them in some way, and I hoped this would provide some pleasure in their lives. I believed they had probably never heard any Bible stories. I was not a particularly religious man, although I had heard the Bible stories at school.

I sat on a rock at the top of the island, preparing for my visitors, I had no idea how many were likely to turn up, maybe none at all. I had only been there a few minutes when I saw a large group of children heading towards my location. They varied in age from about four years to 13 or 14 years of age, and I estimated there were a couple of dozen. There were a couple of women among them, no doubt the mothers of the smaller children.

As they arrived I got them to sit in a semicircle in front of the rock I was sitting on, they looked at me with wide eyes, not knowing what to expect.

I had chosen the Nativity story, and by the time I had finished, the numbers of women in my audience had increased. There were ten or twelve mothers sitting on the grass. Everyone there appeared to enjoy the story. Nobody thanked me but I did not expect that. I said I was going to tell another story the following day, depending on how many turned up; it was the only way to gauge my success. I was pleased to bring that little bit of joy into their lives, and to be honest it did me no harm either.

I went to my hut until it was time to go to the inn for the evening. There was no need to prepare myself for the evening's excursion: even having a wash was out of the question. I lay on my bed and decided on a late afternoon nap.

That evening at the inn the atmosphere was electric. Vicary and Landon had not yet made an appearance, and this in itself was a surprise as they were usually the first customers. Maybe the sorting out of the shares had taken longer than expected. I sat in my usual seat and the food arrived. It had started to taste good; was my palate changing with the times? The glass of rum was always most welcome.

I had been there about 30 minutes when the door was flung open. It was Vicary and Landon, and they carried a large bag. I assumed this contained gold from the strongbox. They immediately went to their places at the bar, and their rum was served instantly. Vicary then called each crew member in turn, the most senior first. Each was handed a handful of coins, then they moved away to count their share. I have no idea the value of each share, but everyone seemed happy. The coins certainly looked like gold coins.

Vicary then stood up in front of his crew and spoke about the weapons haul. He explained that the weapons needed to be sold in a private deal, and this was going to take some time to negotiate. Until that time they remained where they were. When the weapons had been sold, each crew member was to get a share of the money gained. The crew cheered at this prospect.

I was unsure whether such a transaction was likely to take place, and I felt Landon had persuaded Vicary to leave the weapons alone, possibly by explaining the dire consequences of selling the Crown's property, because there was no doubt that these weapons were headed for the Crown.

This was something we must find out from Alan at our midnight meeting. There was a great deal to discuss tonight, principally Alan's future on the island. He had already shown his intention to leave, and perhaps sooner rather than later was now the best idea. Tonight we had many decisions to make.

I left the jovial atmosphere of the inn just before midnight, making my way to the meeting place. Colin turned up a few minutes after me. He appreciated the seriousness of the situation. I asked Colin what he thought of Vicary's speech, he agreed with me that Alan had played some part in it, as we did not think Vicary had the slightest idea of how significant the haul was, until it was pointed out to him.

It was my opinion that Alan's position on the island was in jeopardy, and we needed to persuade him to leave with us. He then had a choice to stay in 1985 or to move forward with me to the present day, that was his decision. We were going to talk to him when he turned up; he was certain to realize the island was doomed, that the muskets were the beginning of the end for the good life.

A noise behind the rock heralded the arrival of Alan, looking splendid as Landon.

'The weapons we seized on the raid were almost certainly destined for the King, along with the gold in the strongboxes. This is as bad as the original raid which resulted in the crew's execution. There is no way the Crown is going to accept this lying down. The King will use all his resources to find the perpetrators,' said a very nervous Alan.

'We know what justice awaits the crew. Do they have any idea what has happened? What about Vicary's little speech, was that his idea or were you behind it?' I said.

'I persuaded him to make the speech; he had no idea of the significance of the cargo. He just wanted to sell the weapons to whoever came along. I explained the weapons were destined for the King, their theft was going to result in a full-scale search and that we had to lie low for a while. He eventually got the message. I think he has started to panic and I would not be surprised if he tries to leave the island. He has accumulated a lot of wealth and will leave the crew to their fate without a second thought,' he said.

The last comment underlined what I thought to be true about Vicary: he thought only of his own safety; he did not have any family on the island, and did not care for the families of those left behind. There was little option for the crew, as their lives were on the island, their families were here. Unlike Vicary they were unable just to move away.

'What about your position, you must also consider your future now.'

'I've thought of nothing else since the theft. I've been weighing up my options.'

'I would suggest you return to the mainland with us, you must have enough diamonds to provide for yourself. If you go to 1985, then the problem you had with creditors will not exist, it will be before you dealt with them. How does that sound? We also have some valuable paintings there. They are to be auctioned off and we expect to make a lot of money, we will give you a share of that,' I said.

Colin nodded his agreement. 'We could not have reached this point without you, Alan. You have made all our journeys possible, you must consider leaving the island with us, your life is in danger. We will have enough money to share if that is the problem. I think you are taking a terrible risk by staying,' said Colin.

This effort was in vain, Alan had his own ideas. 'I feel I must stay to protect the Pathway, although I know you have the key which you have not used. I feel the Pathway is the safest way for Pat to return to his time. If we were all staying in 1985, it would not be such a problem, but Pat must return to his present. I will ensure he does that and return with him. I know the chance I am taking. If the crew and I are caught we will be executed. I will try to persuade them not to go to sea for a while, at least until Pat returns; we may only be talking a couple of days. If you consider the weapons were taken from a ship off Portsmouth, it is going to take the Royal Navy months to locate the ship in Ruby Bay. They will naturally assume the ship was local to the Portsmouth area and that will give us time. If I mention to Vicary the likely punishment if he is caught, although I think he already knows, that will persuade him not to sail for a while. I think I can survive here until you return, it will take the Navy months to find us,' he said.

'Are you sure about this? You are taking a great chance. Surely if you leave the Pathway in your cellar, I can return and I will know where to find it,' I said.

'I will not change my mind, I will remain here until you return. I want you to have an ally here when you get back.'

'Another option is that we all go to 1985, then Alan and I could return to the island, then make the final trip home, how does that sound?' I said.

'What you are failing to grasp is my concern to protect the Pathway. If I leave the island it is unprotected. My safety is secondary to the safety of the Pathway. It might sound stupid to you, but to me it is important,' he said.

'Alan, you are a brave man. You have the chance to return to civilization, but you choose to stay in the past, to guard a valuable commodity. In a selfish way I am glad you will be here on my return,' I said.

'I will bring the diamonds on the night of your departure; make sure you both have the pouches. I have written the note. They are to be placed in a deposit box at the bank, the note verifies I am the owner of the contents. I would appreciate it, Pat, if you could organize that for me in 1985,' he said.

I said I would be happy to carry out his wish. We left the meeting place and returned to our huts. It was two nights before our departure, and I was eager to move forward to Colin's destiny. We had discussed the situation a little, and he was adamant that not only was it necessary to save his wife, but it was imperative that we caught the murderer. If the murderer had a grievance against his wife, preventing the burglary was unlikely to solve the problem, the burglar was simply going to return at another time and complete the gruesome task.

We were due to return about a week before the incident, this allowed us time to formulate a plan, maybe even to involve the police, but doing that was going to pose a problem. If we approached the police and said we knew a murder was going to take place on a particular evening at a particular location, and we knew the approximate time, they were certain to put us in a cell or summon a doctor to certify us insane. The whole thing needed very careful planning, someone's life was at stake in this matter.

During the afternoon of the following day I sat on my rock at the top of the island, I hoped yesterday's religious story would bring forth another crowd, as I had promised them another story. The size of today's congregation would tell me how successful I had been the day before. I looked down the hill and saw people walking towards me, many were children but there were quite a few mothers. The word had got around, and my audience was going to be larger than yesterday.

Once I had everyone seated, the congregation totalled more

than 50. I had to decide on a story from the Bible, one that was likely to interest and fascinate. I was tempted to pass a hat around for contributions, knowing these people had gold coins from the share out at the inn, but my conscience got the better of me. The story I told was of the Sermon on the Mount, a classic tale.

Although I doubted my story had impressed the parents, I hoped the minds of the children had gained something. Their minds were more susceptible to stories of miracles. Maybe my efforts had done no good at all, but least I had tried, and hopefully got some success. I was amused at the thought of the real monk, after I left, being pestered by the children wanting more stories from the Bible.

We met the following night at the meeting place, and Alan brought the diamonds and the letter. There were about 40 small uncut diamonds; the rest were for for our final trip home.

My biggest concern about our new mission was that only the diary was taken; this was not an opportunist thief, he knew exactly what he was looking for, and the jewellery and money were of no interest to him. I concluded that this person had planned the burglary, and was therefore well prepared for the crime. He was able to overpower Colin's wife and batter her to death; had he used a gun the sound of gunfire was certainly going to alert the neighbours, but there was still the possibility that he was armed.

'I've got a friend in the police. I'll have a chat to him; he may be in a position to help,' he said.

'Surely having him on board is a bonus, but is it going to make the predicament easier? Although I would expect him to believe what you tell him,' I said.

'The problem is we can only tell him we suspect this burglary will take place. You know better than me, Pat, the police will need something more concrete, won't they?'

Colin then asked Alan how he could become the 1985 Colin, as we had discussed in 1981.

'You are no doubt basing this question on the fact I studied the deeds in great detail, aren't you? As I see it, you are not to come in contact with the other Colin, you must merely interact with his family or friends. You must meet one of them before the other Colin arrives on the scene, then he will disappear and you will become him. For example if you know what time he gets home from work, you go in and greet your wife before he arrives. You are accepted and he is gone. He takes over when you leave that time, but in your case hopefully that is never,' said Alan.

'What will happen to my car if I turn up at the house before he does?' said Colin.

'You've certainly got your priorities right. Don't worry, it will reappear in a few minutes. Make sure you don't meet your wife outside, she will notice no car and possibly the reappearance of it,' said Alan.

Alan was surprised that Colin was unfamiliar with the contents of the deed, but Colin promised to go inside the house to greet his wife.

We left the meeting place. We would return the following night for our journey. I looked forward to getting out of the habit, and the thought of a bath and clean clothes made me smile.

I walked the island the following day, there was nothing else to do, and my hut was depressing me even though I tried to tidy it up. What the real monk thought of my domestic prowess I shuddered to think. There were the usual conversations with the islanders who spoke to me, a wave and a wink from a certain lady. I was counting off the hours until midnight. I checked the pouch around my neck, the diamonds were still there. I certainly had no intention of losing Alan's future.

My last full day, in my new position as storyteller of the parish, I met my flock at the usual place. They came in droves this time. As well as the women and children, there was a large contingent of the crew. My storytelling fame had travelled around the island, and with that in mind the prostitutes turned up too.

Knowing that this was my last story, I decided to mention the twelve disciples, concluding with the Crucifixion, followed by the Resurrection of Christ. I was concerned as to what they might think of this story, most of their dead lay at the bottom of the sea, and I doubted if they wanted any of them to rise up.

When the story was finished the congregation drifted away, and one little boy actually said thank you. Somehow that made it all worthwhile, I had brought religion into their lives even if most of them had no idea what I was talking about.

Finally my last night at the inn arrived. I ate the stew and drank the rum. I walked to the meeting place before the witching hour, waiting for my colleagues to report. They were both punctual. Alan had the Pathway and set the date as Colin instructed. Our return date was three weeks after that, two weeks after the burglary. This was Colin's decision, he wanted to know who the murderer was and to ensure he was brought to justice.

Once the island fell silent we made our way to the slipway. The tide was in but we expected to reappear on the mainland, as I did not fancy having to swim for it. Alan pressed the appropriate part of the Pathway, and the portal appeared in glorious colour. The storm raged in the usual manner, we shook hands with Alan and I moved forward hopefully to 1985.

7

I arrived on the rocks on the mainland; this had been my entry point when travelling. I was attired in the same duffel coat I was wearing when I arrived in 1941 and 1981, obviously clothing that was acceptable in any time period of the twentieth century. I was once again glad of the coat, with a bitter westerly wind blowing.

I quickly made my way to Colin's house, our arranged meeting point. As I reached the house he was waiting at the door to let me in. The small gas heater he had acquired in 1981 was working at full power, the room was warm, and the sleeping bags from our last visit were on the floor waiting to be occupied.

'How long have you been waiting?' I asked.

'Only a few minutes, I landed near the house. What about you, where did you end up?'

'In amongst the rocks, the same place as my previous visits. I don't know why I can't land somewhere comfortable like you always seem to.'

'Do you still have Alan's diamonds?' he said.

'Yes, they're still there, I can feel the weight. I would think these diamonds are worth a pretty penny. Aren't they worth more in the uncut state? I'm sure I read something about it, a rarity on the market I believe. Do you get the impression these diamonds are probably worth more than our paintings?' I said.

'I don't know really, I'm not an expert in either field,' he said.

I checked the note I was going to give to the bank manager,

which had remained intact on the journey through the portal.

Alan had said I was to get the security box in my name. The letter was to be opened by the manager if someone wanted to open the box. It contained a codeword that only Alan knew, similar to the arrangement for our bank accounts.

Now, getting some sleep was all I wanted to do. We curled up in the sleeping bags, and it was a great deal more of a pleasure than my bed in the hut.

I slept well and woke up refreshed. Today was the day we deposited Alan's diamonds and started to think of a plan to save Colin's wife. The first of these two assignments was the easiest. We decided to go to the local cafe for breakfast.

There was no problem with money in this time, as our accounts had been set up only four years before; hopefully our accounts would blossom when we had completed the second of our missions, the selling of the art. As Colin was possibly staying in this time, it seemed prudent to sell the artwork now. My account would earn interest; Colin had plans to use his money in this time.

Our first port of call was the bank. The manager welcomed us, saying he had not seen us for some time. We decided not to comment on the reason.

'I have something I wish to deposit in a safe-deposit box. What do I need to do?' I asked.

'That depends on the size of the item,' he said.

'It is the contents of these pouches. I need to take the pouches away with me. Is there some sort of receptacle I can use?'

He provided a small metal box. The inevitable question followed: 'How long are you likely to require this service?' he said.

This was the tricky bit, and I had little choice but to state that I had no idea.

'The box is actually to be held on behalf of a friend, I am unsure how long he will require its use. If I could set up a standing order to pay the rental charges from my account – as I say I am not certain of the time span – can I pay this annually? Is that acceptable?' I said.

'If we are talking annual fee, I can only assume the time period is considerable. It will not be a problem,' he said.

He gave that bank manager's smile, a bit like Uriah Heep in the Dickens novel.

'The letter is only to be opened if someone other than myself wants access to the box. That person is likely to have a key, the letter will certify whether that person can open the box or not. As I say, the contents are owned by a friend, he was unable to deposit the goods himself,' I said.

'I understand sir, we appear to have quite a few letters from yourself, but we will always abide by our customers requests,' he said.

Once the standing order had been set up to pay for the box we left the bank. The manager was very helpful although a little confused with the request, but I thought it was reasonable. He had been confused with all our requests.

'This may be a good time to contact my art dealer friend, but there is a slight problem with doing this – his telephone number is in my phone book at the house, the house Helen shares with the other me. I suppose there is only one answer to the problem, I will have to take over from my 1985 version. It is urgent we set this up, we will soon know if Alan is right or not,' Colin said.

'Before you do this, there is something you should consider: you look fifteen years older. Helen is going to see you have aged fifteen years since breakfast. Hopefully you have considered this,' I said.

'No, I haven't but I know I must take over from the other me. I need to contact my art friend, also the police, and I will need somewhere for them to contact me. But how do I get over this ageing process? I think the only way is to be at the house just before I get home, you know what I mean, then the problem of the car should not be a big problem, it will reappear within a short time. I know it doesn't address the ageing but what else can I do? I'll just say it was a stressful day at work.'

'It seems we have a plan, a very flimsy one, but a plan nonetheless,' I said.

'What are you going to do when I go into the house?'

'I'm going to wait outside, either your car will reappear, or the other you will drive it into your drive. I hope it works like it did on the island, except there we were taking the identity of a complete stranger,' I said.

'All I know is that I must get into my house, I need to be inside to plan this whole mission successfully.'

'I agree with you, there is no other option. You must chance it, Helen's safety is at stake.'

We hired a car from a local dealer, and I drove to Plymouth with him as a nervous passenger; nervous not because of his driving, but because of what lay ahead for him. He had not seen his wife in 15 years, since her untimely death. He also had to explain why he had aged so much since she saw him that morning. Or maybe he would automatically take on the age of the other Colin, there were more questions than answers.

'What were you actually doing at this stage in your life, where were you working?' I said.

'I was a solicitor at a practice in Plymouth,' he said.

'That may well be your best option, go to your place of work and take over his identity there.'

'That's not a bad idea, if I walk into the office and they know me, hopefully the other Colin will disappear. What if the other me is in the office? But I doubt he would be in reception, and the receptionist is a friend, so it might work. It would save putting Helen through it, we would know if it worked before I got home.'

'Let's check the car park to see if your car is there. If it's not, when you enter the building it should reappear, that will show you have succeeded,' I said.

We then changed our route and headed for the city centre; I took over the driving. I pulled into the car park of the solicitors offices. As he got out and walked towards the building, he gave a thumbs up. I really did hope this plan worked. He walked cautiously towards the door. Inside was the receptionist who ought to recognize him, and this should be the point when the other

Colin disappeared. He quickly checked the car park and could not see his 1985 car, the other Colin was obviously out and about.

I waited. If the plan failed, we would need to make a quick getaway, followed no doubt by the other Colin. Nearly 30 minutes passed before he appeared at the door, walking quickly to the car. He still looked the same age. He pointed across the car park. I did not see it happen, his car had reappeared, it had worked as planned.

'I checked the whole building, there is no sign of the other me. People noticed I had aged slightly, but it did not appear to be dramatic. They said I looked like I had not slept for a few nights, they assumed it was pressure of work.'

'Are these people you work with completely blind? Fifteen years older and they think you haven't slept for a few nights? You have to assume they were just being polite. I think the big test is with Helen.'

'Thank you for that vote of confidence, but I realize Helen is the stumbling block, she will not be so polite, as you say. The keys to my house and car have appeared in my pocket, I think we can safely assume the other me is gone. If you go to the Holiday Inn in Plymouth, I will come round this evening. We'll have a drink and a discussion. I'll let you know how it went with Helen.'

He left the car and returned to his offices, he had to complete his day's work.

I felt that Helen would be bound to observe how much he had aged. I never saw the 1985 Colin so I had nothing to judge it on, but she had seen that version, only this morning. I hoped she was not going to be the stumbling block I suspected she might be.

I went to the hotel in the city centre. I went to my room although I had nothing to unpack; my lack of luggage caused a few looks at reception. I had forgotten to pack anything on leaving Ruby Bay, so yet another shopping trip was required. I was building up a large wardrobe of clothes, unfortunately they were not all at the same location.

I met Colin in the bar after dinner, he looked excited.

'How did you get on with Helen?'

'She did notice that I had aged. I simply said it was a few worries at work. I'm not sure she believed me, but it got me past that awkward point. I have also spoken to my friend in London, he'll be coming down tomorrow to look at the artwork. I've arranged to meet him in Ruby Bay at lunchtime; I know it's Saturday and the Bay might be busy. We need to dig up the cellar in the morning, so I'll pick you up from the hotel after breakfast. I've told Helen I have a client to see in Exeter, which will give us plenty of time to complete the task. Being the weekend she would expect me to be at home, so I had to make up some excuse. She doesn't known my art dealer friend, we met before Helen and I were an item,' he said.

'Why does it make a difference whether Helen knows him or not?'

'It is simply because I don't want Helen knowing about the paintings, I want them sold without her knowledge.'

'Won't that cause a few problems, particularly with your instant wealth? That is assuming, they are worth anything.'

'Of course they're worth something, they are masterpieces in their own right. But I don't want her to know how they came into our possession, it is too unbelievable a story. I've decided to tell her they are yours and I'm helping you to sell them.'

'If what you say about their value is correct, how are you going to explain the large amount of cash in your bank account?' I said.

'I will just say you are giving me a percentage because I used my contacts to sell the paintings. Our priority is to get the artwork to the auction room and get them sold, then we can concentrate on the burglary.'

'Have you decided to involve the police?' I said.

'I think it is a good idea to involve the police, they have more chance of catching him than us. They have the resources to set up an operation, provided we can persuade them it is going to happen.

I will talk to my friend, but we need to give him a story he will readily believe. Now is a good time to come up with an idea.'

We decided to say that I had overheard two men discussing the burglary in a pub. It was an old story but we felt it had some mileage in this case. We needed to add more detail, to prove that the men were talking about his house. We decided to think it over and discuss it further over the next couple of days, we had to make sure it was convincing. Once we had agreed on a story, Colin would telephone his friend in the police.

I went to bed early. There was some labouring to do in the morning, removing the cement on the tiled floor that had been there for nearly 45 years.

I slept very well and went down to breakfast, then Colin arrived. I was not going to ask him how his first night back with his wife went, it would be undiplomatic. He was in a suit, somewhat inappropriate for the task ahead.

'I take it you're going to change before we dig up the cellar, or is this the new image of a gentleman labourer?'

'Of course I'm going to change. I had to leave the house in a suit, otherwise Helen would have been suspicious. Remember, an appointment in Exeter was my cover story. I also told her I was visiting Ruby Bay on the way back. You had some paintings but did not know how to sell them and I was going offer you advice on the subject. Helen has invited you to dinner tonight, so we need to get our stories straight about the artwork. My art friend is also joining us, but I will brief him before dinner. There is no way I can tell Helen the truth at this stage, but my friend will go along with it too, his only interest is his commission.'

'I don't think you realize this but I am staying in a hotel in Plymouth, so why are we meeting in Ruby Bay?' I said.

'It gives me a reason to be in Ruby Bay, just in case I am seen by some of my clients. I could say you were visiting here and I decided to meet you for lunch or something.'

'It was my intention to visit Ruby Bay at some stage; I want to see Julie again, the Julie I assume is my daughter.'

'I understand, perhaps dinner on the island might be nice,' he said.

We prepared to dig up the cellar floor. Fortunately Colin had a drill at the Ruby Bay house, which would make it much easier. We also had to take good care not to damage this valuable merchandise. I had only his word for how valuable these paintings were, the confirmation was to come from the expert.

We left the hotel and headed towards Ruby Bay. There were several hours before our visitor arrived. I hoped retrieving the artwork was not going to be a troublesome task, but we had to allow for possible complications.

Colin was excited about what his friend would say on seeing the paintings. These works had not been seen since the war.

'What concerns me is that these pieces may not be as valuable as you anticipate. All three artists are unknown to me. I thought the big money was on the likes of Picasso and Van Gogh, not that I'm an expert,' I said.

'I appreciate that to you and me they are not big names, but in their time they were desirable to dealers. Anyone in the business will be astonished that these works have come to auction, they were believed lost during the war. That fact alone will increase their interest to dealers and I think the prices in the sale will reflect that.'

At the house Colin donned his overalls and started to demolish the cellar floor, taking care not to damage the paintings. The whole job took less than an hour to complete, the artwork was removed successfully and placed upstairs in the lounge. We did not replace the tiles on this occasion, there was no need.

We cleaned ourselves up, he put on his suit and we waited for our visitor. We tried to make ourselves as comfortable as possible, not easy in a room without furniture. For the benefit of our visitor, this was to be my house, I had just purchased it and had not yet moved in, but I had left the artwork there for safekeeping. I had no idea if he would believe this flimsy story, but that was what we agreed to say. As Colin said, he was only going to be interested in the paintings, and those were going to excite him, Colin was confident.

Within minutes of midday our visitor arrived. He was called James, this was followed by a double-barrelled surname which I forgot instantly. We removed the covers from the paintings, and he used a small magnifying glass to examine them closely. He said nothing as he examined them, then he straightened up and smiled. He was obviously excited about what he had seen.

'How did you come by these paintings?' said James.

'They actually belong to both of us. They were acquired many years ago and we have now decided to sell them, hoping to get a good price. I would be grateful if you didn't tell my wife I was part owner of these pieces; it is a long story,' said Colin.

'I will of course respect your request. To be honest the paintings are my sole concern. I assume the ownership is therefore down to Pat, as far as your wife is concerned,' he said.

'That is correct, I am merely assisting him in selling them,' said Colin. James then answered our question before we asked it.

'I believe these paintings are genuine, although I will need to carry out further tests to be certain. Do either of you know what you have here? These pieces of artwork have not been seen since before the war. They were thought to be lost during Hitler's scourge of these artists. It will need time to get them auctioned in a way for them to reach their true potential; collectors around the world will want to own these pieces. This is a fantastic find, if we can prove without doubt they are genuine. With your permission I would like to take them back to London to examine them thoroughly. They will need to be in London for the auction. Are you happy for me to take them?' he asked.

'I think I can speak for Colin when I agree to your request. How long will it take to set up the auction?' I said.

'At the minimum I would estimate ten days. I needed to inform dealers around the world. Some will want to come to the auction. It is the best way to achieve the best prices, which is what we all want,' he said.

I was starting to like James, he was saying the things I wanted to hear. Having the artwork verified as quickly as possible was going to mean that the auction took place that much sooner.

'I may not be in the area when the sale goes through, I have some travelling to do, but Colin can handle my part of the deal. We would be grateful if you could make out two cheques of equal amounts, one to each of us. If I am not here Colin will put mine into my account. I appreciate this is a little premature, you still need to verify the authenticity of the paintings,' I said.

'That will not be a problem, I will do as you ask,' said James.

Colin and I knew they were the real thing, but this piece of information we kept to ourselves.

Colin then told James he was welcome to stay at his house, an invitation that was not extended to me. He mentioned that I would be at dinner, which was the best offer I was going to get. James accepted the offer and said he was returning to London the next day.

We left the house and Colin dropped me off at the hotel, writing the address of his house on a piece of paper, and instructing me to get a taxi for 7 p.m. I noticed that his house name was called Heinrich, his real family name. It was an unusual name for a house, I was intrigued.

James followed Colin to his house. James seemed genuine enough, and he was visibly excited when he examined the paintings, no doubt a dream come true for a dedicated dealer.

I dressed casually for my dinner engagement. I was looking forward to meeting Helen, who was the reason for our trip. The taxi driver knew the address and I arrived at the large detached house within 15 minutes. I rang the doorbell and Colin opened it and greeted me. I saw James talking to a lady who I assumed was Helen.

I was duly introduced. She was slightly taller than Colin, with a slim attractive figure. She must have married him for his money.

'Colin tells me you have some paintings for sale, he believes they might be valuable,' she said.

He had a knack of saying too much.

'The value has not yet been determined, hopefully James will confirm that. I suspect they might be valuable, but I have no idea how valuable,' I said.

'James seems to think they are the real thing, I must admit I am not familiar with the artists. How did they come into your possession?' she said.

I had rehearsed for this, so I was able to answer convincingly. 'They were originally my father's, he left them to me in his will. He bought them many years before and they had been left in the loft to gather dust. He never mentioned them when he was alive, it was only because of the will that we discovered they existed. I do know that he travelled extensively before the war, particularly throughout Europe,' I said.

'These artists had works in galleries throughout Germany before the war, but they disappeared when Hitler came to power. Nobody knew where the paintings went. Over the years it had been assumed they had been destroyed by Hitler, as these artists offended him, but these paintings prove that was not so,' said James.

We went into the dining room and consumed a wonderful meal prepared by Helen. She showed she had the ability to hold a conversation on almost any subject. No wonder Colin had felt the loss so much, she was an attractive and vibrant lady. I was sorry when it was time to leave.

Colin felt this evening with Helen helped our future plan, the prevention of the murder and the bringing to justice of the perpetrator. My story to the police was vital, and Helen was more likely to believe it if I was known to her. Colin's mind sometimes worked in mysterious ways, but most of the time his thought process was to be admired.

I left the house just before midnight, accepting Helen's invitation to another dinner. I spoke briefly to James who said he was going to make contact with me through Colin; the verification of the paintings was going to take a couple of days. I was pleased to have met Helen, now I knew why Colin wanted to change history.

On arrival at the hotel I went straight to bed; drinking in the bar on my own was not an attractive proposition. Tomorrow we had make plans to stop the burglary, Colin was using the excuse of a meeting with a client to visit the hotel.

He arrived early the following morning. I had just started breakfast, and he decided to join me as he not yet eaten. I was glad of the company. Helen wanted me to go to dinner on Wednesday, which he thought was ideal for our plan.

'Do you come to the hotel bar each night?' said Colin.

'I usually have a drink before dinner, sometimes a few pints after. Why do you ask?' I said.

'This hotel is open to non-residents, therefore anyone can come in here for a drink. Let's say you were sat here one night and just by chance you overheard a conversation about breaking into a house. It is unlikely the police would be able to trace those men having the conversation. I think I may have a plan,' he said.

'I think you'd better tell me what it is,' I said.

'When you come to dinner on Wednesday, I will mention the fact that Helen and I have been invited out to dinner on Friday. You will then relay the conversation you overheard in the hotel, it would be very pertinent to our dinner date. Helen's apprehension would give me the excuse to contact my friend in the police. Although there is no solid evidence, I feel they will take the matter seriously,' he said.

'What exactly do you want me to say?'

'I will leave that to your imagination. If I don't know what you're going to say, my reaction is going to be more realistic,' he said.

He also mentioned this particular officer was very fond of Helen; I was not sure it had any relevance to the plan, but Colin thought it had.

This plan had to work, if it did not we had few options other than tackling the burglar ourselves.

Colin said he would pop in after work to let me know when James had made contact. After he left I was able to enjoy the rest of the day in peace and quiet, taking a stroll along Plymouth Hoe, enjoying watching the waves breaking against the seafront wall. There were many people walking although it was a chilly morning.

On Monday he turned up just after 5 p.m., he said he had news for me. We sat down in the lounge, then he told me.

'James telephoned me at the office: the paintings are genuine. I appreciate we both knew that, but now it is official. They have the correct paperwork to sell them, it is now a case of preparing for the auction,' he said.

'Does James have any idea how much the artwork is worth?' I asked.

'He estimated millions, his American contacts were keen to purchase. In fact the interest is worldwide, even he is surprised by the amount of interest generated.'

'You do trust James, don't you?'

'I do, but I got him to sign for the paintings before he took them, as well as requiring a report of the validity of the works, along with a stipulation as to who the paintings belonged to. I think James will be more than happy with the commission he gets from the sale,' he said.

'I think you're right, the first part of our mission has gone like clockwork. It is up to me to come up with a story to sort the second part. Hopefully that will be done on Wednesday at dinner,' I said.

He said to expect him the following night, hopefully there was going to be news of Friday's party invitation. If the invitation never came we had a problem.

I ate alone in the restaurant at dinner, it was surprisingly pleasant. I liked Colin but he had a great aptitude for talking constantly, and not always interesting conversations. I had yet to make arrangements to see Julie, and I thought the best time was probably on my last night, as I would be at Ruby Bay that evening, preparing to leave at midnight. Although I had mentioned this meeting to Colin, I had not said when it was to take place. It was something he was not invited to, and I did not think under the circumstances he was going to expect to be there.

The next day was Tuesday, of a week that was going to change Colin's life. I decided to drive to Cornwall, and crossed the Tamar Bridge into the county. I started in Looe, a place I knew well, then drove along the southern coast until I reached Land's End. Along to the north coast and the resort town of Newquay, then I returned to the A38 and my beloved Devon.

I decided to be back at the hotel in time for a possible visit from Colin, perhaps he had further information to impart on his way home from work. He did not arrive at the hotel, but he telephoned me to let me know the Friday invitation had been received.

'At this point we do not know whether one or more of the dinner guests were involved in the burglary. Possibly they would not be involved personally, but maybe hiring someone for the task, which made me think one of the guests had an interest in the diary. It appears they were the only people who were aware of the dinner party, so I suppose suspicion must fall on them. We know Helen was taken ill on the night of the original break-in, but on this occasion she must be protected in some way, by either going in the car to the dinner, or in such a way the police might think fit,' he said.

'Once we involve the police, provided Helen believed there was going to be a burglary, I think she could be persuaded to leave the house as expected. There is of course another possibility, what if Helen was the target, and the break-in was a cover-up, making it look like a burglary that had gone wrong?' I said.

'I feel that is impossible, Helen had no enemies that I was aware of. She was a housewife, it is unlikely she was leading a double life. I know my wife well enough – she was not the target.'

'To be honest I agree with you, I put it forward simply as a possibility,' I said.

On Wednesday evening I arrived at the house for dinner as arranged. We were only two days from the fatal burglary, and tonight our plan went into operation, exactly as Colin and I had discussed. I was met at the door by Helen, looking as lovely as I remembered her. She greeted me and showed me into the lounge for an aperitif. Colin was waiting there and we shook hands.

'Colin told me about the auction, I am very happy for you,' she said.

'I was pleased to hear they were the real article, I thought they might have been fakes. I want to say that I hope Colin will share in my windfall, without him none of this would have been possible. I am adamant when I say he will be rewarded for his efforts.'

'I don't think you need to do that. Colin merely put you in touch with the dealer,' she said.

'I have to disagree with you there, Helen. Following my father's death I showed Colin these pictures. He felt they were worth something, if it wasn't for him I might have sold them off cheaply. He has played an important part in bringing these paintings to auction at the right time and he will be rewarded for that,' I said.

'That is very good of you and we appreciate it,' she said.

I then went into the prearranged story.

'I noticed your house name when I arrived, I thought it unusual,' I commented.

'It's not common at all, in fact I do not know of another with the name,' she said.

'Then under the circumstances there is something I need to tell you. I overheard a conversation in the hotel bar, a house named Heinrich was mentioned and at the time I had no idea how I recognized the name. When I rang your bell tonight I realized. This may seem a strange question, but are you planning to go out on Friday evening?' I said.

Helen looked at me, a little bewildered, Colin looked at her and shrugged his shoulders.

'Strangely enough we have been invited out to dinner. How would you know that?' she said.

'The conversation I overheard worries me. Two men were talking behind me about coming to a house named Heinrich, they said the occupants were out on Friday evening. I did not hear anything else, but I suspect you may have been targeted for a burglary on Friday evening,' I said.

Helen was visibly shocked by what I said. If I could have avoided frightening her, I would have, but her reaction assisted the plan.

'Are you certain of the house name?' asked Colin.

'I am certain. It was only tonight that the house name registered with me: when I turned up on your doorstep, there was the nameplate. The fact that you are going out seems to suggest it is your house. I think we need to contact the police urgently, they will know how to approach the problem. Do you have anything of value that you feel the burglars are after?' I asked.

'I have a few personal items of jewellery, no more than anyone else in the street. Why would we be singled out? There is little of value here,' she said.

'I am sorry, Helen, it was not my wish to cause you distress, but I felt I should mention what I heard. I do not want my friends to suffer at the hands of a burglar,' I said.

She thanked me for my concern. Although the revelation had upset her, she appreciated my motives.

'I will contact John Dawe, he will know what to do,' said Colin.

'John Dawe is a friend of ours, he works at the local CID. We have known him for many years, I think he will appreciate it is not a hoax and maybe he will get some sort of surveillance set up, we'll see what he says,' said Helen.

Colin went off to make the call. Helen was still upset by what I had said. This was unfortunate, but her distress was going to be seen by the police and this made them more likely to act.

Colin returned and said John was making his way to the house. It was decided to delay dinner, at least until the police had been and gone, not that Helen was in a fit state to serve dinner with her usual panache. The plan was coming together well.

The doorbell rang after only a few minutes, it was Detective Constable John Dawe. He walked into the lounge and we were introduced.

'Can you go over what happened at the hotel?' asked John.

'I was sitting in the bar having a drink earlier this evening and there were two men sat behind me. I overheard a short conversation between them. They spoke in a normal manner, there was no whispering, just a normal conversation tone. Suddenly the conversation stopped, I looked around but they were gone,' I said.

'Did you see their faces?'

'I'm afraid not, I had my back to them the whole time. I only looked around when the conversation stopped,' I said.

'Do you remember the exact words that were spoken?'

'Not the exact words, but one said something like "It can be done on Friday evening, the couple will be out." The other asked where it was and that was when Heinrich was mentioned as the house name. There was no mention of a street, so I assume they already knew the street. That was about it,' I said.

'So you saw the nameplate and asked Colin and Helen about their arrangements for Friday.'

'When I arrived and saw the name Heinrich, I thought I would ask them if they were going out. They said they were, and it was too much of a coincidence,' I said.

'I agree. For some reason, Colin, you have been targeted. Do you have anything of significant value to interest burglars?' John said.

'I can't think of a single reason why we should be the victims.'

Of course he had not, but he gave a convincing performance; I was very impressed.

'I think there is something in this story and I want to catch the burglars red-handed. I think my boss will agree with me. Don't worry, Helen, we will catch these men. I will go and see my boss and get the all-clear to set up some sort of operation,' said John.

She looked better for those few words.

'Where was this dinner date?' asked John.

Colin told him and explained that there was a group of eight of them, and they took turns each month to throw a dinner party, so there were six others apart from Colin and Helen.

'Are these the only people who knew of your arrangements for Friday night?' John asked.

'I'm afraid they are the only ones,' said Helen.

Her pallor increased yet again. She knew what he was saying: it was possible one of their close friends had organized the burglary.

'It is possible that someone at the party may not be the friend you thought they were, if they were the only ones who knew about your movements. Is there anyone who is going to be there that you feel suspicious of, or maybe someone you have not known very long?' John asked.

'I consider them all as close friends, I have known them for years. It seems inconceivable that any of them would be associated with such a crime, but what you say makes me doubt what I have just said. I will find myself looking at them again, trying to work out the most likely suspect,' she said.

'We cannot say for sure whether any of the dinner guests are involved or not; only a thorough investigation is going to provide the answer. I will speak with my boss and convey the information you have given me. I am confident there is enough there to convince him a crime is about to be committed,' John said.

He left the house and returned to the police station. I believed our story was convincing enough for the police to do something. Helen's performance had helped the situation immensely; she was of course not acting, to her it was very real. Colin too was confident that a surveillance operation was the likely outcome.

We eventually sat down to dinner, having persuaded Helen that the police were going to deal with what was about to happen. The burglars were going to be caught and prosecuted, and if it was something to do with their friends, it was better to sort it out sooner rather than later.

I think the worst part for Helen was believing one of her friends was possibly involved. Neither Colin nor I knew if this was true, bearing in mind that the offender was never caught. Nobody was to be ruled out until the offender was apprehended, but hopefully the truth would be at our disposal in a few days.

Dinner was sumptuous of course, she was an excellent cook. We talked about the revelations of that evening, trying hard to put her mind at ease. She ate very little, which was a shame; her appetite was affected by the whole incident. Colin on the other hand ate heartily. It was a good job she would never know the truth; she was never going to know that.

The following day I received a telephone call from Colin. John Dawe wanted to see us all at Colin's house that evening: he had approval for an operation in connection with the burglary, and he wanted to discuss it with us. Colin reminded me that Helen was going to be taken ill on the day, we had no way of changing that piece of history. Of course it was not something we were able to discuss with the police, but we both felt that somehow we had to overcome that problem in some way, to protect her.

I arrived at the house just after 8 p.m. John Dawe was already there, joined this time by a female officer who was introduced to me as Lisa. We shook hands and walked into the lounge. Colin and Helen were already seated, waiting to hear what the plan was to be. The officers and I sat down.

John suggested we listen to his briefing on the plan before making any comment; there would be plenty of time to ask him questions. He was happy to hear any suggestions to do with the plan; if it was possible to improve it he was going to be happy to make such adjustments. He said he was here to make sure we were all safe. He looked at us individually, waiting for a nod of approval, which he got from the three of us.

'We do not know for certain how many people are involved in this burglary, experience tells us it will be either one or two, but we will allow for the unlikely scenario that there are three burglars; our manpower will reflect that. We also have no idea if these people will be watching the house on Friday, but we will assume they will be, prior to you leaving for the dinner. If they do watch the house, it will probably only be for an hour or so before you leave, but we do not want them to see police officers around. By that token we will be in the house from lunchtime, four police officers. including our policewoman Lisa.

'I feel it necessary to bring Lisa in on the operation as she can travel to the dinner with Colin if Helen doesn't want to go. It is completely up to you, Helen, it is merely a back-up plan. In saying that, I would prefer that both Colin and Helen leave the house as planned. The rest of us will wait inside for the burglar or burglars to break in. If you two fail to turn up at the party, it will make the guests suspicious, particularly those who may be involved in the burglary. It is therefore imperative you attend the function. Do you all understand the plan?' John asked.

We said we understood.

'What about me, where do you want me?' I asked.

'There will be an unmarked police vehicle in the street with two officers inside. I am happy for you to wait with them. Your information has been paramount in this operation. I thought you might want to listen in to what is happening,' he said.

I was satisfied with that.

'I will turn up at midday with three male officers and Lisa, and we will remain in the house out of sight. Colin and Helen will then leave at the appropriate time for their dinner engagement, while we await our visitors. I hope you have plenty of tea, Helen?' he said.

'Of course, and no doubt you'll want sandwiches as well,' she said.

'Once we have the people in custody, Colin and Helen will be contacted after the party, when they arrive home. It is imperative that you both remain at the party until the end; if one or more of the guests are involved we will not know until the suspect or suspects have been interviewed,' John concluded.

It appeared to be a good plan which had every chance of being successful. In my mind I felt happy that the perpetrator was not going to be able to murder Helen. Although it would now be impossible to charge the person with that offence, we would have saved her life.

The police came to pick me up from the hotel just after 6 p.m. I sat in the rear of the unmarked police vehicle, and two officers were sitting in the front. They were in radio contact with the inside of Colin's house, and relayed to me what was going on. Several officers were inside the house, including Lisa.

Then they told me Lisa was going to be leaving the house with Colin; unfortunately Helen had been taken ill and was too unwell to leave her bed. I had suspected this might happen, in fact I knew it was going to, but the police had covered the situation. Lisa appeared to be a capable officer. Neither Colin nor Lisa had left the house yet, that event was an hour away. I then thought, if Colin contacted the dinner guests and said Helen was ill, why was Lisa accompanying him? The question was put to John inside the house. He asked how I knew Colin had contacted the dinner party, a good point. I merely said that was what I expected Colin to do, being the polite man he was. It was thought if two people left the house the burglars would assume the house was empty, if Colin left on his own the possibility of his wife being in the house may frighten the burglars. I understood why this plan was carried out, giving the appearance that the house was empty.

John stated that Colin was not to contact the dinner party, such a phone call would alert the dinner guests that Helen was in the house. 'If these guests are involved, it is possible they will call off the burglary when they realize someone is in the house. Leave the house with Lisa, but obviously she will not attend the dinner, she will wait outside and bring you home. She is only in the car to give the impression Helen is leaving the house.'

We pulled into the street, and parked about 50 yards from the house, positioning ourselves to be ready in case the officers were needed. There was some radio chatter between the officers, letting each other know that everyone was in position inside and outside the house. Our job was to alert the house of any cars in the road, therefore preparing them for the burglary.

I knew nothing was going to happen until after Colin left the house, but I did not feel inclined to share that information. The conversation in the car was limited, neither officer wanting to miss any car that came into the road. I did mention the paintings to them, when I said how much they were worth their ears pricked up some.

We saw a car pull up opposite the house; from our position we were unable to see its registration or how many occupants there were. It was possible that this was our burglar, but we knew he was not going to approach whilst Colin's car was in the driveway. It was not time for them to leave the house yet, based on the timings Colin had told me of the other 1985. It was important he stuck to that schedule, we had agreed on that. But nobody expected them to break in yet, knowing the residents were at home.

From the radio conversation it appeared that Lisa was definitely leaving and taking on Helen's role. Helen had decided to remain in the house with the police, out of the way of our burglars. Alex, our driver, relayed the details of the car to the officers inside the house. It was a likely candidate, parked as it was opposite the house. One of the officers inside the house took a look from an upstairs window, and said there was only one person in the car. The next message from inside the house stated that neither Colin nor Helen were aware that the car belonged to anyone in the street.

There was still about 15 minutes before they were due to leave; the police decided not to deviate from this schedule. We sat in the quite warm car, waiting to hear that they were leaving the house. Although it was not long to wait it did seem as though it was never going to happen. Eventually the word came, they were about to leave the house. From our position we had a good view of the car after it left the house and came onto the road, Colin took a left turn and headed towards our location. As Colin and Lisa drove past us, they made no acknowledgement of our presence, on the advice of the police. Any such movement might be noticed by the offender.

How soon the break-in would occur, nobody knew. At the time of the original offence, Colin said he had returned home and found Helen's body. He looked around the house before calling the police, but was unable to find a point where anyone had broken in. At the time, he felt Helen had probably let the person in. I did feel this was unlikely, unless the burglar was someone she knew.

Colin passed us as rehearsed, he was to go to the party alone, Lisa would wait nearby in the street, then she was going to return to the house with Colin, but not until the party had taken place. Arriving at the party alone was the exact scenario of his previous incarnation. Before, he had telephoned the party to say Helen was ill; this was not the case this time, on John's instruction. Lisa was only in the car to encourage the burglar to think the house was empty, although that was not the case on the previous 1985. Once the offender had been arrested we were to wait for Colin to return home from the party with Lisa, then he was to be escorted to the police station, that was assuming the offender had been apprehended. The dinner party guests were to know nothing of the operation.

The wait in our car was becoming unbearable. I felt certain the burglar was parked just a short way from us, he was about to commit a crime but had not yet done so, we had to wait for the act to take place. Maybe he was waiting to be sure the two occupants of the house were not going to return, possibly a very cautious burglar. Three sets of eyes were on the car, willing him to make his move, knowing there was nothing to be done until he made that move; everything was going to take place at the instigation of the burglar. We received a call from the house, they wanted to know what our man was doing. Sitting in the car was not the answer they wanted, they were as keen as we were to arrest him.

Then there was movement in the car, he had been sitting upright looking ahead, now he bent over and was picking up something or looking at something in the passenger seat, then he sat upright again. The driver's door opened, and a medium-height slimly built figure stepped out. He closed the door and locked it, he looked around in all directions. Was our burglar about to step outside the law? Alex contacted the house, stating the man had got out of the car, one of the officers inside had seen it from an upstairs window.

The car driver then walked to a house on our side of the road, the opposite side to Colin's house. He knocked on the door and someone opened it and spoke to him. To our surprise the man went into the house. I was as confused as my colleagues in the car. The message was relayed to the house; they were aware of what had happened. It appeared we had watched someone who may have been innocent in this affair, but why did he wait so long to knock on the door?

Then all became clear as the door of the house opened. The man was now accompanied by a lady, and we decided between the three of us that this was probably a blind date, and he was nervous about seeing his date. Unfortunately this did not help the problem, we were still short of a burglar. Colin had said he returned home just before midnight when he found Helen's body. That time span gave us up to four hours to wait.

Now another car travelled along the street, and this one pulled into Colin's driveway. We alerted them inside the house. Our view was now blocked by large bushes, but inside the house they were able to watch the arrival clearly, and they told us what was happening. A man got out of the car and went to the front door. He rang the doorbell. This posed a slight problem, which no one there but me knew about: on that fatal day it was possible that Helen had answered the door, simply because there was no sign of a break-in; added to that, her body was found downstairs. But nobody would answer the door, the police were lying in wait. So the offender might just leave, the problem far from solved.

Then came a revelation: the officers inside said he was pulling out a key from his pocket. He inserted it in the lock, and entered the house. This was something I had not considered, the burglar having a key, therefore it was someone both Colin and Helen knew. But who had they given a key to?

The next words spoken were music to my ears: the man had been arrested, he was about to be escorted to the car in handcuffs, then transported to the city centre police station. The offender was not named over the air, not that I was going to have any idea who he was likely to be.

Colin was unaware of the outcome, Lisa approached the car and said we could go back into the house, the burglar had been taken away. Another life saved I thought. Hopefully Colin might know the burglar, someone who had a key to the front door. was acquainted with the burglar. I was asked if I knew any of their respective friends, which of course I did not; I reminded them that I had only been in town a few days, and had only recently met Helen. I asked Helen if she knew the burglar, she stated she was upstairs all the time, he had been arrested and taken away before she came downstairs, she had not peered out of the window.

We were soon to find out who the intruder was, but one of the officers saw there was a possible problem: he did not think he had actually tried to steal anything, he was prevented from doing so by being arrested first. It was possible he was a family member with a key, he had not done anything wrong. He was only arrested because of what I had heard.

More information would be gained when he was formally interviewed. But was there more to this than Colin had actually told me? He was unlikely to keep vital information back, particularly with Helen at risk. Of course the police were right, it was impossible to say what this burglar intended to do. But this murderer was going free, although he had not committed the act. A man who had murdered Helen in the other 1985 was only going to be charged with burglary, and under the circumstances even that was unlikely. Apart from saving Helen's life, the consolation was that we were about to find out who did the deed in the other 1985. But it was little consolation knowing what Colin and I both knew about the scoundrel.

I waited in the house for Colin to return from the party, which he eventually did, a little earlier than the other 1985, but then he had good reason to want to return home. Lisa said one of the other officers was going to take us to the police station in the city centre, she was going to remain with Helen until we returned, a sensible precaution, although the precaution was unnecessary as the burglar had been caught, but I understood her reasons. On arrival at the police station we were let into the custody area, where other officers from the operation were standing by the desk. Colin was asked to accompany one of the officers, he wanted to know if Colin knew the offender.

'We want to take Colin to another room; hopefully he can identify the man we have arrested. The offender asked for Colin by name, it is obviously someone who knows him. We do not at this stage have anything to charge him with as he entered the house with a front door key. You need to see him, Colin, and establish why he had a key to the house. Possibly he stole it from you, but he could be someone you know. If you could wait here while we clear this up, it shouldn't take too long,' said the officer.

I waited in the corridor of the custody suite for Colin to return. I hoped the whole thing had not been too much of an ordeal for Helen. Lisa was at the house taking care of her. I thought I would go back to the house with Colin, to check on Helen. I waited patiently; Colin was taking his time.

Then the door to the interview room opened and he stepped out. He looked quite pale, and it took him a few moments to speak. He said he wanted to speak with me in private, and we were ushered to an empty interview room. Colin and I went into the room, he closed the door behind us, we both sat down and I awaited what he had to say.

'I've just been chatting to the burglar, he asked for me by name,' he said.

'I know, I was told that. Why did he ask for you, do you know who it is?' I said.

'I know who it is all right and now I understand why he asked for me. The police would not match him up to me, but I was shocked to see who it was. It is someone you also know, but I doubt you would recognize him now. You last met him in 1941,' he said.

My mind went blank, I remembered the ladies I had met, but right then I could not think of any men. I did not know who he was talking about. Then came the bombshell. He was right, I had met him before.

'The burglar is my father. He used his real name Heinrich, therefore the police did not make the connection, they did not know he was my father. He told me quietly he did not want to ruin my reputation by telling the police he was my father – very considerate of him,' said Colin.

'Had you seen your father since we returned?' I said.

'No I hadn't, but he was a regular visitor to the house, he was there a couple of weeks ago, so he tells me. He did say I had aged in the last fortnight. He did tell me why he was at the house, it was to steal something, something very important he said. He knew Helen and I were going to dinner. You know what this means: in the other 1985 my father killed my wife. Do you have any idea how difficult that is to take in?' he said.

The story he told Colin was complicated. During the war his father knew a fellow German named Stuygens, who was also a spy. He supplied his father with information, in particular about when the U-boats were going to pick up whatever information his father was able to give them. He arranged the transportation back to Germany. When we persuaded his father to stop passing information, Stuygens continued his devious ways. His father was a disappointment to Stuygens, he made that clear at the time. Stuygens lived in Exeter and his father had kept in touch with him, not for spying, simply because of their wartime connection.

Stuygens contacted his father a few months ago, telling him a group of fanatics were after him, Jews looking for the Nazis. This group had information that was likely to link Stuygens to a spying ring, but they did not have enough to convict him. That was where Colin's father came into the equation: Stuygens said he knew his father kept a diary during the war and he was concerned about what it contained. However, the fact was that his father did not keep a diary, but his mother did, and she gave it to Helen before she died, making sure she agreed not to let anyone see it. She was told it was an insurance policy against the likes of Stuygens, she did want Colin's father to be the only one who suffered because of the spying. Had there not been a reason behind it, the diary would have no doubt been destroyed. In the other version of time Colin's father had been executed, it has been his mother's wish to hand the diary over and thereby convict the other spies, but this she did not do, she intended to do it just after Colin's father had been executed. She hung on to the diary with a view to carrying out this plan, but as time passed she mellowed, thinking it a nice reminder of her husband, although she did not agree with his actions. She left it to Helen rather than Colin, believing Helen was going to look after it until she felt all should be told to the authorities, ruining any life Stuygens had made for himself, a sort of revenge she felt she was able to take through her daughter-in-law.

His father knew about the diary, and he had no doubt mentioned its existence to Stuygens. He had no idea what it contained, but Stuygens obviously thought it was possible there was something in the diary that was damaging to him. His father was told to get the diary: he had access to the house, it was going to be a simple task for someone with a key. His father agreed.

Colin said it was very likely that his mother had put things in that diary that would be detrimental to Stuygens health. He knew for a fact that details of his father's activities had been recorded in that diary, his mother had told him that in her later years. She said that what was written could possibly hang a few German spies. She had very little time for what the Germans had done in the last war, and although she did marry a German, she always felt he was one of the weak ones, 'unable to hurt a fly' was her expression for him.

Stuygens needed the diary, and he told Colin's father he was going to take him down with him if this organization got hold of him. His father had little choice but to help. He had a key to the house, given to him by Colin some time ago; he rarely used it. And somehow his father had obtained the combination to Colin's safe, possibly by watching him use it. Initially Colin had thought the safe was opened by his wife, but it now seemed more likely it was opened by his father.

No signs of breaking into the house or the safe, it all fitted into place now. We knew there was nothing taken except the diary, that was exactly how it was in the other 1985. There was nothing else to discuss, it was cut and dried as far as Colin was concerned.

'Colin, you have not thought this through properly; it is not as simple as you thought. There are several aspects of this burglary that throw a different light on who the perpetrator was, and I am glad to tell you it was not your father. In the original burglary, when Helen was murdered, it was impossible for your father to have been the burglar: he was executed in 1949, he was not around at that time. These are in fact a new set of circumstances involving your father, who should not be here,' I said.

Suddenly the whole impact of what I had said was shown on his face. He smiled at knowing his father was not the murderer.

'What you must realize is that we are no further ahead: the man who killed Helen is still at large, although in fact she is still alive. We have another problem: is another break-in to be attempted, thereby putting Helen's life in jeopardy yet again?' I said.

'I will get my father released from custody. He has not actually committed a crime, and as you say he was not involved in the original crime. This evening's events have shocked him,' said Colin.

'If your father took the diary to Stuygens, surely that would solve the problem. There would be no need for anyone to break-in and Stuygens would have what he wanted. I think it is fair to say Stuygens had something to do with the original crime, that is a logical conclusion,' I said.

'Of course you're right, Stuygens only wants the diary. If we give it to him there is no need to commit the crime,' he said.

'I have a better idea. Why don't we visit Stuygens? We still have our government passes, we could put the frighteners on him. It is a great opportunity to tell him that we knew of his war exploits, such a revelation is going to cause him great discomfort and would be an advantage during our negotiations with him,' I said.

'I think it's an excellent idea,' he said.

There was one thing niggling me. We know on this occasion his father was in touch with Stuygens, but how did Stuygens know the address in the other 1985, when Colin's father was dead? I asked Colin if he knew the reason.

'I do know the reason, but I need to go back to my childhood to explain. Following the death of my father, my mother brought me up on her own, which as you can imagine was quite a struggle in those days, just after the war. We were never short of money, but I then began to realize why. Although my mother went out to work, we had more money than other two-parent families. She received a letter once a week, I remember seeing her open one of these letters, it contained pound notes. At the time I did not know where they came from, but these letters were postmarked Exeter. Stuygens had lived there since the war. The money was almost certainly from him, maybe a thank-you for my father's silence. From what I found out about the trial, my father never murmured a word about who else was involved,' he said.

'If Stuygens knew your mother was using the name Wickham, it would be easy to locate your address. With both your parents dead he concluded the diary was going to be in your possession, a logical assumption. In this 1985 it was easy for your father to take the diary, he had access to your house. Was Stuygens the burglar in the other 1985? He must have rung the doorbell and

Helen answered the door. He had not expected to find anyone at home, the rest as they say is indeed history,' I said.

'He must have got her to open the safe first, then he murdered her,' he said.

'The next question is how Stuygens knew Colin and Helen were going out that evening. The information must have come from one of the dinner guests, there was no other way he would have known. How well do you know these people?' I said.

'Not very well actually, they are Helen's friends. I would suggest Stuygens is the best man to answer that question. I will speak to my father and get Stuygens' address in Exeter,' he said.

'You do realize that at some point you will have to tell Helen about your father's actions in the war?' I said.

'I know I will. I will try to avoid using the word spy, I'll try to make it more subtle, but I don't know how that can be done,' he said.

Colin then left to see the duty officer. I was at a loss to understand a more subtle way of describing a spy: he was what he was. At least we knew his father was not a murderer, just a burglar working for a murderer, an important breakthrough.

Colin appeared with his father, and Mr Wickham Senior looked at me strangely.

'Do I know you? I feel we have met before,' he said.

'We have, it was a long time ago, I doubt you will remember the circumstances. One day when I have time I will refresh your memory,' I said.

'It has not been my best day, I have been caught doing something I was not proud of. I will explain everything when we get back to your house. I owe you a huge apology,' he said.

'There is no need, we know everything,' said Colin.

This surprised him, with good reason.

'How on earth do you know what I planned to do?' he said.

'We have a plan of our own and with your help we can end this once and for all. We will prevent a certain person from contacting you and our scheme will put your mind at rest,' said Colin.

This confused him even more.

We left the police station and caught a taxi to Colin's house. During the journey we agreed that Helen was not to be told the true facts, just that a burglar had been caught, as we did not want to ruin her relationship with Colin's father on that score. Although the revelation that he was a German spy was unlikely to help the situation.

Helen opened the door for us, she looked quite recovered now. She was completely unaware of her father-in-law's involvement.

'What happened at the police station?' she said.

'The burglar is being dealt with, there is no need to worry,' said Colin.

She looked at his father, expecting an explanation for his presence.

'I rang Dad to tell him what was happening, he came to the police station to offer his support. I mentioned to him you were not very well and he wanted to make sure you were all right,' he said.

'I appreciate that,' she said and gave him a hug.

We retired to the lounge where Colin fetched four glasses and poured us each a fine brandy. We sipped this as I waited for him to break the news of his father's previous occupation. But he had clearly decided to say nothing; he did not want to upset Helen and alienate his father.

'The police interviewed the burglar, he broke in to get the diary. Do you know why the diary is so important?' he asked Helen.

'The only diary I am aware of is your mother's. She asked me to keep it for her. I have no idea what it contains, but she did say it could be important in the future. I have never even read the contents, I assume it was your mother's reminiscences of the war years, private only to her. But the burglar never actually broke in, did he? I cannot find any damage to the door,' she said.

'The police caught him before he forced entry. The police want to see the diary, it is evidence in the case. Is it all right if I give it to the police? I ask because it was left in your safekeeping,' Colin said.

'They are welcome to it, if it causes people to break in I don't want it. You can tell the police to destroy it when they have finished with it,' she said. Colin thought it might have been prudent for his mother to have destroyed it many years, no doubt she would have if she knew what problems it was going to cause. It appeared she had told Helen very little about the diary, but she was quite ill when she bequeathed it to Helen.

Knowing what we were going to do with the diary Colin agreed with her.

'I will tell the police to destroy it when they have finished their investigation.'

I felt we needed to know the contents of the diary before seeing Stuygens, who we knew from Colin's father now called himself Green, which he had done since before the war, he was accepted to be a British citizen by all who knew him. Helen invited me to stay the night, which was fortuitous as Colin and I wished to discuss our visit to Mr Green in Exeter, after she had retired for the night.

Helen went to bed just before 10 p.m., having not completely recovered from her illness. The three of us sat in the lounge ready to hear what Colin's father had to say about this man Stuygens.

'Stuygens is still a loyal German and during the war he was a faithful follower of Hitler; believing he was the man to help Germany rise again, unaware of the atrocities that the papers in Britain said Hitler was part of, he did not believe these reports. He was not a Nazi in the true sense of the word, just a German patriot who took to spying for his country, it was his way of helping the Fatherland. He is older now, he has seen the war criminals brought to justice and he fears for his own safety; not in the war criminal sense, he had nothing to do with that, simply because he was a spy. If you visit him you must be forceful in your approach, especially about the consequences of his wartime activities; he will be frightened if you approach him in this manner.

Do not let him off the hook, or let him think he has got away with it. You will need to make him feel nervous,' said Colin's father.

I then made a comment that I regretted as soon as I said it.

'We are going to make Stuygens as nervous as we made you in 1941, when we warned you off,' I said.

He looked at me closely. At first he clearly had no inkling as to how I knew that, then it suddenly dawned on him. 'Now I remember you, we did meet in 1941, you made me aware that the authorities knew what I was up to, but that is not possible. That was forty years ago, you have not aged one bit,' he said.

He did not remember his son, but Colin had hidden his face under a large brimmed hat when I confronted his father, part of our plan.

'Actually, the man you met was my father, we look the same, he told me the story many years later, it is only recently I realized that man was you. I apologize for the shock I gave you,' I said.

He continued to look straight into my eyes, then he smiled, accepting my explanation.

Colin and I breathed a sigh of relief. There was no way we could have told his father the truth, that would be stupid; he was not going to believe such an outlandish story of time travel.

Colin now got up and went to the safe, he dialled in the combination, opened the door and pulled out a black book, the diary. He said he wanted to know what all the fuss was about, I did not think his father had been privy to the information in the diary, he had no idea what his wife had recorded, he was as interested as we were.

Colin opened the diary and started reading it. I waited in the hope he was going to share the contents with us, but he continued reading, turning the pages slowly as he did so.

'Are you going to tell us why the diary is so important?' I said.

'It contains lists of names and addresses, including our friend Stuygens. In fact he is very prominent, no wonder he wanted it.

It has the same address we have for him in Exeter, no wonder he was so worried. Were you aware that Mother was detailing the names of these people? There are about forty different names and addresses,' Colin said.

'I was not sure what she had written down, I never actually saw the contents. It was her way of ensuring no harm came to us, an insurance policy. I suspected she was recording names, but whose I did not know. I don't know how she got Stuygens' address, but your mother was a resourceful woman,' he said.

I did not know how this diary was unable to help her husband in the other 1949, when he was executed for spying. I suppose the evidence against him was so strong she was unable to help, but she kept it for revenge in her future.

'What do you mean she was resourceful, she knew nothing about espionage. You were the spy, isn't that so?' said Colin.

'I did the donkey work, your mother was the brains of the operation. She had the idea to spy, I just did what she wanted me to do. The operation would have been very poor if it wasn't for your mother. She turned it into a successful operation,' he said.

This piece of news was devastating for Colin. He was visibly shocked at what he had heard. He had known his father was a spy, but the fact that his mother took part in the operation was hard for him to believe. He thought the world of his mother, and in his eyes she was incapable of doing any wrong. This appeared to explain the money she received when he was young: his mother was being paid for her part in the spying operation, not as he thought in compensation for his father's execution. What part did Stuygens play in this whole affair, apart from passing information about the locations for passing information? Was he in fact the brains of the whole spying ring in the area? I felt Colin wanted to know the answer to that as much as I did.

Colin's father went to bed, no doubt feeling it necessary to leave after passing such devastating news to his son about his mother.

'We need to approach Stuygens. What he tells us could be vital in deciding who was the spy. I think Stuygens is the key, he knew the truth. Your father may be lying to protect himself, your mother is unable to answer for herself. By seeing Stuygens you can find out the whole truth, get all the skeletons out of the cupboard,' I said.

'I agree, but what if Stuygens doesn't want to tell us? Why should he tell us the truth? He has his own problems, he believes some Jewish faction is out to get him for war crimes or the like, he has no reason to tell us anything. We can offer him the diary, which of course he can destroy if he wishes – in theory that will leave no evidence against him. What concerns me is this faction that are after him. They do not have the diary, therefore it is reasonable to suggest they have their own evidence. The diary will not help him against these people,' he said.

The next day I went to Ruby Bay. It was my intention to meet a young lady I had not seen for four years, someone I had become attached to: Julie's daughter, who was quite possibly my daughter as well. I intended going to the shop to see if she was there, then to invite her to dinner at the hotel that evening, or possibly lunch in the village. It was up to her whether or not she wanted to see me.

I walked into the estate agents and was surprised to see them both there, mother and daughter, the second and third generations. They both appeared pleased to see me. Then Julie came towards me and shook my hand, saying she had hoped I was going to return, Juliette remained seated, she did smile at me.

Then I asked if she was too busy to have lunch with me. She looked at her daughter, who nodded her approval. We left the shop and walked along to the Pilchard, which was more modern now, not quite as I remembered it.

As we walked Julie placed her arm inside mine, just as her mother had done 40 years ago. It was if she knew something. Perhaps all was going to be revealed over lunch. We sat down in a quiet corner and ordered drinks and our food.

Then Julie looked straight into my eyes.

'You look exactly like the photograph my mother had of your father, the resemblance is uncanny,' she said.

'I have been told I am the image of my father, as you are the image of your mother,' I said.

'There was no photograph of your father in my mother's possessions, just as you have never seen a photograph of my mother,' she said.

I was beginning to think this was one of those moments in a film, the one where the truth comes to the fore. But how was I going to tell her the truth? I hardly believed the story myself. It was time to go on the defensive.

'What do you mean by that?'

'It is obvious, you must have met my mother at some point. You must have met her here in Ruby Bay, possibly just before she died. The only people who know I am the image of my mother, live here, those that have seen me grow up. There are no photographs of my mother: she hated being photographed, she thought it was bad luck, it was a sort of witchcraft thing. Anybody who knew her would tell you the same story. You are right, I look very much like her, but how did you know that? I do not recall you ever being in Ruby Bay when my mother was alive. If you had met her I would have known. For the last ten years of her life we chatted every day, you were certain to have been mentioned if she had met you. So there must be some other explanation, one which I think I know, but I'm sure you'll tell me in your own good time,' she said.

I was knocked completely off balance by what I had just heard. How was I going to get out of this one? She was looking me straight in the eyes, and beautiful though the eyes were, they were piercing, waiting for some kind of explanation.

'What do you think the reason is?' I said.

I was hoping she was going to give me something to work with, all I had was the truth, and the chances of her believing that provided impossible odds.

'When you left here four years ago, I looked closely at my daughter Juliette. We both have something in common, something my mother never had, it is a slight blemish, but enough to notice. Our noses are shaped slightly differently, your nose has a similar shape, therefore I think we are related in some way. I think you knew that and tried to make contact for that reason. I only noticed it on your last visit. You say your father met my mother in 1941; I was born in December 1941, the result, I think of their union. How does that sound as an explanation?' she said.

'It sounds like a likely explanation,' I said.

It was a better explanation than the real one.

'The thing that confuses me a little, is the way you looked shocked when you saw me at the hotel, as did your friend, as if you had seen a ghost. You had seen Juliette, we do look very similar, but my resemblance to my mother is closer than Juliette's, in fact I am near enough the same age as my mother was in 1941. You had no reason to be shocked, certainly not after seeing Juliette first. There is only one explanation for your reaction; you thought I was my mother when I walked into the hotel, as did your friend. How close am I to the truth?' she said.

'Tell me exactly what you are thinking by making that remark. You tell me what you think, and I promise I will tell you the truth, although I don't expect you to believe it,' I said.

'I will say what I think, and this is pretty crazy as well. Not only do I believe you were the person my mother met in 1941, but I think there is a strong possibility you may be my father. What I need to know from you is, how is that possible?'

'This is probably the most difficult conversation of my life, but I will tell you everything.'

I explained about my time travel to 1941, and she did not laugh but looked interested in what I was saying. I did not tell her everything: she still did not know that I was from 2000.

'Your mother visited Colin and me on many occasions for dinner at the hotel, we got on very well. One thing led to another, as inevitably they do, and you were the result, but I did not know that until a few years ago when I first visited your premises. It was quite a shock to find that I not only had a daughter, but also a granddaughter, hence the reason I have come to see you again. I so much wanted to tell you, but I had no way of knowing how you would take such a fantastic story. You have made it easier for me.'

I saw she had tears in her eyes. She actually appeared to believe what I had told her. I was relieved I had got it off my chest, and I thought it had helped her as well.

'The story is beyond belief, not that I don't believe what you're saying, but a DNA test would prove it, if you agree. I want to verify that the relationship is what we believe it to be, just to be sure you're not a raving lunatic. I will not mention anything to Juliette until we are sure.'

The next day we made the trip to Plymouth. This test was going to prove it beyond doubt, it was about to help all three of us. It is not easy to get such a test unless one is prepared to pay for it, and I decided to do that to speed up the process. The results would take a few days, and they would be sent to Julie's address.

I dropped Julie off in Ruby Bay, and this time a hug seemed appropriate. I said I was going to explain more when I next saw her; she needed to know for sure that I was not from this time.

I then went back to Colin's house to discuss our plan to visit our neighbourhood spy in Exeter. We decided to go the following day, each wearing the suit of a War Office/Secret Service man. Colin would bring our false identity cards. The cards looked believable even in 1985, and hopefully would be enough to fool Green; they had fooled Colin's father in 1941.

I was thinking about the pieces of artwork we had rescued. There must have been other items of value before the paintings haul, and perhaps Green was the middleman who sold on the items. Perhaps Colin had thought the same: that was something to discuss with him on our hour-long journey to Exeter.

Colin and I both went to bed early. He looked shattered by what we had discussed; I had seen him look that way before, in

1941 when he had a harem to keep satisfied. He was looking forward to meeting Stuygens, tomorrow was the day everything was to be put into perspective. I think he was prepared for the worst but hoping for the best.

At breakfast, Helen was told of the truth about the arrest of Colin's father. We were able to explain that it was all a big mistake, he was thought to be an intruder, but he was merely visiting Helen because Colin had told him she was ill. Helen accepted this, she did not think her father-in-law was a burglar.

We had decided she was not likely to want to know the details of his past, nor the real reason for our visit to Exeter. Colin had clients all over the West Country, and this was described as another business meeting. Helen was not told I was going as well; Colin said he was going to drop me off at my hotel on the way to Exeter, which she thought a very kind gesture.

Colin's father left after breakfast, and privately thanked us both for what we were doing. He knew the true facts were never going to be spoken about in front of Helen, and he was certainly not going to implicate himself.

We left the house around 10 a.m. Helen said she hoped I was available for dinner again later in the week.

I went into the hotel with Colin, going to my room to put on the suit I had bought recently in Plymouth, it looked the part, even Colin thought it appropriate. Colin had the ID cards, which he produced in pristine condition. He said the diary was in his briefcase in the car. This was hopefully our trump card in negotiating some sort of truth from Stuygens, and I hoped for Colin's sake that it was going to work. We left the hotel looking very official in our dark suits.

Colin was now about to hear more about his past than he had ever thought possible, and I was concerned about the possible revelations he was likely to hear from Mr Green. I was also sympathetic to how this might affect Helen. At this point in time she was not aware her father-in-law was a German spy, she had looked upon him with affection, sheltered from his past.

In the fullness of time, following our meeting in Exeter, she might learn that both her in-laws were spies, this was going to be devastating news indeed. Although it was not for me to question Colin's judgement in this matter, the fact he had probably lied about his father's involvement in the war was not going to assist his position if he suddenly decided to tell the truth. I felt he should have confronted this many years ago. What was Helen's attitude going to be to this sordid matter? Or did he intend never to tell her the true facts. I felt his mind at this point was probably going through a turmoil of infinite proportions. He knew decisions needed to be made, particularly if the Exeter mission proved disastrous to his family name.

8

We left Plymouth and took the main dual carriageway towards Exeter, it was a slow journey because of the amount of traffic, but this gave us time to talk. We needed to discuss what we were going to say to Mr Green, and our initial approach was crucial: we were intending to get information from him, information that he was probably reluctant to hand over without some sort of guarantee.

Colin made it clear that what mattered to him, as well as ensuring his wife was safe in the future, was to know how involved his mother had been. Not for one moment did he ever consider his mother to be anything less than worthy of the pedestal he had put her on. Suddenly everything had changed, following what his father had said. His mother rarely spoke to him about his father, she tried hard to protect him from that period of his father's life, and he believed she knew the truth was going to come out one day; she just did not want to be the one to tell him. That reason was possibly because of her involvement: only now did he consider that possibility.

The regular payments of money she was receiving were some sort of hush money, she was being paid for what she knew. But Green was the best person to discuss it with, he had all the answers, it was just a matter of whether he was going to divulge them.

'What sort of area does Stuygens live in? You know Exeter better than I do,' I said.

'It is quite an exclusive part of town, a nice area,' he said.

'Stuygens, or should I say Green, has become wealthy as a result of his spying,' I said.

'I think he has amassed his money off the backs of people like my father.'

'I don't think your father lost much, he seems to be well enough off. I'm sure he had his cut as well. You need to change your attitude if we're going to get information from Green.'

'Don't worry, I will be calm, I will be politeness itself. I appreciate it is the only way to get the information we want,' he said.

'I can understand how you feel, you are angry with Green and although he sent your mother money, you think it was a small amount compared to what Green got. It is possible that Green got his wealth after the war, although the ventures were paid for by his spying money,' I said.

'I am entitled to my opinion and I think Green is one of the bad guys.'

I changed the subject by telling him about my meeting the previous day with Julie. I related our conversation, and told him that I had told her the truth.

There was a layby approaching, he indicated and we pulled in and stopped.

'Did you actually tell her we were time travellers? What was her reaction to that?'

'She sort of believed it, then she thought there was a way of clearing it up, if we had a DNA test, privately of course.'

I wished I had a camera to take a picture of his face, his mouth was wide open and he was staring at me.

'If the DNA test goes as we think it will, she will know she is your daughter. Do you think that is a good idea, bearing in mind you're going to leave soon for fifteen years in the future? Are you going to explain that to her?'

'I have not mentioned that yet, we have to see how the DNA test goes first. Maybe I am not the father, it is possible Julie had another relationship in 1941. After we left, how could we know whether there was someone else or not?' I said.

He looked at me and shook his head. 'You know as well as me, she did not have casual affairs. You're the father all right.'

'I know you're right, I feel certain I am the father. There is little to discuss until the DNA results came back, it is a near certainty they will be positive. I have decisions that need to be made about my future. Alan is waiting for me to return to the island, he is not going to leave without me. The longer I remain here, the greater danger he is in. I know I will return to my own time,' I said.

'I am amazed you broached the subject of time travel with Julie. Even if the DNA shows she is your daughter, do you think she will just accept time travel?'

'Surely she has no alternative, I am her father and I am a little older than her. She must accept there is something in it,' I said.

Our final destination was about 25 minutes away. We had discussed using our Secret Service identities from the off, to put him on the back foot. We would then move into sympathetic mode to get his cooperation. There was going to be no mention of the diary until it became necessary; we must try to get as much from him before we spoke of the burglary.

Our reason for the visit was to be simply that we had heard about the organization that was after him, and we wanted to help if possible. Nothing was to be mentioned about his exploits in the war, not unless the subject was unavoidable. If he quizzed us on the organization that was after him, a reference to the Israelis was all we had to offer; they were always looking for war criminals. We decided to make it up as we went along. We could say what we wanted about the break-in, even to the point that someone was killed. He was not going to want to be associated with a murder, and our plan was based on his initial reaction.

There was of course the possibility that Mr Green was not at home. We had prevented the murder, but the man we believed had originally committed the crime was a short distance away, although without going back to the original crime scene, we were never going to know the true facts. The saving of Colin's father in 1941 had changed the events of that fateful night; and perhaps the murderer was someone other than Green.

We rounded a bend in the road and the house appeared on the left, a large detached property surrounded by a brick wall. We approached the electronic front gate and I pressed the intercom button. I was not sure what to say.

A voice at the other end greeted us, calling us by our first names. We were both amazed by that. He said everything would be explained over coffee, provided neither of us were going to refuse his hospitality. He invited us into the house.

The electronic gate started to open slowly. I looked at Colin, who seemed as confused as I did. Then we realized a telephone call had probably been received from his father.

We drove up a driveway which circled round the front of the large house. As we pulled up outside the large oak front door it opened, and an elderly man stood in the doorway. Was this Mr Green or the butler? It must be Green. We got out of the car and walked towards the man.

'Before we say anything, please do not insult me by showing those false identities. I know who you are and why you're here. Colin, I see the family resemblance. Your father told me you were coming, and I promised to answer all your questions,' he said.

We were invited into a very large lounge, paintings adorning the walls. I got the impression they were not fakes. The offer of coffee was accepted and we sat down to discuss the matter at hand.

'I am prepared to tell you everything you want to know, in return I want something from you. I appreciate Colin knows most of what there is to know about his father, but maybe I can add a little more,' he said.

We of course knew why he was in this frame of mind: he was keen to get the diary. It held information he did not want broadcasting, information we were able to barter for.

'Your father knew the importance of the diary, although I do not believe he ever examined it. He knew your mother was meticulous in her note-taking, it was unlikely she would leave out any detail. There are many names she recorded, but I think you already know that.'

'My father told me something that caused me great concern, something which I prefer to hear from you. I am not convinced I can trust what my father has told me, he might simply be protecting his own reputation,' Colin said.

'I understand what is it you want to know and I will tell you the truth. I have no reason to lie at this stage in my life

In fact we were sure that he had a very good reason to lie. We both nodded our agreement, we were willing to listen to Green. We hoped that the many inconsistencies in Colin's life were about to be cleared up.

'I am German by birth, you are probably aware my real name is Stuygens, but I changed it when I arrived in Britain in 1937, I thought an English name might be more preferable. Like many Germans I was aware of what was happening in my country: Hitler had come to power and to us in Germany war was inevitable, although Hitler did not spell that out, his speeches told most intelligent people he was not going to settle for a few pieces of territory, territory he believed belonged to Germany before the First World War. Rather than go and fight in the trenches, I thought I was going to be more use to the Fatherland by being in Britain. Although war was not declared until 1939, I knew that Hitler's ideals were going to be unacceptable to Britain, and eventually Germany and Britain would be at war with each other. I felt my usefulness to my country could be served by remaining in Britain. I had false papers which made me a British citizen, I applied for a job at the Ministry of Defence before the war actually started, my English was good and I spoke like an Englishman. I thought I was in the ideal position for when war broke out, I might be in a position to help Germany.

'I had worked in the equivalent organization in Germany,

and my skills in this field were to prove useful to my new occupation. Until relations with Germany changed dramatically, that is, but I was prepared for that. Strangely, my colleagues were not. I contacted the authorities in Germany before war broke out, then once the war started I was recruited as a spy by the Fatherland. My fluent English was something they needed, along with the fact that I was loyal to my country. I was completely unaware at this stage of the treatment Hitler showed to ethnic minorities, in particular the Jews. I know the English papers mentioned it at length, but I thought it was simply propaganda. I was happy to spy for my country, but it was not spying at that point, until it was felt that I was trustworthy, then my role changed.

'A network of spies had been set up all over the country, and the one in the West Country was among the most important, because it faced the Continent, and access by sea at isolated places was possible. That was the reason your father set himself up in Ruby Bay, it was off the beaten track, so German submarines could pass unnoticed. I worked in Plymouth with your father, and we got on well because we were both German: although I did not know it when we first met, he had moved here as I did. I was able to get him into the loop to assist me, then the government realized we both spoke German, so we were asked to spy for Britain; they still believed we were British citizens. The government purchased the house in Ruby Bay for him to use as a base to deal with the Germans, they wanted us to pass useless information to the Germans, which we agreed to do.'

'What about my mother's involvement? How far did her loyalties go, not only to my father, but was she loyal to her country, was she in fact a spy?'

'Your mother was important to the operation, she was an intelligent woman, able to put the information that was being passed in an orderly and believable fashion, thereby passing information that sounded more important than it was. Your father was unable to put the information together in such a way. During this period

I was alarmed that we were passing false information, because I wanted to help Germany.'

They were all at that time working for the British, passing false information to the Germans. Green was not happy about that, he wanted to be a German spy, but Colin's father and mother were happy to work for the British. Neither of Colin's parents were aware of Green's loyalties, they thought he was spying for Britain, until Green turned Colin to the dark side as it were, with relative ease it has to be said. Green told Colin's father that there was an opportunity to make themselves rich. Payment from the Germans was always made in goods, which the authorities got, while the two men were paid a wage for their efforts. Although the wages were generous by the standards of the day, the Germans were far more generous. They both felt the amount they got was not comparable to the goods received.

'What did the Germans leave as payment, what sort of goods?' I asked.

'Gold was their favourite currency, usually small bars, which they transported by submarine into Ruby Bay. All the gold was then handed over to the government official, he was liaison for the Treasury. We assumed it went into the Treasury pot, to help the war effort, but you never actually knew that, there were no receipts or anything. We suspected the liaison man probably made a bundle, he only needed to take one bar at a time. Whatever the government paid us we shared, straight down the line. It was after a while we realized we were not getting the lion's share, that was going to the government. Our share was quite paltry in comparison, so we decided to change the rules. I decided to deal directly with the Germans, I could speak the language and I knew how to contact them. It was decided to deal in artwork, the Germans were keen on that. Unfortunately it only happened once, on the second occasion the paintings were destroyed when a bomb hit your father's house, he then decided not to continue, someone had warned him. I have to admit I carried on for one more mission, it was enough to make me wealthy. Then I ceased to trade, the war was starting to go against the Germans at that point,' he said.

'What did your last haul consist of?' I said.

'Paintings. That's where the money was. I had four pieces but I sold three, it has allowed me to live out my life in comfort. That painting on the wall is the one I kept, it is my insurance for the future, in case the money runs out, which I don't think it will. I worked for the Ministry of Defence until the end of the war, then retired permanently,' he said.

We both left our seats and walked over to the painting Green had indicated. I recognized the artist instantly, we had two of his works at the forthcoming auction. I decided to impress Green.

'It does appear to me that your past has come back to haunt you. Do you know who these people are who are looking for you?' I said.

'It is a choice of several organizations, perhaps they think I was a double agent, except all the information passed to the Germans was of little use, that was the idea of our little set-up. I appreciate the artwork is likely to show I was working for the Germans, that can be the only reason. They have located something from German files, or they've mixed me up with someone else. The only possible evidence they would have is in the diary. Did you bring it with you, it all depends on what was written down?'

'I am happy to let you have the diary under certain conditions: you are never to contact my father again and he is never to be implicated in anything at a later stage, be it a government enquiry, or the people who you suspect are after you. Do I have your word on that?' Colin said.

'You have my word, which does mean something,' said Green.

Colin handed him the diary. He flicked through the pages quickly, and it appeared to confirm what he thought it was going to contain.

'That Nolde painting on your wall, do you know how much it's worth at auction?' I said.

'I have not had it valued, I would estimate over £1 million. That's only a rough estimate, but I hear two of his works are up for sale in London.'

Neither of us commented on that.

As we walked to the front door, Colin was deep in thought. Then he came out with it.

'I would appreciate an honest answer to this. Was my mother involved in anything that might make her a traitor?'

'You do not have to worry, Colin. Your mother was a true and proud British citizen. She was unaware your father had done anything other than what the government wanted; she would never do anything against her beloved country.'

'What would you have done if we had not brought you the diary, was there another burglary planned to get it?' I said.

'That was a possibility, I would have employed someone to break in, I have plenty of contacts, someone would have been hired for the job,' he said.

'Why did Colin's mother put you in the diary, surely she knew you were working for the British?' I said.

'She knew I was a good German, she also knew that I would spy for Germany if the opportunity arose. As it happens she was right, as the artwork will testify,' he said.

Colin now had the satisfaction of preventing another break-in, a satisfactory day's work. I was glad we had offloaded the diary on Green, removing the possibility of further a break-in to Colin's house which would put Helen at risk. He was now able to live in peace with his wife, without fear of further danger to her.

We left the house on reasonable terms with Green. Colin was a lot happier then when we arrived, as he had learned his mother was not involved in any treachery. This was important to him, his mother's memory was not to be tarnished. Green was in theory the only one with loyalties to Germany, he saw the opportunity to help his country, surely British spies did the same thing, maybe not for money but the principle is the same.

We discussed the fact that the murderer from the first 1985 was likely never to have been traced; it was someone hired for the job, just a paid burglar who had got carried away. This was something we decided not to pursue with Green.

From what Green had said the arrangements for the auction of our paintings were going well. I hoped it would happen before my return to the past. I was returning to that island past on my own, although Alan in the form of Landon was going to join me for my repatriation to my own time. But the whole of this adventure had been done in the company of Colin, and it was going to seem strange him not being there. However, he was definitely in a better place.

Colin dropped me off at my hotel, and I promised him that I would see him and Helen the following night for dinner. I was looking forward to that, now our work in this time had been successfully completed.

I sat there in the hotel lounge smiling to myself, not because I was going crazy, simply because Colin and I had achieved our goals in this time. He was returned to his wife, and he was going to live with her in the certain knowledge that our return had made that possible. We were both about to amass a fortune, six paintings were to be sold on our behalf, and each one was likely to command£1 million. My smile grew wider at that thought.

I still had a week before my return to the island, and I had another plan of my own. I had decided to visit my old street, the one where in this time my father now resided. It was impossible for me to make contact with him for obvious reasons, but he had passed away in 1989 and I thought it would be nice to see him again. It was a sort of personal pilgrimage. I had not shared this plan with Colin, this was personal to me.

And I had another errand of my own to complete, to find out if I had a new family in this time. If it was the case, I decided provisions must be made; I had neglected them for over 40 years, although I was unaware of their existence. I was going to meet

Julie in the near future when the DNA results were received, maybe to celebrate.

Colin contacted me the following day. Was there anything I wanted to do? I told him I was going to see someone today, then I was meeting Julie at some point. I did not tell him that, the person I was seeing today was my father.

Colin told me had been contacted by the auctioneers, and our paintings were going under the hammer in three days' time. It seemed that I was going to be in this time to see what the artwork fetched. I was glad of that, especially as some of the money was going to my new family, if that was in fact what they were to become.

I took a bus to the area of Plymouth where I had spent my formative years. I left this area at 18 years of age to join the Royal Air Force, but always returned during my leave periods.

My father took a daily walk to the shops, not necessarily to buy anything, on most occasions merely to chat to people he knew. He always went at the same time of day. I waited near the shops, looking down the street he was eventually going to walk along, hoping I was going to see him again. Having waited only a few minutes he appeared, wearing the trilby he had always worn, slowly making progress with the use of a walking stick. It was good to see him again. The moment became too emotional for me, and I decided to leave and catch the bus back to town. He continued his walk, unaware that I was nearby, chatting to everyone he passed, he was a sociable person. It was a very strange and moving experience.

That evening I caught a taxi to Colin's house and arrived in good time for dinner, knowing that a drink in the lounge was the accepted aperitif, always a pleasure with his extensive drinks cabinet, which he was pleased to open for his guests.

'I have heard from the auctioneers that interest in the paintings has been unprecedented, his words not mine,' said Colin.

'I'm pleased about that. I might still be here when the auction happens,' I said.

'Where are you going? Surely you can stay a little longer,' said Helen.

'Unfortunately I have to go abroad for a while. I have to leave on a particular day, it is out of my hands. If it were possible I would love to stay, sometimes you have no choice in these matters.'

'Where exactly are you going?' she asked.

'It's a little island, where they have no contact with the outside world. It has no modern conveniences, the people are way behind the times. I am not expecting to be away that long, relatively speaking that is,' I said.

'What job do you do?' she asked.

'I deal in ancient artefacts.'

I was hoping she knew nothing on this subject.

'Pat doesn't like talking about his work. What are you going to spend your fortune on when you return?' asked Colin.

I was very tempted to say wine and women, but decided against the obvious quip.

'I've always wanted to live in Ruby Bay. Since I was a boy I always thought it would be nice to retire there and live by the sea. Colin had said he was going to sort out a property for me, is that still the case?'

'Leave it me,' he said.

'I think you know the one I like, hopefully I can move in on my return,' I said.

'When do you intend leaving on your trip?' she said.

'Next Wednesday, I have no idea when I will be returning. It was a long trip time-wise, but we'll meet up on my return,' I said.

'I think we should arrange a meeting about the house in Ruby Bay before you leave, perhaps one evening when I finish work,' he said.

We had to be careful what we said, Helen was a very astute lady. This so called business meeting at Ruby Bay was obviously to cover my departure back to the island, and she never infringed on his business matters.

'Dinner is ready, let's not talk business,' she said.

We had achieved what we intended to do. Colin smiled, knowing well how to put Helen off the scent; she had responded exactly as he had anticipated, those years away had not change his understanding of her, he knew how to bore her.

Dinner was again very palatable, and the conversation was far away from any business deals, except that concerning the paintings, a subject which Helen was prepared to discuss at length. I persuaded her the paintings belonged to my father and were passed down to me, they had been kept in various lofts over a period of time, nobody knowing if they were valuable. I had at first thought my father's purchase had not been very astute, but he knew more than he was letting on, I remembered seeing them in the attic of my home during my formative years, little did I know then.

When I discovered what they were, along with Colin's assistance, we decided it was possible they were very valuable pieces of artwork, which is when we called on expert help. I again emphasized how priceless Colin had been during this period, not only checking records for me but also contacting the experts, his contribution had been invaluable and he deserved his share of my windfall.

As long as Helen never actually saw his bank statements, maybe he had a chance of getting away with it. He could tell her he had invested the money I gave him, and that his investments made money. Helen was happy that he was getting something from the venture, talking of a new dress and a new piece of jewellery. If she knew the truth her sights would likely be set much higher: maybe a holiday home in the Algarve.

Back at my hotel that evening, my thoughts turned to my imminent return to the island. It was less than a week away. The money from the sale would be safely tucked away in my account by then. I had no idea what sort of interest £3 million was going to earn in interest over 15 years, and I was looking forward to seeing the bank manager's reaction to this large deposit. Colin had arranged for his auctioneer friend to telephone him on completion of the sale, he was then going to contact me with the news.

The next few days were nail-biting; we knew the paintings were valuable, the estimate was a £1 million for each one, but we knew that auctions can sometimes get out of hand and the price becomes inflated. The day of the auction I was very nervous. I spent the day walking around the town, and made frequent trips back to the hotel to see if I had been contacted. The receptionists must have been fed up with my enquiries.

Eventually the telephone call arrived from Colin: the paintings had been sold, James was flying down to Plymouth with our cheques, and we were to meet him for dinner at the hotel that very evening. I booked the table, excited by the prospect of a windfall. Colin did not know how much we were to receive, James only told him to prepare for instant wealth.

I waited for them in the reception area of the hotel. I found it difficult to sit and continually paced the carpet. Finally their car arrived, and sitting in the front passenger seat was James with the double-barrelled surname. He greeted me with an outstretched hand, like a long-lost friend. We made our way to the lift, to take us up to the restaurant on the top floor. Not that food was on my mind.

I asked if James had enjoyed his flight from London.

He said he had and it took less than an hour. We decided to have a drink before we ate, thinking a drink might help us to take in the size of the cheques, the detail of which he was about to divulge.

'I think you will find the sale was worthwhile, it was quite a grand turnout,' he said.

We thanked him for what he had done, then he handed us each a cheque in a sealed envelope. I opened mine quickly, I had waited all day for this moment. I was not disappointed by what I saw. In my hand was a cheque for £5 million. I was very rich.

Colin smiled when he opened his envelope. His lack of emotion told me that James had already confided in him, he was aware of the windfall.

'This is considerably more than I expected, not that I knew what the paintings were worth,' I said.

'These pieces of artwork had interest from all over the world, but I thought they would. If something comes up for auction which the art world thought was destroyed during the war, all those in the know want to own it, pushing the price up considerably. I thought that each painting might fetch £1 million, but the dealers thought they were worth more than that,' said James.

We celebrated as we ate dinner that night. It was the best dinner I had eaten since I left my own time, not because of the quality of the food, but because our plans had all succeeded. Back in those far-off days in my bungalow when Colin came out with this fantastic story, I had not believed anything of what he said was going to happen, it was such an outrageous tale. But I had agreed to it because I had nothing better to do; retirement is not always exciting.

Once dinner had finished we sat in the bar and drank a few brandies, James had to fly back to London on the late flight, we thanked him for all his hard work.

After James had departed, we remained in the bar. There was a great sigh of relief from us both. We wondered what to do with our new-found wealth. I had not really thought as far ahead as that, although I had earmarked quite a bit to a young lady living nearby. Undoubtedly a lot of good could be done with such a vast amount of money, and I needed time to think about it. My priority was to bank the money and see Julie again, she was an important option in this sequence of events, the rest of my options were to be thought out when I returned to my own time, if that was where I was going.

It was different for Colin, he was finally home, this was his final destination. He was of course unable to tell Helen of this windfall, so he needed to be careful about spending his share.

'I will tell Helen eventually where the money came from,' he said.

'That is a strange thing to say, or do you think Helen will

believe we got the paintings from the past. How are you going to explain that? Your only option I suspect, is to wait for my return in fifteen years time. I think it is something you need to consider,' I said.

'I am very keen to tell Helen about the time travel, I have £5 million burning a hole in my pocket and I am unable to spend very much of it. I will need to find a way to tell her,' he said.

'It is unlikely she is going to believe what you tell her. Who in their right mind would believe such a story, it was preposterous to think time travel was possible, I think you are desperate to spend the money. The only time you can tell her the truth is when you have evidence to back it up,' I said.

'When will that be?' he said.

'She is only going to believe your story when she sees me coming through the portal in fifteen years' time, you know that is the way it is. There is no other option for you; you can spend some of it of course, but that is your commission, not £5 million.'

'You're right of course. When you return in fifteen years, Helen and I will be there to meet you. If you tell her the story she will be more inclined to believe it, it will add credence to my story. Maybe then she will have little choice but to accept our glorious past.'

We chatted for a long time, deciding to visit Ruby Bay the following day; Colin was taking time off work to meet a client, I intended to drop in on Julie. The money was going to be deposited in our respective accounts in Ruby Bay, and he had to buy property in Ruby Bay. He said that if he bought another property there, a property not known to Helen, any correspondence relating to his secret bank account could be sent to that address. The house he had lived in with Jane was up for sale; in reality it was another five years before he purchased it, but although it was changing history we had done plenty of that so far. He decided he was putting in an offer the following day, once the money had been paid into his account.

For myself I was looking into the possibility of earning a truckload of interest, placing money in accounts that maybe had a ten-year life, although some was going to remain in a current account. The rest I had other plans for.

Colin left the hotel just before midnight, after arranging to pick me up the following morning just after ten. I did not sleep well that night, with the thought of all that money, and the thought of my return to the land of Vicary, the latter being only a few days away. This event was closing in fast, I knew I had to do it to get back to my time. I had enjoyed this relatively short stay in 1985.

After breakfast I waited for Colin in reception. The cheque was in my inside jacket pocket, and I was hoping beyond hope that it was not the bouncing kind. This was panic taking over.

He arrived on time and we headed towards Ruby Bay. Colin was obviously fretting about the amount of money he now had, and being unable to share his joy with Helen. He was thinking of saying that the money I was about to give him, his consultancy fee, had earned massive amounts of interest, and that the house he was about to purchase was left to him in a will. Whichever way we looked at the problem it was going to be difficult to account for £5 million.

He needed to be very careful as Helen was not a fool. His wife was very strait-laced and honest, and if he admitted to such a bank balance she was certainly going to think he stole it; she was not one of those wives who was happy with the money wherever it came from, and would spend as much as possible. Although lucky to have such a devoted wife, he felt this detracted from his good fortune.

We arrived at Ruby Bay and I went to the bank, while Colin went off to make an offer on his house. I was to meet him at the bank when he had concluded that piece of business; he desperately wanted to secure the property to use up some of his money. I was taken to the manager's office immediately, having discussed with the teller the reason for my visit. The bank manager looked pleased to see me, and greeted me by name, saying it was a delight to see me again. This was old-fashioned politeness I had not witnessed in my own time. He was aware I had a large deposit to make.

I sat down and pulled the cheque from my pocket. It was still in the envelope, as I wanted to keep it in pristine condition. I took the cheque and placed it on the table in front of the manager. His smiling face changed instantly, he looked at the cheque and gulped.

What I had not considered was this amount was probably enough to supply the British Army with vital supplies in their war effort in 1941; even in 1985 it was still considered a large amount of money, as the bank manager was able to testify. He quickly regained his composure. He assumed I wanted some investment opportunities. I told him I was leaving England soon, and my travels might keep me away for several years, so I need a long-term investment for some of the money, earning the highest possible interest rates.

I also made enquiries as to whether Julie had an account with the bank. He was obviously not allowed to discuss that with me, which I understood completely, but I explained I wished to transfer a large part of my cheque into her account, so I needed to know if she had an account before that was possible. He understood my predicament, he stated that Mrs Winters did have an account, but he suggested payment by personal cheque was the best option.

He then asked what amount, and gasped when I said £4 million. He commented the money was going to help her and her daughter greatly. She had lost her husband only a few years previously, killed in a car accident, and her business was not exactly doing well. He made out the cheque and handed it to me, stating what a generous offer it was on my part.

During the next hour we discussed investments. I wished I had read the financial pages in my own time, I would then have been likely to know what he was talking about, but I was prepared to accept his advice on these matters. Eventually we agreed on my portfolio, leaving a small amount in my current account, the rest was to be invested long term at the discretion of the bank. The manager assured me the money was going to be safe in his bank. I was sure my money was going to be safe until I returned again. Or perhaps I needed to check that more thoroughly: I had an idea that 1987 was the year the stock market crashed. But I was going to discuss my portfolio with Colin.

I left the manager's office to find Colin sitting in the foyer, he was the manager's next client. I wished I was able to sit in on the visit, to see the manager's face again. Colin said his offer on the house had been accepted. It was a way to offload some of his money.

His visit was somewhat shorter than mine, then the manager called me back into the office with Colin, suggesting that as we were business partners, it was a good idea for Colin to keep an eye on my investments in my absence. I signed a form giving him the right to reinvest my money with the assistance of the bank; he was not going to have access to the money, but could use other options if the market was flat. It was a sound idea. All correspondence in relation to both accounts was to be sent to Colin's new house in Ruby Bay.

It was a satisfactory conclusion to the day's business. I had not however told Colin that the majority of my money was going to Julie. Colin confirmed that 1987 was the year that stocks and shares took a nosedive, and he agreed to take my money out of such investments when the time came.

Colin travelled back to Plymouth on his own, and I was off to see if Julie was available for lunch. Things had to be sorted out quickly, soon I was going to be back on the island. Colin was not aware of my turmoil over this matter; I was not looking forward to living in squalor again. At least I now knew the maximum stay on the island was one week.

I intended to enjoy my last two days in this time. I took the bus to the next village, stopping near the estate agents I knew so well. I entered and saw a vision, both Julie and Juliette were there. They both looked up and smiled, and Julie said they had been talking about me. She said we needed to talk, and whisking me from the office she left Juliette in charge of business. We went to the Pilchard to have a drink.

'I have received the result of the DNA tests, I tried to contact you at the hotel, but they told me you were out. Do you think you know what the tests show?' she said.

'I think so, but I still want to hear it from you,' I said.

'They said with tests like these they cannot be 100 per cent, but we know that anyway. The result indicates that we are related, or to quote what they said: "very closely related", although again they cannot state categorically that you are my father.' She was visibly excited by the news and to be honest so was I.

'With this news I am prepared to believe your time travel adventures, I must accept it with the DNA results. I don't know how time travel works, and I really don't want to know. It does sound fantastic, but it proves there was something between my mother and you. I am excited and a little confused by it all, it has taken a while, but I now have a father, and Juliette has a grandfather. I don't know how I will explain it all to Juliette, do you have any ideas on the subject?'

This was the time to tell her that I was actually not from this time, but from a time 15 years in the future. This was not going to be easy to say. There was only one way, just to come right out and say it. And I was in a position to prove it, explaining things that were going to happen. I told her the story of when I made my first trip, from the year 2000. She looked at me with astonishment. I told her there was going to be a Live Aid concert in London in July to raise money for victims of famine-stricken Africa, in August they would find the remains of the *Titanic* on the sea bed, the actor Rock Hudson would die in October, as would Orson Welles. All these things were in the future, how was I likely to know this if I had not passed this way before?

'I understand what you're saying, but you don't just expect me to accept what you say? As the year rolls on your predictions will prove your point, you must understand my position,' she said.

'In a few days' time I have to take the return trip back to my time. I will come and see you in fifteen years' time and I will look as I do now. This will help you to believe what I am saying. I'm sorry it is so long to wait, I have wondered whether to go back or not, but I have a family in that time who have never been without me. You have survived very well without me. I intend to leave you with something to make life more comfortable for you and Juliette, it is my way of repaying you for all the years I was not around. Here is a cheque for the two of you.'

She stood there speechless as she read the amount, her mouth was wide open.

'If you want to stay it would make me very happy, but I understand why you can't. I will tell Juliette you are a long-lost uncle, if you agree to that. The truth will be harder to explain. I can't thank you enough for the money, it will certainly make a difference to our lives. Tell me, was this cheque a result of selling the 1941 paintings?'

'Yes it was, this is your mother's share.'

We parted with a hug, and I asked if she was able to meet me for dinner on my final night. She thought that was a good idea, and suggested perhaps her Juliette could come along and meet her uncle. We agreed to meet at the hotel in a couple of days, with Juliette in the party.

I was invited to Colin's house for dinner on the night before that. Helen was aware that I was leaving for a distant place, little did she know how close that place was, about 15 miles away.

Once dinner had finished Colin said he would return me to the hotel. In fact we were heading to Ruby Bay. I would stay at the Ruby Bay hotel for my last night. I had told him I had a dinner date on my last night. He did not need to ask who it was with, he knew full well. I agreed to meet him at the house after dinner; the portal would open around midnight, and I was eager not to miss the journey back, although at the same time I did not want to make this journey. Colin told Helen he would have a drink at the hotel with me the following night; this allowed him to have a reason for arriving back late. She wished me a safe and pleasant trip. I told her I was going to see her on my return, but I did not mention the time lapse.

This was the last time I would journey to the island, my next trip was to my own time. Although I detested living on the island, I was hoping time had not passed too quickly, knowing that if it had, things on the island might be very different. Alan knew, as did Vicary, that the pirating was going to end in bloodshed, and the time to get off the island was already drawing near on my last visit. Alan had told me where the Pathway was going to be located, in case he was no longer there when I returned. Very soon I would find out. Alan's high-profile position on the island was not going to help if the Royal Navy captured him. His bravery in this matter was beyond doubt, he waited on the island for my return, he had the option to leave with Colin, he stayed to protect the Pathway and make sure I got home.

In the morning I moved out of my city centre hotel and made my way to the island's hotel, preparing for my last night in 1985, and dinner with a daughter and granddaughter I had newly acquired, knowing I had helped to secure their future. Their mother would have been proud of my actions. I was pleased to be back at the hotel, it held many happy memories for me, spanning more than 40 years.

I dressed for dinner and waited in the bar, Julie and Juliette arrived on time, and this time I had a hug from both of them. Julie's daughter had been informed that I was her long-lost uncle.

We chatted over drinks, and throughout dinner. I had to be careful what I was saying, as Juliette was not aware of my complicated past. I was amazed that they were both so similar to the Julie I had known; not only their beauty, but even their mannerisms took me back 40 years. I was sad when the evening ended. I saw them to the slipway to meet the tractor. There was a longer hug this time from them both, and Julie whispered in my ear, wishing me a safe journey and a safer return. I waved them off with a great deal of sadness in my heart. Hopefully we were going to meet up again in the near future, they were a wonderful addition to my family.

I arrived at 2 Ruby Bay, my house of the future. Colin agreed to have it fully furnished for my return, at no cost to me. I changed into my scruffiest clothes, including the duffel coat which was always present on my return. We had about an hour in the bungalow, talking about what we had achieved. Colin promised to be there for my return, which we knew would be the day after our initial departure. He also promised not to have any of my money tied up in shares in October 1987, when the markets crashed.

He said he might write a book on what really happened on the island during Vicary's time, and I told him I was likely to have something to add to that, depending what happened on this final visit.

Eventually the time arrived, and we took the long walk across the beach. The cloud activity began, a sure sign that the past was close at hand. The rain drove down on us with ferocity and the beach was of course empty, as we strolled across the small expanse, neither of us talking. I was sorry Colin was not coming with me. This time I was alone, except for the assistance of Alan on the island.

The storm was raging as we approached the portal. It started to open, allowing me to pass through. This was the moment. I looked at Colin and we shook hands, then hugged me, and wished me luck. I waved to him as I walked through the portal, then the portal closed behind me.

9

I stepped out of the light that was the portal. I was back on the island. I knew the period simply by the smell, the odour was as bad as I remembered it. I was at the bottom of the island, it must have been just after midnight, and I needed to make my way to the meeting place. I deviated around the huts to avoid passing close to the inn, reaching the meeting place in quick time. All was quiet as I sat waiting, hoping Alan was going to turn up. I wondered if he was having difficulty leaving the inn, which might be particularly difficult when Vicary was in full swing. But there was little noise from the inn. I peered over the rock but was too far away to see the reason for the quietness.

I waited some 30 minutes before I decided to make my way to my hut, Alan was obviously not turning up tonight. There was no one around, in fact it was very quiet, as I started to walk towards my abode. I was tired and felt that sleep was going to come easy. I wondered how long I had been away in the island's time; I trusted it was more than seven days otherwise the Pathway was of little use until the seven-day period was up. The thought of spending more time than necessary here filled me with dread. There was one good point to consider: this was to be my last visit, my greatest wish at that moment.

The uphill climb was quite tiring; the good life of 1985 was beginning to tell on my fitness, and my overindulgence in the hotel bar was returning to haunt me. I reached my hut a little out of breath, strangely glad to reach the hovel that was my sanctuary, away from the general vileness of this island. Even the smell of the island was a little weaker inside the hut.

I closed the curtain at the window, it was more of a rag than a curtain, with more holes than material, and reached for the bottom of my habit in order to take it off. I was shocked to find that I was not wearing a habit. How had I not noticed the trousers and boots? Who was I? There was a type of mirror in the corner of the room, I picked it up and looked at the reflection. It was someone I recognized, but it was not the monk. My reflection showed the face of Jefferson; this was of course Colin's disguise when he was on the island. Had I for some reason been promoted? I did not understand why.

Another thought hit me at that moment: I was in the wrong hut. I felt sure the monk was not going to be pleased with my intrusion, he was likely to put a different slant on my reason for being there. I left the hut immediately. To make my way to my new home was the best course of action. Fortunately I knew where Colin had resided, but knowing what he said about his wife I felt a drink was in order first.

My walk to the inn was brisk. I had a new position on the island, a very senior position which was likely to demand certain respect from the crew. I walked into the inn expecting to be greeted cordially by the crew, but none were present. Apart from the prostitutes I was the only other person in there. It was not usual for the crew to decide on an early night. Then I appreciated the reason: the ship was clearly at sea carrying out another act of piracy. That was in some ways a blessing, but if that was the case then why was I here, and not on board?

The ladies looked at me and smiled, I was their only potential customer tonight, something I had no intention of being. I had a large wife to go home to, and I felt it unlikely I was going to manage both in one night.

The landlord greeted me as Mr Jefferson, making enquiries about my health, perhaps this was how he greeted the crew; this was my first experience of being a member of that cutthroat group of vagabonds.

He mentioned that my wife had said I had been laid up with 'the sickness'. That was obviously the cause of my not sailing, I had been laid up with something unknown that they called 'the sickness'. I was glad this illness had stopped me from sailing.

The three ladies who I shared the inn with were not particular about the sickness, they still offered their wares in the crudest manner. I refused, stating that I had to go home to my wife, but this confused them as all their customers had wives, and none of them ever refused sex to go home to their wives. Refusal was something they did not expect, particularly when they were not shy in showing their wares, in a few cases very well-proportioned wares. They allowed me to finish my rum in peace.

The landlord remained in the cellar, no doubt clearing space for a few new items to be stored. Vicary used the inn to store items other than rum, no doubt paying a small gratuity for this service.

I looked at the monk's seat near the door. No more stew for me. But Colin had said his wife was a good cook; this appeared to be her only good point, and soon I was going to find out how true that was.

I said goodnight to the three prostitutes, something they were not accustomed to, the way they looked at me showed that. Obviously politeness was not a requisite when dealing with these ladies, and a few choice words of abuse were aimed in my direction, which I duly ignored.

I walked the short distance to Jefferson's hut. It was larger than the monk's, but then Jefferson was third in command, and the monk was treated like something you wipe off the bottom of your shoe. I walked into the hut to find a single large room, with an area for cooking and dining. In the corner was a bed, much larger than the monk's, and beneath the blanket was something also very large. This was my adopted wife. Colin had underestimated her size.

If anything of a sexual nature took place tonight, which in my mind that appeared unlikely, was it going to be classed as committing adultery? I decided not to enter into those sort of relations with her. The problem was that if she wanted sexual relations I was unlikely to have a choice in the matter; my chances of fending off this woman were slim indeed.

I started to undress, which was more complicated than I thought, the monk's habit was easy in comparison, with not as many pieces that needed untying. Having freed myself I got into bed. This was not easy, as the monster had claimed most of the mattress. I did not want to disturb her sleep, as much through fear as anything else.

I awoke to the sound of pots and pans being clanked together, it was the wife preparing breakfast. I got out of bed and dressed as best I could. There was no conversation as I dressed, and I began to wonder if she spoke at all.

I enquired as to how she was this bright morning, and a frown appeared across her forehead. Clearly this was not something she was asked on a regular basis, her welfare was not supposed to be of any concern to me.

She put a metal plate full of food on the table, and indicated that was my breakfast. I thanked her for her efforts and the frown reappeared. Still no conversation had passed between us. I had a feeling that this was going to be a difficult relationship. I was treating her as a human being, something she was obviously not familiar with. Treating my wife like a slave was more normal in this place, she seemed to accept it without any complaint. She either was unable to speak or such an action was likely to bring reprisals, I had no idea which was true. There were no signs of children in the hut, and I did not remember Colin mentioning any.

Following breakfast I told her I was going to the inn. She grunted but still did not speak, then she picked up the empty plate and took it away. The thought of kissing her goodbye came and went with terrifying speed.

I walked up the hill to check that the ship had returned safely. It was tiring after a good breakfast; Jefferson was right when he described his wife as a good cook, so perhaps my short stay was not going to be so bad.

I reached the hut and climbed down the ladder to the walkway, then I realized that the ship was not there. Surely it should have returned by now, no matter how long the trip? I decided to go to the inn and enquire as to why the ship was missing, surely it was not feasible to carry out raids during the day, that was certainly be the action of desperation? Landon was unlikely to allow that, particularly as he had shown his intention to leave the island.

My walk to the inn was pleasant, I mused over what I had seen, or more to the point what I had not seen. It was still very quiet, and there were a few children around. I entered the inn to complete silence; even the prostitutes were not there. I did not think there was much daytime trade, but then there was no trade at all last night, and their choice was limited to one very uninterested party.

The landlord greeted me again, this time he asked what I wanted to drink. Of course I was Jefferson, so I ordered rum. It would be going against protocol to order anything else, and at least I knew how the rum tasted.

'I thought the place might be busier,' I said to the landlord.

This brought a look of surprise.

'Why did you think that?' he said.

I realized my mistake.

'Of course, it is obviously too early for the crew, what with the ship being at sea, now I understand why they are not here. No doubt when they return it will be very busy. I wasn't aware they had sailed, but I looked around the back and saw the ship had slipped anchor, do you know what time they are returning?'

'Was that some kind of joke, Mr Jefferson?' he said.

'It is no joke, the ship is definitely not there. Do you know where the ship is?'

'Of course I do. I appreciate how lucky you were not to be

with them the other night. Your sickness was your good fortune, but surely you are aware of the fate of the crew, or has your wife failed to tell you?' he said.

I did not like the words 'fate of the crew'. This sounded very serious. Was the landlord going to elaborate?

'My wife has said nothing to me. What about the fate of the crew?' I asked.

'A few nights ago the ship was stopped in the Channel, by a Royal Navy frigate. The ship was taken and the crew arrested. The crew are in a prison on the mainland, they are awaiting trial for piracy, as you are no doubt aware, the most serious of offences.'

'My wife has not told me this. When were they captured?'

'It was three nights ago. The ship was close to the island, it was on its way back, it was boarded by the Royal Navy, along with Revenue men. There was a fight and some of the crew were killed, they were the ones that resisted. The rest of the crew were put in chains. It appears our crew had sunk a Spanish ship. The stolen cargo was on board, so there was no way of denying it – they are guilty even before they go to trial. It was all because of those muskets they had taken on a previous trip, they were destined for our king. This required the Royal Navy to step up patrols in the Channel, which they did and caught our ship.'

'What about the crew that were captured, where are they being held?'

'They are on the mainland, and the trial is set for tomorrow, in Ruby Bay itself. The authorities wish to set an example of the crew in front of their families, that it why it is taking place locally. Some of the women are going, those that are interested. I will of course attend, there is little trade at the inn to keep me here. My livelihood has been taken away, I shall be looking for some other form of employment,' he said.

'Would you mind if I accompany you tomorrow, I think I should be there. Do you know which of the crew were killed?'

'I have no idea who they were, it was four of the crew and a Royal Navy man. The rest of the crew will be sentenced to death for piracy, a special gallows has already been erected. It is a foregone conclusion, the verdict has been decided even before the trial has started,' he said.

'Is it safe for the two of us to go to the trial? What if the crew pointed us out to the court as fellow pirates?' I said.

'That is very unlikely, there is nothing to be gained by doing that, as well as it being thought dishonourable to do such a thing, I think we are quite safe,' he said.

I left the inn, saying I would be back in the bar that evening. It was either that or stay at home with the wife, it was the lesser of two evils. My biggest concern was that Landon was the only one who knew the location of the Pathway for sure, he had told me it was going to be left in his hut, but with the events that had passed maybe it was somewhere else, although that seemed unlikely. My route home could be in jeopardy, this was a major concern. Landon had indicated on my last visit he was going to leave it in his cellar, which if Landon had died I could only hope was correct. If Landon was in court it was possible he could give me some sort of sign, maybe to confirm the location of the Pathway in the cellar. I was in great fear of spending the remainder of my life on this island, even though there was always the prospect of a large deduction in price from the prostitutes, being one of only two men left on the island. I could check his cellar without interruption, there was nobody left to worry about such an action. I was not sure how long I had been away, it was surely more than seven days. I decided to check the cellar after the trial.

I went back to my hut; my wife was there. I decided to leave after an hour of intermittent grunting, perhaps she really was dumb. I strolled around the island to clear my head, it was even more desolate without the crew. The women of the island went about their daily tasks, none seemed upset at the impeding trial, although tomorrow was the day justice was to be administered.

Maybe they accepted the demise of their menfolk, they probably knew since they started the piracy that they were going to be caught one day. I was not altogether surprised that they did not care too much about their husbands. How often did they see these men? They spent more time at the inn than at home. Most of the wives had been hit by their husbands, most of the children as well. From what I had seen there was not one marriage on the island that was a true match; for the women it was necessary to find a husband, and I had no idea what the attraction was for the men.

My walk took me past a certain hut, one I had frequented as the monk. The lady was stood at the door, and she beckoned me over. I decided this was one way to pass the afternoon. I had very little money on me but she accepted this paltry amount, bearing in mind that business was bad for her. We entered the hut. She was another lady who had very little to say, maybe in her profession it was the best way. Having completed the liaison to my satisfaction, I left to go and rest. She was very good at her profession, or maybe I was easily pleased.

I went home and consumed my evening meal. I told my wife I was going to attend the trial the following day, as was the landlord. She did not comment, merely gave a grunt. This grunt appeared to have more feeling than before.

The inn was my next stop, where the landlord had time to chat. The prostitutes had taken a night off.

'Did they take the full crew? Except for me of course, was everyone else on board?'

'Yes they were, you must have a guardian angel watching over you, you've had a lucky escape. It is strange to think that an illness has saved your life, it's usually the other way round,' he said.

It also explained why I had returned as Jefferson: he was the only crewman left. From that it appeared even the monk was to meet his maker, hopefully he was better prepared than the rest of the crew.

'What do you think will happen to the crew?'

'They will be hung, remember they are being made an example of. But the only sentence for piracy is hanging, as it is for most things. You don't think they would build the gallows for nothing, they intend to hang them all,' he said.

I was concerned about the man I had once been, the man of the cloth.

'Surely they won't hang the monk?'

'He'll be hung with the rest of them, he was on board when they were caught. Religion plays no part in this, he was with a bunch of pirates, therefore he is a pirate, he will not be treated any differently to the rest of the crew. But they have their prizes, it was Vicary and Landon they were really after, and I suspect they will deal with them at the end of the trial. The ringleaders are always dealt with last, I don't think either of them were killed, we would have heard about that.'

'Are all the wives going tomorrow?'

'Only a few, the majority will remain on the island. They all expect their husbands to be executed, the crew themselves are aware of what awaits them. The wives have other things to do, caring for the children and the livestock are their priorities. I expect most of the women to leave the island, some will try prostitution, anything to survive.'

He was absolutely right. The women had a terrible existence on the island, no doubt that was the same everywhere if you came from the poorer classes, and sadly turning to prostitution was their only outlet. By the look of some of them it was not going to be a profitable occupation.

I looked at the following day's trial as an opportunity. I was about to witness an important part of the history of the island at first hand. What was about to happen did not coincide with the history that I knew to be so; Landon was supposed to have escaped the island, yet another version was that he returned, and tomorrow was to give me a third version.

I slept well that night, considering I had only a fifth of the bed. My wife merely wanted to sleep, she had no intention of taking advantage of me, and I was grateful for that small mercy. I lay there thinking that possibly the seven days for using the

Pathway had passed: the crew had been arrested several days before, and when I left last time there was no talk of an imminent voyage, so I felt I was close to the seven days at worst. I was in a position to leave if I so wanted, but the chance to see the events of the following day was an opportunity I felt was too good to miss.

My wife was up before I was. If she was happy that her husband was not among those arrested, she kept it very much to herself; breakfast was eaten in complete silence. I thought maybe if I offered an olive branch it was going to help the relationship, merely on a talking level.

'Do you want to go to the trial? I am going with the landlord, you are welcome to come with us if you wish,' I said.

'No, it will be sad to see them sentenced to death,' she said.

I was shocked by this. Not only was she speaking, but her refined voice did not fit the person I saw before me, and she even showed a caring side.

'What do you think the future holds for us, with no ship and crew? Perhaps we can discuss it when I return from the trial.'

She was very surprised at this comment.

'Why do you want to discuss it with me? Are you saying these things because there is nobody left on the island? I can survive on my own, I have been doing it all my life, but what are you going to do?' she said.

This lady was right, the strength of the island was in the women, the men were weak and easily led by Vicary and Landon. She did not need Jefferson, but perhaps he needed her.

'Maybe we can leave the island, try to make a better life on the mainland,' I said.

I knew I was talking for Jefferson, I was soon to be out of this lady's life forever. It was strange to make decisions for him. What would be his thoughts on the subject when he reappeared, then was faced with this bombshell?

'Leaving this place will be good for the children as well,' she commented.

That was a shock, something I had not realized: Jefferson had children. I did not know how many and it did not seem wise to ask. My stay on the island had to end soon; I did not want to be a father to someone else's children.

As I left the hut I considered this life, one which I had not made for myself, but was forced upon me by circumstances. I walked to the inn and saw the landlord waiting outside. We went down the slipway, across to the mainland. The walk was a sad affair. Although I appreciated that these men were thieves and scoundrels, their lifestyle was out of necessity. They had no education to speak of, they lived on a small island, there had been little choice as to the road they took. A few of the wives crossed over too, but the landlord and I avoided them, approaching the mainland across the rocks. Coming up the beach with the ladies was likely to underline that we were also islanders.

On the mainland I saw the newly erected courthouse; it was obvious it had been built in a hurry. Next to it was the scaffold. The verdict was clear for all to see. We entered the court from the mainland side.

The courthouse was packed. Some people had travelled from Exeter, as the trial was big news in the area. We sat at the back of the court, not wanting to give the crew the slightest chance to pick us out. I was not convinced of their loyalty as stated by the landlord, I was taking no chances. Landon, or rather Alan, was about to face the end of a rope. Even so, it was my intention to make eye contact with him; he was hopefully going to assure me the Pathway was safe, along with confirming its location, a forlorn hope I knew.

The first batch of crewmen entered the court, ten of them, looking more bedraggled than I remembered them. Vicary and Landon were not among them and it appeared that the landlord was right, Vicary and Landon were going to be left to the end. The charge of piracy on the high seas was read out, but none of the men were given the opportunity to speak, none of them had any right to plead their innocence, their guilt was a foregone conclusion. All ten were sentenced to hang, the sentence to be carried out after the trial had finished. All ten were taken from the court.

The next ten crewmen were brought in, the monk was one of them. Again the charge was read out, followed by the inevitable guilty verdict, they were to meet the same fate as the first ten. A further eight crewmen appeared in front of the judge, and the same procedure was followed. This was justice on a conveyor belt.

Then came the moment most of the court had been waiting for with great excitement: Vicary and Landon appeared, with chains on their ankles as well as their wrists. This was a prize capture by the Royal Navy.

Landon looked straight at me. He knew it was me in the guise of Jefferson: he had enough intelligence to appreciate that it was the only possibility, as I was the only surviving crew member on the island.

The conviction and sentencing of these two men was a more drawn-out affair, as evidence was read out by a Navy officer. The judge nodded as he read out his statement. Surely this was again a foregone conclusion.

To my surprise, on this occasion Vicary was asked if he wanted to say anything. He shook his head. He knew nothing he had to say was likely to protect him, his fate was sealed before the trial started.

Landon was offered the same opportunity to speak, and he accepted the offer although he must have known it was futile.

'This court has made a decision on my fate, along with all the crew, this is not justice, so I accept my punishment without further complaint,' he said.

'Is there anything else?' said the judge.

'Yes just one more thing, it's in my cellar,' said Landon.

The judge looked at him strangely, asking him to repeat what he had said. Alan looked at me. I nodded that I understood. He refused to repeat the comment, and it was passed off as the ravings of someone about to die. Although I had guessed where the Pathway was, Alan had confirmed it even in his darkest moment. I was going to check the cellar, but since my return I did not seem to have time.

The judge passed a different sentence on these two: they were to hang in irons. I knew what this meant, and so did the landlord; he shook his head at the verdict. The punishments for all the crew were to be carried out the following day, the judge stated the time of the hangings. Whether he did this to attract a bigger crowd I did not know, I felt there were going to be many there to watch.

The whole trial had been peculiar. Perhaps the fact the prisoners were in court legitimatized the proceedings, but there was no evidence provided in the true sense of the word, and most of the prisoners were not allowed to speak. I was confused as to why Vicary and Landon were given the opportunity to plead their case. But no doubt if the crew were invited to speak the proceedings would last all day, and the judge was in a hurry to conclude the trial. From start to finish the trial was over in an hour, 30 people sentenced to death, swift justice indeed.

I left the court with the landlord, and he suggested we drown our sorrows at the inn. Although I knew where the Pathway was, I had now decided to leave the following day; I wanted to watch yet another piece of history taking place, the execution of the crew.

I was thinking about the punishment given to Vicary and Landon. They were to be hung, but instead of being buried like the rest of the crew, their dead bodies would be dipped in tar, then they would be fitted into a cage in the upright position. The tar preserved the body for a while. It was a way of frightening off prospective pirates. It was customary to exhibit the body in a prominent place, leaving it there until it rotted. I was about to see barbarism in action. This practice was used for those classed as the ringleaders, and it was easy to identify them in this case.

I said farewell to the landlord, and he agreed to accompany

me to the big event in the morning, but I was going to be at the inn that evening, for a conversation with the only other man on the island. It was not his first execution, he had witnessed something similar outside Exeter prison.

I went home to my charming wife, intending to visit the inn that evening. I walked into the hut and was greeted by her. This was a shock: she had started to talk, was I going to be able to stop her?

'How did the trial go?' she asked.

'They were all sentenced to hang,' I said.

'Did you expect any other verdict?'

'Of course not, but I wanted to see what form the trial took. It was disappointing, nobody had their chance to plead their case. Only Vicary and Landon were allowed to speak.'

'Are you surprised, we are the little people, nobody cares about us, we do whatever we can to survive. Unfortunately that usually means breaking the law, and the King is happy to punish us for that.'

I was impressed with this conversation. This lady had an opinion on what was a grave matter, and she also spoke a lot of sense. I wondered if all the wives felt this way.

'What do you think can be done?' I said.

'It is all down to wealth, we do not have any wealth, therefore we have nothing to offer. We'll struggle through like everyone else in our position.'

I was surprised at that, little did she know but her thoughts were those of millions of people, not only in this time, but also in modern society. Those with money rule, those without follow. I was tempted to remain in the hut and continue this fascinating conversation, but the lure of the inn was overwhelming. It was expected that I go there, even my wife expected it, and I had also promised the landlord.

On entering the inn I found myself in the company of three prostitutes. How these ladies intended to survive now was a matter of conjecture. The landlord suggested these three were going to take the opportunity to seek their fortune on the mainland. They were unlikely to be made welcome there, all the inns had their quota of prostitutes, and two of the three were going to find slim pickings.

The one who I had visited as both the monk and Jefferson approached me, knowing I was all that was available. But even the offer of buy one get one free did not help her situation. It was very difficult to refuse her, as I knew exactly what the quality was underneath her grubby dress. She left me then, clearly feeling rejected. She chatted to her colleagues, no doubt explaining my lack of finances. I had enough for the rum though.

My thoughts turned to my departure tomorrow. I had not yet secured the Pathway, but I was intending to check on it as I made my way back to my hut. I knew exactly which hut was Landon's. With few people out and about on the island, my departure was going to be easy. I was saddened by the fact that Alan was not going with me, knowing that he had intended to return with me. I was grateful that he had indicated where the Pathway was, even at such a desperate time, in the last hours of his life. If only he had returned with Colin and me to 1985.

Here I was in the company of the only other male on the island, the landlord who I had become friendly with; it was a pity it was under circumstances of distress for the islanders, but he seemed relatively jolly about the whole situation. This in itself surprised me, as his business was about to go to the wall, he knew that as well as I did.

He asked me if I was looking forward to the events of the following day. He was referring to the multiple hangings, and I was not looking forward to this, I was only interested in watching it for the historical value. Such affairs usually took place in the larger towns, a sort of day out for the family. I did appreciate there was not much in the way of entertainment for the locals, but this was taking pleasure to new heights, imagine taking your children to a hanging! They were also a show of force from the authorities, and in this case they wanted the remaining islanders to see what the consequences of piracy were. Unless the women were going to crew a ship I found it unlikely there was likely to be much piracy from the island in the foreseeable future.

I left the inn and went to check out Landon's hut. I stopped at the door, and putting my ear to it I listened for noise inside, just in case someone had moved in since his arrest. There was none. I made my way inside, lit the lamp that was on the table, and quickly found the cellar door. I pulled it back and found the box containing the Pathway. I opened it to reveal the Pathway and a note, I took the note out and moved closer to the lamp to read it, it was from Alan.

Pat, If you are reading this I am either dead or in custody. The Pathway is set to the date you require, you only need to press the sliding piece on the shaft, the portal will open, it remains open for about ten minutes. You do not need to be outside the hut to activate. Remember the Pathway must remain where you found it. Please return it to the cellar once you have activated it. Remember not to activate until midnight, hopefully Colin will be waiting for you on your return. I wish you good luck and a long life, sorry things did not work out for me. Alan.

Having read the note I returned the Pathway to the box. I now had the necessary equipment to carry out my return journey tomorrow night. I felt sad. Alan had allowed for his possible demise, remembering to help my return. It was an unselfish act. I felt he had been somehow at home in this environment, as he had said, he had not made a name for himself in our time, but he had in this time, as the history books were going to show.

I continued to my own hut. My wife was still up, and she made advances to me. She said she was feeling amorous, and I had no choice but to oblige, as a refusal might bring dire results for me. This night I was definitely going to remember for the rest of my life, not in a good way I must add.

I was pleased when morning broke, and I was out of bed before the wife, in case she wanted to repeat last night's performance. I certainly had no intention of getting too close to her. She eventually arose and cooked the breakfast, smiling continually. What a changed situation was I leaving for the real Jefferson? Soon that was not going to be my problem.

I walked to the inn where I met the landlord, and we made our way down to the beach. Looking across to the mainland, we saw that a large crowd was gathering, surrounding the scaffold. This was a big event in the village's history, everyone knew that and wanted to be present. As we stepped onto the mainland, again going by the jagged rock route, I saw there were many women and children waiting for the big event.

The scaffold was nothing like the ones I had seen in Wild West films. There were two uprights and a horizontal piece of wood going across the top, no trap door whatsoever, just the earth floor beneath. I was not sure how this contraption was going to operate.

The first four men were brought out, their hands still chained. Four ropes with nooses were thrown over the horizontal bar, and the nooses were placed around their necks. Then I saw how this was going to work. Four horses were brought forward, the ropes were attached to their harness, then the horses moved forward slowly. This pulled the men off the ground, each one struggling violently. It was a slow form of strangulation, and no doubt very painful, just what the justice system required. This method did not break their necks instantly, as a trap door would. But an instant death was not required: painful and lingering was the order of the day. The procedure was repeated for each group of four men. The bodies were loaded onto a nearby cart. The crowd were quiet throughout the ceremony; everyone watched uneasily.

Then the last two appeared, Vicary and Landon. The method of execution was the same, and both men struggled violently before the end. The bodies were then taken down, but they were not put on the cart, they were taken behind the courthouse where their final humiliation awaited them. After a long wait their bodies were brought back. Each body was inside a metal cage, black from head to foot with tar. They were unrecognizable; the tar was thick so that no features could be seen. The crowd started to cheer as both cages were hoisted up on the scaffold, where they were to remain for the foreseeable future.

I found it difficult to believe that one of these was Alan, someone who had assisted both Colin and myself on our journey. His journey had finished here, in a desolate place in an ungodly time, by a barbaric method.

The landlord and I left the mainland. I was disgusted by what I had seen, and even the landlord was quiet as we walked across the beach. He had been affected by watching the crew he knew so well executed in that manner.

My thoughts turned to what Alan had said, he had gold hidden somewhere, he was of the opinion Vicary had a stash somewhere as well, and bearing in mind Vicary never left the island it must still remain there.

'Do you think there is gold hidden somewhere on the island? You knew Vicary very well. Did he ever mention a hiding place?' I said.

'That's a bit mercenary after what we've just witnessed,' he said.

'It may sound that way, but it is not for me. If we find this gold, we have an opportunity to help all the wives that are left. God knows their husbands did little for them. There are also plenty of children, let's try to do something for them,' I said.

'It is a good proposal, I have no idea where Vicary's fortune is, but it must be hidden somewhere on the island, he only ever left the island on the ship. Are we assuming Vicary had a hidden stash?'

'He must have, don't you think these ships carried more than Vicary shared with the crew?'

'I think you're right. These women only have the vegetables they have grown. They will not last very long. When the food's gone they will be forced to leave the island and where they go is another problem. The mainlanders will not welcome them – no matter how far they travel it will take time for them to be accepted. People are very wary of strangers, these women are in for a hard time. Most of the crowd today travelled a long distance to see the hangings, the women will have to travel further to be away from the scandal,' he said.

'If I said I was going to try and find Vicary's loot, would you help me? I am doing this to help the women, I want nothing from it. Do you have any idea where Vicary might have a hiding place? It might be a step in the right direction.'

'You say there is nothing in this for you, if we find the gold you do not want any part of it, is that correct?' he said.

'I want nothing except to know my wife and children will be taken care of, but you must have a share, your business has been affected by events. What do you think?'

The landlord nodded his head in agreement. 'I still have no idea where the gold is. Perhaps Vicary's hut was a good starting place, but that is unlikely, it is too obvious. I would say our best option were the rocks at the top of the island, near where the ship was anchored. Did Vicary or Landon ever confide in you? Being third in command I thought you might have some idea.'

That was not an easy question to answer, having been Jefferson for only a few days. I had never sailed as Jefferson, merely carried out his duties with his wife.

'I was never privy to that information, I did not think even Landon knew where Vicary hid the gold. They seemed to be in dispute about the treasure, I was aware of the animosity between them.'

'To carry out a search with only two of us would be monumental. Why don't we get the wives to help? It is in their interest. I will get them together and discuss it. I will round them up and meet you at the top of the hill.' He rushed away to visit the remaining residents.

I wondered if this was when the treasure was found; that would explain why in the future it was never located because it had already been found at this time. My confidence in the venture grew, if there was a way of helping these poor people, my departure from the island was going to be a satisfactory one, although tinged with sadness for the demise of Alan.

I walked up the hill towards the hut, the door was open. I looked inside and saw the steps leading down, it was lit by the sunlight off the sea. I decided not to go down until the search party arrived. I hoped the landlord was successful in his quest, he was correct in believing the two of us were unlikely to cover the area of the rocks, help was certainly required to find the treasure.

Soon the women began to come up the hill in small groups, some still carrying their children. Hopefully the numbers were going to increase substantially. The landlord appeared at the bottom of the hill, he had more than a dozen women with him, even the prostitutes were providing their services; their trade was not immune from the seriousness of the situation. In all I counted 30 women, a good number to check out all the nooks and crannies within the rocks. Our jovial landlord was a persuasive man, but then the rewards were exceptional.

One by one they descended the steps, and I asked them to wait on the ledge above where the ship moored. We would coordinate the operation from there, not wanting too many people checking the same area.

Once we had arrived at the walkway I surveyed the large area of rock. There appeared to be many small tunnels. Lamps were lit to assist the search parties. I suggested the routes for each search party, and the landlord directed the ladies as he knew them better than I did. They went to their task with enthusiasm, which was understandable as their futures depended on it.

The landlord and I waited on the ledge; we felt we had all the tunnels covered with search parties, and it was now a case of waiting and hoping. We were both sure there was nowhere else Vicary was likely to have hidden the treasure.

We had briefed the women to look out for broken rocks that appeared to have been replaced, anything out of the usual in the tunnels. I think they understood what we were saying, they appreciated that Vicary was going to hide the treasure well, but hopefully their enthusiasm was going to bear fruit.

'If we do locate the treasure, is it possible for you to sell it, no doubt you have many trading outlets, is that possible? Finding it might be the easy part. Bearing in mind the authorities are aware this treasure has not been recovered, do you have reliable contacts?'

'Don't worry, I can offload it safely. I have made many contacts over the years, by what you say it sounds like you may not be around to help me. Are you not staying here for some reason?' he said.

'I'm going to be here,' I said. In reality I did not intend to be.

'It's just that I thought you might be leaving soon; not Jefferson, but the real you.'

This comment shocked me. What did he know? Obviously a lot more than I had given him credit for. Who was this landlord?

'Apart from being the landlord of the inn, have you ever had another occupation?' I said.

'If you ask me a direct question I will answer you with the truth, then we will both know who we are dealing with.'

'Were you born in this period of time? If not, where are you from?' I said.

'That is two questions, but I am prepared to answer both.'

I waited to hear the answers, I knew what I expected to hear.

'As you now suspect, I am a traveller, I arrived here in 1947, and I have been here ever since. I arrived with my wife, but unfortunately she died here many years ago.'

'I'm sorry to hear that. I intend to return to my time this evening, that is why it is vital we find the treasure as soon as possible. I am very pleased to know you are a traveller, from a different time it is true, but at least we were from a civilized time, not like this place,' I said.

He then told me his story. He arrived on the island in the 1940s, with his wife, they had read the deed and thought it was rubbish but they were going to see if it worked. To their surprise it did work. He started on the island as a member of the crew, this was because he had arrived with his wife, if he had been alone he was no doubt destined to be the monk, and to his astonishment his wife remained his wife when they arrived here. It was their intention to write about the place, therefore they had to observe everything that was going on, live the same crude lifestyle, be part of the smuggling trips. They only wanted to stay as long as it took to get all the information, then return to the world they knew. Like all big ideas, things do not always go as planned. His wife died here, from a disease which he thought was flu, very manageable in our time but on the island it had a disastrous effect.

He decided to stay, without his wife there seemed no point in returning, he continued as a crew member until he got injured, then Vicary and Landon suggested he run the inn. He had been there ever since, how long in normal time he had no idea.

'Every time a traveller arrives from the future time goes back, and as I expect you know, as a traveller I am aware of a new arrival as well. I have seen time go back several times. No doubt you have some idea how many times this has happened from your present.'

'I am aware of several people that have travelled, one of those men was called Alan Donald, he took on Landon's identity, and we both know what happened to him. That is why I knew Landon had no idea where Vicary's treasure was – he told me. Two other friends of mine have travelled, one remained in 1981 and the other in 1985. I will be travelling back to my present which is the year 2000,' I said.

'I am amazed at what you've just said, you are talking about times in your past, which are in fact in my future, if I had remained in my time. I arrived here in 1947, does that mean I have been here over fifty years in our time? It is all very confusing,' he said.

'Do you want to return with me this evening? It is possible as I have the Pathway.'

'I think there will be too many changes in your world. At my age I will find it very difficult to cope with. I think it best I stay here, I am old now and probably have very few years left. I appreciate your offer, but I think you know it would be too much for me,' he said.

'How did you become the landlord of the inn? I thought travellers moved from monk to crew members? I appreciate that because you were married you missed out the monk phase.'

'Vicary in fact owned the inn, I appreciate nothing in his will ever confirmed that. There is no doubt in my mind that he owned it in this time. I was a member of the crew and I injured myself on one of the trips. I was made landlord on a temporary basis until I recovered, but it became a permanent position.'

'I have come to the conclusion that the deed and Vicary's will were not penned by Vicary. This I suspect was done by Landon, although I am not certain about that; it seems Landon produced all the paperwork on the island. One point, I will show you the Pathway, how it works. If you change your mind you can use it. If you set it to 1947, maybe your wife will be waiting for you,' I said.

'I'm not sure I understand that, my wife died in this place, at a time much earlier than 1947, how is that possible?'

'I don't know how it works, but I can tell you I went back with a colleague whose wife had been murdered; we prevented the murder and saved his wife,' I said.

'Even if I can go back to 1947, and my wife is there alive and well, what about me? My wife is going to be a young woman, I am going to be an old man.'

'I don't know how it works in that respect, but I think you should think about it. By being there you could prevent her taking the trip to the island, that alone would prolong her life. Just think about it, I will show you the Pathway before I go.'

I was not convinced he wanted to take the chance of turning up as an old man with his wife being young, but he thanked me. I was glad to give him that small glimmer of hope.

'If you come along with me when I leave, I will ensure you are in a position to use the Pathway if you so wish. I must emphasize that the Pathway must not leave the island, it is important it remains where it is, in Landon's cellar. Anyone who leaves with the Pathway has a scrap of metal only, it can never be used again.'

'I'll come with you when you leave, if only to satisfy my own curiosity. I read about the Pathway in the deeds, now I can see what all the fuss was about.'

Suddenly there was a scream from one of the tunnels. We both ran over to find out what was causing the commotion. We entered the tunnel that was furthest from the ledge, both of us carrying our lamps. We travelled about 50 feet along the tunnel where one of the women searching indicated behind a rock. She had found something, and with the assistance of a second women had pulled it from its resting place.

It was a joy to see. On the floor of the tunnel was a large strongbox which the two women had hauled from its hiding place. It was a large box, bearing a very large padlock. The landlord and I shone our lamps into the hole from which the strongbox had been pulled, there were smaller boxes visible. We pulled out everything that was inside. A total of four other boxes were retrieved, all were padlocked.

Now we needed to take them out and break the padlocks. The boxes were taken to the surface, and the landlord went to the inn to find some tools. All the women had returned to the surface, there seemed little point in continuing the search as we were all sure that we had found the treasure.

The landlord returned with some tools, and he quickly demolished all the padlocks. We opened the large box, which contained coins. The others were stuffed with gemstones. We had achieved the impossible, bringing some sort of future to the womenfolk.

It was the first time I had heard many of these women speak, now it was impossible for them to stop. The landlord explained that he was going to sell the treasure on their behalf, everyone having an equal share of the profits. They all agreed to this course of action. The boxes were moved to the cellar of the inn, the landlord opened the bar and provided free drinks all round. The bar was packed with women, many of whom had never set foot in the place before.

The landlord pulled me to one side, he had something to say. He introduced himself as Jim Merrow. I introduced myself by my real name, and we shook hands following the introduction.

He wanted to thank me for what I had done, organizing the search so these people were going to have a better life. They were going to appreciate greatly what had been done for them. I told him it was partly down to him, he had persuaded the women it was a good idea. Now their lives were going to change forever, they would be able to avoid a future life of begging and in some cases prostitution.

'I am tempted at the prospect of going back to 1947, but the age problem does deter me,' said Jim.

'I'm not certain how it works, but my friend Colin returned to his past, but he did not get younger, he retained the age he was when he first made the trip to this island. Using that principle, it is possible if you return to 1947, which was in fact your point of entry when you first came here, you might return to your 1947 age. I can only compare it with Colin's case, I am not a persistent time traveller, it is merely supposition. Is it worth chancing it?' I said.

'If I did return, would I make the same mistake and buy the bungalow, thereby coming to the past, allowing my wife to die in this place?' he said.

'I can only tell you what I have gained from experiencing a few trips. I think you will remember the time travel, but your wife will be unaware of it. In other words you will tell your wife in 1947 that it is not a good idea to buy the bungalow, knowing what you remember of this experience. She will not remember anything because it hasn't happened for her, she is not under these circumstances the traveller. I hope that has not made it more complicated, but that is how I think it works. There are of course no certainties, it is just my opinion,' I said.

'I actually do understand what you're saying. It is up to me whether I want to take the chance or not, don't you agree?'

'It is your decision, Jim.'

He then said a very strange thing.

'Were you confused about the silk found in Vicary's hut, before it was supposed to be stolen?'

'Yes I was, I had forgotten about that,' I said.

I was a little confused by what was said, how did my new friend Jim know about that?

'Being a traveller, as I said, I was aware of the imminent arrival of new travellers, time going back and all that. When time rolled back I kept a look-out for the new arrival, that was when I saw what Landon did. I watched him take the silk into the side of the portal. The portal was opening at this stage, he placed it inside and walked away, no doubt hiding out of sight. We know the silk could not pass through the portal, but how did Landon know? I know you said one of your friends was Landon, but I wonder if he was this Landon. If he was not that means there is only one other conclusion: there was another Landon who was also a traveller. By placing the silk in the portal it did not disappear when time went back. It does make you think how many travellers were on the island.

'He was aware the silks were not able to travel through the portal, but he figured if they were placed just inside the portal, once the traveller had passed through, the silks were going to reappear. He could have done that with the gold I suppose, but it was pure luck on his part that he saw the portal open. I have no idea how he knew that, unless he was another traveller, but it worked.

'I used my position of landlord quite wisely, I knew most of what was going on. I saw you leave the inn and go to the hut Landon had left the silk in. That was when I thought you were a traveller. I knew finding that silk would throw you into confusion, so I thought I would clear up that point. I did not know you had forgotten about it. It still poses the question, if your friend was not that Landon, who was that Landon?'

'I fear we will never know the answer now,' I said.

That solved a small problem I had about the silk, it appeared to be a well-thought-out tactic by Landon, but it still did not explain how he knew it protected the silk, perhaps it was simply a case of trial and error.

On my return to my hut my wife was jubilant at the prospect of wealth, she had even started packing, preparing for her new life on the mainland. It was difficult to refrain from telling her the truth: the treasure was going to take time to sell, maybe years rather than months, but I did not want to ruin her euphoria.

To my surprise she wanted to visit the inn that evening, stating that the other women were going to be there to continue celebrating their good fortune. I thought it a good idea, and it meant nobody was likely to be around when I left, then the real Jefferson was going to reappear.

The inn was packed, and Jim asked several of the women to assist with serving. There was no money changing hands tonight, everything was free. Whether my prostitute friend had the same idea about no payment seemed very unlikely as she looked at me, knowing I was the youngest of the two men present. But I had other plans for tonight.

Just before midnight I signalled to Jim it was time to go. He was not going to be missed as everyone was helping themselves by then. We walked out of the rear of the inn, looking back to make sure we were not followed. The short journey to Landon's hut was made at speed, soon we were inside.

Lifting the cellar door I produced the Pathway. Jim looked at it with complete surprise. I gave him a quick lesson in how it worked, and Jim understood easily. My lesson ended with the same words told to me: under no circumstances must the Pathway leave the island. Jim nodded that he understood. I was hoping he was going to join me, but he said he needed time to think about everything I had told him. Any decision he made was going to be a momentous one for him.

I looked outside to check there was nobody around. I set the Pathway for my return to my present, and shook hands with Jim. I said I hoped he would find it in his heart to return to his wife in 1947, if that was his wish. I pressed the button.

The Pathway was returned to the box and placed carefully in the cellar. We closed the door and made our way outside. The storm clouds had started to gather, soon the portal was going to appear.

Jim looked at this phenomenon in awe, it showed him what happened if he decided to take the trip, although as he said he had seen it before. He had seen people appear from the other side, but the storm was not as violent on this side, and it was the first time he had seen anyone leave this time. The mist came down, then the portal appeared, very brightly lit. Jim looked on in amazement. We shook hands again and he wished me good luck. I again wished him luck and moved into the light, leaving behind a piece of history that had been rewritten. I wondered what effect that was going to have on the future.

I was returning to my own time, no longer would I endure the awful conditions of the island.

10

It was early morning when I walked across the beach towards the mainland, my feet sinking in the wet sand as I left the island. I had been through a considerable amount in the last couple of months a life-changing experience.

I had travelled back to the seventeenth century and watched as the poor, unfortunate inhabitants of the island made a meagre living. I had seen the notorious Captain Vicary treat his crew with contempt, having taken more than his share from their smuggling exploits. Travelling back to war-torn Britain, hoping to use this period in time to obtain a fortune for myself in fine art, I had watched with understanding and pride as the people dealt with the rationing and shortages, learning to cope with all difficulties facing them. Moving forward to the 1980s I had assisted in saving the lives of two people, with careful planning and strategy.

There were people waiting on the mainland. Was I the object of their patience? At this point I had no idea; soon I would find out. My biggest concern was to do with what I had seen: who would believe anything of what I was about to tell them? I hoped there was one particular person there who would have the courage to confirm what I was about to inflict on the world. Whether I was part of some vast event that had changed history forever, I was about to find out, for good or bad. My step quickened in anticipation of what was to come.

As I drew near to the waiting group, I was able to pick Colin out. Although he had aged 15 years since I had last seen him, I recognized his walk as he moved towards me. We met about 50 yards from the mainland, some distance from the other onlookers, he obviously wanted to say something in private to me. He approached me with outstretched hand. He was pleased to see me safely returned, I was very pleased to see him. Our adventure had come full circle, and we had achieved all the things we had wanted to do. I was soon to find out how much we had changed history between us by what we had done in the past.

'I have lots to tell you. My last visit to the island did not turn out as we expected it to, it was far from uneventful, things happened that neither of us could have envisaged. What happened is certainly going to change the history of the island,' I said.

'I know it has been eventful for one reason alone, Alan is not with you. I think I know what you are about to tell me; there is only one reason why Alan is not with you. We need to go to your bungalow; don't worry it is paid for and furnished, as I promised you all those years ago – or was it a couple of days ago in your world? There are people waiting to meet you. They are all known to you, but this is where it gets slightly confusing, as some of them will not recognize you. That is the reason I have come to meet you on your own, to explain who knows you and who doesn't,' said Colin.

'I think it was a good idea of yours to warn me,' I said.

'Helen and Jane are there, Helen will recognize you but Jane won't. That is because you met Jane in this time, before we went back and changed the past. I will explain things as we go along,' he said.

I thought it very modern of him to bring both wives to meet me, I was not sure how they felt about that situation.

'Helen is part of what we changed, she is going to remember you as our house guest, is that clear?' he asked. 'John and my father are here; my father will know you, but John will have no idea who you are. John is here because of the note we initially left him when we prepared for the trip, when he was your neighbour. Although we changed his life, we never actually met him, so he will have no idea who you are. In fact he has already asked what he is doing here. You do understand what I am saying, Pat?'

'I sort of understand what you're saying; it all depends on what we changed during our travels. Because of the changes we have made, even Jane has no idea who I am,' I said.

'That's about it, just play it by ear. By the way some elderly gentleman was here. He didn't give his name, he said he would call at the bungalow tomorrow, I didn't recognize him. He said he knew you some time ago; sounds like your past colleagues have caught up with you. I told him your address, hope that was all right?' he said.

'I think my priority at the moment is a good night's sleep, the whole experience has already been quite tiring. Meeting people I know but do not know me, I understand the theory but it is still a little confusing,' I said.

'Are you ready to meet your adoring public?'

'It's as good a time as any,' I said.

We then walked towards the slipway onto the mainland. The tractor was parked there, what a lovely sight, reassuring me that I had finally come home. Colin commented that I still retained the duffel coat. I had been glad of it on other trips, it did protect me against the biting wind, particularly when I landed in the rocks.

The first person I saw was Helen. She had aged very well, she hugged me and kissed me on the cheek, a wonderful welcome home. She commented that I looked the same as when she last saw me. That was only a few days ago in my experience. She asked me how my trip was, and I wondered whether Colin had told her everything, I assumed he had. She grabbed my arm and led me forward, saying she wanted to introduce me to someone she thought I already knew, but appreciated this person may not remember the occasion. This showed me Colin had told her everything.

Jane moved forward and we shook hands. I still had admiration for Colin, bringing his second wife to meet me, or rather the woman who was not now going to be his second wife. Helen then introduced her as their daughter Jane, adding that Colin had no doubt told me they had a daughter. Now it started to make sense.

He had mentioned his daughter, but I had no idea Jane was that daughter. What John had told me was completely wrong, because Colin and Jane lived in the same house he thought they were husband and wife. Colin had never introduced Jane in any capacity, he simply introduced her as Jane.

Jane said I looked surprised at the introduction. She had no idea how surprised. I tried to cover my tracks by saying her father had mentioned his daughter, who was at university.

'I've graduated now, I was working for my father, until I was able to find something in banking. Welcome home, although to be honest I have no idea how you got here. I remember the blinding light from the island, maybe you can explain that to me tomorrow. I'm sorry I should explain, I have got the job here as the local bank manager. My father told me you would probably be visiting me tomorrow, you have an account that needs activating. I have made an appointment for ten in the morning. Will that be convenient for you?' she said.

It was of course very convenient, I was keen to check how rich I was, the sooner the better I thought, and I agreed to the meeting.

'Jane does not know everything that happened, I will explain things to her tonight. Helen knows everything, there is only Jane to tell,' he said.

'It is important she knows the truth, otherwise she could ask me embarrassing questions. It is better for you to answer them before I get asked. Promise me you will speak to her tonight?'

He promised to tell her everything. He took me over to John, and introduced us.

'It's great to see you again,' I said.

That was of course my first mistake, which John quickly picked up on this.

'I was not aware we had ever met before,' he said.

Colin looked distraught. He had warned me, and here I was falling at the first hurdle.

'It was many years ago, in Plymouth. It is unlikely you will still remember me; do you still live in Plymouth?'

I felt I was digging a larger hole for myself.

'I do, but I have no idea why I have been summoned here tonight. I had a note in my wallet, it has been there as long as I can recall. It has this time and date with the location, and I thought it might be important. My inquisitive side got the better of me, but all I've seen is someone coming from the island in a beam of light. Perhaps someone could explain why I needed to be here, I really don't know,' said John.

Colin spoke calmly to John, explaining that he would know the reason soon.

'We need to meet up with you in a few days and sit down together, I will explain everything to you, why you have the note, and why it was important you were here. You may not believe what I'm going to tell you, but you will be fascinated by the story,' said Colin.

John agreed to attend the meeting, he desperately wanted to know the reason for his presence.

'How is your wife, John?' I said.

'What makes you think I am married?' he said.

'I met your wife many years ago, when I met you.'

He then told a sad story. I was not prepared for what followed. 'My wife died many years ago, in a car crash, I have missed her ever since, I'm actually thinking of moving away from Plymouth. Ruby Bay looks like a nice place to live.'

I then started to think to myself that Colin and I had failed. We had returned to save his wife, we thought we had done so, but what he had just said confirmed otherwise.

Colin stepped in, having seen the look on my face, and asked him when the crash was.

He said it happened in 1989, and there was no doubt that she was at fault. He admitted she was a terrible driver, and he never liked her driving the car. He warned her about her driving, but she took no notice of what he said. On that particular day they had an argument, again about how unsafe she was on the road. She stormed off and got into the car, he tried to stop her from driving off but to no avail. She was trying to prove to him she was a good driver, but she crashed into a heavy goods vehicle in the city centre. He believed she was speeding at the time, and she died on impact, that was some consolation he felt. He had lived with the guilt, knowing her driving was the cause of the argument, and that she was trying to prove her point. Instead she proved his point.

I told him I was sorry to hear that sad news. So our efforts in 1980s had prolonged her life by a few more years, but she was obviously destined to die that way. Although he had had a few more years with her, our attempts with the original crash was not the success we thought, this new crash made him feel guilty. Perhaps it would have been better if we had not tried to help him.

'The house next to Pat is for sale and if you are serious about the move I will check it out. Was that something you might be interested in, John?' he asked.

'I would definitely be interested, but I'm not sure how my neighbour would feel about it,' he said.

'I think it would be an excellent idea, I think I know what sort of neighbour you'll be,' I said.

He appreciated that, not aware the relationship was going to be rekindled.

Colin and I then left the small throng of people, agreeing to meet them individually in the future. We walked to my bungalow, but it was not the one I had remembered leaving. As the purchase was made in the distant past, thanks to Colin's generous act, the builder never purchased the property, therefore the rebuild had never taken place; I was intending to see to that in the months to come.

We walked into my bungalow and I was pleased with what he

had done, all new furniture with matching accessories. I felt Helen must have had a lot to do with this, and he admitted that she was the creative one.

We now had the chance to chat. I needed to tell him what had happened to the crew, in particular the fate of Alan Donald, someone who had helped us both through our various expeditions.

'How do you feel about picking up the friendship with John?'

'I think it's a good idea, we know John better than he knows himself,' I said.

'I think you were surprised that Jane was my daughter. Like everyone else in Ruby Bay you assumed she was my young bride. It was partly my fault, I never actually introduced her as my daughter,' he said.

'Actually it was John who said she was your wife.'

'I always introduced her as Jane, from that people make assumptions, it was quite amusing.'

'I also assumed John knew.'

'I did not mean to embarrass you, but the look on your face did amuse me,' he said.

'What have you told Helen?'

'I've told her about the time travel, which of course she did not believe. The crowning glory was to see you reappear in a flash of light, I know she is more inclined to believe it now. Jane of course knew nothing about it. I will broach that subject tonight, hopefully with Helen's assistance; I think it will be difficult to persuade Jane. I set up your meeting at the bank to help you, I knew when you were returning, I knew you would want your account up and running, I have no idea what the interest is you have accumulated over fifteen years.'

I asked him if Helen had actually recognized me, or was it because of what he had told her.

He emphasized the point, the only people who were going to recognize me were those who had shared the experience, in other words only travellers, although John did not fit into that category, as I did not know him on the island. Helen did not know you, me. Colin asked her to behave like that to please me.

'Is there anything else before I relate my tale of woe about Alan?'

'The elderly gentleman who came to see you. All he said was he had good news for you, but he didn't share that news. Maybe it's an inheritance,' smiled Colin.

'If it's anything like my last inheritance, I really don't want it. Although I agree it made us wealthy, in your case very rich,' I said.

This comment made him smile.

'So what happened on the island? I have an idea but you'd better tell me.'

'I really need to tell the story in its entirety, maybe if you sit down and make yourself comfortable,' I said.

I decided to be as brief as possible, and related everything that had happened on my final return to the island. I wondered what the history books would say now. I also wondered if there was still more treasure to find on the island.

'I think we should visit the inn, it will be interesting to see how the story has changed. Tom Maxwell always said he knew everything about what went on in those heady days, maybe you could put him right on a few facts. But I think that can wait, you need to get some rest, we will take on the inn tomorrow night. Remember you have the appointment at the bank in the morning. I will return after my daughter has dealt with you, or is it my wife? Even I'm getting confused,' he said.

I went to my new bedroom, where the bed was made with new sheets and a matching duvet cover. Colin and Helen had done an excellent job, even the clothes I had bought on several visits to the past were in the wardrobe. It was wonderful to finally be home, back where I belonged. Now the next part of the adventure was about to begin: I was eager to find out what we had changed during our travels.

I slept very well, time travel can be exhausting. I had breakfast on my verandah. I looked towards the island, it was the first time I had studied it since my return. Everything looked as I expected it to look, the inn and hotel were where I expected them to be.

Then as before when I had first moved to Ruby Bay, a figure appeared in the garden. This time it was Colin, not John.

'I thought I would call round. The elderly gentleman is visiting this morning, and if you're at the bank you might miss him. I'll stay and wait for him,' he said.

I suspected his inquisitive mind had something to do with his offer to wait. Was this being neighbourly or Colin being nosey? I thought it was possibly a bit of both.

'Thank you, but aren't you neglecting your work?'

'I own the business, and as you rightly said, I am very rich, I don't need anyone's permission to take time off.'

He was indeed wealthy, and so was I, although it was to a lesser degree.

'On the subject of wealth, where do you live now?' I asked.

He laughed loudly, and winked.

'In that large house they call Ruby Bay House. I bought it again and made some alterations, necessary to reach the standard of a man of my means. Hopefully you will visit soon and check out the alterations.'

'It will be a pleasure, I would like to see the place again, hopefully that includes a dinner invite, I don't care which wife does the cooking.'

I left him at the bungalow and walked to the bank, it was a great feeling to smell the ozone off the sea. Even better was what I was about to find out: had my £1 million increased by a substantial amount?

On entering the bank I was shown into the manager's office, where Jane was sitting behind the desk, elegant and well dressed, the position suited her very well. We shook hands and I sat down. Jane opened the envelope which produced my codeword, and this she verified along with my signature. Then she told me how rich I was.

I was delighted with the result of my investment. She smiled and said she was pleased about my shrewd decisions. What amazed her was that I had a great deal of money tied up in stocks and shares, but they were all sold in September 1987, one month before the stock market crashed. She complimented me on a clever piece of business, carried out by a third party acting on my behalf. I was glad I had mentioned this financial disaster to Colin, fortunately he remembered to sell everything. I enquired as to what was the likely outcome had I left my money where it was? She was quick to say I was very likely to have lost three-quarters of my wealth; whoever carried out the transactions was a wise man.

She then started to talk about what her father had told her the previous night. I think she was looking for some sort of confirmation from me. The story was about how we had become rich by travelling through time, a concept she admitted was difficult to take in, but she appeared willing to listen to my version of events.

'Did you believe what your father told you? I appreciate is not an easy thing to grasp.'

'My first impression was that it was rubbish, then my mother said she had met you fifteen years ago, when your account was set up at this bank, an account with a large amount of money in it. She also mentioned that some rare paintings were sold, hence the large amount in the account. What I found strange was the account has not been touched in all that time, except in 1987 when the third party sorted out the shares before the market crashed. It was as if you knew what was going to happen in 1987, which of course you would if you were from the future,' she said.

'That alone is not likely to change your mind, whether or not I had travelled through time. Do you know who touched the account in 1987?'

'I have no idea, it was confidential, I wasn't working here then, it would be impossible to find out. Surely you know?'

'Indeed I do, but that must remain a secret I'm afraid.'

From what Colin said Helen knew none of these details until Colin had briefed her. She did not recognize me at all, she was saying these things to persuade Jane, but Helen probably accepted time travel having seen me return through the portal, just as Colin had predicted.

'It was not just that. My mother said you had not changed in appearance in fifteen years, not aged a bit. On the beach I saw you appear from a beam of light, it made me consider that there might be something in your story,' she said.

I decided not to mention that her mother did not recognize me: she was acting to help her father, possibly to make me feel better. But she had certainly made her daughter think again.

'Did your father mention anything about our adventures in the past?'

'My father said he returned to 1985 to save my mother, she had been murdered in a botched burglary. Was that true?'

'I only know that what we did saved her life. Your father was the only one who knew about the original burglary. I know it is difficult for you when we talk about preventing your mother's death, but it is what happened. What else did your father say to you?'

'I think he told me everything, I even know all about John. I saw this person called John there, he did not seem to recognize anyone.'

'It was the same John your father had mentioned. He was there because of a note your father left him. Because we changed things in the past for John, he never actually met your father and me, therefore he did not know who we were,' I said.

'Had you met me before?' she asked.

'I had met you before, but as in John's case, things were changed after we met, so you did not recognize me. I'm sure your father will explain it one day, it is a little more complicated than my explanation, I'm not convinced I understand it completely. But to try to explain, when we saved your mother, that one event changed the past. Our intervention, by keeping your mother alive, was likely to change the direction of your life, and it also meant your mother was around, whereas she should have ceased to exist after 1985. By saving John's wife, he did not move to Ruby Bay, therefore I did not meet him, so he did not know who I was. I hope that helps a little. Ask your father if you have any questions,' I said.

'But she didn't recognize you, my dad told her to pretend that she did,' she said.

This I already knew, it meant only one thing: Colin had explained it to her. Perhaps the initial reunion was just for my benefit, in the moment as it were. That meant that time had changed since our last meeting, which was strange as I had only been on the island. My mind was racing. Helen had been made aware of events, the selling of the paintings, but I did not figure in her past, and Colin knew she was not going to recognize me.

'I'm not sure how changing something hundreds of years ago could to affect this time,' she said.

'Anything that is changed in the past can affect the future, no matter how small the change,' I said.

'So what changed on the island on your last visit? Something must have done so, for my mother not to recognize you. Perhaps it was something minor, but as you say, no matter how small the change it has repercussions on the future.'

'I helped the islanders find the gold and jewels that the history books thought were lost. In fact that was the reason many people visited the island, hoping to find Vicary's lost treasure, the treasure that is no longer there. This action was going to have certain effects on the future, although at this stage I don't know what they are. That was the action that changed everything,' I said.

She agreed I was probably right. We shook hands again and I left the bank, almost convinced Jane believed what we had discussed. She was an intelligent woman who would try to find holes in my explanation. If I were in her position it was something that I was going to find difficult to accept. I was going to have time to speak to her again, as Colin had invited me to the house for a dinner engagement. I was aware that she and Helen were both good cooks.

Happy that my finances were in a very healthy state I walked back towards my bungalow. How was I going to spend all this money? It meant security for the rest of my life, no purchase out of my reach.

My front door was opened by Colin, smiling in that knowing way. I had seen that smile on numerous occasions, particularly in his film-making days in 1941.

'Why the large smile? Are you all right?' I said.

He opened the door to let me in.

'Your guest from last night has arrived, we've had a long chat. I think you are in for a pleasant surprise,' he said.

I walked into the lounge and an elderly gentleman rose to his feet, holding out his hand he called me by my Christian name. I had no idea who this man was, I looked closely at his face but did not recognize him.

'I'm very sorry, I have no idea who you are,' I said.

'That's understandable, you have never seen my real face. I'm Jim Merrow from the island.'

I was amazed: our jovial landlord had left the island.

'I obviously knew where the bungalow was, being a previous owner. I knocked on the door and there was no reply, then your friend Colin arrived and said everyone was waiting for my arrival. I thought I would come back today when all the fuss had died down,' he said.

'I'm surprised to see you. The last time I saw you we had found the gold on the island, and you were going to share it out among the women. You said you were going to the mainland with your share, to live the life of an aristocrat. What happened to that vision?'

'I decided against it, instead I used the Pathway as you showed me. I returned to 1947, hoping I was going to arrive at my former age, which thankfully I did. It worked a treat. My wife was there as we'd hoped, and I persuaded her not to buy this bungalow, thereby avoiding travelling back in time. We moved to Plymouth instead.'

I decided not to ask him about his wife, I had made that mistake with John, but as we chatted he mentioned her. I was pleased to hear that he was still married to her. He would have brought her along to say thank you if she had been well enough.

'How did you know I was coming back last night?' I said.

'I saw the Pathway when you set it, it was just a case of waiting fifty-three years to see you.'

'I'm glad you did. Now we should treat you to lunch. I think we'll go somewhere which you know very well, will you join us at the inn?' I said.

'There is something I want to discuss before we go to the inn, something you may not be aware of. Jim is in a position to clarify a few points, these points are historically very important,' said Colin

'What exactly do you want to confirm with Jim?'

I was intrigued by this conversation, I assumed I had a good grasp of world affairs. I did not know why Jim needed to be part of the conversation. Soon I was to find out his reasons.

Colin asked his question only to Jim.

'Jim, you went to the island in 1947, you stayed there a considerable time. How long would you say you were there?'

'I would estimate about thirty years, give or take a year,' he said.

'When you returned from the island, you went back to 1947. Did you notice anything different about the 1947 you returned to?'

Jim was stunned by that.

'I certainly did, but how did you know that? I thought I was the only one that noticed, it made me feel like I was losing my sanity.'

'There is an explanation for it, you were not losing your sanity, things had changed dramatically, and only the three of us here are aware of it. Pat, you are not as yet accustomed to this time, but the history books of today will tell a story unknown to you. Jim, have you checked any history books since your return? I'm sure you have; were you surprised by the results?'

'I purposely checked them, I have been confused since 1947, with no answers to what I thought was our history, I thought the events I believed were in my mind, I am glad I came here today for some sort of explanation. From what you say I assume you had something to do with the changes, is that correct?'

'What changes are we talking about?' I said.

'Pat, I have to admit both you and I had something to do with these monumental changes to our history. At the time we were not aware of it, and at this point you have no idea what I am talking about. Just one small action on our part caused the history of the world to be changed forever.'

'Perhaps you can explain what you're talking about,' I said.

'Indeed I will, this will include a short history lesson. On the 6th of June 1944 a momentous event in the war took place, the invasion of Europe by Allied troops, known as D-Day, when the troops stormed the beaches at Normandy with the intention of getting a foothold in Europe.'

Jim and I nodded our heads in agreement, it was a part of history nobody was likely to forget.

'Jim, what was the result of this action?'

'That's a silly question, we all know what happened,' I said.

'Just let Jim give his answer to the question, you may be surprised at what he tells you.'

'The Allies stormed the beaches, from there they moved on towards Germany, bringing ultimate victory to the Allies in 1945, that is the short version,' said Jim.

'Thank you, Jim, as you say short and to the point. What do you think of that answer, Pat?'

'I must say, a little confusing, not exactly how I remember it. Obviously I wasn't there, but the history books told a different story.'

'Yes they did, they tell it just as Jim has told it: the Allies successfully defeated the Germans, D-Day was a success, the start of the push to victory. Why would you disagree with Jim's answer, perhaps you have another version of events?'

'It is not what I was taught at school. Yes, D-Day happened, but the Allied troops were slaughtered on the beaches of Normandy, the Germans had predicted the landing spot and were waiting for them. The Allied commanders had hoped the Germans were going to think it was Calais, the shortest distance, and the Allied commanders used tactics to make the Germans think it was Calais, but they did not fall for all the ruses the Allies tried to pull. It was thought the Germans would not anticipate a landing in Normandy, yet it appeared Hitler and his commanders were smarter than their Allied counterparts. I have no idea why you should think Jim's account is accurate, it bears no resemblance to actual events. I like the idea of an Allied victory, but I'm afraid the Germans were victorious,' I said.

'Jim's answer was to the point, he described exactly what happened: the Germans did not anticipate Normandy, they thought Calais the best option. Do you recall what the codename of the Allied operation was, Pat?'

'Of course, every schoolboy knows it was called Operation Overlord,' I said.

'So in your world, Pat, who won the Second World War?'

I thought this was some kind of strange joke, but decided to play along; maybe the relevance of all this was soon to become apparent, sooner rather than later.

'Germany of course. Like many we lived with the humiliation for years, the Germans made sure of that. I appreciate it makes little difference in this day and age, but growing up in the fifties it did. I remember the German boys at my school, many fights were started because of the events of the war.'

'You may not be aware of this but Operation Overlord was a strategy that had been discussed for years, virtually from the start of the war, because the Allies knew they would need to invade Europe to obtain victory. Logically it was the only way to defeat the Germans. You do of course remember our trip to 1941. It took me some time to convince you of the merits of the trip, but you eventually agreed. Remember how we saved my father from spying for Germany, as well as retrieving the paintings for ourselves? Do you remember if there was anything else we brought back from 1941, apart from the paintings?'

'Not really, we moved the paintings before the bomb hit. I don't remember picking up anything else, you said you wanted the six paintings,' I said.

'What about the envelope, do you remember that?' he said.

'Oh that, but we didn't need it in the end, it was probably some useless information your father was giving to the Germans. If you remember, he was working for the British,' I said.

'Do you still have the envelope?'

'I believe I do, I left it in the work coat we used when digging up the cellar. It should still be in the cellar, I'll go and check,' I said.

I went and fetched the envelope from my coat. It was quite dirty, it had been in the cellar for some time.

'You may be surprised to hear this, Pat. I think I know what the envelope contains. Since my return in 1985, I suddenly realized the significance of what was in that envelope. When I saw that the world had changed from the one I knew, it dawned on me that we had done something huge in historical terms, but at the time I did not know what. I am pretty certain now, but I would like you to confirm my suspicions. History has in fact been changed by the contents of that envelope, the same envelope we thought was of little use to the Germans. The contents are in fact sinister, as well as life-changing for many thousands of people.'

The envelope had remained in the inside pocket of my jacket, left in the cellar we had dug up, there for almost 60 years. I had felt it was of little importance, particularly as we had completed the tasks we intended to complete. At no time had I thought of opening it and checking the contents, there was never a need to do that. I had no idea why I had hung on to it, maybe deep down it was for this moment.

'Would you like to open the envelope Pat? Read to us what it says,' said Colin.

I looked at the grubby envelope, still sealed as it had been in 1941, and opened it quickly. What I saw shocked me to my bones. He was right, the contents were of significant importance, now I understood what the talk had been about.

'What does it say?' asked Jim.

'The main title reads, "Operation Overlord",' I said.

'That, gentlemen, is what I thought it was going to say. My father was going to pass information about an event that was not going to take place until three years later. Although it was unlikely to be important to the Germans at that time, it was something they were going to file for future reference. When the Germans started discussing where they thought the invasion was going to take place, the filed information sounded a feasible alternative for Hitler. Believing the Allies might cross at Calais, he changed his mind and selected Normandy. By preventing this one note getting to the Germans, we not only saved lives, but we altered the final outcome of the war. Unfortunately we are the only three people that can ever know that,' said Colin.

Jim and I sat silently. Nobody was ever going to know how big a part we had played in winning the war. It was an awesome thought: we saved the world and made a lot of money in the process.

Colin said, 'We have to agree between the three of us, the details of the letter are not to be revealed to a living soul. Nobody is going to believe we saved the world. Let the government believe they masterminded the Normandy landings, there is little to be gained by telling the truth. Many films have been made about the big event, stories have been written, there is no need to say anything; like I say, nobody would believe that we helped win a war before we were born.'

I then asked Colin about his father's involvement, was he not working as a British spy before the chance of financial gain? He agreed that he was, but Stuygens turned him into a German spy. It was the prospect of great wealth, the wealth that we now have, that changed his allegiance, but we stopped the vital piece of information being passed. So our wealth was down to his father turning against his country, I think they call it the spoils of war.

We then made another decision: it was time to go to the inn for lunch. Jim was looking forward to this, wondering what had changed since his days as the landlord. The walk across the beach was quiet, we were all pondering the contents of the letter. It explained a lot for Jim: he had wondered how the things he remembered had changed so drastically. It meant very little to me, as I was not aware of any drastic changes. But I had only been back a day, and the significance of these changes would become apparent in the fullness of time.

When we reached the inn, I was pleased to see Tom Maxwell was the landlord. He of course did not recognize me, history had been changed since I last met him. Tom was introduced to both myself and Jim; he knew Colin well enough.

'Tom, if you've got a few minutes these chaps are very interested in the history of this place. In the meantime we'll have a drink,' said Colin.

'I'll be pleased to tell you a potted history, it's part of the job to tell customers about the inn. I'll be with you in a moment, I'll just get your drinks,' he said.

Jim sat with a large grin on his face. Having run this place for 30 years, at the height of its history, he was interested to know what Tom had to say.

Tom returned with the drinks as promised, and sat down with us. Jim had agreed to say nothing, he was not going to criticize the storyteller, he was just going to listen with interest to what tale was told; maybe it was going to be close to the real facts.

'This place was the haunt of the infamous Captain James Vicary. All his crew drank here every night. It is possible he stood at the bar just there.'

'What about Landon, wasn't he one of the crew?' I said.

'He was second in command, something of a monster by all accounts.'

'Wasn't there a Jefferson, wasn't he the second mate?' I asked.

'That's right, not much is known about him. Do you want me to tell this story, or do you just want to ask questions?'

'Just one more, if you don't mind?' I said.

'Go on then, what is it?'

'Did any of those tankards over the bar belong to Vicary?' I said.

'Could have been that one there,' said Tom pointing at one.

'No it wasn't, it was the one next to it,' said Jim.

'You're right, it could have been any one of them,' said Tom.

Jim smiled and sat there contented. He had been a part of the history that was never going to leave this place, a bygone day of skullduggery and pirating, no romance, just hardship.

Tom continued with his story at length.

'There was talk of treasure never found, although it is unlikely any of it is left. The islanders had recovered a great deal before they left the island, abandoned everything they did. Nobody ever knew how they located the treasure, it was supposed to have been well hidden by Vicary. Vicary and his crew were all executed after a piracy trip went wrong, and it was rumoured these executions took place in Ruby Bay. I find that hard to believe, but the fact cannot be proved.'

Following that comment Jim and I looked at each other and smiled again, nobody was ever going to know what we knew. We finished at the inn and made our way across to the mainland.

Colin then asked me the strangest of questions.

'Have you ever thought of selling your bungalow, Pat?'